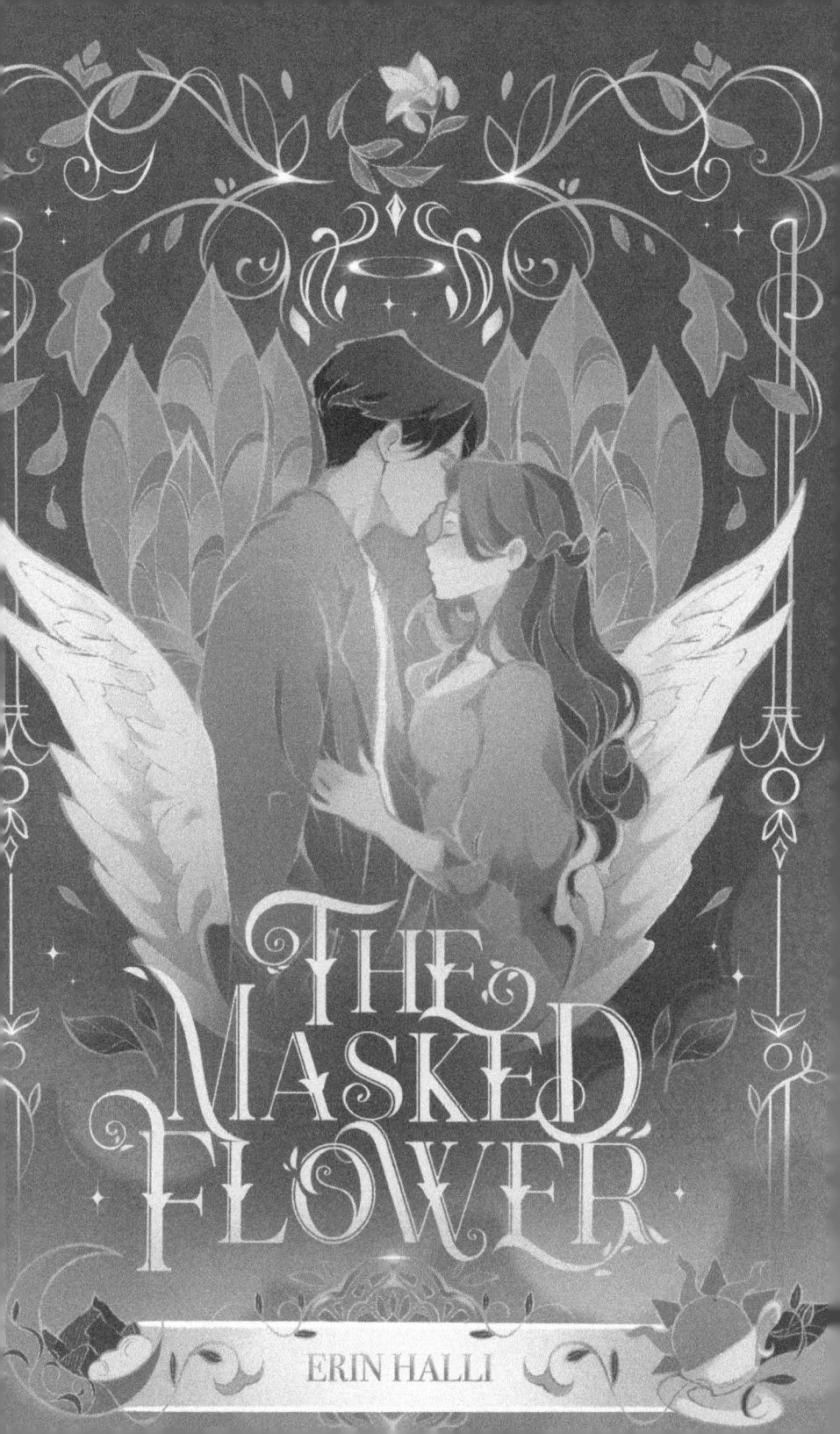

THE MASKED FLOWER

ERIN HALLI

The Masked Flower

By Erin Halli

Erin Halli
Publishing

Book Cover Design by Lara Klein @ 2024 (@laaraaklein)

Character Art by Michela Fiori (@michi_illustrations)

Proof Read by Samantha Jayne

First Edition Published August 2024

Published by Erin Halli Publishing

Paperback: 979-8-218-45557-6

Hardback: 979-8-218-46539-1

E-Book: B0D388LZD1

CONTENT WARNING

Please read with care. The contents of this book are intended for mature adult audiences only. It touches on the sensitive subject matter as follows: Loss of a loved one, blood loss, depression, trauma healing, panic attacks, anxiety, drinking alcohol, slight suicidal ideation, and coping with grief. It also contains profanity and explicit sexual descriptions.

To grieving wanderers who find solace in the sun, comfort in the clouds, and peace in the moon.
And to my mother—you were my muse.

PROLOGUE

T he girl meant to glance outside to see if he had arrived. Instead, she found herself getting lost in the clouds. Strands of fluff floated across the pale midday sky, seeming to drift without a care in the world. As she fell deeper into the trance, her mind wandered. *Oh, to be a cloud—simply floating in the sky without worry, stress, or pressure.*

Thanks to her unprecedented ability to overthink, Iris Adelaide Greene often got lost in trains of thought. After recognizing her brother's '76 Chevy Camaro horn honking *incessantly* in harmony with its revving engine, she snapped out of it, looking down and locking eye contact with him, rolling her eyes.

On that note, she hurried to her mirror for one last check. She wore leggings and an oversized navy blue university sweatshirt, keeping her hair tied back in a messy bun, allowing wavy brunette wisps to frame her olive-toned face. She lugged her suitcase down the hall, kissed her sweet cat, Truman, goodbye, and stepped outside of her apartment to say hello to the chilly winter air and farewell to the comfort of her home for the next three days. She loathed the winter holidays. Kai met her at the bottom of the stairs and held out his hand to take her luggage.

"No thanks." Iris continued walking, not pausing to consider his offer for even a second after his honking escapade. Her apartment complex was quiet and full of elderly folks; his honking alone may have caused someone severe distress. She went straight to his project car's trunk and jimmied her luggage into the only open spot amongst Kai's coaching gear.

"Someone didn't eat lunch today," he teased while trailing her. She opened the door and sank into the red sedan's old front seat then situated herself.

She'd been in this car hundreds of times, and it never ceased to smell different. Kai prided himself on the way his car smelled. He claimed he only rotated scents "once in a blue moon," but based on the assortment of smells ranging from *Pine Woods* to *Birthday Cupcake* she'd wafted just over the last month, she knew he was being modest. He wanted his project car to smell good.

If Iris were to guess, today's scent was a mix of pears, pine trees, and fresh snow. He settled into the driver's seat and took off. As much as Iris dreaded seeing her parents during the holidays, she couldn't wait to spend quality time with her brother. He took center stage in all of her childhood memories.

The commute to their parents' home was roughly two hours. He always drove, not that Iris minded. No, she believed the term "passenger princess" had to have been coined for her exceptional skills as a passenger. She chose a career opportunity in a small town where nearly everything was within walking distance for a reason–she preferred walking. She did *not* move there just because her brother coached at the high school there; she insisted that was merely a coincidence but a significant plus, nonetheless.

After getting gas and a quick bite, they settled back into the car, bracing themselves for what this weekend would hold.

"I'm feeling the scenic route this time, yeah?" He glanced at her through his peripherals.

"The scenic route is just about the only thing that makes this trip worth it," she replied almost immediately.

"Oh, don't sound too excited, Irie." He winked at her while keeping one eye on the road. She never understood how he could multitask while driving so well. Iris couldn't even eat french fries while driving straight, let alone look at the person beside her.

"I'm not looking forward to seeing Mom and Dad, but we have to; it's part of the agreement. Visit them during Christmas or Thanksgiving every year, and *someone* celebrated Thanksgiving Eve a little too hard this year, resulting in us needing to spend Christmas with them," he reminded her. Thanksgivings with their parents were usually more bearable. Rather than sitting around the fireplace silently, they got to do one of her favorite things: eat *delicious* comfort food without restraint.

He wasn't wrong, though. She decided to host a Friendsgiving with him and their friends on the day before Thanksgiving this year. Iris was not a big drinker; however, she did drink socially occasionally. When his friend, Jake, pulled out the classic red wine, she happily obliged. When done responsibly in the company of loved ones, holiday drinking can be a blast. However, when done in the company of friends who just so happen to be enablers, holiday drinking can be disastrous. Iris learned this the hard way. She was in no shape to visit their parents the following day.

"Okay, guess who didn't stop me?" She playfully slapped his arm. "I don't want to talk about Thanksgiving."

"Aw, is that because you didn't have a good time or *can't* talk about it because you forgot it even happened?" He mocked. "You are a responsible, 23-year-old woman who deserves to make your own decisions. I, nor anyone else, have the right to stop you from being the mess you are."

Her jaw dropped. Then, she punched him in the arm and burst into laughter. "Whatever! If we really want to talk about Thanksgiving, we should discuss *Katherine*. Remember who showed up super late to our dinner? I couldn't have forgotten that detail even if I tried. Your ridiculously smitten smile is permanently ingrained in my memories."

He leaned back, allowing his head to hit the headrest as he sighed while running his fingers through his light brown waves. "I am a responsible 27-year-old man who deserves to make my own decisions."

"Kai," Iris whined. "You've gotta give me more than that. Are you guys still talking? Do you think she wants to get back together?" She nudged for more. He didn't open up about his dating life often, but he didn't need to. He wore his heart on his sleeve. It wasn't difficult to tell when someone was tugging his heartstrings—he called it her "sixth sense," but she chalked it up to being an observer. She often enjoyed observing others. People make peculiar choices all the time, and it felt nice seeing living evidence that she wasn't the only one.

"Katherine was the best girlfriend I've ever had. Those years we had together were pure bliss—through the good and bad, we were there for each other. In the end, it hit me. She was ready for something I wasn't. It'd be wrong for me to keep dating her, knowing I may not ever be able to commit to a lifetime with her, whereas she'd be ready to tie the knot by the next spring," he paused, contemplating. "The only emotion that equates to love is fear. I guess I chose fear. Even if she wanted me back, I couldn't do that to her. She deserves someone who will be with her forever without hesitation. I invited her over on Thanksgiving because I knew she didn't have plans and didn't want her to be alone. We're still friends, but yeah, it's over."

The only emotion that equates to love is fear.

"When did you become so wise? Don't you coach baseball or something?" She lightly held his upper arm for a moment. Sometimes, she had a difficult time showcasing her vulnerabilities through words. So, she chose to express her love for him through a soft touch this time.

He shrugged. "Eh, I just listen to motivational podcasts during my workouts sometimes." Iris giggled, but then she remembered their current destination. Her childhood home in the mountains was a dark place she kept tucked away in her mind. Her only bright memories from that time of her life involved her brother. He did a substantial job of distracting her during the drive, but alas, her anxiety won as it always did. Often, she felt like the underdog running up against her own mind.

Being the golden child in the Greene household wasn't easy for Kai either. He was held to nearly impossible standards, whereas their parents felt the need to apologize for Iris. Her parents thought she was *shy*; that was the first word they used to describe her to anyone and everyone they met. They didn't like how reserved she was in public seeing as the rest of her family were practically socialites in their small community.

"Oh, I'm sorry my daughter is being rude; our Iris is just shy," her mom would say to anyone with a pulse. Her parents didn't know what to do with her. When Iris dozed off and shut down, her mom often snapped at her to "knock her out of her annoying funk."

Ironically enough, she wasn't shy. They just weren't her safe place.

"Hey, Irie, looks like the scenic route has paid off yet again," Kai interrupted her spiraling thoughts, pointing toward what lay beyond her window.

Iris peered outside, seeing her clouds, except this time, they were melting into the most striking mural of hues. Golden flames etched across the sky, masking pastel pinks and blues. The clouds no longer drifted as they had earlier; instead, they seemed to fade away into the canvas.

She looked over the cliff into the snow-tipped forest trees below, seeing the sun reflecting on the lake's glistening surface. From a distance, the lake appeared composed of a million microscopic crystals, shimmering for the world to see.

This view makes the whole trip worth it. It didn't matter who they were going to see. Kai was her rock.

Iris took a deep breath and let her nerves go. She turned up the music, rolled down the window, and closed her eyes. When she opened them, he grinned wide at her and clearly felt as weightless as she did. She rested her eyes again. This was their moment.

Everything would be okay—everything *was* okay.

Until it wasn't.

Chaos erupted faster than she could've ever imagined possible. She opened her eyes to see the world spinning. No, *they* were spinning. She heard a gut-wrenching scream. He held onto her waist with a death grip. They inevitably lost control, crashing directly into something hard.

Chaos.

So much *chaos.*

Iris didn't know when the tears came, but she couldn't withhold them. A jolt of pain shot up the back of her neck when the car halted abruptly to a screeching stop, wedged directly into the gray mountain from the driver's side. Her entire body ached. She realized very quickly that she couldn't lift her right arm, and then she glanced down to see Kai's arm still wrapped around her waist.

Wait, not wrapped... draped. His arm draped across her waist and was covered with streaks of blood, shards of thick glass poking out. A trail of thick dark blood gushed from his right forearm, seeping into her sweatshirt. She refused to look at his face. Instead, she gripped his arm, holding onto it with all her strength, ignoring the glass piercing her hands.

"Kai... *Kai*..." she pleaded with her eyes squeezed shut, a lump forming in her throat, blocking her airways. Her breaths grew shallower with every passing second as she desperately tried to tune out the thoughts her mind practically screamed at her. Still not daring to look in his direction, warm tears streamed down her cheeks.

"No, no, no..." her voice faded into a broken whisper. "*Please.*"

Kai did not stir. His arm remained drooped over her.

Even in his final moments, he shielded her. Her brother, her confidant, her rock was *gone*. She gently opened her eyes and barely turned her head, glancing to her right to witness the sun setting and the moon rising to claim the sky as its own. She continued holding onto her brother, slowly reaching for his hand to intertwine her small fingers in his.

After the chaos, stillness settled in, making itself at home.

Iris was alone.

The quiet was deafening.

ONE

IRIS

NEARLY TWO YEARS LATER

To no one's surprise, I am running late. Again.

No, not because I woke up late, but because I have spent an ungodly amount of time lying in bed after waking up. One thing led to another, and suddenly, 7:00 a.m. turned into 7:45 a.m. *very* quickly, leaving me approximately fifteen minutes to prepare for the day ahead. Rest assured, as a notorious procrastinator who claims to thrive under pressure, I've dealt with worse deadlines before.

Truman, however, has had enough of my laziness. He leaps into bed and brushes his face against mine, signaling it is time for his breakfast. I'm convinced he would pinch me if he had opposable thumbs. I sigh, but I can't blame the poor guy. I resonate with his hangry nature more than he knows.

"Okay, okay, I'm getting up," I groan. I shimmy out of the peach-toned bedding and walk straight to my bathroom, turning on my favorite mix of Indie Pop music. I have a busy work day ahead, so I don't have a second to waste. Especially after wasting the first thirty minutes of my morning in bed. I stand over my vanity and begin. First, I spritz water on my face, then reach for my cleanser.

On an ideal day, I would've showered, blow-dried my hair, styled it, then started my skincare routine before applying makeup, finishing my morning routine well before leaving. However, I only have a handful of ideal days quarterly, so this will have to suffice. Some people call this look "minimalistic." On the contrary, I know I'm far from a minimalist—the sheer amount of wall decor and trinkets in my bedroom alone can attest to that.

After finishing the world's quickest skincare and makeup routine, I brush my teeth and hair, then glance at my phone for the time: 7:51 a.m. I sprint to my closet, stumbling over a fluffy orange blob, who is meowing rather aggressively now. *Shoot, I need to feed him.* I turn fast in my tracks toward the kitchen to supply him with fresh food and water. After feeding my hungry fur baby, I resume my routine.

Routine. If running around my apartment like a mad woman blasting Conan Gray's latest album while hustling to get ready even qualifies as a routine. After gazing at the plethora of hanging clothes in my closet, I piece together the perfect light academia look: a flowy off-white turtleneck sweater with flowy sleeves, a high-waisted gray plaid skirt, knee-high black socks, and black Doc Martens platforms.

Unfortunately, I'm a chronic mood-dresser, so I choose to save this outfit for a different day, a better day. Instead, I slip on an oversized beige sweater, tucking it into high-waisted black trousers, and finish the look with a black leather belt and flats.

8:03 a.m. *It's go-time, Iris.*

I sling my work tote over my shoulder, bend to give Truman one last snuggle, and head outside of my apartment to greet the chilly autumn air. I'm interviewing candidates for an opening in our department today, so I need to put on my professional business woman shoes and step into motion.

But before I get to those, what I *really* need is an iced pumpkin spice latte topped with caramel cream to carry me through my 9-to-5. Pumpkin spice should not be limited to the seasonal menu—it's downright cruel that the basics of the world, like myself, can't order a pumpkin spice latte in June.

I pace down the block sauntering past several local shops to my safe haven: Little Falls. This local cafe has been the only constant in my life—outside of event planning—these last few years. I'm a Little Falls regular, which is exciting because I've always wanted to be a regular for some sort of small business. The fact that the owner, Davis, knows me by name and always remembers my order makes me giddy. I've lived in Chrysocolla Cove for over four years, and this coffee shop is still the best part of the Cove for me. I'm a simple girl.

As I step inside, the aroma of artisan coffee beans, freshly baked sourdough bread, and apples engulfs me. I lean against the front counter, ready to order my usual. Little Falls has several velvet sofas and comfy chairs strategically placed throughout the shop, along with tall wooden bookshelves filled with fiction books and card games.

"How's it going, Iris?" Davis peers my way from behind the counter, working on another order. I don't know his exact age, but I'm guessing he's in his mid-forties; his wrinkles, smile lines, and silver hair give it away. Without those features, he wouldn't look a day over 35. People tend to dread aging, but I've always found it fascinating. There's something so beautiful about looking into someone's face, seeing their fine lines and crinkles—pure evidence that they've *lived*.

"Oh, just ready to inject pumpkin spice into my veins. Nothing new here," I smile. "What's the loaf of the day?"

"Oh, you'd never guess," he chuckles, then reaches behind the counter and slides his knife through the loaf. He hands me a small piece of it. "Here, take a gander."

My mouth waters as I nibble on the small slice he gave me. "Mmm, you can never go wrong with banana-nut bread. Compliments to the chef."

"Definitely a fan-favorite at Little Falls, I'll let her know you liked it." Davis grins. His wife, Lilly, is the cafe's world-renowned baker—a true artist in the Cove. "Do you want the usual today?"

"Always!" I pay, then sit in a cozy green accent loveseat at a table meant for two in front of the counter. After settling in with my back toward the counter, I reach into my tote and pull out my laptop, bracing myself for today's hectic schedule while waiting.

Monday, October 2, 2023
9:00 a.m. - Clear Inbox
9:30 a.m. to 12:00 p.m. - Interviews
12:00 p.m. to 1:00 p.m. - Break + Reset
1:00 p.m. to 4:30 p.m. - Interviews
4:30 p.m. - Clear Inbox

Jam-packed. I have a total of eight interviews today. Interviews can be daunting for wishful applicants. Honestly, leading interviews makes me sweat sometimes, too. Ultimately, it's all about experience and connection for me, though. I'm the Head Events Director at Soi Connect, a small Marketing Agency downtown. I may be biased, but the agency's culture is immaculate; our Human Resources department takes the hiring process very seriously so as not to tamper with the "feng shui" of the office. By the time event-loving candidates make it to my office, they've already gone through two other interviews.

In other words, they've reached the final interview—the moment that will either make or break their job search. If I overthink each candidate's job hunt, I may or may not get a little too emotionally invested, so I make a conscious effort to avoid overthinking it. While awaiting my order, I glance over the candidates' resumes. I see some apparent standouts but can't rely on their resumes alone. A piece of paper does not define a candidate's worth. The former Director, Lena, hired me straight out of college. She took a chance on me, teaching me I could grow. If the opportunity arises, I would love to do the same for someone else.

I glance at my phone to check the time. Soi Connect is a fifteen-minute walk from here, so I still have time before I need to head out. Thankfully, I'm not running as late as I thought. I gaze to my right to peer out the shop's window.

I see an arrangement of copper, brown, green, and rustic red leaves falling in clusters. The overcast sky composed of gray and pale blue makes my clouds difficult to admire today. I spot people in beanies, thin coats, and boots descending the cobblestone streets. Fall is in full swing in the Cove, and I couldn't feel more relieved. Something about this season invigorates my soul.

While getting lost in my mind, I suddenly feel eyes lingering on me—from what direction, I'm unsure. Albeit alarming, this is not an odd occurrence. It's become quite ordinary in recent years.

I often feel like someone is watching me. I carefully turn away from the window to my laptop nonchalantly.

While turning, I scan the warm, inviting cafe and see nothing particularly unusual: a couple sitting on a couch together, cuddling and whispering sweet nothings into each other's ears—*okay, moving on.* A dark-haired man scrolling while eating a sandwich, AirPods in. A young woman highlighting several lines in a textbook—likely a student. A couple of young employees stand near the front counter, anxiously waiting for their bosses' orders to be ready.

Although someone may be watching me, I don't observe anything worth noting. I feel fine. Thankfully, Little Falls is bustling this morning. I'd be more uneasy if the cafe were slow. I'd rather wait fifteen minutes in line at a busy time than have no wait and no company.

"Iris, your order's up!" Davis shouts. I nearly topple out of my seat to meet him at the counter. He's smiling brightly as he casually hands me my holy grail.

"My hero," I grab the drink and immediately enjoy a mega quick sip before stepping away. "Thanks as always!"

And just like that, I'm jogging past the counter and back outside. Now, it's *officially* time to step into my badass business woman shoes.

Two

Jasper

O h, boy. I'm in trouble.

Was moving back to my hometown the biggest mistake I've ever made? Probably, but only time will tell. I used to know who I was. I *was* a music enthusiast, a self-proclaimed food critic, a realist, and even a scholar at one point. All those things led to my true self's grand reveal—I fooled everyone. At my core, I'm *actually* just a Masters School Dropout.

I chuckled at the irony of it all. *Jasper Alcott, valedictorian of his graduating class, hopes to move to the big city and make a difference.* My graduating class and parents sent me off with honor. I was overjoyed to start somewhere new after spending my whole life in the Cove.

My undergraduate experience was typical—early morning classes, parties, stressful midterms and finals, cranky professors, dating, hookups, on-campus jobs and extracurriculars, dorms that reeked of sweat and despair, the usual stuff we all go on and on about. I was lucky enough to study abroad for a semester in Italy. I enjoyed school. Loved it, even. In fact, I loved school so much that I chose to dive headfirst into a master's program focusing on finance roughly five years after working as an accountant in Seattle.

And I failed.

After spending so many years priding myself in my work ethic, study skills, and passion for learning, I failed. Now, I'll be frank: I failed one class in my third semester, but it was enough for me to reconsider my entire career path. Then, I kid you not, the same day I found out I failed the class, I got the call. My dad fell.

I drove home that night, roughly a four-hour commute from the city, meeting my mom at the hospital. In hysterics, she said, "Jasper, it's bad. Really, really bad."

I embraced her momentarily and then went to his room to evaluate the situation. In my undergraduate schooling, I was taught to wait to assess the damage until I saw concrete numbers or results. So, when I walked into his room and saw him sleeping, motionless, I started looking at the numbers.

I glanced at the heart monitor—eighty beats per minute, sitting at the average rate for a person his age. I looked at his casts at length and in full detail. He had a full leg cast on each leg and a neck and back brace.

"Damnit, Dad, did you fall off a building?" I whispered while staring at my old man.

"Not quite, but he did fall from about twenty feet up," a deep voice said. I turned to see a man in a lab coat and scrubs, presumably the doctor. "I know your mom has been having a hard time coping, so I imagine she hasn't given you details yet."

"Your assumption is correct." I nodded. "What happened?"

"He was on the second floor of his shop when he tripped over an extension cord and stumbled backward over the railing, landing on his back. Your dad's injuries are severe, but he will live," the doctor affirmed. "However, his life will be different moving forward. Due to the severity of his injuries, he will need to receive physical therapy and chiropractic treatments for the next several months, if not years."

I gulped subtly and nodded.

"Additionally, he will be unable to use the stairs like he once did. He won't be able to lift heavy items again. In order for him to live a long, healthy life, he will need to rest for the remainder of it."

"Come again?" I asked, unable to hide my shock.

"Your dad's busy days are over; he needs rest," the doctor firmly stated. It was a fact, not an opinion. Then it hit me. Dad wouldn't be able to run the shop like he had for the past thirty years. All of it started making sense.

"I see—thank you, doctor," I said, sitting next to my dad, staring off into oblivion. Well, that settled it. I had to move back to the Cove. From that point on, our family business was my business.

All of that led to today. It's a normal day in the Cove for everyone else. For me, it's the first day of a new era. I've been drowning in self-pity in Chrysocolla for the last two months. I am not proud of it. Believe it or not, before pursuing a master's degree, I was at least *somewhat* tolerable. Now, I'm worse than an elderly neighborhood grouch. Am I a failure? Undoubtedly. But I once heard that making small choices to nurture yourself can lead to large rewards.

With that in mind, I've decided to try something new this morning. Rather than waking up at 10:30 a.m., barely before the shop opens, I wake up at 7:30 a.m. to try another coffee shop my mom won't stop raving about. I gaze in the mirror and run my fingers through my dark hair, noting I really need to shave. I feel good to go after splashing some water on my face and brushing my teeth. After putting on a dark green sweatshirt and jeans, I head into my garage and start my 2020 Subaru Crosstrek, feeling ready for this place to wow me. With only a three-minute commute, I'm at Little Falls Cafe almost immediately. The scent of bananas fills my nose as I step inside. Fun. While waiting to order, I look at their assortment of breads and desserts and settle on a sourdough sandwich.

"What can I get you?" The employee asks.

"I'll get a black coffee and egg sandwich," I say. The employee—Davis, according to his badge—enters the order swiftly. I pay and sit in a chair next to the cafe's front window. I can't help but notice how noisy it is here. I slip in my AirPods and listen to music to drown out the commotion. Yep, I'm definitely not used to being up this early anymore.

When my order is ready, I thank Davis while grabbing the warm cup of coffee, then head back to my spot and begin to devour this sandwich. I'll admit, I wasn't expecting it to taste *this* good. I guess I will have to visit this cafe more regularly than anticipated. As I take a swig of my coffee, I look around and see one too many smiling faces. I don't mind that other people buzz with excitement at this time of day, but that is not my vibe. As of recently, I'm practically dead to the world before 9:00 a.m.

I have a good view of the front door from where I sit. While eating my sandwich, the bells chime, and I glance up to see them walk in; they're hard to miss. She's shorter than me and walks with confidence in each step, practically prancing. Her deep brown hair drapes along the slope of her back. I can't see her well from here, but I'm sure she has a wide grin stamped on her face.

How is she beaming this early in the morning? Ah, it must be the coffee. Wait—she probably hasn't even had coffee yet. Color me impressed.

Davis seems to know her personally, showing her more teeth in one conversation than I've seen from him all morning. Must be a regular. With my AirPods in, I can't make out the sound of her voice, but I imagine she's ordering *a pumpkin spice frappuccino with extra whipped cream* based on her vibe alone. She has to be a pumpkin spice girl. You can always tell.

A towering man with honey-brown hair trails in behind her. After she orders, she sits at a table for two, facing me. I make out the details of her face better from this angle. She has light olive-toned skin, light eyes, and bold eyebrows. At this point, I realize I've been staring for who knows how long as her boyfriend is sitting right next to her on the sofa.

Coming on a little strong, Jasper. Slow down on the coffee.

I glance down at my phone and start scrolling through the endless void of social media for a change of pace. After a few minutes of scrolling, I finish my coffee but choose to hang out a bit longer to bask in the cafe's ambiance. After all, it's my first morning outing since moving back here. My eyes wander around the shop again, landing on her briefly, only to catch her boyfriend casually staring right at me. Feeling guilty for getting caught, my eyes dart away.

I glimpse at my phone again to avoid his intense smolder. My eyes flicker back to him to ensure he's not looking anymore. And, much to my dismay, his eyes remain fixed on me. *Fine.* I take a different approach this time; I stare back. If this is a test of dominance, screw it. I'm in.

Then, within a matter of seconds, he breaks his intense stare, smirks, and *winks at me.*

What. The. Actual. Hell.

I start scrolling again, ignoring the urge to see if he is still being weird as shit.

Deciding I've overstayed my welcome at Little Falls, I get up. After taking my AirPods out, I hear, "Iris, your order's up!" I discreetly peer over to see her practically running to grab her order.

Iris. Her name is Iris.

Well, Ms. Iris is a girl on a mission—after taking a sip and thanking Davis, she dashes outside like her life depends on it. Just before stepping outside after her, the man with her turns to me again in no immediate rush to accompany his girlfriend. Not that it seemed to matter; she didn't pause to wait for him either. After assessing him, I notice he is only wearing a charcoal henley button-up shirt with jeans in the middle of fall. *Weird flex, but okay.*

His eyes linger on me, then he leaves. While driving home, I fixate on how odd this whole interaction was, but I decide I need to drop it. I have plenty of other things to think about anyway, like how to enjoyably run my old man's shop for the rest of my life.

Why didn't she acknowledge him at all during their coffee run, though? Why the hell did he wink at me like that? While pulling into my driveway, I realize I'm thinking about this so... excessively. Too excessively.

For fuck's sake. I'm definitely in trouble.

THREE

IRIS

I arrive at work precisely on time. Walking into my office, I take a whiff of my wallflower air freshener: eucalyptus and mint. I gaze at my birchwood desk, taking note of the stack of resumes waiting for me. I set my latte down and after I take a seat, I lean back for just a second, staring at the decor lining my walls and resting atop my desk. I'd describe my office style as Bohemian but colorful. I love adding pops of color to minimalist spaces—especially varying shades of green.

I could stare off into space for hours. Honestly, a break from thinking would be pleasant. Instead, I lean forward and accept defeat. It's time to get lost in my inbox. I used to have a hard time clearing out my inbox, but in recent years, I have gotten into the habit of responding to every single email I receive within one business day. I find it is a good way to keep myself busy during slower event seasons. I start sifting through emails, losing momentum with the click of each key.

"Good morning, Iris!" Soi's receptionist, Pen, peeks into my office. "Your first interview is here."

How have thirty minutes already passed?

"Great, thanks, Pen! You can tell him I'll meet him in the conference room in about five minutes. Thank you."

Pen swiftly nods and rushes out. She has been working at Soi for over five years after relocating to Washington from the South. I wouldn't be remotely surprised if her diet were composed of cheerios and sunshine. Her enthusiasm and sweet southern charm helps us all get through the slow season. I grab the top resume staring at me to re-acquaint myself with our first candidate.

Aaron Jones earned his B.S. in Business Marketing and walked across the stage just one year ago. His skills lie in Microsoft Excel, Budgeting, and Events Music Playlist mastery. Choosing our next hire is our top priority in the Events department right now, so I cross my fingers and head to our conference room to begin.

After six interviews, my confidence in finding our next event planner today is dwindling. Don't get me wrong; I've met various talented candidates today. I thoroughly enjoyed some of the interviews, and no one seemed overly nervous so far. Hell, I might have been more anxious for them than they were.

However, they all had one thing in common: their pitch lacked passion. For this interview, we require candidates to pitch an event idea for our annual fundraiser event. Soi sets aside a generous amount of funds to host one local fundraiser event annually. The candidates each pitch a local cause Soi could support and why. Then, whoever gets hired gets the opportunity to help organize that very event with our Events team as their first major project. The new candidate doesn't run the event, but the experience is always very valuable. When Soi hired me, I pitched a *fur* baby blanket drive event. I helped when needed and raised tons of funding for the local animal shelter to purchase new bedding for their surplus pets.

So far, our final candidates have shared some creative ideas, but the proposed events lack passion. Not to mention, I have not made a genuine connection with any of these applicants yet. Lena used to make interviewing look so effortless—she tends to make everything look effortless, though. Lena, my predecessor, left this past spring, promoting me to Head Events Director. I miss working with her fiercely, but we still keep in touch. For the most part. I snap out of it and refocus on the task at hand. It looks like our next candidate is named Joy. *That's a promising name, right?*

Pen ushers Joy into the conference room. Her blonde waves and freckles make her appear youthful and bright as she introduces herself. The energy in the room shifts for a split second, and my sliver of hope returns.

"So, Joy, what interests you about this opportunity?" I ask.

"Well, I've lived here all my life except for college, and I've watched Soi Connect become what it is today. It didn't happen overnight; it took years for Soi to build up its reputation locally. In a way, I want to go on a similar journey. I know I just graduated this past April and I started college a bit later than the average student. It's clear I don't have as much experience to offer as I probably should, but I'd love to be given the opportunity to grow as Soi has. I have always enjoyed event planning and feel like I could help make a difference."

I find her enthusiasm refreshing. After answering several interview questions, Joy pitches her fundraiser event idea to me. She shares that an antique shop downtown, Aged Emporium, recently underwent new ownership after the previous owner fell and could no longer run the shop. The previous owner opened and ran the shop for over two decades. While listening, I feel an outpouring of empathy for the former owner—he must be devastated. I haven't visited Aged Emporium in years, so I had no idea this even happened. I'm willing to bet other people in town aren't aware either.

"Even if you don't select me, I think it'd be amazing for Soi to consider hosting a grand reopening event for the antique shop, providing the funding we earn in the fundraiser directly to the family. I've known the family for years; they truly deserve all the support they can get," she says. I can't explain why, but this idea feels so *right*, goosebumps spread across my arms. This type of event ignited my passion for event planning in the first place all those years ago.

We conclude the interview, but it's clear as day: Joy will fit right in at Soi. The amount of thought she put into each answer struck me. As a courtesy, I'll still host the last interview, but the odds of my decision changing now are slim. We don't have enough locals at Soi anyway, so adding her to the mix will spice things up.

Once I conclude the last interview with Craig, a rather monotoned fellow, I head back to my office. My inbox isn't too out of hand, so I do some quick research on Aged Emporium.

The website can definitely use some work. After clicking through what feels like a million tabs, I finally find the current owner's name and email address: *Jasper Alcott*. I jot down his information on a sticky note and add the note to my planner, tucking my planner back into my tote. I am beyond ready to go home and snuggle with Truman. I close my laptop and prepare to leave when Pen sneaks into my office.

"How did the interviews go?" she asks brightly.

"I am proud to announce I think we found our next hire, Pen." I sigh in relief. "She is a local who has lived here most of her life, and the idea she pitched for our fall fundraiser is perfect—it's almost too good to be true."

"Oh, thank goodness," Pen exclaims. "Can I just say I am so relieved you found someone? You're so picky; I was totally worried."

"I'm not *that* picky." I slide my tote's leather strap over my shoulder. "I'm honestly just usually indecisive."

"Whatever you say, honey," Pen winks, heading out into the lounge. "Well, I'll see you tomorrow; get home safely tonight. The roads are slick."

"The perks of walking everywhere," I say, flipping my office's light switch off. While walking to the front entrance, I put on my coat and slip my AirPods in as I step outside. Immediately, I get chills from the brisk cold air. Daylight hours in the Cove are pleasurable; I typically only need a sweater to get by. But evenings are a different story entirely. Now that the sun sets earlier each evening, the cool air consumes the Cove starting at around 5:00 p.m. daily.

While passing by old-fashioned streetlamps decorated with autumnal wreaths across the street, I gaze up at the dusky sky, seeing the clouds fully masking the sun. In an instant, I lose my footing and slip on black ice while crossing the crosswalk. I *can't stand black ice*. I use my hands to push myself up off the ground, and *again*, I plummet. I glance around to make sure no one notices because I'm downright embarrassed at this point. I'm not typically this inept at simply walking, but getting lost in the clouds has hurt me yet again.

C'mon, Iris. Just. Stand. Up.

I attempt to stand on my own two feet again, and this time, I see a silver car approaching swiftly from around the corner. At this moment, I realize if I'm having difficulty rising after slipping on black ice, cars may not be able to brake properly. My throat tightens. I panic. I need to get up, but the grip on my black flats is insufferable. I pause and focus, attempting to drown out the panic flooding my mind. I place my hands firmly on the crosswalk and use all my strength to push myself. Miraculously, I finally manage to lift myself off the ground and then walk as carefully but quickly as possible to the other side of the crosswalk. During my final attempt to rise, it wasn't complicated at all to stand up for some odd reason, so I thanked my lucky stars and finished the journey home.

FOUR

IRIS

U pon entering my apartment, Truman greets me at the door, rubbing against my shin as I slide off my heavy tote. Being the most dog-like cat I've ever had the pleasure of loving, Truman strolled into my life about three years ago on my way home from work.

On that rainy day, as I walked into the old parking lot of my apartment complex, I noticed an orange tabby cat with white mittens sipping leisurely from a puddle of water. Inching closer to him, unable to restrain myself, he took an interest in me. He looked me up and down, then slowly approached me, placing one foot in front of the other, careful not to step in puddles along the way. I crouched to meet him on his level, and he recoiled away instinctively.

"It's okay, angel. I just want to be your friend," I whispered, gently reaching out my hand, hoping he'd give me the benefit of the doubt. I'd always loved cats. My parents loathed them. He hesitated, then gazed directly into my eyes. I pointed at my green eyes and stared back into his. "Looks like we already have something in common."

Recognizing his nervousness, I retreated my hand and slowly stood up. The poor thing was obviously malnourished, but I didn't want to scare him further, so I decided to finish the walk home and bring back fresh water for him. As I walked away, I heard a faint whimper. I turned to see his eyes locked on me. He meowed again, then trotted to me, rubbing against my leg. I reached down to pet him, and he nestled his forehead into my hand. He had surprisingly soft fur for being a stray.

After gaining his trust, I carefully scooped him up and brought him to the local shelter to see if he was microchipped or reported missing, but alas, he seemed homeless. He wasn't too skinny and was oddly friendly for a stray, so the veterinarian assumed he could have once lived with humans. Deciding to take him home was a no-brainer. I spent nearly a third of my savings on a vet exam and cat necessities, then snuck him into my apartment, promising to add him to my lease contract the next day. As I think back on that experience, I remember Kai being absolutely shocked I adopted a stray cat... this little guy sure loved Kai.

While I enjoy alone time, I ironically hadn't particularly enjoyed *living* alone, so little Truman has been my saving grace. I can survive alone, but living with another being brings me comfort. At this point in my life, that someone happens to be an affectionate feline named Truman.

Dragging my feet to my bedroom lazily after giving Truman a sufficient amount of kitty love, I change into a cozy loungewear set and transition from my bedroom to my kitchen. As much as I love dressing up, I prioritize comfort, so immediately changing upon returning home daily is non-negotiable. I open my fridge and stare at all the options for tonight's dinner: pre-cooked tacos, lasagna, or leftovers. This is what I call gourmet living as a 25-year-old woman. After deep consideration, I settle on the lasagna as I can guarantee it will require the least effort.

I turn on my oven and then begin scrolling through social media when the name Jasper crosses my mind. Right—*Mr. Alcott*. The new owner of Aged Emporium. I end up looking up the shop on Instagram to see if they announced the ownership change, and unsurprisingly, Aged Emporium doesn't even have an active Instagram account. Of course, Aged Emporium has yet to announce the ownership change on social media. *Wow, this really could be a great cause for our fundraiser.*

Yikes. I forgot to clock out of work again mentally. I can't be the only one who has a hard time leaving work at work. Recognizing I need to stop hyper-fixating on business, I slip my phone into my pocket, wander across the room to my leather sofa, turn on the TV, and remove my AirPods. I've found that reality TV is the perfect escape from my own reality. With today being Monday, a new episode of my current favorite dating show will be airing later tonight.

I don't date much these days. After dabbling with online dating and striking out time and time again, I chose to take a brief dating hiatus. Well, that brief break ended up lasting several months. In fact, it's been over two years since my last relationship and over a year since my last date. Between my forty-hour work weeks and the weekend events I often facilitate, dating hasn't been a priority.

It's difficult to comprehend how much I used to enjoy dating. I adored connecting with new people and exploring them both mentally *and* physically. I've grown tired of exploring, though. Once upon a time, I craved spontaneity and butterflies. I craved not knowing what would come next. I craved adventure. I wish I could say my cravings changed gradually over time. I wish I could say I grew dull because of age or dutiful obligations. But no, my zest for life changed in the blink of an eye on a winter day as I watched the moon claim the sky and my sun lose its light. Now, I crave the mundane.

Running my fingers through Truman's velvet soft orange fur, tuning out his faint purr is nearly impossible. Cuddling with this little guy always centers me. As I wait for my dating show to start, I get a FaceTime notification.

At this point in my life, I have two friends—other than Truman, of course—Lena and Callie. Lena was my manager at Soi before accepting a greater opportunity across the country in Georgia, of all places. In her thirties, some of Lena's best qualities include her assertiveness, honesty, and wit. Amongst all of these unnaturally superior traits, she also maintains a regal sort of beauty. She has a blunt, short black bob, dark brown eyes, and stunning deep bronze skin.

When I first met Lena, I felt immensely intimidated. I stuttered when simply sharing my name with her—pitiful, I know. That's when I knew the interview would be disastrous. I was half-tempted to walk away right there, but Lena isn't a fan of surface-level conversations. Taking note of my nerves, she sat upright and directly asked me why I was interested in an Event Planner position at Soi. I told her I'd always dreamed of becoming an event planner. She smiled politely and told me to "cut the fluff." I realized she was testing me. She pressed for a deeper answer.

She openly acknowledged that pursuing event planning in a small town like the Cove could be challenging, given the lack of growth opportunities available. At first, I told her I liked charming towns, and Lena saw right through that response. So, I folded.

I confessed I wanted to live closer to my family—specifically, my brother. I never would've admitted it to Kai, but he was the primary reason I chose the Cove. Lena considered me. After a moment of silence, she acknowledged the extensive event planning experience in my resume. She asked for the real reason behind my desire to work for Soi because, in her words, I was overqualified to work in a town as small as this one after interning with one of the most reputable event-planning agencies in the country. My jaw must have dropped because she smirked.

"You're candid. I like it. Most people would have lied straight to my face, even after I pressed them more," she said matter-of-factly. "Your willingness to swallow your pride and be honest attests to your character."

One thing led to another, and I landed a position at Soi at the age of 22. I moved to Chrysocolla Cove with high hopes. Little did I know, my scary manager would ultimately become my best friend, the person I would turn to the most after Kai's early departure. As cliché as it may sound, Lena has become the older sister I've always yearned for. I don't have to mask my feelings in front of Lena *as* often as I do with everyone else. She relocated and promoted me a few months ago, just shy of three years after my initial onboarding date. Since then, we haven't talked much, but that's life—I still cherish our friendship.

I peek back at my phone to see it's *not* Lena calling—this should be fun. Where do I even begin with Callie? If Lena is my sophisticated, intimidating sister from another mister, Callie is my golden retriever hype girl.

We met at a baseball game at the high school where Kai worked and coached. She's only a year older than me, and we clicked instantaneously. I was excited to learn she was an art teacher at Kai's school. However, don't let Callie's teaching background fool you. Despite her innocent persona—her words, not mine—she is a *wild child*. With her freshly dyed cowboy copper locks and curvy petite figure, she lives for socializing and going out in general, which is excellent for me. When we go to social events, I never have to worry about carrying on conversations in group situations. Callie takes care of it for both of us.

Her loyalty outshines all her other traits, though. She stands by my side and helps me step outside my comfort zone. She doesn't take it personally when I reject invites to go out, too; she has been exceptionally patient over the last couple of years. Just last month, I opted out of celebrating my own birthday because I didn't feel like leaving my apartment; she handled that with grace, too. I answer her call.

"What's up?!" Callie shouts into the phone's speaker while sitting in the driver's seat of her car, parked somewhere.

"Legitimately nothing, what about you?" I hear my oven beep upon replying to her. *Finally.* Why does preheating an oven take forever? I clearly don't have enough patience to enjoy cooking. I walk to my oven as Callie begins telling me about her day. "So, I'm thinking we deserve Thai food."

"Thai sounds so good my mouth is watering, but I'm putting a lasagna in my oven as we speak. You know my lasagnas are a labor of love."

"STFU, Iris! If by 'labor of love' what you really mean is 'test of patience,' sure, but we both know pre-cooked lasagna is your low-maintenance go-to," she cackles. Callie loves using acronyms like "LOL" and "WTF" aloud—wild child tendencies, I suppose.

"Ugh, okay, fair. But I just put it in the oven." I'm usually always up for Thai food, especially with Callie, but I'm not sure I'm good company right now.

"Well, take it out, and let me treat you to Thai. I'll pick it up and bring it over, then we can watch your reality TV shit show together and talk shit." She frowns. "Please?"

"Okay, fine." I take the lasagna out of the oven and wrap it, planning to eat it tomorrow. Let's be real, this lasagna didn't stand a chance against Thai takeout. "But you don't have to cover it. It's totally fine."

"Nah, I'll cover it because you'll deserve it after listening to me rant endlessly about my last class of the day. It was brutal."

"Ah, well, I'll cover it next time."

"Don't worry about it! I'll be over soon." I can see her opening her car door and stepping out. She must have already been parked at our Thai place. She hangs up, and I sink back into my sofa when I hear a knock. To my surprise, I see my chipper friend holding takeout and a bottle of wine through my peephole. I answer the door, and we both burst into laughter.

"Okay, so maybe I initially called you just to make sure you were dressed and okay with company." I don't think Callie enjoys alone time very much. Although I fancy alone time, I thrive in clamorous environments, which she is great at providing.

FIVE

JASPER

From behind the intricate hand-carved wooden counter, I gaze around the room to find the chestnut grandfather clock. Some would call this clock "antique." Personally, I think it looks prehistoric. Thankfully, vintage is timelessly popular. Otherwise, I am not confident Aged Emporium would still be in business.

Squinting to see the time, I sigh in relief. *Hallelujah.* My favorite time of day has arrived: closing time. I stride away from the counter and walk upstairs, skipping one step at a time. My closing routine is simple. First, I saunter around the entire shop to ensure no soul is in sight, starting with the upper level. After walking up and down each aisle and seeing nothing out of the ordinary, I trudge downstairs to continue my regimen. Passing by the vinyl records, old British tea sets, and creepy glass dolls, I don't see anyone. Once I determine no one else is still here, I lock the front door, turn off the Welcome sign, and secure the old-timey register. There is a reason why the shop is named Aged Emporium—everything inside is archaic, including the register itself.

I find old items neat. They're fun to hold and interesting to look at—especially old records, I'm a big fan of classic rock. However, I can't quite pinpoint why our customers often go out of their way to collect items like this. I can't complain, though; those same people are the ones keeping my old man's business afloat—well, *my* business now, I suppose.

After locking everything and flicking the warm-lit lights off, I head out through the back door. My home is practically calling my name, but I'd be lying if I said I didn't feel a sense of anxiety surrounding the topic of Aged Emporium. Sales have gone down significantly over the last couple of months.

When my dad first got injured, sales skyrocketed for a solid week and a half. I remember my dad saying that if sales continued like that, I could retire by age 40. But the momentum didn't last. By the end of August, the initial hype died down as people began to forget why they supported us in the first place, and our sales decreased significantly. My days at Aged Emporium have been slower more often than not. I don't want to consider what will happen if things don't improve from here.

You can't let them down, Jasper.

I feel refreshed as the crisp cool air surrounds me like an old friend. Determining it's time to stop thinking about work, I shift my thoughts to the forefront of my mind—tacos. I've always enjoyed cooking. I find it gives me time to decompress and think. Over the last several weeks, my typical nightly routine consisted of dinner, working out, showering, then heading to the local bar if I'm in good spirits.

Rest assured, I don't go to the bar to get plastered every night. In fact, I like to think I drink fairly responsibly. I got all of that partying out of my system in college—which I'm not particularly proud of—so I mainly go to the bar to have a drink or two and watch whatever game is playing. As surprising as it may sound, I sometimes even *socialize* at the bar. Old-fashioned, I know. I do have a few old friends who never left the Cove, so I meet with them from time to time. Oh, the joys of returning to your hometown when you're pushing 30. I only go to the bar two or three times a week. Nothing too crazy.

Chrysocolla Cove has grown a lot over the last decade. A *lot* being a subjective term. My high school graduating class was composed of only one hundred students. Now, the graduating class sits at a little over *two hundred* students. Look, I know it's still a relatively small number of graduates, but it's doubled within just ten years, which is thrilling to most of the Cove's locals.

After a quick drive home, I pull into my garage and get to work on those tacos. I gather the ingredients—chicken, pepper, salt, cilantro, lime, bell peppers, jalapenos, seasoning, rice, cheese—the good stuff. I take my time in the kitchen. The more time it takes to cook a meal, the more time I have to think. My mom is the one who taught me the basics of cooking, and she'll never let me forget it. At about age 5, I asked my mom if she needed help in the kitchen one evening while my dad was working late; she accepted my offer. She loved having a helper in the kitchen. I continued joining her throughout my life because she enjoyed cooking with me. It just stuck. I know cooking isn't for everyone, but my mom's face lights up when we cook together.

We don't have much in common, so cooking is something we've always been able to fall back on.

As I chop the onions, my eyes water outrageously, and my mind drifts back to the yummy sandwich I ate at Little Falls. *What was in that sandwich?* It's been a couple of days since my less-than-ideal encounter at Little Falls, but it still plagues my thoughts during every quiet moment. To distract myself, I finish chopping the onions, wipe my hands, and check my inbox. When I worked in finance, I had to check my inbox nearly every hour of the work day.

With my career transition to Aged Emporium, I no longer have to check my inbox more than once a day, which is undoubtedly one of the most positive things about the transition. However, every now and then, I fall back into old habits and check my inbox during a particularly uneventful evening. Looks like I received an email from an unrecognized emailer.

Subject Line: Soi Marketing Agency Events

Mr. Alcott,

I hope all is well. I'm Iris Greene, the Head Events Director for Soi Marketing. I am writing to you to gauge your interest in Aged Emporium partnering with Soi Marketing in an upcoming fundraiser project. I could explain more via email, but I feel it would be best to discuss this proposal face-to-face. Do you have availability to meet anytime soon? I'm at your disposal, so let me know what day and time works, and we can coordinate from there. Thanks so much for your consideration.

Warmly,

Iris

There's no way. Could this be the same Iris I ran into at Little Falls? What are the odds? I set my phone down on the counter to begin plating my tacos. After arranging three tacos on my plate, I grab my phone, stroll over to my mahogany dining table, and sit at the head of the small table. I take a bite—I knew I should've added more cilantro to the rice. While eating, I read the email I received from Soi Marketing again—Iris Greene. I respond:

RE:Subject Line: Soi Marketing Agency Events
Ms. Greene,
I'm happy to meet with you to learn more. How does meeting for coffee at Little Falls at 10:00 a.m. sound?
Jasper

I shoot the email, not expecting a response any time soon. Corporate Jasper used to set a strict no-emailing-after-business-hours rule. That is in the past, though. I put my phone down and continue to scarf down my tacos when I hear a ping. Sure enough, I received a new email. Despite it being nearly 7:00 at night, she already responded.

RE:Subject Line: Soi Marketing Agency Events
Mr. Alcott,
That's actually my favorite spot in town. I'll see you at 10:00 a.m. on Friday.
Warmly,
Iris

> **RE:Subject Line: Soi Marketing Agency Events**
> *Great, it's a date.*
> *Jasper*

Ah, Little Falls is her favorite place? My gut is telling me this is the same Iris I saw on Monday. I smirk before setting my phone down. Let's see how her boyfriend feels about this email thread. I am sure using the word "date" will cause him to have an aneurysm. I scoff. Sure, *maybe* I don't like him, I don't exactly feel inclined to be nice after Monday's incident. At this moment, though, I'm more interested in why Soi Marketing has taken an interest in Aged Emporium.

Six

Iris

I begrudgingly decide to skip Little Falls for coffee before work because I'm meeting with Jasper Alcott, Aged Emporium's new owner. After receiving the green light from Human Resources on Tuesday morning, we extended Joy an offer later that afternoon. She accepted, so her official start date is next Monday. I ran her fundraiser idea by other marketing team members, and of course, they ate it up. I decided to schedule a meeting with Mr. Alcott to discuss the opportunity. I have no idea whether or not he will bite, but I'm feeling jittery nonetheless and I haven't even had caffeine today.

Just before 10:00 a.m. I stroll into Little Falls, greeting Davis, and choose to sit in a plush rustic orange loveseat in the back corner. I'm still drying off from the rain outside. Not packing my umbrella today may have been a rookie mistake, but I had other things on my mind. Across from the loveseat sits two forest green chairs, and a quaint rectangular wooden table connects the seating. I take out my laptop and planner, resting them on the table's coarse surface.

Soft bells chime, leading me to glance up at the front door. I see a tall man with tan skin, likely in his thirties, stride inside. He has dark brown—nearly black—tousled hair, the smallest hint of facial scruff, and a sharp jawline. His attire consists of a black coat, navy blue button-up, fitted charcoal jeans, and some leather lace-up boots. I don't recognize him. I turn away to avoid getting caught staring, and to my surprise, he makes a beeline toward me, standing next to the table I'm currently seated at.

"Ms. Greene, I presume?" Oh, my. *This* is Mr. Alcott? I greet him immediately, nearly fumbling out of the oversized seat to do so.

"Mr. Alcott! Hi, it's a pleasure to meet you. Please feel free to take a seat." I motion toward the chairs, attempting not to get lost in his deep gray eyes. Shockingly, he chooses to forgo the seat across from me and sits on the loveseat beside me instead.

Be cool, Iris. You're a professional.

Noting my hesitation, he says, "Sorry, I prefer this soft spot over the hard one," while grinning—he has dimples. Up until now, I haven't been close enough to look at his face. His eyes gaze into mine, unwavering. "I'm happy to sit across from you if that's what you had in mind?"

"No, that won't be necessary, I mean, honestly, who wouldn't choose the loveseat over those hard chairs?" I angle my body toward him, taking note of his defined arms. Suddenly, it feels hot in here. I won't be surprised if I start sweating. "Well, I imagine you're curious as to why I've asked you to meet with Soi Marketing today, so I can get right to the point. A little birdy told me that Aged Emporium recently underwent new ownership due to less-than-ideal circumstances." He nods. "I don't know how familiar you are with Soi Marketing, but we're a local agency that's been around for about ten years now. Every fall, we host a fundraiser for a local business or organization. We typically set aside funding for this, so the organization's costs for the event are at a minimum price point. We feel Aged Emporium would be a great choice for this year's fundraiser."

He stares off into space, seeming to contemplate what I just shared. The silence lingers, so I take that as my cue to continue my pitch. "Regarding the timeline, we could host the event as early as November 10 and as late as December 16. Given that your shop is founded upon vintage and older items, I am leaning toward organizing a masquerade ball or art auction event if you're open to either of those ideas. It really depends on what you're comfortable with."

"Wow, I'm impressed; it seems you've already put a lot of thought into this. What would the fundraiser be for, exactly?" he asks, scanning my eyes.

"Well, that's the *fun* part of the fundraiser—it's up to you. Typically, our fundraiser partners use the funds for renovations, marketing, or upsizing the business. This is a special case, though, considering what led us to reach out to you. Honestly, we just want to help. Based on what I gathered, the previous owner didn't choose to stop running the shop, right? He fell and no longer could. There is a distinct difference between choosing to let go and having no other choice. We'd love to support his family in any way we can." I hope Mr. Alcott understands Soi Marketing values authenticity above all, so I mean it when I say we want to help his business and the family thrive. He considers me.

"This almost sounds too good to be true—so you organize the event to raise publicity and funding for us? What's the catch, *Ms. Greene*?" I don't miss the playful tone coating his voice when he uses my last name.

"Like I said, we really just want to help, *Mr. Alcott*. You can take some time to think it over and get back to me if you'd like. Here," I hand him my business card. "Call, email, or text me, whatever works for you. I'm at your disposal until I hear back from you."

"Okay, sounds good. I'll think about it and let you know." He puts my card in a leather vintage-looking wallet—he's so on-brand. I glimpse away and begin shuffling items in my work tote when he says, "I'll be sure to share your sentiments with my dad, too. I know he'll appreciate the support from you and your team at Soi."

I pause, unsure how to respond, gazing at him with wide eyes. "Your dad?"

"Yeah, my old man is the one who fell. I took over Aged Emporium shortly after," he says while looking outside through the window, seeming to get lost in the gentle raindrops streaking down the window's surface.

"Oh, wow," I gawk, completely unable to hide my shock. "I am so embarrassed, I should've done more research. I am so sorry you're going through this." He looks back at me with a flicker of emotion, then dismisses it.

"Don't worry about it; my parents are the ones who need support here. I'll be just fine," he affirms assuringly. I continue settling my laptop in my bag as several questions cross my mind at once.

Before I can stop myself, I ask, "Do you have any brothers or sisters? Why did you take over?" The voice in my head that sounds oddly like my mother scolds me: *Mind your own business,*

Iris. The thing is, though, I can't stop myself from asking. I'm not prying to get a juicy scoop of gossip. For some reason, I care about his answer—more than I can understand. He pauses for a moment, then carelessly shrugs.

"I'm an only child. I chose to take over Aged Emporium because my dad poured his entire soul and life savings into the business. As you mentioned earlier, it would've been a shame to be forced to let it go." His eyes twinkle. I can sense there's more to this story, but I don't want to intrude. We aren't even on a first-name basis yet; I don't feel like I've earned the right to know the information I keep seeking out.

"I see—well, that is commendable. I hope it's going well for you. What I said earlier still stands. We want to help support *your* family, so please consider our offer and get back to me when you can." I rise to leave. I have a meeting soon, so as usual, I need to hustle. Being a procrastinator is great and all until times like this when it really matters.

"Thanks so much for meeting with me, Mr. Alcott. I look forward to getting closer—" I panic. *Get closer? What the hell, Iris?* "I mean, working together and getting closer to accomplishing some goals together." *Great. That's just great, Iris. You arguably made that moment even more awkward.*

He quirks an eyebrow while the corner of his mouth curls upward. "Sounds good, *Ms.* Greene." There he goes again, using my last name in a mocking tone. I walk toward the exit, taking off my coat to raise it over my head as a shield before trekking into the rain.

"Are you walking?" Suddenly, he is at my side, practically towering over me. I'm about 5'5, so I'm guessing he is around 6'1. We pause at the doorway, stepping out of the way for any Little Falls customers entering or leaving.

"Oh, yeah, it's a pretty short walk back to Soi—less than fifteen minutes actually, and I have a meeting soon, so I've really got to hustle." I glance at my watch. I'm cutting it close this time, causing my anxiety to settle in and make itself at home.

"Are you always in a rush?"

My brows furrow. "Um, sure. But what do you mean by that?"

"Nothing, just wasn't sure." He runs his fingers through his ink-toned waves. "Well, hey, I think your agency is actually on the way to Aged Emporium, so do you want to hitch a ride with me?"

"Oh no, it's totally fine. I walk in all sorts of weather—rain, snow, hail—heck, I'd probably even venture out during an earthquake." I laugh. To my surprise, he doesn't.

"It's no big deal, Iris. I insist," he says earnestly. Typically, when strangers offer me rides, I am quick to reject them politely. Who am I kidding? I don't think a stranger has ever offered me a ride. And to be honest, Mr. Alcott doesn't feel all that much like a stranger for some reason... Screw it, I might as well. I don't want to be late.

SEVEN

JASPER

I ris smells like a spoonful of vanilla dipped into a jar of honey.
I wouldn't have known this had I not offered her a ride. I
don't know what's gotten into me. I glance at her using my
peripherals—she's wearing a pair of leggings that hug her thighs,
knee-high boots, and an oversized burgundy sweater that nearly
swallows her. As promised, I'm simply giving her a ride to Soi
Marketing, then heading to Aged Emporium. Technically, Aged
Emporium should already be open, but I highly doubt a line of
customers will be waiting.

"Do you mind if we turn on some music?" Iris asks softly. I
glance at her briefly and take note of her fidgeting with her hair.
She wore it up in a high ponytail today, using a thick hair tie to
keep it up.

"Yeah, sure, feel free to play whatever music you want." I hand her the aux cord and look back at the road. Before she even begins playing music, I receive an incoming call from none other than my mom. She calls me often, so I reject her call this time, promising to call her when I get to the shop.

"Sorry about that," I grumble then let out a sigh.

"Are you close with your parents?" I don't know Iris well, but she clearly doesn't shy away from asking personal questions. I'll admit, I was taken aback by how formal she was during most of our meeting today. Based on my first impression of her at Little Falls earlier this week, I assumed she would be more peppy, but today, she was all business. A woman of many hats, I suppose.

"Yeah, we're relatively close. I have dinner with them once every other week and do a breakfast thing once a month," I share. "What about you? Are you close with your family?"

She hesitates before answering, still fidgeting. If I'm not mistaken, I'd say she looks nervous. "Somewhat."

Somewhat. Who would've thought a one-word answer could be so telling? We sit quietly, listening to music. Again, I subtly glance at her just in time to see her squeezing her eyes shut.

"Who sings this?" I blurt out, trying to distract her from whatever is plaguing her mind. She gapes at me, clearly shocked by my question.

"This is "*All Too Well*" by Taylor Swift," she says matter-of-factly. Geesh, I didn't realize this was a touchy subject. "You know who Taylor is, right?"

"I mean, I know who she is, but you won't catch me belting out lyrics to "*Anti-Hero*" in my spare time," I say, keeping my eyes on the road. I take a left turn and pull into Soi Marketing's lot. Soi Marketing is right next to the forest; my shop is nearby on the other side of the road.

"Aha! You're more than familiar with her. You were able to reference a song casually without me even asking." I fold and crack a smile. Earlier this week, it was hard to miss the amount of smiles Davis threw her way. I think I'm starting to understand why. I park in front of Soi Marketing's building and turn to look at her—she's beaming. She likes pop stars. Note taken.

"Well, thank you so much for the ride, Mr. Alcott. I appreciate it and look forward to hearing from you." There she goes with the formalities again. I'm happy to play along.

"Of course, Ms. Greene. Anytime." She opens the door and jumps out, dashing into the office building like a track star. I pull out her business card. This is the most feminine, dainty card I've ever seen, and I used to work in the industry amongst plenty of other businesswomen. Her name, written in cursive lettering between the pale pink corners of the card, catches my eye. *Iris Adelaide Greene.* Sure enough, the card includes her cell phone number.

Just before pulling out of the lot, I notice a man with light brown—or maybe dark blond—hair leaning on the outer wall of Soi near the forest, his hands in his pockets. I look closer, and upon further inspection, I recognize exactly who he is. Damn, this man is *obsessed* with his girlfriend. Frankly, I'm beginning to feel concerned for Iris. I lock eye contact with him—*oh, please, for the love of everything, not this again*—this time, he simply nods his head, inclining for me to follow him. Feeling confused but too curious to walk away, I shut off the car and follow along.

I walk toward him hesitantly, and then he trots into the evergreen forest. While following in his footsteps, I recognize the sun has come out of hiding for the first time today. Its rays shine down on the forest, enfolding us and accentuating the fresh dew drops on every leaf and stone. The sound of the running stream captures my attention. Chrysocolla Cove is surrounded by forests. Several tree-covered groves connect to the greater forest, even in the central part of town. I glance around, realizing we're entirely secluded. I remind myself of the way this man regarded me earlier this week. I'll admit, in hindsight, *maybe* following him into the forest was a shitty idea, but how badly could this go?

"Hey man, you won't kill me out here, right? I'm already late to opening my shop for the day," I call out, getting goosebumps. He abruptly halts before reaching a small creek. At this point, we're within reaching distance of each other, enveloped by mossy trees, fallen leaves, and large rocks. Standing only a tad taller than me, he slowly turns around, and his golden eyes ensnare me. When he looks at me from this close, it feels as though he's peering straight into my soul, seeing every choice I've ever made, good *and* bad. Suddenly, I feel lightheaded, and the green-hued forest is spinning, losing its color as it spirals. It's taking strength not to faint, and I don't quite understand why.

"I've been told my looks can be blinding." He flashes a tantalizing smile. I strain to keep my eyes open, and then he blinks, breaking our intense stare. As he does, his eyes fade from gold to hazel. In an instant, the world stops spinning, I can stand up straight again and no longer feel like I'm going to pass out.

What. The. Actual. *Hell.* Is. Going. On.

"Hey, Jasper," he reaches out his hand, presumably to shake mine. "I'm Kai."

EIGHT

JASPER

While recovering from the mind-warp, I gaze at his hand in a daze, hesitating to move a single muscle under his watchful eye. I don't feel inclined to trust *Kai*, let alone shake his hand while alone in the forest, after the sensation I experienced seconds earlier. He catches my drift and pulls his hand away, shrugging. "Suit yourself, buddy."

Buddy? Absolutely not.

"Look, Kai, I followed you out here thinking we would talk, man-to-man, about Iris. I didn't expect to be nearly blinded, so please *forgive me* if I'm not ready to be *buddies*," I say, looking into his eyes pointedly. I've never been one to cower away from a challenge—especially if that challenge comes in the form of an overconfident guy who may or may not have superpowers. *Oh shit, am I losing it?*

He chuckles and motions toward a massive gray stone perched on the creekside.

"Understood—let's start fresh. You're going to want to sit down." He eyes the stone. I look at the time, seeing I'm already thirty minutes late to opening the shop. At this point, I'm too dumbfounded to leave this conversation, so I prop myself up against the stone.

"So, want to start by telling me what that was all about? Is the golden eye thing a magic trick?" He rakes his fingers through his golden brown hair and sighs as if I'*m* the unreasonable one here.

"Before we get into that, I need to divulge more important information, Jasper. I've never been one to beat around the bush, so I'm just going to say it: Iris is essential to me. Her safety is my utmost priority. Everything I do, I do for her." He picks up a silver pebble, tossing it into the creek. I watch it skip a couple of times before it plunders into the clear mountain water.

"I understand, man. I can tell she means a lot to you. I don't know if she's told you, but she and I are just working together from a business standpoint, so there really isn't anything for you to worry about—"

"Excuse me?" Kai interrupts. "What are you suggesting?"

"Well, I'm just saying you don't need to worry about me pursuing her. We're all good here," I assure him, feeling uncomfortable about this entire situation. Suddenly, Kai bursts out into an obnoxiously loud roar of laughter. He's laughing so hard that it transitions into a faint wheeze while I feel thoroughly confused.

He grins, looking down at his feet and shaking his head. "Dude, Iris and I aren't together. I'm not her partner. I'm her *guardian*."

Strange. They seem close to the same age which is uncommon for guardian-child relationships.

"Oh... how does that work?"

"Alright, we're going to go all in now. You sure you don't want to sit down?" He waits. "Okay, fine, here we go. I'm dead. Well, not quite dead I suppose, seeing as I'm here, having this conversation with you. But I can assure you, I died, and at this moment, I'm not alive either. I don't like using the term *angel*, but if that helps make it easier to understand, just think of me as a guardian angel, I guess. Although, I denounce the second part of that."

He can't be serious. Wait, is he serious? I expect him to admit he's joking, but he stares at me with a serious expression instead. My mind is whirling, but not from an eye-piercing gaze this time.

Ah, *fuck*. Is this it? Is this my breaking point? I really must be losing my damn mind. I mean, throughout my childhood, my mother often talked about angels. Our family is not particularly religious, but she firmly believes in angels. She would've fainted upon hearing the words I just heard. Quite frankly, I'm surprised I haven't fainted yet.

"I'm sorry, didn't you say earlier, 'I'm not one to beat around the bush,' and then you proceeded to do exactly that? Why didn't you start with this?"

"I didn't know if you'd believe me," he admits. "I'll be honest. You're the first living mortal being who's ever been able to see me, so I'm not used to talking about this."

Truthfully, I don't have the slightest clue what to believe. As someone who's always relied on numbers and logic, this defies all reason. But logic can't explain the mind-warping number he performed on me earlier by simply staring into my eyes. How is this possible? Why on Earth can I see him? *Why me?*

"So, no one else can see you?"

"Not that I know of."

"Great. Well, I need to get to my shop right now, I should've been there an hour ago." I turn around and begin trudging back to my car, crunching leaves with every step. He catches up instantly, keeping in step with me.

"You just found out guardians exist, and you are worried about being late for work?" he questions me. He's got a point, but I'm just going through the motions right now, hoping my mind can make better sense of this later. Maybe I'm in shock. Who knows. "Okay, that's fine! I don't actually have to be next to Iris 24/7 to guard her anyway; as you may have noticed, guardians have special abilities. Earlier, I actually used my soulsight on you. I also share an unbreakable tether with her. If she is severely distressed, I feel it in my gut, and I can teleport to wherever she is."

As you may have noticed. I scoff. I couldn't have ignored the soulseeing madness from earlier, even if I wanted to. We reach my car, and I settle inside, turning the key in the ignition and taking a deep breath to steady my nerves. As I grip the steering wheel, I realize I have chills. It's not every day someone peers into your soul and you find out guardian angels are real. Kai appears in the passenger seat beside me without having to open the car door himself. I eye him. "So, you're connected to Iris as her guardian. What does your job description entail, exactly?"

"Eh, it's pretty stereotypical, honestly. I protect her from harm, lift her up when she's down, you know. The types of things you'd expect a guardian to do," he says in a nonchalant manner as if he didn't just turn my entire world upside down in a single conversation.

"Damn, you really are an angel, huh? I'm not just seeing things." I reverse out of the parking lot, heading to Aged Emporium, speeding the entire way. I'm still feeling lightheaded, but the sooner I can get to Aged Emporium and rid myself of his company, the better.

"Again, I don't love the use of that word, but yeah... I guess I do 'angelic' things to keep Iris safe." He rolls the window down, resting his arm on the window frame. "Man, I've missed sitting shotgun. Iris avoids driving; she walks nearly everywhere. It *drives* me crazy." He winks.

This guy is a trip.

I consider what he said, connecting the dots. When I gave Iris a ride, she seemed unsettled. "Have you ever actually prevented her from harm?" I can't help but ask and hope the answer is no.

"Yes," Kai says somberly. He pauses, leaning his head back on the headrest while staring off. "Just earlier this week, Iris slid on black ice while walking across the street. She was wearing shoes with zero grip, so she managed to slip two other times while attempting to stand back up. On her third try, I saw a car fast approaching, so as she stood, I lifted her up the rest of the way and made sure she could stay balanced before letting her go."

That damn black ice. We need to set down more salt on the roads after dark. "I see. Does Iris get into situations like that often?"

"Wouldn't you like to know?" He grins. He has a point. Why did I even ask that?

"So, who were you to Iris?"

Kai stares off, evidently contemplating before speaking. "No one. What matters is I'm her guardian now—until I complete my mission."

"Which is?"

"To help Iris embrace her emotions and find the peace she deserves."

I haven't known Iris long, but she exudes an extremely upbeat, positive energy in every environment I've encountered her in thus far. "So, is that why you are her guardian? Does every human have one?"

"I signed up to be a guardian after my death. When I died, I was given the choice between being a guardian or immediately ascending. Yes, she needs a guardian to help carry her through this turmoil. No, not every human has a guardian. Contrary to what many humans believe, guardians are not lifelong companions for their assignments. Guardians are not meant to be permanent fixes—they serve a purpose for a specific period of that person's life." I pull into Aged Emporium's little parking lot. "Let's say someone is struggling with addiction. They may be provided with a guardian to help them conquer their inner demons instead of turning to the substance they crave. Other people receive guardians during hard times when they need help healing physical, mental, or emotional wounds. People can receive guardians for plenty of reasons."

"So, why does Iris have a guardian, then?"

"That isn't my story to share." Feeling puzzled, I open my car door and approach Aged Emporium's doors. After walking in, I set my keys down and step behind the front counter. Kai follows, taking in the many wonders of Aged Emporium. He glances at the grandfather clock first, then his eyes wander over to a glass doll in a little rocking chair, lingering on her. "Side note: that doll's energy isn't great. I'd consider rehoming her."

"Uh, yeah, that's kind of the point of her—it—being here at the shop." I roll my eyes. "Anyway, you said I'm the only human who's ever seen you. Why?"

"You tell me. I imagine it has something to do with Iris." He pauses, turning to face me directly. "You have to understand: I am here to help Iris feel whole. I want her to feel happy, safe, and *free* again. Now, I'm not expecting you to swoop in and mend her. The amount of progress Iris has made up until this point is no small feat, but it will continue to take time and effort for her to heal. If anything, you having the ability to see me might be the secret sauce I've been needing."

"Okay, you had me all the way up until the 'secret sauce.'" I scoff.

"Look, I'm her guardian, so I'm not asking you to protect her; I've got that handled. But maybe, out of the little kindness in your heart, could you be there for her if she calls? She can't see or hear me the way she can communicate with you. I think Iris needs more friends in her life who she can open up to." *Friends.* Right. "It wouldn't hurt for me to have someone to bounce ideas off of from time to time, too."

Just before he steps outside, he eyes the jewelry in the glass display case. I follow his gaze to the shiny silver, gold, and rose gold jewelry boxes. He abruptly puts his hands in his pockets, then turns to look at me, all humor in his expression gone. "Jasper, it's imperative you do *not* tell Iris she has a guardian. All the growth she's done will vanquish if she finds out. Please, do not tell her."

Nearly tangible, the vulnerability in his eyes catches me off-guard. I'm definitely missing something here. I nod a single time, and he lets out a sigh of relief then smiles warmly at me. "Thank you, Jasper. As for everything else—no rush. Just think about it. I don't want to force you to be friends with her. She would hate that. In the meantime, I'll be around." He turns to walk away, seeming to fade into mid-air.

Screw it. Instead of flipping the Open sign, I whip out the Closed For Today sign. I haven't been drinking much lately, but a drink is warranted and entirely necessary right now.

Angels are real. Angels are real. *Angels are real.*

What an unprecedented situation. Numbers and facts have always been my friends. I worked closely with numbers throughout my schooling—this simple statement defies all logic I've stored in my mind up until now. I stop at the town bar after my run-in with Kai, and even the bartender looks surprised to see me at this time of day. *You and me both, dude.* While sitting alone, I spend an obscene amount of time thinking about what the hell just happened and, more importantly, what happens next.

NINE

IRIS

I set my phone down atop my desk after checking my inbox for the hundredth time since Friday, determining hyper-fixating on this has led to unwelcome anxiety. A crucial part of event planning consists of successfully pitching events and building relationships. I thought I did a decent job on Friday, but it's been seventy-two hours, and the crickets have grown insufferable.

Typically, if we don't hear from the prospect within forty-eight hours of the pitch, the sale is a fail, as Lena always says. Mr. Alcott seemed interested, but I suppose I could have read him wrong. Or maybe he was just being polite, when really, he wasn't interested at all. I can't blame him. I know that feeling all too well—feeling the need to please the other party at all costs, even if it costs you a piece of yourself in the process.

Tucking my anxiety back into bed, I glance at the time and head to the lobby. Joy should walk in at any moment. I don't think I'll ever live up to the high standard Lena set as my predecessor, but I do want to provide Joy with all the support she needs to succeed as an Event Planner. Right on cue, Joy walks into the lobby, grinning from ear-to-ear. I remember the jitters I felt on my first day at Soi—that girl had no idea what her future had in store for her, which is probably a good thing.

Pen greets her first, asking her if she'd like some coffee and complimenting her lipstick. Joy is wearing a maroon blazer, a flowy blouse, and trousers. She undoubtedly dresses to impress. I step out of my office to welcome Joy, shaking her hand. "We're so happy to have you here, Joy! Today, we will start with some basic onboarding."

I invite her to follow me to her new desk. Upon walking into Soi, the front desk rests in front of a backlit cream-colored divider with our peach Soi logo branded on it. We walk beyond the front desk area to find Joy's new home away from home. Her white desk is situated amongst several other desks in a large room just behind the divider.

Soi is composed of just two floors; our financial, legal, and executive teams occupy the upper floor. The ground floor is for the creatives—the marketing, social media, and event planning teams. About forty people work on the creative side of the company. My events team is composed of ten stellar souls, including myself—we're known as the "upbeat" department of the company, which I take pride in, considering I haven't used that word to describe myself in years. Not that anyone I work with needs to know that.

"You're welcome to decorate your desk however you'd like." I hand her a stack of paperwork. "And this is your onboarding documentation. After you get through this stack, we will have you watch some brief training videos about event planning etiquette here at Soi, then you and I can meet to discuss any questions you have about the job. Following that, we will do some fun introductions."

"Perfect, sounds great!" She beams and peers around at her surroundings. "Where is your office?"

"I'm right over there." I look over her head and to the right, nodding toward my office, less than twenty feet away, lined up amongst the other directors' offices. "Also, before you have to dive into this ridiculous amount of paperwork, I want to share an update. I pitched your Aged Emporium fundraiser idea to the team and they were obsessed, so I met with Mr. Alcott on Friday to discuss the opportunity. I haven't heard back yet, but I will let you know as soon as I do."

She holds back a squeal, obviously trying to reign in her excitement. "I just know he will say yes! This is going to be the best, I can't thank you enough for taking a chance on this. I won't let you down."

I'm only just beginning to get to know Joy, but I feel like I can trust her. My mother taught me that trust must be earned, not given freely. Much to her dismay, I often find myself too trusting. Giving people the benefit of the doubt comes naturally to me—it always has.

"I'll be in my office if you need anything, Joy." I stroll into my office when my phone pings. My heart skips a beat. *Finally.*

And it's a text from Callie. Not an email.

Callie

What are you wearing to the halloween party?
Wanna match?

Callie may have caught me at a bad time this weekend, leading me to commit to accompanying her to a Halloween party. The high school is hosting a late-night party for adults after the student party this Saturday. I should've known I'd regret that choice, but at the moment, I felt guilty for rejecting so many of her invites to go out and she promised it'd be fun.

Iris

I have no idea, what are you thinking you'll dress up as?

Callie

I'm leaning toward dressing up as a devil this year! I think it'd be so fun for us to match, what do you think??

Iris

Cute! I will let you know what I find.

I can't wait to see your costume. :)

I settle back into my office and unlock my computer. I haven't dressed up for Halloween since college. I loved socializing during my university days. Halloween was actually my favorite holiday. While growing up, Kai and I dressed up together often. One year, he was Dash and I was Violet from *The Incredibles*, which cracked everyone up considering how much taller and older he was than me. Another year, I dressed up as Toadette with him being Toad at my side. We coordinated costumes on and off for years, but when I turned 15, I decided I was too old for that and wanted to impress some guy at school I liked, choosing to dress up independently as a witch. Kai felt bummed, but he understood. He gave me a hard time, though, like he always did.

"Irie, this boy won't remember what you wore for Halloween this year forever, but guess who will? Me." He furrowed his brows. Then, when Halloween came, I walked downstairs to see Kai dressed up as a warlock, still finding a way to collaborate with me even without my consent. I let myself envision his radiant smile while wearing a blue mystical wizard's hat for a few seconds longer before abruptly stopping myself.

No, not today. I will not go there today.

I receive another message, and to my surprise, it's *not* from Callie. An unknown number texts me.

Unknown

I'm in, Ms. Greene.

Mr. Alcott *texted* me? And he's *in*? I bite my lip while fighting an embarrassing grin. Now, I can't contain my excitement, although I don't fully understand why. I tread outside my office to capture the attention of the events team.

"I have great news, everyone. Aged Emporium is a go! I will meet with Mr. Alcott ASAP to solidify the contract details, then we can get to work. Let's make this our best fundraiser yet!" I exclaim, clapping.

Everyone in the room claps excitedly, then Joy rushes to my side before I exit. "I am so excited Jasper said yes, I knew he would!"

Jasper? I find it surprising they are on a first-name basis, but try to ignore the ping of emotion I feel. It doesn't matter. Hell, the closer they are, the better this event will go. My cohorts poke fun at how formal I am with clients, but I couldn't care less. Blurred lines between business and personal life lead to mistakes. After settling back into my office, I reply to his message.

Iris

Thanks for getting back to me and agreeing to work with us, Mr. Alcott. Do you happen to have time to stop by Soi today to discuss contract details? We just want to get started as soon as possible.

Jasper Alcott

How does this afternoon work?

Iris

Works great for me!

My stomach drops—similar to the way it does when descending on a massive roller coaster. The nerves consume me. I haven't felt this way in years, and I'd be fooling myself if I said I was mad about it.

TEN

JASPER

A couple of sleepless nights later, I conclude it won't hurt to help Kai complete his mission. Shocking, I know.

I mean, I obviously have a lot to learn about Iris—for instance, I haven't got the slightest clue about why she feels the way she does. But the idea of her fighting a silent battle seemingly alone gets to me, regardless of how well I know her. Primarily, for this reason, I choose to work with Soi. Working with Soi will help Aged Emporium in the process anyway; it's a win-win. The shop will gain the funding it needs to excel, and I'll get to help Kai help Iris. While sitting at the front counter of Aged Emporium, I take my wallet out to find her business card. I try to avoid emailing unless absolutely necessary at this point in my life, so I shoot her a text instead. She quickly replies. Of course, she is still calling me Mr. Alcott.

We settled on a time to meet at her office this afternoon. I haven't had any uninvited guests visit me since my angelic encounter on Friday, which I find relieving. I assume Kai is serving his purpose at Iris's side. Throughout the weekend, I thought about their dynamics. He cares a lot about Iris. Sure, he can chalk it up to it being their tethered bond or whatever, but he can't deny how deeply he cares for her. Just as I'm getting sucked into that stupor of thought, the bells chime. We've been open for two hours already and we're just now greeting our first customers of the day. I hope this fundraiser helps as much as Iris thinks it will.

I glance at the middle-aged couple wandering in, carefully taking in all of our shop's belongings. The jewelry entrances her at the front while he sorts through the watches. They both pick different pieces for each other and chuckle like they're sharing a secret only they know. For a moment, time halts, and I see my parents in them, but before the accident. If I can just get this shop back on its feet, maybe they'll recover.

I stride in through Soi's front doors, not knowing what to expect. From what I've gathered since moving back home, Soi is one of the newer establishments in town. A woman with black hair greets me. "You must be Mr. Alcott! Welcome! I'm Pen. Iris should be finishing up with a meeting. If you'd like, I can take you back to wait closer to her office."

"Sure, thanks." I take note of Pen's warm energy. Does everyone working at Soi eat rainbows and sunshine for breakfast?

"Not everyone, but a lot of them do," a hoarse voice whispers into my ear, over my shoulder. Great. I guess I can officially add mind-reading to his bag of tricks I don't care for.

"Dude, you can't sneak up on me like that—it's too much," I mutter. As Pen leads me to Iris's office, she turns her head ever so slightly over her shoulder to glance at me.

"Everything okay, Mr. Alcott?"

"Uh, yeah, sorry about that—I was replying to Siri, she has a mind of her own." I hold up my phone. She nods in a friendly, reassuring but tentative way, then turns back around. I cringe, and to no one's surprise, Kai snickers.

"Oh man, this is going to be fun. I love that you can see me, it's my new favorite game." Kai walks next to me. I grit my teeth and attempt to brush this off, accepting this is my life for the foreseeable future. The faster we can mend Iris, the better. I can't acknowledge everything he says, otherwise people will think I'm a lunatic.

"Jasper!" a high-pitched voice shouts to my left. I gaze over to see Joy? Just when I thought I couldn't possibly be more surprised than I already am.

"Joy? What are you doing here?" I approach her desk, grinning. "I haven't seen you since high school."

"I know, it's crazy. Today is actually my first day at Soi as an Event Planner. I'm the one who pitched Aged Emporium to Iris as our fundraiser, and I can't tell you how happy I am that you agreed. I knew you would, though," she says, playfully punching my arm. It's wild seeing her here. We spent time in the same crowd throughout schooling, but she was much younger.

As we're catching up, I see movement out of the corner of my eye. I turn slightly to see an open office. Natural light pours in through a large window, illuminating her brunette waves cascading down her back. She's vigorously taking notes in her planner while sitting at her desk with her legs crossed. Upon closer look, she appears flushed. *Is she blushing?*

"Before you get carried away, her cheeks are naturally pink. Don't feel too special, buddy." I jump, forgetting Kai had even been next to me. This is getting old fast.

"Whoa, are you okay?" Joy reaches over and gently grasps my arm. I pull away politely.

"Just peachy. If you'll excuse me, I've got to meet with Iris. It was good talking with you." I turn to walk toward Iris's domain. Upon approaching, I thank Pen quietly, then lean on her door frame, taking in all the elements of Iris's office that make it her. The scent reminds me of soft rain on a cloudy day. Her cozy office features several minimalist art pieces lining the walls, alongside an assortment of greenery—from faux plants to the chairs. How fitting it is for Iris Greene to fancy the color green. I find tuning out the faint music echoing throughout the space to be nearly impossible, not that I actually mind. When I worked in corporate, I never cared about decorating my office. I saw it as a means for work only, not taking time to make it my own. I never understood why people decorated their offices so intensely until now. Her office is an expression of herself.

"Hi, *Ms. Greene.*"

"Mr. Alcott." She looks up from her planner, startled. Did she really not notice I was here? No wonder she needs a guardian. "I'm so glad you could stop by! I already heard back from Legal. They'll send you a contract to review sometime today. That will cover any additional costs we may need you to cover, but your financial investment should be minimal. I was thinking we could use this time to discuss what exactly we want to do, when to do it, and where to focus our efforts."

Not wasting a single second of time, she motions for me to take a seat. As I approach the chair, I gaze at her. Subtle, hardly noticeable purple shadows lie directly below her emerald eyes, and yet, her smile doesn't falter.

"I'm all yours. Hit me with whatever you've got." I pause. "Just know, I've never been a marketing guru—I worked in finance previously, so that's my forte."

She appears taken back for a second. "Oh, fun—let me guess. Accounting?"

I smirk. "Not so fun, but yes, accounting. You've got me pegged." Suddenly, I hear a rumble of laughter that does *not* belong to Iris. I see him sitting in the seat next to me, using my peripherals.

Oh, great, he's back. He just comes and goes as he pleases with zero notice either way.

"I'm sure that makes running your business a bit easier," she says softly. "Do you ever miss it?"

"Accounting? Nah, I just pursued that as a means to an end while obtaining my master's degree in finance."

"Oh, wow! A master's degree is definitely something to brag about," she says excitedly. Here we go again.

"I actually didn't earn the degree," I say nonchalantly. "I flunked one of my classes the same day my dad fell. Instead of heading back to class after the accident, I stayed here, taking over Aged Emporium for the unseeable future. Appreciate your sentiments, though."

Her brows furrow. "You said all of that as if any of it was your fault. Sure, you failed a class, but I am certain you still would've been able to get the degree eventually. Instead, you chose to support your parents, which was pretty selfless if you asked me. Honorable, too."

I stare at her, stunned. Iris doesn't know me, but she singlehandedly soothed a tainted part of my soul without even trying. After another beat of silence, she clears her throat and warmly says, "Well, I want to respect your time, so let's get started."

Eleven

Iris

Joy actually *knows* him. She doesn't just know who he is—she knows *him*. I shouldn't be surprised. Joy is a local. He is a local. They're both bound to know each other. If they went to high school together, then that means he is closer to my age than I initially anticipated. *Ah, there I go again, exercising my ability to overthink.* He looks up, waiting for me to continue. For some reason, I cannot focus. Today he's wearing yet another sweater, but this time the light gray tone brings out the smoky clouds in his eyes. *Focus, Iris.*

"So, previously we discussed a pretty open timeline for the event. Have you thought any more about when you would like it to take place?"

"When would you suggest it takes place?"

His question surprises me. Nine times out of ten, usually the client has unrealistic demands and expectations. Rarely do they ask for my opinion at this point. Jasper isn't like every other client I've had, though. Based on what he shared earlier, something tells me he is a bit self-critical, too.

"Well, it depends on the type of event. If we host a masquerade ball, it'd be wise to shoot for December so we can roll with a Winter Wonderland aesthetic." I say as a swarm of decor ideas for a Winter Wonderland ball flow in. He suppresses a laugh, swiftly cuts a glance to his left and then his eyes wander back to me. I would've missed it if I hadn't been watching. *Oh, good, I'm not the only one who can't focus right now.*

"December it is. I'm good with a ball, too; those always seem to go well in movies," he says. Now, I'm the one laughing.

"I mean, if we're being real, masquerade balls almost never go well in movies," I tease. "Have you ever heard of that one princess? Cinderella? Her prince couldn't find her for weeks following the event."

He rolls his stormy eyes playfully. "I may not be cultured enough to know Taylor Swift's voice live, but I'd have to be living under a rock to not know who Cinderella is."

"So glad we've covered that," I poke fun. "Let's settle on Saturday, December 16, if that works for you?" He nods, so I continue. "On another note, I checked out your social media accounts for Aged Emporium—they could use some work. Do you use social media?"

"Eh, I use it a fair amount. I've been meaning to use it for Aged Emporium, but the market in the Cove is so small, I didn't realize it'd make a difference, honestly."

"I understand; it'd be great to focus on building Aged Emporium's online presence through Instagram and TikTok, especially leading up to the event. Do you have updated pictures we could use?"

He pulls out his phone, scrolling through pictures, pausing on one to show it to me. "Well, this is all I've got at the moment." I stare at the picture. It's an image of the Aged Emporium sign outside in a golden sheen, the sun's rays shining behind it. I'm shocked he doesn't seem to like this picture.

"Wow, this is a great start! I could totally see us using this. Well, considering you don't have additional pictures, do you mind if we stop by to take more pictures sometime soon?"

"Sure, want to stop by today?" I consider his offer, but decide against it.

"I would, but I need to complete Joy's onboarding before going anywhere. Would Wednesday work for you, maybe? I'm sorry I can't stop by today," I apologize. He knits his brows, peering into my eyes.

"Why are you apologizing? It's not a problem, Iris. Wednesday works just fine, and even if it didn't, there's no need to apologize. Taking pictures of the shop is your idea anyway."

He has a point. I don't even know why I apologized this time. It just comes naturally, I suppose.

"Fair point. I rescind my apology." I smirk. He chuckles and leans back into his chair, running his fingers through his hair. "Hey, you called me Iris for the first time."

"Not the first time, Iris." My name rolls off his tongue like honey. I think back, failing to remember the first time he actually used my name. He glances at the wall on his right, catching a view of my diploma. I graduated with a degree in Public Relations, focusing primarily on Event Planning throughout college.

"How long have you worked here?"

"I've been working here for over three years now."

"Wow, so you've lived in the Cove for a while. What made you move here in the first place? It's not exactly an oasis."

"The Cove is what you make of it. I'd wager that any place could be an oasis to someone." I pause, contemplating how to answer his question. "I wanted to live closer to my family. My family lives upstate, just a couple hours away in the mountains."

"Fair enough, I mean, the Cove is... fun." I can't contain my laughter. "Look, I've lived here almost my entire life. Forgive me if I can't fully understand the allure."

"I get it, I feel the same way about my hometown." I scoff. "How does it feel being back?"

"As good as it can feel, given the circumstances. It may sound strange, but coming back to the Cove almost feels like it was meant to happen. I don't really believe in fate, but being back just doesn't feel coincidental."

I find myself wanting to know every little detail, but something tells me not to dig for more this time—he will tell me more if he feels inclined to. I peek at my watch, noting the time. I don't want to take up too much of his afternoon, so I decide we can table the conversation for now, regardless of what I *really* want.

"Well, I don't want to commandeer the rest of your afternoon. You're free to go, Mr. Alcott. Just keep an eye out for the contract, our Legal team will email it to you."

"And what if I want to stay?" His question catches me off-guard.

"Oh, well, you're welcome to hang out at Soi! Whatever works for you!"

His lips tug upward into a smile.

"I'm kidding. If that's all for now, I'll leave you to it and see you Wednesday." He stands up, walking toward my office's exit. "Oh, and Iris? Don't be afraid to call me by name, too."

I gawk. "What? I'm not afraid to call you by name."

He smirks, clearly amused by my reaction. "I'll be waiting for you to prove that."

Puffy clouds stretch across the midday sky, covering the sun once again. Typical for this time of year. Joy picks me up from the office on the way to Aged Emporium—this is a great real-world experience for her to shadow. I'll also confess I did not want to go alone.

Joy, similar to Callie, is great at keeping a conversation alive even if the other party would be fine with it sizzling out. We talk about everything from the weather to TV shows she's currently watching. By the time we arrive, I know her sister's name and zodiac sign. I love building connections, and Joy's warmth is contagious, but my nerves are making it challenging to focus.

It appears his car is the only one in the parking lot other than Joy's. Aged Emporium's exterior has a classy, timeless feel, with its varying shades of brown bricks meshing well together. Sure, it could use some tender love and care, but this shop has been open for decades. Quite frankly, I'm surprised it still looks this good.

We approach the wooden doors to enter, each door including an arched window that allows visitors to see inside. As we step inside, the familiar scent of Everwood pine greets me. I move further into the shop, seeing Jasper behind the front counter, and suddenly, I'm transported to a different time—a warmer time.

The yellow lights brighten the entire front entrance. Christmas music plays throughout the establishment, and a fresh plate of chocolate chip cookies rests on the front counter, sitting beside an epic gingerbread house.

I venture deeper into the shop, looking for him, taking in all the novelties and gems of Aged Emporium. I brush my fingers across the vintage scarves, marveling at the different prints and patterns, knowing I can't pull these off but choosing to try them on anyway. I pick a blue scarf with embroidered suns on it. After putting it on, I rush to find him, calling out his name. I've always loved vintage items, especially the ones I've collected from Aged Emporium. I can't wait to show him this one.

I hear creaking coming from deeper into the store, so I approach that area and stumble upon a small rocking chair with a Victorian glass doll propped in it, the shelves behind it filled with even more glass dolls. My imagination must be playing tricks on me, because the chair is most certainly moving. Yep, now I'm most certainly getting out of here. I'm not going to be one of those girls who investigates it only to lose her life. I back away, not taking my eyes off the doll, beginning to panic when I bump into something—no, someone. I slowly turn my head to see him.

"Gotcha!" He lets out a maniacal laugh. "I swear, you were breathing so hard that the man at the front probably heard you."

Kai. To think, I was so excited to show him this scarf only for him to repay me by scaring the living daylights out of me. It all starts to click. I couldn't find him because he was too busy preparing for this scare. Ugh. He's good. I'll have to get him back for this one.

"Okay, I'm leaving." I rip the scarf off and walk past him to exit Aged Emporium, then he grabs my arm.

"Wait, there was something I wanted to show you." He practically drags me to the jewelry counter. "Look at this."

He holds up a dainty rose gold jewelry box with an intricate flower engraved on the lid. "It's an iris." *He hands it to me, and the second it touches my fingertips, I fall in love. I turn it around to look at the price tag and fall out of love as quickly as I fell in love.*

"Wow, this is so stunning! I love it." *I pass it back to him.* "But I haven't saved up enough at Soi to buy something like this yet."

"I saw the price; I just thought I'd show you." *He softly smiles and sets it down.* "Maybe another time."

Another time. That's right. This is another time.

I take a deep inhale then exhale slowly. *Not today. I will not go there today.* As I repeat these words, his all-consuming smile haunts me, but I don't give in. I repeat this over and over in my head until I can at least somewhat regain focus. Usually, this works—but ironically, *not today.*

Realizing I need to face this alone and in private, I tell Joy I'm going to the bathroom—she seems more than content to keep Jasper company in the meantime. I flash the brightest smile I can muster, and my eyes flicker to his for just a second before diverting elsewhere, anywhere but here. I hustle to the bathroom, shut the door behind me, then continue repeating my mantra. I haven't been here since he passed. I used to love visiting Aged Emporium with Kai. I thought I could handle this, but I must have overestimated myself.

Not today. I will not go there today.

TWELVE

JASPER

I don't need a guardian angel to tell me something is clearly wrong here. I can see it all over her face. Other people may fall for that bright smile, but I don't—with or without Kai's influence. She excuses herself to go to the bathroom, and before I can check on her, Joy steps up to the counter. In true Joy fashion, she already has a lot on her mind. I try to listen as she talks, but my thoughts are elsewhere.

"I see the way you're reacting. You can see through it." Kai appears next to me; if I didn't know any better, I'd say he sounds taken aback.

"Anyone with eyes should be able to see," I mumble, causing Joy to pause mid-sentence. *Shit.*

"I'm sorry?" she says, uncertainty lacing her tone.

"Anyone with eyes should be able to see how nice this piece is." I point to a random ring in the display case. Of course, it happens to be a diamond engagement ring, which causes Kai to absolutely lose it. I bite my tongue.

"Oh wow, yes, that is so stunning! I would love a ring like that one," she exclaims while looking into my eyes. "Hey, are you going to the Halloween party this weekend?"

I want to leave this conversation, but she isn't easy to deter. "I didn't know there was a party." Maybe a party is just what I need to loosen up. I've been on edge since Kai started paying me unexpected visits. "What are the details?"

"'*What are the details?*' How old are you again, bro? 50?" He snorts. My brows crease in frustration. She pulls her phone out, tapping on her screen and then I hear a ping from my phone.

"Just airdropped you the invite—don't forget to dress up!" Now, it doesn't feel like I have much of a choice on whether or not I attend. I wonder if Iris is going. *Iris.* My heart is pulling me to go check on her. I look around and see no trace of Kai.

"I'll be right back, Joy. Feel free to start taking pictures or doing whatever you need to do—behind the counter is strictly off-limits, though." I hastily walk away. As I get closer to the bathroom, I realize I have no idea what I'm doing. If Iris is upset, how will I comfort her without really knowing her?

Just as I'm about to knock, the door opens. To my surprise, she isn't alone. As she stands in the doorway, Kai's arms are wrapped around her shoulders tightly—he's embracing her. She appears paler than earlier, but when she smiles at me now, it seems more... genuine. I haven't seen this side of her guardian before. All the humor in his expression has vanished. Instead, his eyes remain closed as he seems to channel all his energy into Iris. He's even glowing.

"What's up?" she asks, all smiles now. This is a problem. She is too good at masking her emotions. It makes her nearly impossible to read. I, on the other hand, don't see the point in hiding anything.

"You were gone for a while, and I thought I'd check on you. Are you okay?"

"Oh, yeah, I'm just feeling a little sick; it's probably something I ate. I'm ready to get started! Where do you think we should take pictures first?" He lets her go and she begins to walk out of the bathroom toward the front entrance. It looks like Joy is already taking pictures, which is great because I feel like Iris needs more time to regain composure than she lets on. He follows us to the front, patting me on the shoulder.

Iris takes her AirPods out of her purse and puts them in her ears, then turns her Canon camera on. My eyes linger on her fitted white turtleneck that accentuates her curves and patterned loose pants. I haven't ever really cared for turtlenecks—until now.

She and Joy have cameras wrapped around their necks. I didn't dabble much with marketing, social media, or photography during my undergraduate studies, so I find this interesting. She begins perusing, stopping in several different spots to capture images. She gets far enough away for Kai and me to finally have a moment.

"So, how did that work exactly? The whole hugging thing?" I quietly ask.

"Oh, I just do that when she's struggling. It's not a permanent solution because I won't always be here, but it usually helps her in the moment." He assesses the old Vinyls hanging on the wall behind the front counter. "Jasper, are you a fan of rock music?"

"Um, yeah. Anyway, about Iris—"

"No way! I finally figured out something we have in common." He grins, holding up a "rock on" sign with his hand. I stifle a chuckle, looking down and shaking my head. "Okay, I can tell you're dying to know how the supernatural hug works. Basically, I funnel my golden energy into her—think of it like magical medicine. It provides her with some comfort, but not enough to raise suspicion, and unfortunately, it doesn't work long term."

"I'm curious—how long have you been her guardian? Did you have to do formal training or anything to secure the position?"

"I've been her guardian for years. As far as 'securing the position' goes—" He cracks a smile. "I was given the freedom to choose. I awoke in another realm after dying, which was wildly unexpected, I might add. An archangel greeted me and presented me with the choice. After choosing to become a guardian, I did some general training. Time works differently in the Middle Realm, so I'm not sure how long I trained for, but after refining my gifts and understanding my purpose, I ventured back to this realm and was assigned to Iris."

"What is the other realm like?" I can't help but find all of this fascinating.

"You'll see it one day," he affirms. "It won't do you much good to know what exactly comes after this life while you're living it. If you know all the details, living in the moment will be harder. Trust me."

"Fair enough. Well, what can I actually do to help you and Iris?"

"Like I said before, being her friend would do wonders. She has a couple good friends, but one lives across the country now, so that leaves just one in town. Well, aside from her cat—Iris would be annoyed if I failed to consider him her friend." I've never had many female friends. In college, I talked to a lot of girls, but I would not actually consider them friends—well, not in the way

Kai is suggesting, at least. "I've been worried about her. Don't get me wrong, she is resilient and damn strong, but that girl has trouble leaning on others."

As if on cue, Iris and Joy appear back at the front desk, giggling about something together. Ironically, she is leaning into Joy, forcing me to suppress a smile. Kai shoves me and I barely feel it. I don't know if I'll ever get used to that.

"Thanks for letting us stop by. We should be good to go for now! Next step is scheduling tours to see our venue for the ball," Iris says. "Would you want to come along?"

"I can be there. As you can see, the shop isn't too busy these days." I motion toward the emptiness surrounding us. She frowns in response to that comment.

"We'll try our best to help with that." Iris perks up. "In the meantime, maybe put that record player to use and play a fun vinyl to set the mood because the vibes are off in here right now."

"The vibes are off? I'm wounded, Iris." I cock a brow, resting my hand over my heart, as Iris gazes at me with a mischievous glint.

"Well, we've got to get going," Iris says. Joy walks outside, waving goodbye on her way out. Before stepping outside, Iris turns back, coyly smiling. "I'll be in touch, Jasper."

Embarrassingly, I gulp.

I could get used to hearing her say my name.

Thirteen

Iris

"**I** can't believe you're going out tonight. To a party. With actual people," Lena teases while taking a sip of her apple cider. "I can't remember the last time you went to an event you weren't involved in planning."

Lena and I haven't been talking as often recently. She has been busting her ass at her new office in Georgia, and as a workaholic myself, I can't blame her. Between balancing work and spending quality time with her girlfriend there, *our* quality time has decreased significantly. So, the little moments spent FaceTiming mean a lot to me now.

"You and I, both. Callie asked me at the most inopportune time. I know if I wouldn't have been multi-tasking, I would've said *immediately no*." I stare at myself in the mirror, evenly applying my moisturizing primer to my bare face, bracing my skin for what's to come. Screw it. If I'm going to a party, I'm going all out.

I glance back at my phone to see Lena relaxing on her couch—I keep my phone propped up against my vanity so Lena and I can continue talking as I apply my makeup. My mom never took the time to teach me how to do makeup, but that did not mean she didn't want me to wear it. In fact, my mom *told* me to wear makeup throughout my adolescence, claiming my imperfections needed to be hidden at all costs. My dad never stepped in to correct her, leading me to conclude they both felt the same on the matter. So, I caked my face in foundation and concealer daily throughout high school and most of college. Now when I apply makeup, I can't help but think of her.

"So, how has the fundraiser planning been going so far?" Lena graciously disrupts my train of thought.

"It's been great, honestly. I'm just waiting for the ball to drop at this point because it feels like it's been going a little too smoothly, you know?"

"I'm happy to hear that." She pointedly looks directly into the camera. "I don't know if you've heard this recently, but I'm so proud of you."

Who knew such a simple statement could make someone feel so good? Lena isn't overly emotional, so hearing these words come out of her mouth feels indescribably good.

"Ugh, I wish you were here, Lena." I peer into the camera at her, feeling a wave of emotion hit me. Instantly, I look up, waving my hands at my eyes to prevent tears from cascading down my cheeks. "I just applied foundation, so I've got to stay strong."

We both cackle and proceed to catch up about everything, from our crazy work lives to our current fall coffee orders. As we talk, I delicately continue to apply my makeup with as much precision as possible. After blending my foundation, concealer, and contour, I begin to work on my eyes. I use matte neutrals as the base alongside an iridescent golden shade on my lid. Once I finish the shadow, I put on black mascara, lengthening and volumizing my lashes. Mascara is my favorite part of any makeup look—it's the one step I hardly ever skip on a day-to-day basis. Now, it's time for tonight's magic touch—highlighter.

I know highlighter isn't as popular as it once was, but tonight's look absolutely requires it. No ifs, ands, or buts about it. I brush the shimmery golden shade onto my upper cheekbones, then paste some stick-on golden gems to my brow bone and temples. Settling on a nude glitter gloss, I complete the look with setting spray, then look at Lena for final approval.

"It only took five hours, but I'm finally done," I joke. "What do you think?" I angle my face upward, downward, left, and right, then cross my eyes for Lena.

"One word: flawless," she says resolutely. "Let me go get Tina! I've got to show her your look, she'll freak out."

Lena and Tina—yes, they're so perfect their names rhyme—have been long-distance dating for years. Lena ultimately chose to look for job opportunities in Georgia where Tina lives so they could finally move in together. They've been living together for several months now, and it's safe to say it's going well. Tina comes into frame and immediately drops her jaw.

"IRIS." She gasps. "You're such a babe!"

"Means a lot coming from you!" I exclaim as Tina and Lena lean in toward each other. I've never seen Lena so at ease. I'm endlessly happy for her, if not a little envious of the peace they must feel.

"Well, I'll let you guys go." I grin. "Thanks for getting ready with me, Lena. Miss you always."

"Miss you too, friend. We'll talk again soon. Have fun and be safe tonight, okay?" She uses a serious tone. We conclude the call, then I turn on music. I find myself feeling excited about the party for the first time since agreeing to go. Now, I just need to change, then I'm good to go. Fingers crossed my introverted self can pull off pretending to be an extrovert tonight.

Callie picks me up late—attending a party I have no part in planning means I can arrive leisurely. She is also known for being notoriously late herself. We stroll into the high school gym to see it's no longer a gym at all—it's an exotic dark garden. A thin layer of mist shrouds us, and I gaze around the room to see it's entirely shadowed in dark, shimmery sheer curtains complete with flowers of every species. White lilies with black tips, black roses, daisies, and tulips surround us all. Satin onyx tablecloths lie atop each round table, paired with lacy white table runners. Immediately, I survey these items, trying to estimate the costs, when suddenly, a pitchfork interrupts my thoughts.

"Nope, not happening." Callie wags her pitchfork at me. "You're not here to work—you're here to party with me and anyone else who interests you. I see what you're doing and that's a major no for tonight."

"Ugh, okay, fine. I'm just impressed they managed this using city funding, that's all," I say, still getting lost in the dark magic garden surrounding us.

"Is that your way of complimenting the event staff? If yes, why thank you." Callie mockingly bows. "I dipped all the flowers with my students this week, and we created the balloon arcs."

"What?! You've been holding out on me! How much do you charge per hour?" I tease, punching her arm playfully. I'm not surprised she helped put this together—her artsy mind amazes me. As I take in the rest of the event's decor and moody indie music, I get a better look at her costume: she's sporting a short burgundy leather dress, black horns, and striking red eyeliner. She is the color red personified. The best part of her costume has to be the glitter-bombed pitchfork, though. She's already having way too much fun with it. Callie, being the social butterfly she is, gets pulled away into a conversation with other teachers. So, I stand there alone momentarily before someone steps into my view.

"Iris, it's been so long!" Jake bends down to hug me. "How have you been?" I haven't seen him in ages. He and Kai used to be close friends. His short golden blond hair is styled with gel, complimenting his Ken costume. We haven't ever been too close, but I'm relieved to see a familiar face in a crowd of strangers.

"Ah, it's so good to see you! I'm doing great! How has work been for you?" I ask excitedly as the music seems to grow louder.

"Oh, you know, same old, same old. What's new with you? You look beautiful, by the way." He shouts, his brown eyes look me up and down.

Electricity pulses through me as someone's hand brushes against my back, delicately but deliberately. I turn slightly to see Mr. Alcott—*Jasper*.

"Just thought I'd say hi before the crowd sweeps you away," he whispers into my ear, sending shivers down my spine. He's wearing a charcoal sweater over a white collared button-down shirt with black jeans. A single streak of deep red liquid trails down from his lips, and when he grins, I catch a glimpse of gleaming fangs. Well, *that's* unexpectedly attractive.

"We haven't known each other long, Jasper, but you should know by now that I'm not exactly the life of the party." I peer into his deep gray eyes. He's staring intently into mine, and only for a moment, it feels as though the music halts. But surely, that can't be the case.

"I don't know about that, Iris. All I've been able to look at since arriving is you." *Am I hallucinating?* Before I can respond, someone grabs his arm.

Oh, joy. It's Joy, dressed up as a Powerpuff girl. "Jasper! Blake and Jess are just over there. They want to catch up." He smiles politely at her and obliges, strolling away arm-in-arm with Joy. Jake asks who that was, and I attempt to explain, still at a loss for words after what he just said to me. Jake presses for more, then proceeds to ask if we're dating. His question puzzles me—*why would he ask that?*

"C'mon, I feel like I've made it pretty obvious," Jake says, leaning closer to me. "I've always liked you. I just didn't want to break bro code when Kai was still here. Now that he's not here, maybe we can give it a shot."

"Give *what* a shot, exactly?" My patience is wearing thin.

"Dating. Let me take you out on a date." He pulls me in closer to him, and I scoff in his face, thinking he must be joking. His expression sombers—*oh.* He isn't kidding.

"Jake, you're like an extension of Kai in my eyes. We can't date," I affirm apologetically, pulling away from him.

"I don't see why not—maybe I'm just what you need to get back on your feet." He grins, pulling me back in.

His words pierce me like a dagger to my chest. "What the hell is that supposed to mean, Jake?"

"We all know you haven't been the same since it happened, Irie," he says.

I snap.

"Do *not* call me that. You know he is the only person allowed to call me that."

"Was, Iris. *Was.* He's gone. He isn't coming back. I mean, I'm sure he'd be thrilled if we got together." He leans in even closer to me as my stomach twists.

"You can't speak for him."

"Let's go somewhere more quiet to talk this out." He grabs my hand and pulls me away from the party, out into the hallway—where it's quiet. At first, I pull away from his hand tugging on mine, but I don't want to make a scene, so I follow him. I've known Jake for nearly a decade. He went to college with Kai, who warned me to steer clear of Jake years ago. Right now, he thinks I'm playing along, but really, I'm playing him.

Fourteen

Jasper

I attended the party tonight, intending to see old friends from high school. I thought I'd drink a bit, catch up, maybe talk to some girls. And, of course, upon walking in, she was the first person I laid my eyes on. From that moment on, I have been unable to look away despite my best efforts.

Iris dressed up as an angel, which I couldn't help but laugh at initially—*the irony*. As I study her more closely, even from afar, I notice flecks of gold glitter on her eyelids and gems resting on her olive skin. Her skin glows, nearly translucent under the strobing lights. A cream-colored silky slip dress drapes along her curves perfectly, and her full lips appear *wet*. No one in the room can deny it. Her ethereal beauty is otherworldly. Forget being an angel—Iris is the epitome of a damn goddess tonight.

"Okay, so when I encouraged you to get closer to Iris, I meant as *friends*," Kai shouts over the music. This is the twentieth time he's reiterated this message to me. I'm over it at this point. I'm here to have fun. I've been too uptight since meeting this dude. A little flirting never hurt anybody.

"You know, I'm still confused about the nature of your relationship with her," I mutter to Kai. I try to keep our conversation discreet, considering we're out in public, and at any given moment, someone could spot me talking to myself. "You said you were no one to her, but she seems like a lot more than 'no one' to you."

Kai chuckles. "Iris is my assignment. As her guardian, her well-being means everything to me."

"Well, you should know by now I wouldn't do anything to harm her well-being. You don't need to protect her from me," I whisper.

"Buddy, with all due respect, I've known you for less than two weeks. Trust is not given freely. It's earned. It'll take more to gain my trust," he says earnestly.

"For the love of everything, can you please stop calling me buddy? We're practically the same age."

"Time in the afterlife works differently—I feel like I've basically lived for eons at this point."

I sigh. It does feel nice being around old friends, but Joy pulled me away from Iris too quickly earlier. As Jess and Joy chat, I notice the man with Iris cozying up to her, pulling her into him. I look away, finishing my second drink since arriving.

"That's Jake—he's always had a thing for Iris, but the feeling isn't mutual." He leans over. As I watch them from a distance, I see Iris subtly fidget with her bracelets. She's anxious. *Stay in your lane, Jasper.*

Jake grabs her hand and leads her away from the party, out into the hallway. Kai goes into full protection mode, not even saying goodbye before teleporting instantaneously. I'm well aware I'm not Iris's guardian. That role belongs to Kai, rightfully so. But I can't stop myself from going after them. Sure, Iris can take care of herself, but that doesn't mean she should always have to. I step out into the hall from another access point quietly, so they don't hear me approach. I can hear their conversation from here.

"I've been feeling something between us for years, Iris. You can't deny our chemistry." The prick leans in too close, his mouth nearly grazing her lips.

"Jake, I told you. This is not going to happen." She pushes him away as I clench my jaw.

"I don't see why you can't give me a shot. I've seen your exes. They don't come close to me. I'll be the best you've ever had." He strokes her cheek, leading her to slightly flinch in response. *That's it.* I step toward them, but find myself getting pulled back.

"Wait," he simply says, not appearing uneasy at all. "Just wait."

I glance at Kai like he's lost his mind when I hear a loud smack and turn back to see Jake holding his hand over his face. "What the hell, Iris?"

"You're right. I haven't been the same since it happened. I may be fragile, but I'm *not* broken." She stares into his eyes, unwilling to look away. Jake's face reddens, then he stomps back into the gym, visibly pissed off. Serves him right, I was about two seconds away from decking him myself, and I wouldn't have been half as graceful as she was. Jake's departure leaves Iris and me alone in the hallway, but she doesn't know I'm lurking in the shadows. She takes a deep breath, puts her hand over her heart, and then exhales, strutting back into the party without missing a beat.

"I've never liked him," Kai says resolutely. "I mean, okay, I did at one point, before realizing he was a tool."

"This sounds personal to you," I note.

"I just hate watching guys treat her like that. It makes my blood boil." He grimaces.

"That makes two of us." The words slip out of my mouth before I can register the impact.

"Why is that, bro? Are you into her?" He raises his eyebrows.

"What? Don't be ridiculous." I brush him off. He chooses to ignore me, so I head back inside to the party. While walking in, Joy greets me instantaneously, grabbing my arm.

"Where'd you go?" She glances over my shoulder. For a second, I wonder if she can see Kai, but as I follow her eyes, I discover he has disappeared again—big surprise. I can't lie, it'd be pretty nice if someone else could see him, too.

"Nowhere," I answer, looking around the dimly lit room to try to spot Iris. "Have you seen Iris?"

She looks taken aback for a second, then grins. "Yeah, I'm pretty sure I saw her take some shots a few minutes ago with some friends. Hey, do you want to dance with me?" She pulls me toward the dance floor. Begrudgingly, I oblige, figuring I need to blow off some steam anyway.

"I'm so glad you moved back to the Cove." She leans into me as we dance. "It's crazy that we both moved back around the same time."

"Definitely," I agree. As I dance with Joy, though, my thoughts are elsewhere.

Thankfully, the fluffy white wings are hard to miss—I see her bouncing on the dance floor with a drink in her hand and a friend by her side, seemingly without a care in the world. She's laughing, letting the music carry her away. If I didn't know any better, I'd think she was the happiest person in the room.

"I'll catch up with you later, Joy," I shout over the music, excusing myself. She nods, then continues to dance. I approach Iris through the sea of bodies. Upon reaching her, I rest my hand on her left shoulder, gently urging her to turn toward me. When she notices me, I see the mask slip for only a second before coming back.

"Jasper! Hi! Are you having fun?!" She's never *this* relaxed with me.

"A blast. Can I steal you away from the crowd?"

She glances around, just now seeming to realize she was even in this swarm of people. "Turns out I was swept into the crowd after all." She gleams. "Lead the way!"

She grabs ahold of my hand playfully, catching me off-guard. I lead her off the dance floor toward an empty table and prompt her to take a seat, asking her if she needs water.

"No, I'm fine. What's going on?" she asks, her eyes twinkling under the string lights. I take a seat next to her at the table.

"I'll be frank—I saw you in the hallway earlier. I just wanted to make sure you're okay."

She pauses, seeming to gather her thoughts before speaking. Even tipsy, Iris makes an effort to think before speaking. Remarkable.

"I'll be okay." She gazes at me with warmth in her expression, resting her hand on my knee, causing a jolt of electricity to shoot up my thigh. "Thank you for checking on me, I appreciate that." She leans back in her chair, looking up at the ceiling. "Those little lights remind me of stars. I love stars almost as much as I love clouds."

I chuckle, running my fingers through my hair, unsure of what to do. She clearly has had a hell of a night.

"Iris, would you like to stay or go home? You've had a long night, but the choice is yours. However, I'll be with you the rest of the evening regardless of your decision."

She scrunches her nose and eyebrows. Confusion crosses her features. "Why?"

"Because we're friends. I want to make sure you are okay."

"We're not really friends, we're working together," she corrects. Ouch. "At least, that's what I thought... I don't usually befriend my clients." She closes her eyes, leaning her head back again.

"Well, I don't befriend my event planners, so this is new for both of us." I smirk. She quirks a brow and releases a loud laugh, then covers her mouth after noticing how boisterous it was.

"I think I want to go home," she sighs. "Can you maybe give me a ride? I don't want Callie to have to leave early because I'm a grandma."

I chuckle and nod, letting her know I'll be right back. Little does she know, I have absolutely no idea who Callie is. I assume she is the friend Iris was dancing with earlier, so I venture back to the sweaty dance floor to find her. Upon finding her, she turns toward me with a confused expression on her face.

"Iris wants to go home and asked me for a ride—I will get her home safely," I quickly pull a business card out, handing it to her. "This is my cell. You can call or text me if you have concerns." She seems skeptical at first, but then she looks back at the table Iris is still sitting at, noting her providing us with a double thumbs up.

"Okay, can you please have her text me when you drop her off? She shares her location with me too, just so you know," she says cautiously.

"Duly noted, Callie. I'll have her text you." I walk back toward Iris, who definitely seems ready to go.

"I'm with Callie, dude. Iris is sharing her location with me, too, just so you know." Kai cackles, elbowing me.

"I'll get her home safely—not that it matters to you. I imagine you'll be crashing in the back seat anyway." I grit my teeth as he grins. As we reach Iris, she glances into my eyes hesitantly.

"I'm ready. I drank a lot of water, so I'm sobering up. I apologize in advance for anything I said earlier. I'm a bit of a lightweight when it comes to tequila." She blushes.

"If that's you under the influence, you do *not* want to see me wasted," I joke, making her smile, carelessly wrapping my arm around her as we exit the party and stroll out to my car. She takes off her wings and situates herself in the passenger seat while Kai obnoxiously jumps into the backseat. I see his bright grin in my rearview mirror. She's visibly more calm in my car this time than she was last time. I reverse out of the parking space, head to the main road, and hand her my phone so she can fill in her address.

"Thanks for, uh, being my friend," she says shyly, handing my phone back to me. "Tonight was... unexpected. I'm so ready to get out of this ridiculous costume, shower, and change into a T-shirt."

Just imagining her in an oversized T-shirt without pants causes me to jolt. I'm envisioning her in one of *my* T-shirts.

And I realize, for the second time since she walked into my life, I'm in trouble.

FIFTEEN

IRIS

Jasper opts to walk me to my door despite my protests against it. While trudging up the stairs, I shiver from the frigid air then sigh in relief, knowing I'll be resting in my warm, cozy bed *very* soon. As much as I pride myself in my ability to embrace chaos, tonight has tested my limits. My apartment being the closest unit to the staircase, it doesn't take long for me to know something is not right. For starters, my apartment door is ajar, and I distinctly remember shutting it before leaving earlier.

I inch to my front door slowly, when Jasper reaches out to pull me back. "Why don't I check things out first?" Immediately, I panic. I didn't even clean my apartment before leaving today, it is in no condition for guests—let alone the hot vampire I'm working with.

"No, really, it's fine." I smile sheepishly, I'm sure. "I've got this." I step ahead of him, bracing myself for whatever waits on the other side of my front door. I open it as quietly as possible, peeking my head inside. The smell hits me like a ton of bricks.

As I walk inside, my feet sink further into my living room carpet with every step. Water is *everywhere.* The carpet—soaked. The couch—soaked. Poor little Truman—soaked. I hustle to my linen closet to grab a towel, then bundle a very grumpy Truman into my arms. A burly maintenance technician is currently leaning over my kitchen counter, trying his best to dry the countertops with a towel.

"Oh, hey, you're home!" he exclaims as if we're friends seeing each other at the local grocery store. "So, the bad news: a pipe froze and burst above your unit, setting your kitchen and living room's sprinklers off. The good news: I was alerted fast, so I was able to shut off the water before it flooded your entire unit."

I should've known the good news wouldn't be the kind of good news I'd hoped for.

"Long story short, your carpet is severely damaged, but everything else should dry out and be okay—with the exception of your TV." He cringes. I guess it's time to upgrade my old TV anyway; I used this one throughout college. I take notice of several box fans propped up throughout my living room. "We will replace the carpet for you. We can come first thing on Monday to get started."

"Well, thanks so much for your help tonight." I nod at the technician as my eyes skim the room, landing on Jasper, who has a front-row VIP seat to the shit show that is my life. "Anything else I need to know?"

"We typically advise tenants who experience flooding to avoid spending time in their apartments until the carpet has been repaired or replaced. Mildew can build up pretty quickly, and we wouldn't want you to inhale that." He hesitates. "So, I'd suggest staying elsewhere for the next few days. Terribly sorry for the inconvenience. I can talk to management about discounting next month's rent if you'd like."

This is fine. Everything is fine. I am fine. I set Truman down and brainstorm what to do as the technician grabs the soggy towels and hurriedly vacates my unit.

"Thanks again," I call after him, then gaze at Jasper, who's leaning against the door frame with his arms folded, casually displaying how defined they are.

"You're officially relieved of your duties, sir." I salute him jokingly.

"I don't know if you recall, but I told you I'd spend the rest of the evening with you, Iris." He shrugs. "And it doesn't look like the evening is over quite yet. In fact, it just got even more exciting."

His eyes glitter with mischief as I roll mine. "Okay, well, I just need to text Callie and see if she's cool with me crashing on her couch for the next few nights, it's no big deal." I pull my phone out to text her. Of course, the message fails to send, so I call her. It goes straight to voicemail. Callie is still at the party—duh.

"No answer?" he asks from my doorstep.

"Not yet, but it's all good. I'll figure it out. Really, you're good to go. Thanks for tonight." I turn and step toward my room. Time to pack for an unplanned getaway.

"Stay with me tonight."

I pause, then turn back toward Jasper, still standing outside. Avoiding his statement, I say, "It must be cold out there, why don't you come inside for a few minutes while I pack?"

"Oh good, I thought you'd never ask." He hastily steps inside, closing the door behind him and rubbing his hands together for warmth. "Even if I wanted to come inside, I couldn't."

Confused, I look at him and raise my eyebrows. "You know, the whole vampire thing." He quirks an eyebrow, then grins, pointing to his sharp canines.

"You're something else." I hold back a laugh, then walk into my bedroom, knowing he's a few steps behind me at this point. Despite its current disheveled state, I'm surprisingly comfortable with him being here in my apartment.

"I meant it, though," he says quietly while assessing my Bohemian wall decor. "The easiest option here is for you to stay with me—at least for tonight."

"*Jasper Alcott*, we just became friends like five minutes ago, and now you expect me to sleep with you? We're moving too fast," I joke, trying to hide my nerves. He casts a wicked grin, fangs out and all. *Damn.* I guess my vampire phase never really ended after all.

"I have an extra room, Iris." He says plainly, as if I should've known about his spare bedroom. "Although I wouldn't mind the company. It's been a while since I had anyone stay over."

"Same," I whisper thoughtlessly hoping he didn't hear me. I quickly grab my weekender bag to load my belongings into and take a mental note to remember to pack Truman's necessities, too.

"What can I do to help?" he asks from the dimly lit hallway. I feel bad asking for help, but since he offered and it'll save time, I figure it won't hurt to take him up on his offer.

"Maybe you could pack Truman's overnight bag? His food is in the pantry on the bottom shelf. Other than that, we just need to pack his feeding bowls and some treats." I shove as many clothing items as I can fit into my weekender. I have the tendency to overpack—I find it's usually easier this way. I close my door to change out of my angel costume into a hoodie and leggings. I check my phone to see that Callie still hasn't received my message. *C'mon, Callie. Please.*

I sling the beige bag over my shoulder and venture back into the kitchen area to see Truman cozying up to our guest. Jasper runs his fingers along Truman's spine, then gives him a good chin scratch. As if prompted, he looks over Jasper's shoulder, stands on his hind legs, and meows. Definitely abnormal behavior for my fur baby.

"Truman?" I interrupt. He drops, landing on all-fours, keeping his eyes fixed just over his shoulder.

"Has she replied?" He averts my attention elsewhere.

"Nope," I grumble. "But I can't blame her; she was really looking forward to tonight."

I pause, thinking. What other option do I have? I could go to our local motel for the night, but I'm not sure if it's pet-friendly, and as tempting as it is to hide Truman in my weekender, it's not realistic. His orange fluff would give us away in an instant. I could wait on Callie's doorstep for her to get home, but it's freezing outside, and there's no telling on what time she will get back. If she even comes back tonight.

Think, think, think.

Staying at a client's home is unorthodox. Unheard of for me. But no one has to know, right? I mean, I've already completed one thing I've never done tonight—why not cross another off my Do-Not list?

"I've made my decision," I say, glancing at Jasper. He looks up, peering into my eyes.

"Go on, I'm on the edge of my seat over here." Sarcasm laces his tone.

"Is it really okay for me to spend the night with you?"

"I wouldn't have offered it if it wasn't." He continues petting Truman. "Besides, you were really looking forward to sleeping in a bed tonight. Her couch won't satisfy you the way my bed can." My cheeks grow warm. *Get a hold of yourself, Iris.*

"Okay, then I will stay the night with you—just for tonight." I reach over and pick up Truman, putting him in his plaid carrier.

"Just tonight." He salutes with a crooked grin, offering to hold my weekender for me. I gaze at his hand. This action alone reminds me of *him*. Old memories never fail to sweep me away at unprecedented moments, whether I want them to or not.

"I've got it. Thanks, though!" I walk past him, leading him back outside into the brisk night. After I lock up, we head back downstairs to his car. "I'm sorry for the inconvenience."

I hand him my bag so he can load it in his car how he sees fit, then walk over to the passenger side. "New rule: no more apologies, Iris. If you think I'm remotely upset you have to stay the night with me, then you've got it wrong. You have no control over this situation, so you don't need to feel sorry."

You have no control over this situation. If only he knew how heavily these words impact me. If only I could believe him.

Moments later, we arrive at his home, and to my surprise, it's an *actual* home. Like a physical house. It's older, too. He invites me inside and encourages Truman to explore. I release Truman from his carrier, to which he happily hops out, scurrying across the hardwood floor curiously. The one-story home is immaculately clean, minimalistic, and homey, and instantly, I'm feeling embarrassed by my humble, cluttered abode full of color and nick-nacks. We both seem to share a preference for warm

ERIN HALLI

tones, though, as his home has mahogany, oak, and other light wood accents throughout, complete with an old-fashioned brick fireplace.

"I haven't really had time to decorate yet," he says, scratching his head. "Well, actually, I've had time, but I just haven't yet, so here we are."

No way. Is he embarrassed, too? By *this*?

"Your home is so nice. I'm speechless." I gawk, trying to reign in my adoration. I've always wanted a home like this. My family's home is spacious but cold and gray. His home may be minimalistic, but for what it lacks in decor, it makes up for in warmth. His lips twitch in response.

"Here, I'll show you the spare room." He ushers me toward a hallway lit by a single tall floor lamp. A couple of hipster prints line the hallway walls leading up to the room I'll be staying in. The room is small, but it has more than enough space for me. He sets my weekender down on the floor as I struggle to keep my eyes open. He notices and chuckles, pulling out an extra blanket from the closet and laying it on the bed. I plop down onto the bed and glance up at him.

"You must be an angel," I taunt. "You outdid me tonight and you weren't even dressed up as one." Yep, I'm definitely drowsy, and when I'm drowsy, I have a hard time filtering. Oh, well.

The corner of his lips curl upward. "Good night, Iris—my room is across the hall if you need anything."

After he leaves the room, I sluggishly get ready for bed, changing into a huge T-shirt. Not even a flood can stop me from sleeping comfortably tonight. I set my phone on the table, turning on some indie folk music to keep me company alongside Truman, who snuck in as Jasper walked out. As I drift off, it's nearly impossible to ignore this feeling in the air. What a whirlwind of a night. Ironically, though, as I lie awake in an unfamiliar bed under a roof that isn't mine, I feel like I can breathe for the first time in months.

SIXTEEN

JASPER

I shut my bedroom door and then get ready for bed, hoping for a peaceful night's rest despite knowing better. As if on cue, he clears his throat. I walk by without giving him the time of day. I stroll leisurely into my bathroom, grab a towel, and wipe the paint off my face. After removing the fangs and brushing my teeth, I edge toward my bed to see him sitting there, staring blatantly at me. Again, I pay him no regard—I'm not in the mood to be lectured by an angel tonight. Well, not *this* angel, at least. I'd make an exception for another who just so happens to be sleeping across the hall.

"That's enough," he says without a hint of humor. I continue my regimen by taking off my socks and shirt, remaining in only my pants for now.

"It's awfully quiet in here tonight," I taunt, hoping to get a rise out of him. To my utter shock, he lies down on the bed cozying up under the sheets with his *shoes on*. I was having fun, but this? Too damn far.

"What do you want?" I grunt, shoving his feet off the bed with gusto.

"To talk," Kai says, remaining in place, smirking. "Jasper, I want to make sure you have Iris's best interest at heart here. You may have forgotten, but let me remind you: I've peered into your soul."

"How could I forget? I nearly blacked out."

"Soulsight is a wild gift. Because people can't see me, typically, peering into their souls just feels like a small, brief headache for them. I reckon the sight affected you so much because you looked directly back into my eyes," he concludes while removing the sheets and rising. He begins pacing back and forth. "My point is, I caught a small glimpse of your dating history, and I am telling you right now, Iris needs stability—not a distraction. She isn't just another girl you can—"

"Who says a little of both wouldn't be beneficial for her?" I chuckle, cutting him off before he can finish that sentence. "Relax, you don't have to worry, man, I'm not planning on pursuing her." Kai gazes off, seeming to get lost in thought.

"So, I've been curious," I start. "Can you read all my thoughts at any given moment?"

"No, not all of them, and no, not all the time. I just read bits and pieces here and there—similar to how some people skim-read just for keywords, I skim-read minds. The difference is those people could technically read every word if they wanted to. I, on the other hand, mainly read the keywords. When I focus extremely hard, I can read your thoughts pretty clearly, but it takes a ton of effort. I don't read your mind as often as you may think."

Well, knowing Kai isn't hanging out in my head 24/7 is comforting. I'm not sure if he'd like the thoughts I've had about my current roommate. I was being honest when I told him I hadn't been planning on pursuing her. It's clear Iris is hurting. I'd be a jackass to make any advances while simultaneously aiding her *guardian angel*.

"Well, if we are done with the pillow talk for tonight, I'm going to sleep." I settle into bed, finding warmth under the silk sheets. I glance around the room, noticing I'm alone. *At last.* I turn off my bedside lamp. While wading into sleep, one sentence repeatedly echoes in my mind.

I may be fragile, but I'm not broken.

I wake up at the ass crack of dawn feeling more motivated on this fine Sunday than I have in weeks. Last night was just what I needed to feel alive again. However, I assume Iris may not share the same sentiments toward today, so I decide to do what I do best: cook. Okay, I'll fess up. I haven't cooked breakfast in months—years, maybe. As a night owl, I typically stay up so late that I don't wake up in time for breakfast. But not today.

After changing into joggers and a T-shirt, I venture into my kitchen, determining toast, eggs, and potatoes should be a safe bet for breakfast. I open my pantry, grabbing the bread and potatoes. I set those items on the counter, then open my fridge to grab the eggs, only to notice there aren't any. *That's just great.* Luckily, it's so early that I should have enough time to go on a quick grocery run, so I grab my keys and set off in haste.

I live less than five minutes away from Susie's, the local grocery store. I hustle inside, grab the goods, and get going. Thankfully, the sun is just now starting to rise. I pull into my garage and enter as quietly as possible, careful not to disrupt her slumber. I turn the corner toward the kitchen, and my jaw drops. She's awake. Not only is she awake–she's wearing a T-shirt. A big T-shirt. Seemingly pantsless. In my kitchen. Iris is awake, in a massive T-shirt, standing in my kitchen. *Fuck. Me. She looks even better than I imagined.*

Iris turns to face me, flashing a chipper smile my way. "Morning! Do you mind if I make some coffee?" Her hair is up in a high ponytail, and wavy dark wisps frame her face, highlighting her cheeks. To no one's surprise, Kai hastily walks into the kitchen and hurriedly blocks my view. *Of course. He must have read my mind.*

"Why are you awake?" I say without thinking. *Why the hell did I just ask her that?* She scrunches her nose. "I mean, it's early. Do you always wake up this early?"

"Um, no, actually, but I slept really well, so I guess that's why I'm awake?" she says lacking confidence while waiting for the coffee. With Kai persistently shielding her from me, I can hardly see her clearly from behind his bulky frame.

"Sorry, I'm not used to being up this early myself, honestly." I run my fingers through my hair and make my way to the cabinet, ready to start cooking. Finally, Kai meanders away, leaving Iris and me alone.

"Did you just go to the store?" She reaches into Truman's bag, propped against one of the wooden barstools, and grabs his food.

"Yep, do you like eggs?"

"I haven't eaten eggs in forever." She sighs as she bends down to fill Truman's bowl.

"Great, breakfast will be ready in about 30 minutes." I rinse the potatoes one by one, setting them aside to chop them while Iris finishes brewing her coffee. She takes a sip and instantly spits it out, all over the kitchen counter.

"Oh my gosh, I'm so sorry!" Her face turns tomato red. Instead of laughing it off, she darts across the kitchen to grab paper towels, wiping down the counter in record time.

I approach her from behind, my chin lingering just above her shoulder. "Well, now you've done it."

She turns slowly to face me. We're standing just inches away from each other. I stare into her emerald eyes, then carefully assess the damage over her shoulder. "Looks like I'll have to replace the countertops first. Then, the flooring."

She gawks, smacking me. I catch her biting her lip.

"It's no big deal," I say. "But I'm dying to know. What's wrong with my coffee?"

"Well, I checked your fridge for creamer earlier to see you didn't have any." She throws the paper towels away. "I figured I could survive drinking one cup of black coffee, and well, I overestimated my abilities. That was... unpleasant, to put it lightly." She looks into my eyes, waiting for a response. I nod, biting my lip to keep myself from laughing. I reach for her cup of coffee, lift it up to my mouth, take a large gulp, then set it back down.

"Oh, *so bitter*—just how I like it," I drawl. "Sorry I don't have pumpkin spice creamer. I do have milk and sugar if that'll help though." I walk back toward the stove to resume cooking breakfast. I feel my stomach growling and, at this point, I'm wondering if this will even be worth the wait.

"She won't say it, but she doesn't actually like eggs," Kai obnoxiously whispers into my ear. "She clearly just noticed you purchased them for breakfast and feels bad."

I ignore him and put the diced potatoes in the oven, dressing them with oils and seasonings, then get started on the eggs.

"I'm telling you, you're wasting your time," Kai taunts. "But oh man, I wish I could eat your breakfast; it smells delightful."

"If she doesn't like eggs, she can tell me that herself," I whisper, keeping my back turned away from Iris. Thankfully, she is listening to some music on her phone, so it doesn't seem like she can hear me.

"Sounds good to me, bro," he says, then sits on the stool next to Iris. Truman leaps onto the counter almost immediately, inviting Kai to pet him. I veer away, realizing I have stared in her direction for far too long.

While working on the eggs for a few minutes, Iris appears next to me out of nowhere, invading my personal space. "What can I do to help?"

That's new—I've gotten used to cooking solo. "You can make the toast if you want?"

"I'm on it." She hustles to my pantry, peering inside. I watch her walk away, letting my eyes linger on her smooth legs a smidge longer than I'd like to admit before I clear my throat to get her attention. I let her know the bread is already out on the counter. We both cook together in harmony, and after we finish up, she sets the table and then I dish up our plates, noting that Kai is nowhere in sight.

As we're both sitting next to each other at the bar, my eyes betray me, flickering again to her bare thighs. Turns out, she's wearing short biker shorts, yet I *still* jolt. I've always been attracted to the oversized T-shirt look on girls. But Iris lounging around my home in a massive T-shirt showing off her voluptuous legs will clearly be the death of me. *I'm a wreck.*

"Well, dig in," I say, attempting to drown out my inner thoughts.

She nibbles on her toast, then proceeds to taste the potatoes, letting out the smallest moan after taking the first bite. *Well, shit. Wasn't expecting to hear that during breakfast.* Her eggs, suddenly looking very lonely, sit untouched as she eats every last bite of the potatoes and toast. She begins to swirl them around with her fork, clearly trying to make them look poked over.

"Thank you so much for breakfast, that was seriously divine," she sighs, patting her lips with a napkin. "I'm stuffed. I appreciate it." She reaches over, grazing my arm with her petite hands.

"You didn't like the eggs?" I taunt, locking my eyes on her sultry lips.

"Oh, um... okay, so maybe I'm not a big fan of eggs," she mutters. "But I saw they were the only thing you bought at the grocery store, and I didn't have the heart to tell you."

I grin. "Iris, I don't really like eggs either." Her eyes widen in response.

"Stop, you're kidding!" She glances at my plate, noticing I've barely eaten any of my eggs. She bends over in laughter.

"Next time, just let me know before I cook, okay?" I smirk, grabbing her plate, when I feel a hard smack on my back. I nearly drop her plate. He's goading me, of course.

"Are you okay?" she asks, raising her eyebrows in confusion.

"Hate to say I told you so, but..." Kai says with a smug expression on his face. "I will say, it's pretty cute that you both don't like eggs."

"Yeah, totally fine, Iris," I answer.

"Are you, though?" Kai asks, wiggling his brows at me.

"Yes, I'm *fine*." I grit my teeth without thinking, causing Iris to quirk a brow.

"Got it, so you're *extra* fine," she says, and I'm instantly cringing. I throw Kai a death glare as his smile widens. I've got to get better at schooling my facial expressions when talking with Kai in front of people. Especially her.

SEVENTEEN

IRIS

C onsidering myself a morning person would be a stretch, but if every morning felt like this one, I might be a morning person after all. Between Jasper's disheveled morning hair and the divine breakfast he cooked for us, I'm overwhelmed—but not in a negative way. I mean, I don't know if a man has ever cooked breakfast for me, so it's a shame the first time it happens is with my *client*, who is rightfully and justifiably in the friend zone. It's just been a while since I spent the morning with someone in general, though. It's something I didn't know I was missing.

Kai and I used to spend mornings together every once in a while. We enjoyed going to Little Falls, bracing ourselves for long work days and sleepless nights. Little moments seem insignificant in the grand scheme of it all until you lose the person you shared them with. When those moments are all you have left, they aren't so little anymore—they become consequential. I glance through the dining room window, taking time to admire the backyard's greenery, when I hear a ping.

Callie

OMG, I'm sorry, I just turned my phone back on! Are you okay??

Iris

Totally fine! Can I crash on your couch for the next few days until my flooring is replaced by any chance? I'm sorry to ask.

Callie

Girl, you know you're welcome here anytime. My sister is visiting this week though, so as long as you're cool with splitting the couch with her, we should be good!

Splitting the couch with a friend: no big deal. Splitting the couch with a stranger: no can do. I outwardly sigh, acknowledging I don't have a choice if I don't want to have to pay for a last-minute hotel stay. As I'm typing a response, Jasper clears his throat. I glance at him as he's leaning against the countertop with his arms folded.

"Everything okay over there?" He cocks a brow at me.

"Yep, couldn't be better. Just coordinating my stay with Callie, that's all." I look back at my phone.

"And that's going well?"

"Yep!" I want to tell him the truth, but I can't burden him. I've got to figure this out on my own.

"Cool," he says, heading out of the kitchen. Just before he steps out, I realize it can't hurt to simply tell him a little more about my predicament.

"Wait," I say, giving in to my temptation pitifully quickly. He pauses and nonchalantly leans against the hallway door frame. "Hypothetically speaking, let's say it isn't going well, and I am not sure if I'll be able to stay there."

"Well, if we're being hypothetical here, I would ask for more information." He stalks nearer to the bar I'm sitting at.

"Let's say she has someone else staying with her this week, and she lives in a studio apartment, so the three of us may be getting a little too cozy," I say, scanning his unreadable face.

"I suppose I'd offer you to stay at my place for a bit longer." His gray eyes dance as he leans over the counter. "Free of charge."

I contemplate his offer. Usually, it takes time for me to feel comfortable staying over at a guy's place. But this is different—it's not like we're dating or hooking up, even. He's trying to be a good friend. I haven't had a male friend in so long. I guess I've just forgotten what it feels like.

"Perhaps I would accept that offer—hypothetically speaking, of course." I bite my lip, then break eye contact, glancing at my phone. "Okay, so you're 100 percent fine with me crashing here a little longer?"

"Sure, just make sure to put the toilet seat down, roomie," he jokes, striding out of the kitchen.

Iris

No worries, Jasper just said I could extend my stay here, so I'm covered for the next few days.

Callie

Okay! Jasper is the vampire from last night, right? He's hot as hellllll. Is he single? ;)

Well, isn't that the question of the hour? For his potential partner's sake, I hope he's single. I would be furious to find out my boyfriend offered a random colleague a place to stay without running it by me. Wait... maybe he did run it by his partner. Oh, maybe he isn't single.

My feet begin wandering before I can stop them. I inspect the living room area, searching for pictures of him with his partner. After taking a closer look at the framed photos in the entertainment center, I determine his partner isn't showcased out here. I see one more framed picture on the side table I decide to tune in on. I lean over the couch, grab the frame, and lift it up to my eyes to see Jasper with... his parents. At least, I think they're his parents. He has his dad's eyes and mom's smile. He can't be older than 12 years old in this picture, and he's grinning from ear to ear. I don't think I've seen him smile that wide since meeting him. I marvel at how smitten his family looks. I crave that feeling so much that my desire to experience it with Kai again burns a hole right through the center of my heart.

"That was my eleventh birthday," his gravelly voice startles me. "My parents surprised me with a trip to the Great Wolf Lodge and I was so excited, I couldn't handle it. I've always loved swimming." *How fitting,* I ponder, *considering sometimes, deep inside, I feel like I'm drowning.*

"Have you ever been?" His question interrupts my thoughts.

"No, I haven't—we didn't go on fun family vacations growing up. We tagged along on some of my dad's business trips, but those didn't really feel like vacations, considering he was tied up the whole time."

"Oh, didn't realize he was into *that* kind of business," he drawls from right next to me. I lightly punch his shoulder.

"Jasper! Stop it." Rolling my eyes, I fight back a grin.

"I'm sorry you didn't really get to spend quality time with your parents away from home," he murmurs.

"It's okay. I wasn't ever really alone," I say plainly. Jasper doesn't pry.

"Well, what is on your planner for today, Ms. Greene?" He plops himself down on the couch. I set the picture down and join him, our legs nearly touching.

"Mr. Alcott, my planner is off-duty on weekends. She deserves a break, too. I work her to death." He responds with a mischievous glint in his eyes.

"Then I say, we go to Little Falls to overcome your trauma from this morning's coffee," he offers.

"Say no more, I'm in."

"Before we go, do you mind if I ask what you were looking for out here before you noticed me?" Jasper smirks. *Of course, he caught me snooping around like a maniac.*

"I just wanted to look at all your fun decor." I glance around at the near empty living room walls and shrug. "There wasn't much to see."

"I don't know." He inches closer to my face. I lean away slightly. "You looked like you were on a mission," he murmurs. Suddenly, I'm sweating. *He knows.*

"Callie asked if you were single, so I was checking to see if I could find any pictures of you and your significant other before responding," I blurt out and immediately grimace, resorting to fidgeting with the bottom of my T-shirt.

He bursts into laughter. "I don't know what's funnier. You snooping around my living room to find pictures of my girlfriend and me." I must be bright red right now. I feel it. "Or you thinking I would print pictures of us and frame them in the first place? I'm not sentimental enough to do that."

"What? Oh, like it's so ridiculous for two people in a committed relationship to decorate their home with pictures of themselves?" My face burns. I'm not remotely surprised he isn't very sentimental.

"You know, it's kind of cute when you're flustered, Greene."

Greene. That's a new one. I think I like it.

"Whatever." I scoff, looking away, masking my blushing cheeks. I'm no stranger to the feeling of shame—we're on a first-name basis at this point in my life.

"If you had just asked if I had a girlfriend, I would've answered honestly," he says. "And you would've quickly learned that I do *not* have one."

Just when I think I'm done blushing, it comes back with a vengeance. "Great, I'll let *Callie* know."

He nods, smirking yet again, then stands up. I quickly change into a pair of black leggings and throw on my cardigan, kissing Truman goodbye on the way out. While sitting in the car, I type a response to Callie.

Iris

He's single.

But instead of sending the message, I erase it. I'll be seeing Callie later anyway—we can chat about this more at another time if it even comes up.

Eighteen

Iris

After another peaceful night of rest in a bed that isn't mine, I awake earlier than usual—again. To my surprise, I am not running late to work this Monday morning. In fact, I'm in no rush at all. Shockingly, I didn't think about work once this weekend despite spending an extensive amount of time with one of my very own clients. Today, that same client and I are touring the venue for the fundraiser masquerade ball along with the events team, so I'm jumping back into work mode.

I slip on a flowy blouse with puffy half sleeves, buttons, and brown pants, completing the look with leather booties. Thankfully, I packed at least one work-appropriate outfit in my overnight bag, but if maintenance can't swap out the flooring soon, I'll need to stop by my place to snag more clothes tonight.

I shove my laptop into my work tote and wander out to the living area, searching for any sign of life. *Looks like he's still sound asleep.*

Truman, however, signals me with a meow, clearly ready to feast like the little prince he is. I feed him a scoop of food, then check my watch. I'm early enough to make a coffee run, and Little Falls is only a ten-minute walk from here, so I set forth to visit the most consistent man in my life—Davis.

I recall Jasper saying he isn't a morning person, so yesterday must have been a fluke for him. He had a long weekend; he deserves to sleep in. I sneak out the front door, closing it as quietly as possible. I step off the wooden porch, breathing in the fresh autumn air. Rustling rich-colored leaves on a maple tree in the yard catch my eye. The fallen leaves on the front lawn compose a canvas of vibrant yellows, oranges, and reds of every variation. As a gentle breeze sweeps the leaves away, I observe how willingly they give in and let go, some flying higher and higher until they seem to reach the clouds. *Ah, the clouds. My clouds.* The silver sky embraces me, reminding me I am not alone—shielding me from the sun's rays, allowing me to embrace the storm brewing inside me.

"Ready to go?" A voice startles my innermost thoughts. Jasper is leaning on his car inside his garage with his muscular arms crossed—I suppose he must have already been waiting there before I even stepped outside.

"Go where?" I look back and forth between him and his Subaru. Beyond his car, I see a bench press alongside weights, dumbbells, kettlebells, and other various pieces of gym equipment.

"I figured I could give you a ride to work," he offers.

"Oh," I pause. "Well, I'm actually walking to Little Falls right now, so I won't be going to work for a bit longer."

"Perfect, I've been craving that breakfast sandwich."

"You mean the sandwich you legitimately ate yesterday?"

"I said what I said. Come along, let's go fuel my newfound addiction, Greene," he says while getting in his car.

"Okay, sure. I mean, I guess we're touring the venue this morning anyway, so it isn't too much of an inconvenience for you to give me a ride to Soi, right?" We plan to finish the tour before he opens Aged Emporium at noon.

"Right," he affirms from the driver's seat. I settle in on the passenger side. I realize I've been riding in cars a lot more lately than I usually do. I can thank Jasper for that, I suppose. We head over to Little Falls; it is far too quiet for my comfort. I reach over to increase the radio's volume, to which Jasper gently stops me, handing me the aux cord.

"Feel free to play whatever you want," he says. His observance never fails to impress me. Sometimes, it feels like we are on the same wavelength, moving in sync. Within seconds, music calms my troubled mind. I glance over at him, fixating my eyes on his hands steering the wheel. His subtle scruff adds an extra level of maturity to his look, and his sweatshirt, being more fitted than usual, accentuates his toned arms. For a split second, I wonder what it would be like to be held in those arms. But only for a second.

We arrive at Soi just in time to meet Joy along with a couple other event planners. Rather than traveling separately to Marble

Grove, the proposed venue, we decide to all ride together in the company SUV, which Joy volunteers to drive. Tanner, a senior planner, sits in the front seat beside Joy, seemingly eager to mingle with her. Anna and Courtney, our social media gurus, request the middle aisle, leaving Jasper and me to sit in the back row.

Joy can't help but strike up a conversation with every passenger in the vehicle during our twenty-minute commute to Marble Grove. I don't mind her chit-chat—her ability to talk keeps the quiet away. Of course, her conversations steer back to Jasper more than anyone else.

"So, Jasper, what are you hoping to get out of this event? Are your parents super excited?" She beams, glancing at him through the rearview mirror.

"Just hoping to help bring Aged Emporium back to life," he says, keeping his answer brief. "My parents are stoked for sure. Probably even more excited than I am, honestly."

"We know you're not super into the whole social media marketing thing, but we are running some ads for Aged Emporium and created a Facebook event for the fundraiser," Courtney says.

"And Aged Emporium has already received twenty new followers in just one day, which is astronomical given your previous state," Anna finishes Courtney's thoughts. They both went to college together, graduating with the same degree and everything. They're the epitome of soul sisters.

"You'll definitely be getting more business soon," Courtney affirms.

"Wow, that's really cool," he says, flashing a quick smile. "Hopefully, the momentum sticks."

Anna and Courtney grin, turning back around in their seats. I glance outside, recognizing we're only a few minutes away now. I hyper-fixate on his comment—is he concerned this won't help Aged Emporium long term? Why would he be worried about that? I wonder if Aged Emporium is struggling even more than I initially realized. While deep in thought, the vehicle's silence takes over, forcing me to remember things I don't want to remember right now. *Not today. I will not go there today.*

I take a deep breath in and search for my AirPods. I'm unable to find them at first, but I attribute that to my frazzled state and try sorting through my tote once more. There's no way I would've forgotten these. I bring them everywhere to keep the quiet at bay. However, after searching again, I recognize they clearly aren't with me. I know a person of sound mind would simply start up a conversation at this point, but my logical side has vacated. Instead, I close my eyes and repeat my mantra over and over again until it works, not daring to display any sense of discomfort outwardly.

Not today. I will not go there today. No one can know.

Suddenly, a strong hand gently grasps my thigh, barely above my knee. Stunned, I cut a glance at Jasper, who's staring adamantly into my eyes.

"You okay?" he whispers quietly, his ashen eyes searching mine for answers. I simply smile and nod. His hold doesn't weaken.

"Hypothetically speaking, would you tell me if you weren't okay?"

No, I wouldn't tell you. However, instead of sharing the truth, I do what I do best: dance around it. This is my burden to carry. "Probably."

His grip tightens while his eyes bore into mine harder, and somehow, he knows. I know *he* knows I withheld the truth.

"Well, if you ever want to talk, I'm here," he whispers directly into my ear. "Truthfully, I don't have many friends here, and I plan on keeping you around, Greene. So, I'll be waiting."

He smiles reassuringly, then leans away, peering outside, all while keeping his hand on my thigh. Despite knowing this isn't appropriate for work, I make no move to push his hand away. In an instant, my crippling anxiety morphs into something new and refreshing but just as harmful: *butterflies*.

My client, new friend, and current roommate, Jasper Alcott, just gave me butterflies. Great.

Nineteen

Jasper

K ai uncharacteristically didn't ride with us over to Marble Grove, so I am under the impression he will meet us there. Iris said she would tell me if something was wrong, but I know better. I don't blame her for not being comfortable enough to open up, she's obviously been through something traumatic.

Growing up, my parents had the tendency to butt their noses into my business incessantly. Anytime I seemed remotely off, they asked what was wrong, pressing me for details every time without fail. When I was younger, I didn't mind sharing details as I was usually upset because of something minuscule. As I got older, though, my issues became more complex, adding an extra layer of depth to my emotions, and I grew tired of constantly having to open up to them. My parents would press and press until I gave in every time, causing me to have to enforce major boundaries with them. Consequently, I intentionally do not pry with others. When or if Iris ever feels ready to talk, I'll be here, but until then, I will not pry.

We follow the winding road through the evergreens and pass by several picturesque ponds along the scenic route to Marble Grove. It's been over a decade since the last time I visited this area with my family. The large iron gate is already open allowing us to pass through casually. I catch a view of the show-stopping mansion surrounded by a greenscape garden, flowers, and a pond. The off-white home seems to emit light. Built in the late 1800's, Marble Grove used to be a home for many. Now, it serves a different purpose as a historical home museum and event venue. Apparently, Soi has an ongoing partnership with Marble Grove. In exchange for hosting Soi's annual fundraisers at a discounted rate, Soi offers Marble Grove heavily discounted advertising for their event management services. Marble Grove also loves giving back; something tells me this works out well for both parties.

We park in the brick driveway directly in front of the mansion's entrance and hop out one by one. After getting out of the car, I sneak a look at Iris to read how she might be feeling now. *Where was Kai when we needed him?*

"What's wrong?" Kai asks. Impeccable timing, as always.

"I don't know, but she isn't 100 percent right now," I answer, glancing her way. "She had a hard time during the end of the ride here for some reason. Where were you? She needed you."

Kai stares at her, appearing unsettled and folding his arms. "To tell you the truth, she's been doing better lately, so I've been keeping my distance more than I used to."

"But why?" I find his hands-off approach confusing. We walk under a garden arch trellis laced with flowers and begin walking up the steps to the front entrance.

"I'm trying to help Iris get used to coping without my embrace. As I mentioned prior, guardians aren't permanent fixes for the guarded," he says with a tense expression.

"Well, it would've been nice to know that," I mutter quietly, leaving Kai behind me. "I don't understand. Shouldn't a guardian angel always be with their assignment?"

"Jasper, bro, I've already told you." Kai catches up to me, rubbing his temples. "We are tethered together—I can feel her emotions and distinguish the difference between her feeling safe and alarmed. I didn't sense any inherent danger, so I concluded it'd be fine for her to ride over without me by her side. It turns out she had a hard time, but she seems okay for now, so was I mistaken for not riding with you guys?"

As I consider his question, I glance around the foyer. The furniture in this venue is mid-century modern, and the color palette consists of greens, burgundies, browns, and gold.

As an antique shop owner, this old home is a gold mine, yet my eyes still land on her. She's laughing with the girls while waiting for the host to show us the ballroom—I can't seem to look away.

"I guess it turned out okay this time," I mumble. Kai flashes his teeth at me.

"Welcome, welcome!" An older woman ushers us toward the west ballroom like a flock of chickens. "Mr. Alcott, I presume?" She reaches out her hand to shake mine. "I'm Mrs. Sally Nelson, but you can call me Sal. If you have any questions or concerns, please feel free to interrupt me, sugar."

She swings open two large wooden doors to showcase the grand ballroom. The first item that demands my attention is the massive crystal chandelier hung in the center of the domed ceiling. To my surprise, the room is composed of two stories connected by a pristine staircase. The windows allow a gracious amount of natural light to enter the room, capturing the chandelier's iridescence. The ballroom appears nearly empty, so I imagine Marble Grove allows their clients to decorate the space however they see fit.

Joy approaches me with a friendly smile and asks, "Have you ever been here, Jasper? My cousins host events here every now and then."

"Yeah, I've been to Marble Grove several times, but this is actually my first time entering the venue," I say. As we're chatting, I notice Iris staring, but she's quick to avert her eyes after I catch her.

"Well, we have about forty-five minutes before we need to head back to town," she announces, all smiles, interrupting my riveting conversation with Joy. "Feel free to wander the home and familiarize yourselves with the layout so we can determine how to stage the masquerade best."

I can't lie. It is wildly attractive watching Iris in her element. The way she carries herself with such confidence and grace bewilders me. It's clear she's hosted multiple events here before. Suddenly, Joy reaches down and grabs my hand, tugging me to follow her.

"Come on, we can walk around together." She has a flirty look in her eyes, so I stop following her.

"Hey, I'm good for now, Joy. I'm just going to stay in here a bit longer."

"Oh." She pauses. Joy isn't a stranger—she knows how I was in my younger years. Young Jasper would have followed her to find a quiet space to mess around in a heartbeat.

"Okay, sounds good." She smiles and walks away, catching up with the senior events planner. I turn back around to see Iris slipping outside through the ballroom doors. She's venturing out into the picturesque courtyard.

"You wanna join us?" Kai asks. I stride past him, following her lead into the courtyard. The spacious courtyard leads to an old-fashioned rounded white gazebo with overgrown vines and lavender encircling each supporting pillar. Surrounded by freshly trimmed bushes, magnolias, and trees, the gazebo stands out. Just beyond the gazebo rests a pond filled with lily pads and koi fish.

Leaning over the gazebo railing, Iris seems to be drifting off into her own world. Little does she know, her guardian angel has found a spot right next to her. I move to stand on her other side. Now that I'm closer, I hear the faint sound of music coming from her phone. Still, she stares into the pond and simply says, "As you may have noticed, I'm not comfortable with silence."

"There's nothing wrong with that. A lot of people aren't," I reassure her, following her gaze.

"I just figured you deserve an explanation, seeing as I've subjected you to it. I'm really sorry." She tugs on the edge of her puffy sleeve.

"You don't owe me or anyone else anything, Greene," I say, cutting Kai a glance. To my surprise, he stepped away, walking around the courtyard behind us instead. *Right, he's taking a hands-off approach. At least, this time, he is still in sight.*

"You know, my parents and I used to visit Marble Grove Park once a year to have a picnic," I say, changing the subject. "We would feed the ducks homemade bread—my mom felt like they deserved something better than store-bought bread every now and then. My dad was a hardass, but he never failed to take us to Marble Grove to feed little ducks every year."

"That is so wholesome." She softly smiles, finally looking into my eyes. I stare into her twinkling irises, unable to look away for a moment. "Your parents sound so cute. My parents and I haven't ever been close like that."

"What do you mean?"

Iris pauses, carefully contemplating before answering, as she always does. "My mom and I have never been able to see eye-to-eye, and my dad follows her lead, so he never really gave me much of a chance either, to be frank."

I break eye contact, glancing back at the glistening pond to avoid outwardly reacting. She continues. "I've never been too outgoing. In fact, as a child, I struggled to talk, often bracing myself for people's reactions to what I shared aloud, too. My parents, particularly my mom, struggled with that. They apologized for me constantly. They insisted something was wrong with me because I couldn't formulate my sentences well and never fancied being the center of attention at their gatherings."

She shares this in such a matter-of-fact tone that my chest tightens. How could anyone apologize for their child, especially for someone like Iris?

"Thankfully, though, every time my parents kicked me down, my brother was there to lift me up. So I never really felt fully alone." She releases a quiet sigh, glimpsing up at the clouds in the sky.

"I'm glad he was there for you. I can't imagine how that felt." I clench my jaw. The idea of anyone hurting her affects me far more than I expect it to. Suddenly, it makes sense—the way she constantly feels the need to apologize. "You do not, under any circumstance, need to ever apologize for who you are, Greene. Your parents have no need to apologize *for* you, they should apologize *to* you."

Her breath catches as she looks back into my eyes, emerald pools swirling with emotion before me. Her eyes drop to my lips, flickering back up to my eyes in one fluid motion. "Thank you, Jasper." She checks her watch, noting the time. "Well, we should probably get going."

"Shall we?" I reach out my arm for her to interlink her arm into mine, and my eyes linger on her supple lips. She looks conflicted, so I let out a laugh. "Friends, right?"

"Right." She nods, linking her arm to mine. Something tells me having a friend of the opposite sex is as unorthodox for her as it is for me. I'm still trying to figure it out, and her body's enticing curves aren't making this any easier.

After we completed the visit, Iris and I went our separate ways for the work day. I offered her a ride home, considering Soi is on my route home anyway, to which she accepted without challenging the offer for once. I pull into Soi's parking lot to see Kai and Iris waiting for their ride. Talk about a package deal. She jumps in, whereas Kai just appears in the backseat out of thin air. I don't know if I'll ever get used to his teleportation gift, but I'm mad jealous of that power—I'd be unstoppable. *Literally.*

"Yeah, it's pretty nice," Kai says from the back seat, smirking at me in the rearview mirror. "I legitimately teleport everywhere every day." He leans back, cracking his knuckles. "Another cool thing about being dead: I don't have to wear a seatbelt."

I snicker, nearly spitting out the gulp of water I just took. Iris peers at me, more confused than ever. "What's so funny?" she asks, curiosity filling her eyes.

"Oh, I was just thinking about how serious it is to wear a seatbelt," I say while looking at Kai in the rearview mirror. "Can you imagine not wearing a seatbelt? Wow, it's honestly so exhilarating to think about."

Kai huffs. "Alright, alright, I mean, yeah, it's not like the coolest thing about being dead, you got me."

Iris stares at me. "Yeah, that's so funny." She grins in an encouraging "Are you okay?" type of way. Under any other circumstance, I'd cringe, but I find myself not caring much at the moment.

"Hey, do you mind if we stop by my apartment real quick on the way home, please? I just need to grab some more work clothes and check my mail," she asks while scrolling on her phone.

"Yeah, no problem." Shortly after, we pull into her apartment's parking lot. She chooses to check the mail first, then hustles upstairs. Less than a few minutes later, she's back. I like having Iris in my car. It feels right. As I begin driving back to my place, she sorts through her mail and pauses on one fancy-looking deep red envelope. She opens it and audibly gasps. "Oh my..."

"What? What is it?"

"Um, it's just a wedding invite," she says, her eyes scanning the invite.

"Well, when's the big day? And who is it for? Seems like a big deal to you."

"It's on December 2, and she is an old friend—her name is Katherine."

Suddenly, I see Kai flex his gift yet again in the rearview mirror, teleporting away to who knows where. "Well, what's the big deal?"

"Oh... I just don't think I'll be able to get a date in time, if I'm being honest." She says sheepishly. *That's it? That's why she nearly gave me a heart attack while driving nonetheless, with that gasp of hers?*

"Well, I've been told I'm an exceptional wedding date, in case you were wondering." I throw her a smirk. It isn't a lie, I tend to enjoy weddings. I glance at her in my peripherals and watch her cheeks grow pinker. *She's so cute. Damnit.*

"We'll see," she says, glancing out the window, seeming to get lost in the clouds again. As we get closer to home, I find myself selfishly hoping she takes me up on my offer.

TWENTY

KAI

I never expected to find myself here. I didn't know what to expect after taking my last breath, but man, this wasn't it. Dying felt like losing and gaining everything all at once. In a single moment, I lost my whole life—everything I worked for, my dreams and ambitions, and my connections with the people I loved most. I felt lost. But at that same moment, the stars found me. As I slowly let the reality of my death sink in, I felt a level of peace I didn't know was possible. I am one of the lucky ones. It didn't take me long to accept my fate.

The world looks different from this side. I remember learning something from one of my coworkers—she just so happens to be Irie's best friend. She taught me that millions of different colors exist in the universe. In contrast, humans can only see a million of them. Well, I learned *very* quickly after dying that the dead can see every color imaginable. I can't even properly put some of the colors I've seen over the last couple of years into words—they're incomprehensible. Upon opening my eyes in the afterlife, I could see an endless stream of color flowing right before my eyes. Who knows if I'll ever get used to it? I may see the world in vivid color now, but if my sister's world is in shades of muted gray, none of that matters to me.

I glance around the empty bleachers and take a deep breath, noting the sound of crickets and birds chirping simultaneously. With it being such a small community, there are hardly any guardians in the Cove, we don't spend time together as our objectives are clear as day: heal your assignee, then ascend.

Choosing between immediate Ascension and being Irie's guardian was practically the easiest choice ever. After I awoke in the Middle Realm—I know, not the most creative name for a spiritual waiting room—an otherworldly Archangel adorned with opal wings and icy white long hair greeted me, shaking my hand. Her presence soothed me. After reassuring me that I was okay, she presented me with the choice between being a guardian temporarily or immediately ascending to the Golden Realm—again, not super original, but it wasn't my call. Guardians can choose whom they want to guard. Before finalizing the choice, they even allow guardians to visit their potential assignee so they can assess whether or not it's a good fit.

After selecting Irie, they permitted me to see her. I told myself: if she seems okay, I won't linger. She was always the stronger one of the two of us, so I imagined this would likely be the case. I entered her apartment, recognizing a coolness I hadn't felt before then. While walking around, darkness enveloped me. I entered her room quietly to check on her, glancing at the date on her calendar above her desk. It had been only a week since my early departure. Upon closer inspection, I saw a neck brace and a cast on her left arm. Seeing her in bandages made my stomach turn, but I would rather her be bandaged and breathing than the alternative. She sat in her bed, wrapped under thick blankets, keeping Truman cradled beneath her right arm—man, I always loved that cat.

She released him and grabbed a small rose gold box from her nightstand—one I instantly recognized. *Oh, shit. The jewelry box from Aged Emporium.* I may or may not have secretly gone back to the antique shop to purchase the box, intending for it to be Irie's Christmas present. I hid it in my luggage, sitting in the trunk of my car during the crash. She must have found it after the accident.

As she held the box, she seemed to get lost in it. Her fingertips traced the etched iris engraved on the lid, outlining the delicate design for a couple of minutes. Suddenly, her breathing grew dangerously rapid, and tears welled up in her eyes as she slammed the box down on the bed as hard as she could repeatedly, somehow not managing to break it. Then, I witnessed something I hadn't seen since we were children. Irie sobbed. She wailed. She shrieked. The tears did not subside—no, they kept plummeting, harder and harder with every breath she took. Suddenly, her bloodshot jade green eyes met my own in an instant, stopping her from crying. For a moment, I thought she could see me.

"Irie, it's okay, I'm okay, you're okay," I said, boring my eyes back into hers, pleading. Instead of responding, though, she wiped her tears away intensely using her sweater's sleeve. Her eyes, usually sparkling, were dull and hollow. She tucked her hair behind her ear and took a deep breath, allowing a stoic expression to settle upon her.

Aloud, she whispered defiantly, "Not today. I will *not* go there today."

My heart shattered. That was the moment I knew. Irie needed help. I wouldn't hesitate to put forever on hold for my little sister. What truly concerned me was the way she halted herself from embracing her full emotions. Denying herself from grief would certainly prolong the pain longer than she could fathom. Before finalizing my decision, the Archangel showed me a glimpse of the Golden Realm, which lies just beyond the Middle Realm. Visiting the Golden Realm is prohibited until Ascension, but you can capture a look at it through the large dome-like window encasing the Middle Realm's Greeting Center.

I gazed upward through the massive curved pane of glass and saw endless golden rays shining across the seemingly infinite sky. Amongst the light, I observed clouds and stars of yellows, pinks, and oranges. Of course, if I wanted to see more of that realm, I would've been required to choose Ascension right then. The Golden Realm put the Middle Realm to shame, which was insane, considering the Middle Realm's rainbows alone blew my mind. I gazed at it in awe, but never even considered passing up the opportunity to be her guardian. What kind of brother would I be to force her to bear it all alone when I could be there for her every step of the way instead?

So, I stayed. I underwent rigorous guardian training, learned the ins and outs, and now I'm here to support her until she no longer needs my help. As I stated before, guardians aren't permanent fixes for the assigned, so when she is ready to let go, I'll go. Irie has not allowed herself to cry fully since that cold, dark evening nearly two years ago. Don't get me wrong, she lets herself tear up sometimes—but not in the way her soul desperately needs her to. Although I hate to admit it, Jasper showing up was a much-needed change to our daily routine.

When I said I never imagined myself here, though, I meant *here*—like, literally here. Back at the high school baseball fields. When I was alive, I came here to think when things got too heavy; the habit stuck, even into the afterlife, I guess. Man, I miss coaching. It was my calling in life. As cliche as it sounds, those kids taught me way more than I ever taught them. One shitty thing about being a guardian—the only drawback, really—is I haven't gained inner peace quite yet. So, in short, my emotions still screw me up on some days. I mean, they're not nearly as heightened as when I was alive, but they still hit me. Once I ascend the proper way, that will supposedly change, but we'll see.

Seeing Katherine's name struck me in a way I didn't anticipate. Even in my final moments of life, her bright face crossed my mind, but I haven't seen her since becoming a guardian. Although I'm overjoyed she found someone, a part of me aches, knowing I will never get to be that person. I stare out at the empty field, reminiscing on old memories I share with her. She is the best partner I could've ever had. I don't know how I'll react to seeing her at her wedding, but I refuse to miss it.

Another perk of Jasper being around is I've been able to give my sister more space than I used to, which in turn allows me to spend some time alone, too. Because of my tether to Irie, I can teleport to her instantaneously if something is wrong, but lately, I haven't felt the pull when we're apart as often. Sometimes, when I am alone, I visit the mountains and watch the sunrise.

In all sincerity, I feel bad for not telling him the truth about who I am, but I know it will overcomplicate the situation entirely if he knows. He seems honest, to a fault even, so hiding her guardian is already a lot for him to handle. I don't think he'd be able to handle the full gravity of this situation.

Not to mention, the Archangels would likely *screw me up* if she found out because of me. Guardians are required to remain discreet—our assignments are forbidden to know we're watching over them. It could inhibit their progression significantly. Or something. Who knows. However, I will say that most guardians go *unseen* throughout their guardianship, so I'm already in an unfair position.

Is it naive for me to withhold the full truth from him? Maybe. But at the same time, Irie deserves the chance to tell him about her grief herself if she deems him a worthy listener—which is unlikely.

Jasper's ability to see me does throw me off, though. First off, why *him*? He's a little grumpy for my liking, and his relentless, tactless flirting with Irie is getting on my last damn nerve. Secondly, *why* him? During my training, no instructor ever mentioned the possibility of mortal humans seeing guardians. Household pets, sure, but humans? Nope. Unheard of. I've thought about reaching out to other guardians to ask, but I worry that there could be consequences, and for whatever reason, I feel like we need to see this through. We can't have any interruptions here, especially if he continues to help Irie heal. This flower will come out of hiding to bloom if it's the last thing I achieve in my existence, whether she knows I'm here or not.

Twenty-One

Iris

I set the table as Jasper adds the final touches to dinner. To my shock, he cooked a pasta dinner tonight, and he didn't even use pre-cooked alfredo sauce. Nope, he mixed a bunch of creamy cheeses and seasonings together to make an authentic Italian dish. It turns out he lived in Italy for an entire semester. While there, he took a cooking class and learned how to make various Italian specialties. I asked what I could do to help earlier, and he simply asked if I could set the table, to which I happily obliged. I've never been much of a cook myself, but I enjoy watching him cook. He seems so content when in the kitchen.

After setting the table, I freshen up in the bathroom. Upon looking in the mirror, I discover my hair in disarray. I begin to run my fingers through it, then pinch some life back into my cheeks. Opening Katherine's wedding invite left me feeling... conflicted, to say the least. I've always loved spending time with Katherine—she has the kind of smile that brightens a whole room. She and Kai had that in common. Our mutual friends used to joke around about their pairing being a match made in heaven.

She moved to our hometown when we were in high school, being two years older than me and two years younger than Kai. They remained good friends throughout high school and college and didn't actually begin dating until her senior year of college. They tried long-distance dating for a couple of years while Kai lived in Chrysocolla Cove, eventually leading her to transfer to the Cove for work. Unfortunately for me, her wedding is taking place in our hometown. Truthfully, our hometown is stunning, so I can't blame her, but I haven't visited the town in ages. I don't know how I'll muster the courage to revisit the town without him by my side for the first time.

On top of that, Jasper practically offered to attend the wedding with me, which added a whole extra layer to my confusion. First, he friendzoned me, then gave me a place to stay, and now he's offering to be my stand-in wedding date. *Why is this man so frustratingly difficult to read?* I lightly pat my face in an attempt to look somewhat presentable before wandering back into the kitchen. Pasta is one of my comfort foods; I can't wait to dig in. As I'm about to take the first bite, my phone rings. I sigh and answer it.

"Hi, Iris. This is Tony, your maintenance tech. I just wanted to let you know that you should be all set to return to your apartment tomorrow. We worked extra hard to get this done ASAP. Sorry again for the inconvenience."

"Oh, that's great news! Thank you so much."

I hang up, smiling. "That was Tony, my maintenance guy. Looks like I can move back in tomorrow."

"Wow, they finished that quick?" Jasper raises a brow while taking a bite of the pasta. "Hope they did it right."

"I mean, they only had to replace the carpet in the living room, and given the fact that my apartment is less than 600 square feet, I'm sure it wasn't too time-consuming," I affirm, finally taking a bite. Immediately, I let out a moan, unable to control myself.

"Be careful there, Greene. I think you're giving the Cacio e Pepe the wrong idea." He arches an eyebrow at me, his lips curling upward into a smirk. Suddenly, my cheeks feel warm—I'm definitely blushing. Lovely.

"So, I've been thinking about that wedding you got invited to," he says, wiping his mouth with a napkin. "Did you really react that way because you don't think you'll be able to find a date?"

"Um, well." I pause, determining how to answer this. "Katherine's wedding is in the mountains… my hometown."

"I see," he plainly says, taking another bite of his food.

"It's been years since I last visited the town—I have zero desire ever to move back," I say. "The only reason I'd even remotely consider visiting is to pick up my car."

"Your car?" He quirks an eyebrow.

"Yep, my car. I have been keeping it at my parents' home for the last few years to save money. No car means no parking fees," I share, taking another bite. He nods, seeming to understand. Deciding we've spent too much time on the subject of my family, I shift gears. "So, how did you learn to cook?"

"My mom and I cooked together throughout my childhood. I learned all the basics from her, but I picked up how to cook this dish while in Italy. This is a fan favorite over there."

"I wouldn't have initially pegged you for being a momma's boy," I tease. He rolls his eyes, quirking the corner of his mouth.

"Oh, I'm not." He recoils. "Cooking is just the only thing we've ever really connected on."

"I get that—I wish my parents would've taught me how to cook. Instead, I'm surviving off a diet composed of pre-made frozen dinners, smoothies, and coffee at age 25." I take another bite as he snickers.

"I could teach you sometime if you want," he offers, this being the first time anyone has ever offered to teach me how to cook.

"I'd actually love that." I bite my lip, looking down at my half-eaten meal. I feel oddly comfortable in his home. I haven't felt this comfortable in a long time. "So, will you miss me, roomie?"

"Eh, I've missed being able to walk around my home shirtless, so I think I'll manage." He grins, leaning back in his seat and resting his arms behind his head as I fight back a wide grin. Of course, he's already finished his entire plate.

"What's stopping you from doing that now? With us being friends and all, I didn't think it'd make much of a difference," I poke fun.

"Greene, if you wanted to see me shirtless, you could've just asked." He folds his arms over his chest and shrugs his grin widening. *Well, I guess I walked into that one.*

"That's not what I'm saying, Jasper." I declare. "I was just wondering."

"Fair enough." He smirks, getting up to clean his plate. As he walks away, I wonder if I fancy the company of others more than I thought I did.

The next morning, Jasper loads my luggage into his car. We stop by my apartment complex to drop off my things along with Truman before going to work. He insists on giving me a ride to work yet again, so I hastily accept. We go our separate ways for the day without so much as a single text to each other.

While at work, my events team works hard to promote Aged Emporium's fundraiser event. We solidify ticket prices, the graphic designs for announcements, flyers, and ads, and book our favorite local DJ. I haven't been to a masquerade in years; I only hope it's as successful as our analysts project it to be. I want Jasper's family to gain as much business as possible.

After a long shift, I walk home a little later than usual today, making sure to watch every step vigilantly. Black ice will not vest me again this fall, mark my words. I greet Truman as soon as I walk inside and take in my new flooring. I notice a couple of issues, so I submit a request for the team to fix the loose floorboards. I have never been more thankful for a leather couch than this very moment—it's the only furniture item in my living room that survived the great flood. I'll admit, I thought I'd feel more relieved to be home. Instead, I feel a sense of emptiness I can't quite understand. So, I shoot Callie a text to make plans.

Iris

Hey, what are you up to tonight?

Callie

Bitch, it's Trivia Tuesday at the bar! Wanna come?

I sigh. Do I really want to go to Trivia Tuesday at the bar? No. But alas, I would rather do that than sit here alone in my apartment tonight.

Iris

Yes, actually, I do.

Callie

OMG your first Trivia Tuesday!!! I'll pick you up in an hour.

I react to her message with a heart and begin to get ready. I turn on some pop music and change into a black long-sleeved square-neck bodysuit and washed-out mom jeans, finishing the look with black heeled boots and a black puffer coat. I let my hair down and curl it loosely, pinning it half-up to accessorize. Callie picks me up, more excited than I've seen her in ages.

"Girl, you do not understand how happy I am that you joined me tonight! Trivia starts in about thirty minutes, so we can get drinks and food just before it begins," she says, pulling into the bar's parking lot. We walk inside, and *wow*, it is packed tonight. I brace myself for what could turn out to be a very hectic evening. I peek at my phone and see no new messages await me. I can't help but wonder what Jasper is up to tonight. As if on cue, I receive a text.

Jasper

What are you up to tonight, Greene?

Embarrassingly, my stomach drops.

Iris

I'm at the bar. You?

Jasper

Same ;)

Jasper is *here*? And he just used a *winky face*? I gaze around the bar, searching for a highly attractive brunette male.

Jasper

Try looking to your left.

Jasper

Oops. Your other left, Greene.

My bad.

I turn to my *right*, and Jasper is right there, sitting at a high-top wooden table for two with a direct view of the small wooden stage. I hang my coat up on the old-fashioned coat rack, then tell Callie I'll be back and approach him, breaking out into an embarrassing grin.

"What are you doing here?" I ask, trying to tone down my excitement. I don't know when it happened—I don't know how it happened. In a room full of people, Jasper has become my anchor. I *might* have missed his company tonight.

"Same as you. Can't miss Trivia Tuesday." He chuckles, ushering me to sit in the empty seat across from him. Jasper is wearing a white button-up with the top two buttons unclasped, sleeves rolled up, and a pair of dark jeans. He seems lighter than usual. I glance down at the table to see three empty glasses. *Ah, that explains it.* I bite back a laugh.

"What is it, Greene?" He beams, eyes glittering.

"You've obviously drunk a bit tonight, and it's refreshing to see you so full of life compared to the usual. That's all," I joke, staring directly into his gunmetal eyes. They seem to be twinkling tonight. "Do you come here often?"

"As a matter of fact, yes. I do. I come here a few times a week to watch sports and whatever, but I *promise* I don't usually get carried away," he says, pushing his currently empty glass away. "In fact, I'm cutting myself off. That's right. I don't want to miss a moment of our time together."

The butterflies come back unexpectedly. "I'm flattered."

"I've noticed you don't come here often. Otherwise, I would've met you way sooner than I did. I would've probably asked for your number, too," he concludes, his eyes dropping to my lips. "So what brings you here tonight?"

"Trivia Tuesday," I whisper, unable to stop myself from glancing at his lips, too. Suddenly, a hand yanks me out of my seat, causing me to nearly tumble to the ground. I catch myself, thankfully, but not without an attitude.

"Hey! Callie! What the hell?" In an instant, Jasper stands, narrowing his eyes at Callie.

"OMG, sorry, I didn't mean to tug you that hard." She cackles. She clearly already took a shot. Or two. Maybe three. She is holding a full shot in her free hand out to me, though. "Brought you one!"

I drink it, masterfully if I do say so myself, and look back at her. "There, you happy?"

"Extremely." She smirks and then looks at Jasper, seeming to notice him for the first time. "Jasper, right? I've heard so much about you already."

I elbow her as subtly as possible. Jasper sits back down and leans back in his seat, smirking arrogantly. "Oh, I'm not surprised."

My jaw drops and I rub my forehead. "Oh, please, for the love of everything, you two." Out of nowhere, chiseled arms pull me in from behind. At first, I fight it, but then I find myself leaning into the embrace ever so slightly. Surprised by the gesture, I look at him over my shoulder, but welcome it nonetheless. He tucks a strand of my hair behind my ear.

"We're just fucking with you, Greene," he whispers, unconcerned. His hot breath on my neck gives me chills. *Holy shit.*

"Well, feel free to stop that at any time." I gulp. I expect him to let go, but instead, he keeps holding on, resting his head on my shoulder.

"Have I ever told you I love the way you smell?" He takes a deep inhale and sighs, his lips hovering barely above my neck. "Well, I do. And it's not the only thing I love about you, Greene."

I start to feel warm and fuzzy inside, and as much as I want to attribute the feeling to the sip of alcohol I consumed, I can't. I know, deep down, this feeling could only mean one thing.

"Hey Jasper, you should come to my art show!" Callie interrupts out of nowhere. I'm not surprised; she has been inviting every person she's ever met to her end-of-year show. "It's on December 9. Iris will be there too."

"Sure, I'm always down to see new art." He grins.

Unsure if Jasper is even aware he is still holding me, I attempt to wriggle out of his grasp, to which he holds me tighter. I *should* break free of his hold. We may be friends, but he is still my client, after all.

Despite my better judgment, I make no move to do any such thing. Instead, I lean into him, allowing myself to feel a sliver of warmth in his arms, if only for a single fleeting moment.

TWENTY-TWO

JASPER

I'm not drunk. Buzzed? Sure. But drunk? Absolutely not. Especially not in Iris Greene's presence. I can't lose myself like that in front of her this early on in our... friendship. Whatever this is. I'll admit, if she hadn't shown up when she did, I was on the road to oblivion. When I got home from work tonight, I found myself wanting company, but not just anyone's company—*her* company. So, I hit up the bar.

As soon as she walked in those doors, Kai popped up, alerting me. "Don't do anything stupid, Jasper. You've obviously been drinking."

"Tsk, tsk, Kai," I tutt, watching her stroll into the bar. "I told you—you can trust me, man."

Kai shakes his head in disbelief, crossing his arms. Is he seriously *flexing* right now? "This should be good."

I shoot Greene a text, letting her know I'm here. Clever, I know. Clever, that is, until I tell her to look to her left only to realize that was the opposite direction she needed to look. Damnit, logical, sober Jasper wouldn't have miscalculated that.

From afar, I steal a real look at her. She's wearing a tight top tonight that accentuates her luscious curves—a lump forms in my throat upon noticing her cleavage. And, for the first time since meeting her, she's wearing jeans that showcase the curves of her backside. But that's not even the best part—her radiant smile *beams* when her eyes meet mine. To my surprise, I find myself smiling just as bright. *Hell.* She has no idea what she does to me.

After chatting for a few minutes, her friend comes along—Kaylee, I think? It's been a long day; I can't be held accountable for forgetting her name. As Kaylee chats with us, I pull Iris into my arms. My body has a mind of its own at the moment, and currently, it has no intention of letting her go anytime soon—unless she feels uncomfortable, that is.

I like Kaylee—*Callie.* Callie. She's funny, and she seems to care a lot about Iris. I'm glad she has a friend in town.

"So, what do you think you're doing right now, buddy?" Kai asks irritably, disrupting my moment of peace. He tends to do that these days.

"Whatever the hell I want, *buddy*," I answer in my mind, closing my eyes and leaning closer against Greene, who smells like vanilla and honey, as always. Did I already tell her how much I love the way she smells? I hope I did. She deserves to know she smells like a dream.

"Jasper, I've said it once, and I'll say it again." He stands directly in front of Greene and me, blocking my view. "She needs stability.

If you can't provide that for her, you're wasting her time and yours, quite frankly. This is why I encouraged you to be—"

"*Friends*, yes, yes, I know, Kai." Again, I answer in my head, careful not to outwardly react despite how much he is pissing me off. He's never once asked how I feel about this arrangement. He doesn't have the first clue about my feelings on the matter. "I will *not* hurt her."

Kai processes my answer, then glances at her and sighs dramatically. "Okay, I'll get out of your hair, but I swear to God, if you do hurt her—"

"Is God even real?" I interrupt his threat, then inwardly laugh at my own quip.

"Um, that's irrelevant." He shrugs, rolling his eyes again. "Anyways, I'm trusting you, Jasper. Don't screw it up."

In a wild turn of events, Kai actually walks away, out of view. *Alone time with my girl, at last.* I squeeze her tighter. She turns over her shoulder to regard me.

"Are you planning on holding me like this all night?" she teases.

"If you'll let me," I say mischievously.

"Well, trivia is about to begin, and Callie will kill me if I don't play with her. Care to join us?"

"Sure, let's go kick some ass." I let her go, immediately feeling the weight of her absence. We walk over toward the stage together and sit next to each other. I'm feeling especially daring right now, so I rest my hand on her thigh, similar to the way I did in the car the other day. Her breath hitches.

When I was younger, I flirted with a lot of girls. I hooked up with a fair amount of them, too—especially during my college years. I've never been interested in pursuing a relationship long-term, though. My longest relationship lasted about a year, and honestly, that was pushing it. She was great, but I never even told her I loved her because I didn't. I had love for her, but I didn't *love* her. At least, not in the way I think I was supposed to. I watched my parents throughout my childhood, so I'd like to think I have an idea of what love is supposed to look like. I guess I have a hard time allowing myself to fall. I've logically concluded that's likely because my parents forced me to be vulnerable so often during my youth. But with her, it all feels so natural. My life was mundane until she and her guardian angel casually waltzed in.

During trivia, I sober up for the most part. We play three rounds of trivia before we call it a night. I gulp down as much water as possible before we leave to rid myself of the buzz. As I sober up, my thoughts spiral. Have I been coming on too strong to Iris? Despite my doubts, I still can't stop myself from being near her all night, touching her when possible. Again, it all just feels so natural.

"I cannot believe our team won every round!" Callie cheers as we walk outside. "Jasper, we need you to participate in every Trivia Tuesday from now on. You were our secret weapon! How do you know so much stuff?"

"Eh, I've always loved learning new things." I glance at Iris. She assesses me as a tinge of concern crosses her features.

"Are you good to drive?" she asks worriedly.

"Yes, Greene, I'm good now. It's been a couple hours since my last swig, and I've sobered up significantly. Promise." She narrows her eyes and takes a deep breath. "Trust me."

"Please text me as soon as you get home, okay?" she requests. I can't remember the last time someone asked me to do that. Hell, I don't know if anyone ever has.

"You've got it, Greene."

She sighs in relief. Callie heads back to her car, letting Iris know she will wait for her before heading out. Iris approaches me, landing inches away from me.

"I can't lie," she starts, "it feels weird not riding with you back to your place right now."

"Who's stopping you?" I smirk as her cheeks bloom. I love making her blush.

"It's getting late, and unlike you," she scrunches her nose, "I can't sleep in tomorrow, so I should head home, I suppose." Rejection has never tasted worse than it does right now.

"I understand. I'll see you soon. Good night, Iris." I smile. Again. I've smiled more tonight than I have in a long time.

"Sweet dreams, Jasper. Don't forget to text me." She walks toward Callie's car. To my surprise, she walks to the driver's side. I remember Kai saying Iris doesn't like driving, but I'd assume she doesn't trust Callie to drive at the moment, so she's doing it anyway. Iris always looks out for everyone else, but other than Kai, who looks out for her?

Frantic knocking on my front door disrupts my slumber. I glance at the time, seeing it's just past midnight. Not bothering to put on a shirt, I rush to my front door to see what the deal is. I half-heartedly expect it to be a ding-dong ditching prank, and if that's the case, I'm going to lose it. I slowly open the old wooden door to see a wide-eyed girl breathing hard on my porch. Not just any girl—*my girl*. Immediately, I grab hold of her shoulders, scanning her eyes.

"What happened, Greene?"

Tears brim her eyelids as she works hard not to let them fall. "It's Truman. I've been out all night looking for him, and I can't find him *anywhere*. I kept walking and ended up here. I guess I didn't know where else to go." Her voice breaks as a single tear trails down her cheek.

I brush the tears off of her cheeks gently and look directly into her watery eyes. "We will find him. I promise you."

"How could you promise something like that?"

"Trust me." I look over her shoulder to see Kai standing in my driveway, waiting for us. "We will find Truman. Tonight."

I go back inside and grab the first sweatshirt I see, then hustle back to her side, locking my front door behind me.

"I got to see you shirtless, and I didn't even have to ask. What a treat," she quietly jokes.

Even in her darkest moments, she can muster a smile. She is not even close to fragile—she's *unbreakable*.

Kai leads the way, not that Iris needs to know that. We walk in silence, toward the woods. Eventually, we enter the forest, venturing deeper and deeper into the dark together. Normally, I would try to take her mind off of whatever she was struggling with, but this time, something tells me she should process this on her own. Kai walks in step with us.

"There's no need to worry," Kai assures, knowing I can't respond aloud right now. "Truman is just fine. It's all going to be okay."

In response, I grab hold of her hand. "He'll be okay, Iris."

Instead of letting go, we continue to hold each other's hand. I notice there isn't any music playing—I can't tell if the silence is a good or bad thing at the moment, but I decide she should have complete control over her current environment.

"This is big," Kai says with wonder. "She's trusting you *and* accepting silence—for now, that is." As if on cue, she pulls out her airpods. Screw it, I'm proud of her for walking in silence for as long as she did. She likely walked in silence the entire way to my home, which is no small feat.

TWENTY-THREE

IRIS

When I got home from the bar, my senses tingled. Immediately, I knew something was off. My front door was open, similar to the way it had been when maintenance was over. I slowly crept inside to see a maintenance technician had indeed stopped by—he had left some on my kitchen counter. I imagined it must have been for the request I submitted pertaining to a couple of the new floorboards peeling upward. Our maintenance team is available 24/7, and they felt terrible about the flood. However, when I called out for Truman, he didn't answer. I searched every room, looked under every piece of furniture in my apartment, and even checked the balcony. Truman wasn't home. A wave of panic engulfed me, but I refused to cry.

Instead, I marched outside as quickly as possible and began searching throughout my complex, shouting his name like a mad woman. I glanced under every car, peered around every bush, and even gazed upward at the trees surrounding the complex. It was roughly 11:30 at night, arguably not a safe hour for a woman to walk around alone, but I couldn't care less. I needed to find him. I would find him.

I wandered through the town, cautious not to miss a single trash can and crouching to search under dumpsters in eerily quiet alleys. Never once stopping, not even to turn on my music. I ran into other strays, my hope diminishing with every failure. Eventually, I found myself in a local neighborhood, still looking everywhere imaginable while calling out his name frantically. I began losing momentum but refused to give up. Before I knew it, I was outside his home. I didn't realize I had even walked to Jasper's home until I arrived. Despite not knowing him for long, my soul told me to trust him. I followed my intuition.

He opened his door shirtless, making me forget why I even showed up on his doorstep in the first place for a moment. I always could tell Jasper was fit, but *wow*. I didn't expect him to be so jaw-dropping. For a second, I even found myself intimidated by how sculpted he was. He leaned his head down, frantically scanned my eyes, and asked what was wrong, snapping me out of my hypnosis. I can't even remember what I said. It was all a blur. In a matter of no time at all, he got ready and accompanied me on my mission to find little Truman, which brings me to this moment.

As we walk through the forest, the quiet draws nearer and nearer, calling out to me. After several minutes, I can't handle the lingering silence any longer, so in typical Iris fashion, I play some music. We continue to walk together, hand-in-hand, letting the rhythm of the music carry us forward with the moon's subtle glow lighting the way. Eventually, I hear rushing water from a nearby stream. While walking up a hill consumed by fallen leaves, I notice a small figure curled up on a large mossy stone next to the creek. I break out of Jasper's grasp, running toward the little orange blob. As I inch closer, I see that he's lying still, and my heart races.

Please, please, please be okay, Truman. I can't lose you, too.

I slow down just inches away, careful not to spook him. I brush his fur, waking him up. He lazily opens his eyes, stretching his arms while maintaining eye contact with me.

"So, let me get this straight." I scoop him up carefully, assessing him. "I wander the streets looking for you in distress all night long only to find you lounging peacefully by the creekside as if you don't have a care in the world?" I tighten my hold on him, embracing him harder. "I'm so happy you're okay, little guy."

Jasper stands by my side and reaches out to pet Truman. "Don't scare your mom like that again, okay?" Truman responds with a soft purr. Earlier tonight, I was petrified I'd never hear his purr again. A tear escapes accidentally.

"Thank you so much." I look at Jasper, shivering from the frigid air. "How could you have known exactly where to find him?"

"Let's just call it a sixth sense." He smirks, wrapping his arm around my neck. "Let's head back; it's too cold out here."

As we walk along the dirt path back to his home, I soak in these moments with Truman. My feelings of anxiety slowly dissipate, dissolving into thrills. As a child, I prided myself on being a hopeless romantic. Consequently, I used to love dating, but I didn't get close to my partners often—I wanted to wait for the *one*, whatever that really meant. After Kai passed, though, I lost my motivation to find someone. I have been questioning if love is worth the risk of loss ever since. We approach Jasper's front porch, moonlight beaming overhead. "Your support meant the world to me tonight, Jasper. Thanks so much again." I begin the trek back to my apartment.

"Whoa, whoa, whoa." He steps in front of Truman and me, halting us. "You've had a long night; why don't you stay at my place? Just for tonight?"

Just for tonight. Sounds familiar. Oddly comforting, even.

"Usually, I'd fight you on the offer, but you're right—it's been a long night. Do you really not mind?"

"Not one bit."

"Okay. Just for tonight." I reach out a free hand to shake his, to which amusement floods his expression as he shakes my hand sarcastically.

"Now, let's get you warmed up." He leads me in, navigating me to his cozy couch. As soon as we step inside, he hastily walks over to the fireplace, kindling a fire. Then, he pulls out an extra woven blanket from his linen closet, wrapping me tightly. After efficiently tucking me in, he sits beside me. We turn on his TV, settling on a murder mystery movie. I lean back, settling into the couch, breathing slowly.

"So, do you want to talk about it?" he asks.

"What's there to talk about?" I keep my eyes locked on the screen.

"That was a scary experience—it's okay if it shook you." He angles his body toward mine. I don't talk about my feelings much these days. It doesn't come naturally to me—at least, not anymore. But something about Jasper makes me feel safe, and it's been a long time since I found that feeling in a person. Maybe I feel even safe enough to open up. Just a little bit and just for tonight.

"I thought I lost Truman," I say, breaking the unbearable silence. "When I noticed he was missing, my heart sank. I immediately thought the worst had happened, and I wasn't even close to being ready to say goodbye. I couldn't lose someone else—my heart wouldn't be able to bear that loss, not this time."

Suddenly, I notice my blanket feels damp. Before I can process the teardrops staining the blanket, Jasper pulls me into him, tucking me carefully into his side. He wraps his strong arms around me, cradling me, reminding me of how I cradled Truman tonight. I bask in his scent—fresh sandalwood. I give in, pressing into him rather than away from him. More tears cascade, seeping into his charcoal sweatshirt. I squeeze my eyes shut, unable to share more or look into his eyes.

"You're so much stronger than anyone realizes, Greene," he whispers into my hair, resting his head on mine. "But it's okay to lean on others when things get heavy—especially me."

I open my eyes and gaze upward slowly, looking directly into his stormy eyes swirling with unreadable emotion. Our faces, mere centimeters apart, seem to naturally gravitate to each other with every passing second. His eyes drift down to my lips, lingering there. He draws nearer and then places a gentle kiss on my forehead. Every inch of my body tingles, from my toes to my nose. It feels undeniably right—almost *unnaturally* right. Before I can overthink it, I give in to the moment. I grip the collar of his sweatshirt and pull him toward me, giving in to my intrusive thoughts. I close my eyes and part my lips, silently inviting him, waiting for an answer that will change everything as we know it. His lips—softer than I imagined—brush against mine, as he slowly slips the tip of his tongue inside my mouth. He tastes like mint.

He weaves his fingers into my hair as a groan escapes his mouth, resulting in a little gasp escaping from mine. My body vibrates under his grasp, pleading for more, suddenly believing in magic. *Damn, he's good. I knew he would be.* In one swift movement, he breaks the kiss. His hungry eyes pierce mine.

"I can't do this." He looks away, running his fingers through his hair. Immediately, I feel embarrassed and lean away from him.

"I'm sorry," I mumble, realizing I probably came on too strong.

"What? Oh, you don't have anything to be sorry for," he affirms. "As much as I would love to keep kissing you, I *can't.*"

I pull away even further, folding my arms, flustered by his interruption. Maybe he's afraid of getting too serious. With that in mind, I offer a solution.

"What happened to '*just tonight?*'"

"That's the thing, Greene." He stares into my eyes intently. "I don't know if I can settle for just tonight. I've been fighting it, but I want more than just one night."

TWENTY-FOUR

JASPER

While sitting on my couch with Iris in my arms, I couldn't be happier that Kai took off after we walked into my home. He would *not* be pleased with me at the moment. My criminal eyes drop down to her lips again, now extra pink and swollen, making my arousal even stronger. She tastes like *glazed honey*, even sweeter than I imagined. I'd die a happy—and lucky—man if she were the last woman I kissed.

As much as I'd love to scoop her into my arms and carry her to my bed to devour her, I know it's wrong. She deserves more. So much more.

"What do you mean you've been fighting it?" She scrunches her nose, looking cuter than ever, the glow of the fireplace illuminating her olive skin. She's still wearing the outfit she wore earlier tonight, enticing me with her curves.

"Iris, you've crafted the most striking mask," I remark, messing with a strand of her hair. "It's bulletproof. Most people don't see what lies under your mask, but I do. Not only that—I want to see even more. Quite frankly, I can't get enough of you if I'm being honest. I can't keep kissing you because I may want something more, but I don't want to jeopardize our friendship."

"What if, hypothetically speaking—" she pauses, thinking before continuing, as always, "I want something more, too? But maybe I'm not sure if I'm ready for that?"

"Then, I'd say we're on the same page. Hypothetically speaking, of course." I smirk, caressing her arm.

"So, what do we do?" she whispers, eyeing my lips again. I want to taste her again, but I know better. Kai would be proud.

"How about we change and then figure things out?"

"Um, I didn't pack an extra change of clothes for our impromptu sleepover, so this is it for me." She shrugs, motioning to her outfit. Right. I walk down the hallway to my bedroom to grab a gray T-shirt from my closet, throwing it her way.

"I'm going to change into this right now if that's okay? I am so ready to take off my pants, it's unreal." She sighs. I nod, then gulp as she walks away swiftly to change. I don't know why I assumed she would wait to change until we went to sleep. *Idiot.*

She prances back out into the living room, truly pantsless, taking my breath away in a single stride. *Fuck. Me.* Her smooth, bare legs call out to me. As she is about to plop down onto the couch, I intercept her, pulling her to sit right on my lap, holding her so she can't break free, savoring the feeling of her ass resting on my thighs.

"Jasper!" She squeals. "Let me go, or you'll regret it!" She attempts to break free pitifully, and we both gasp for air from laughing so hard. I continue to hold onto her, refusing to let her go.

"Hit me with whatever you've got," I quip. In an instant, she elbows me, causing me to release her. She rises seamlessly, taking a little bow as a mischievous glint lingers in her eyes. Just when I think it's over, she tackles me, straddling me with her legs on either side of my ribs. She has absolutely *no idea* what she does to me, and she's about to find out. That's great.

She pins me to the couch, looking straight into my eyes playfully. Her eyes widen slightly, signaling that she feels my bulge. Instead of releasing me, though, she chooses to rest her head on top of my chest directly above my heart and collapses on top of me. I wrap my arms around her.

"Does this mean I win?" She whispers.

"Never," I grin, glancing down at her to see her closing her eyes. The flames of the dimly lit fireplace reflect off of her, showcasing the subtle freckles on her nose and cheeks. Her breaths get slower, following a steady cadence. Eventually, she falls asleep nestled in my arms, and I don't have it in me to disrupt her.

"I hope you two had fun tonight." I'd recognize that voice anywhere at this point. It practically haunts me.

"Thanks, we did," I grumble quietly, careful not to wake Iris. To my surprise, Kai chuckles in response.

"The way you dropped everything to be there for her obviously meant a lot to her. You held her steady tonight." Kai sighs, sinking onto the unoccupied side of the couch at her feet and leaning his head back. "You've earned my trust. Feel free to gloat."

Something about Kai's admission gives me chills. Knowing that her guardian trusts me means so much more than I realized.

"Thanks, Kai."

"Thank *you*, Jasper. But don't get too comfortable," he jibes. "I'm not going anywhere—yet."

"Got it, boss," I joke smugly, continuing to whisper. "Do you ever get lonely? On the other side?"

"You know, I thought I would initially." He pauses. "But I feel a sense of fulfillment on this side. Sure, it'd be nice to have a companion, but I feel pretty good."

My fingers stroke her thick hair. "So you feel at peace?"

"Not fully," he admits, staring intently at the lit fire. "I can't find true peace until this one does." He subtly pokes her, causing her to stir slightly in her sleep. "Lately, though, I've been feeling more fulfilled than ever, which I think is a good sign. You're helping more than I thought you would if I'm being real here."

"Well, I'm helping her because I care about her too," I state. "I feel drawn to her in a way I can't fully understand."

"I figured as much. She has that effect on people. She draws them in." He smiles at her. Unfortunately, Kai doesn't get it. This is *more* than that.

"I like her, man. I really like her," I confess, despite how much it terrifies me to admit it aloud. He pauses for a moment. I gaze at the lit flames of the fireplace dwindling down.

"I know." He sighs. "I've known for a while, buddy. That's what makes all of this so much harder."

"Makes what harder?"

"You keeping this a secret from her, of course."

"Oh, well... I figure it's necessary," I affirm. "I've thought it through a hundred times, and in ninety-nine of the outcomes, she thinks I'm a lunatic, so it's best to keep this between us."

Kai bursts into laughter, grinning from ear to ear. "Fair enough. I just hope you continue to feel that way."

"What would happen if I told her anyway?"

"Honestly, I'm not positive what will happen, but I know it won't be good—for her, you, or myself. We'd be screwed across the board." He pauses. "Well, I wouldn't want to disrupt your little slumber party." Kai taunts, rising from the couch. He strides away, disappearing into thin air. I reach over Iris to grab the blanket, draping it over us. I pull her closer, breathing in her scent and committing this moment to memory. For the first time since moving back to Chrysocolla Cove, I actually feel at home.

I awake to the scent of honey and vanilla filling my nose. Cracking my eyes open, I see the most beautiful thing I've ever laid my eyes upon, cradled in my arms. I kiss the top of her head gently, inhaling her scent again.

"Good morning, Greene." She wiggles, stretching her arms and letting out a big yawn, then looks up at me with her hypnotic green eyes.

"Good morning, Mr. Alcott." *Damn, I never thought that could sound sexy.* She turns to face me better, looking directly into my eyes.

"You were so helpful last night. I want to repay you." She bites her lip.

"Oh, do tell me what you had in mind?" She rises up higher on my chest, allowing her plump lips to hover next to my ear. I gulp tightly.

"How about I cook breakfast?" she whispers. Not what I had in mind, but still appreciated, nonetheless.

"I'll never say no to food." I grin, tucking her hair behind her ears. Greene has a major case of bedhead in the mornings. "But wait, you cook?"

"Offer immediately rescinded," she states, pounding her head against my chest.

"I'm kidding, Greene." I chuckle. "Mostly."

"You better be—you'll eat your words after trying my famous pancakes. Just wait." She scoffs, jumping into action. I watch her walk away, paying shamefully close attention to the way her hips sway in *my T-shirt* with each passing step.

"Code red," Kai whispers frantically into my ear. "Don't say I didn't warn you."

Code red? What is that supposed to mean?

"Care to enlighten me?"

"There's no time, you'll understand in 3...2...1..." Suddenly, I hear my front door open. Only one other person in the Cove has the key to my home. *No, no, no.*

My mother struts in through the front door, my father wheeling in behind her. She eyes my sweatpants suspiciously. "Jasper! Don't tell me you forgot *again*!" I look at the date and time: our monthly breakfast hour. I glance over their shoulders, catching Kai cackling. Truman greets them in the front entrance, rubbing against my mom's legs. "And when did you get a cat?"

Of course, my parents drop by while Iris is currently standing in my kitchen, wearing my T-shirt, with her bare legs on full display. Of fucking course.

TWENTY-FIVE

IRIS

While whisking a batch of batter in a mixing bowl, I feel at ease—comfortable, even. It took me a couple minutes to find all the ingredients and materials needed to make some homemade vanilla pancakes, but I'm in no rush. I woke up early again, so I have plenty of time before going home and getting ready for work. I tend to wake up early when sleeping over at Jasper's. He strides into the kitchen, hustling to my side and looking uneasy. He gestures for me to pause my music, so I pull out my AirPods.

"Don't panic, Greene," he says quietly. My heart stops.

"What? What is it?" I've had one too many scares over the past twenty-four hours, I don't know if I can handle another.

"My parents are waiting in the front entrance as we speak." He pauses, trying to read my expression. "Remember how I told you we do monthly breakfasts? Well, it may have slipped my mind due to last night's events. I'm going to go out to eat breakfast with them. Will you be okay here? I'll be back before you have to leave for work, so I can give you a ride."

"Oh, thank goodness, you almost gave me a heart attack!" I sigh in relief. Confusion crosses his face. "Jasper, I thought something else had happened to Truman. I'm great with parents. I could meet them right now if you want, we're not even dating."

"Oh, uh…" His eyes drift down to my legs. I follow his gaze, realizing I forgot a minor detail that isn't so minor.

"*Shit!*" I whisper, pulling down the gray shirt to cover my bare legs, panic rising. "Jasper, go get my pants!"

"On it." He salutes, turning toward the living room.

"Jasper, what on earth is taking you so—" A petite woman in her mid-forties intercepts him. She glances over his shoulder, fixing her dark brown eyes on me. Immediately, almost comically, her eyes drop down to my bare naked legs. "Oh."

Oh? She doesn't even sound fazed.

"Mom, this is Iris. Iris, meet my mom." Jasper motions us toward each other, pinning me with an apologetic expression.

"Hi, Mrs. Alcott, it's so nice to meet you," I smile warmly and reach out my hand to shake hers. This isn't the most ideal way to meet Jasper's parents, but the only way out of this situation is through at this point.

"Hi, Iris." She shakes my hand as thick strands of her black hair fall forward, framing her round face. "And how long have you two been together?"

"We're not," we both answer simultaneously.

"Mom, Iris is running Aged Emporium's fundraiser, she's the one I told you about," Jasper clarifies. *He told his mom about me?*

"Ah, I see." She smiles knowingly at him, turning her gaze toward me. "Honey, there's no need to be embarrassed. This isn't the first time, and quite frankly, it isn't the worst time I've caught Jasper with a girl."

My eyes flicker to Jasper, who is leaning against the hallway door frame, his arms folded.

"We don't have all day," a deep voice rumbles from the living room area. A wall divides the kitchen from the front entryway, so I'm unable to capture a look at his dad.

"Forgive my husband," Mrs. Alcott says. "He isn't known for his patience, and now that he's in a chair, he's grumpier than ever. Will you be joining us for breakfast?"

"Oh, no, but thanks so much for the invitation."

"Well, hopefully, we'll be seeing you again, Iris, it was lovely meeting you," she says warmly. I find myself actually believing she has enjoyed our conversation. She strolls out of the kitchen. "We'll wait in the car for you, Jasper."

"Sorry about that." Jasper runs his fingers through his tousled dark hair. He clearly inherited his thick dark hair from his mother. "She can be a lot."

I smile at him, then turn back around toward the mixing bowl resting on the counter, glancing down at the batter, accepting defeat. "So much for cooking breakfast," I mutter.

"I will gladly save my appetite for whatever you're cooking up." He sneaks up behind me, wrapping his arms around my waist and rocking me. His voice drops to a husky whisper. "You carry yourself so well. Pretty sure my mom was impressed." I feel my cheeks redden.

"Speaking of your mom, could you go grab my pants now, please?" He releases me, spinning me to face him.

"Only if you promise this won't be the last time you wander around my house pantsless." His gray eyes pierce mine. I scoff, rolling my eyes.

"Oh, please, Jasper, I will not promise that." I laugh, assuming he's joking.

"I'm serious, Greene. Promise?" Not thinking much of it, I shrug, giving in.

"Ugh, fine, I promise. You should probably get going." I glance over his shoulder.

"I don't particularly want to, but I suppose I should." He sighs, letting me go. He hustles to the couch and throws my pants at me. "I'll be back soon."

"I'll see you later, Jasper." I watch him walk away. How does he manage to look so good in sweatpants, of all things?

Unfortunately, I don't have the luxury of being able to wait for Jasper to return from breakfast. This morning, my top priority is getting Truman back to my apartment in one piece. After cleaning up, I change into last night's clothes and return to my apartment, carrying Truman in my arms.

The walk to my apartment is only fifteen minutes long, but the cold air isn't exactly encouraging. It's a good thing Truman likes being held, otherwise, this would have been an entirely different experience. I finally arrive at my apartment complex and jog up the stairs. Upon walking into my apartment, everything is as it should be.

I feed Truman breakfast, then hastily begin getting ready for work. First, I shower. This has been the longest week of my year, and it's only Wednesday. While washing my hair, my mind drifts back to what his mom said. Knowing she has caught him in worse settings with girls piques my curiosity. Jasper seems more experienced than I am. As I run my fingers through my hair, my mind wanders, and I imagine him raking *his* fingers through my hair, pulling me closer to him—

Iris. Get a grip. I abruptly finish showering, then jump out, wrapping myself in a fuzzy beige towel. I check my phone to see a couple of new messages.

Jasper

> Where did you go?

Jasper

> You okay, Greene?

I fight a smile. It's been a while since someone checked in on me like this—I'd be lying if I said it doesn't feel good. I still cannot believe we *kissed* last night. At his home. On the couch. In front of a freshly lit fireplace. The producers over at Hallmark would be proud.

I can't remember the last time a kiss took my breath away like last night. I lightly stroke my lips, feeling my cheeks grow warmer as I relive our unexpectedly magical evening together. He obviously knows what he's doing, though—who knows if our night meant as much for him as it did for me.

Iris

> Rest assured, I managed to walk home without any trouble. Shocking, I know.

After responding, I change into a mauve flowy silk button-up and leggings, completing the look with booties and my oversized black puffer coat. I check the time, determining I won't be able to stop at Little Falls today. *Oh, well.* I put my hair up in a high ponytail, adding a ribbon. I find myself putting a tad more effort in than usual, so I conclude that today will be a good one. Before I step outside, I kiss Truman's little forehead. "Don't scare me like that ever again, okay?"

Truman closes his eyes and pushes his face into my hand in response. I slip my AirPods in, then land at the bottom of the staircase, rushing to Soi, when a body blocks my path.

"Jasper?" I gawk. "What are you doing here?" He rolls his eyes in response as if the answer is obvious, to which I raise my brows.

"I told you I'd give you a ride to work," he affirms, leading me to his black car. He opens the passenger door for me, and I begin to protest, but he pushes his index finger against my lips in response, shushing me before I can continue.

The audacity of this man.

"Before you reject my offer, may I suggest you take a look inside the vehicle?" He inclines his head toward the interior. My eyes follow the direction of his gesture and land on the most beautiful sight I could imagine. A Little Falls cup of coffee sits in the front cupholder. Unable to hide my excitement, I jump into the front seat in record time. Yeah, I guess I've missed being a passenger princess. Before shutting the car door, pride gleams in his eyes. I buckle in and take a sip of the pumpkin spice latte, savoring its delightful taste on my tongue.

"You outdid yourself, Jasper. Last night, you were an angel." I raise my cup to his face. "But right now? Right now, you're practically a God."

Jasper chuckles, then looks into his rearview mirror, laughing even harder. I join in, letting the airy feeling in the car consume me. "You're something else, Greene."

"So I've been told." I take another sip of my drink and savoring it. On our drive to Soi, I can't help but overthink our situation. "How does this work exactly?"

"How does what work?"

"Us."

"Us?" Jasper quirks a brow while turning the wheel. My heart skips a beat—and not in a good way—as hesitancy seems to cross his features. "I'm not sure. I'm not an expert in this field."

"Neither am I," I admit, fiddling with my shirt.

"I'm curious; how many relationships have you been in?"

"Not many." I begin using my fingers to count, reaching ten, then continuing to count as his jaw drops.

"Over ten relationships?" he asks when I surpass ten fingers, visibly stunned. "How old are you again?"

I throw him a mischievous smile. "I'm kidding. I've been on a lot of dates, but I have only been in three committed relationships. And you already know I'm 25, thank you very much."

"Ah, three. I guess that's *mildly* comforting as opposed to ten," he smirks. "Only mildly."

My cheeks suddenly grow warm, leading me to turn away to disguise my excitement.

"What about you? And how old are you?" I ask too eagerly. *How embarrassing.*

"I'm 29 years old, turning 30 in April," he answers. *Wow. I thought he was in his 30s. Well, I guess 29 isn't far off.* "As far as relationships go, I've been in a couple, my longest one being a year long."

Wow. That's definitely longer than any relationship I've ever had...

"Interesting, seeing as your mom claimed she had seen you in far more compromising positions with girls before today?" I tease. My parents haven't ever caught me hooking up with guys. Even the idea of that mortifies me.

"Yeah, she has," he says, matter-of-factly. "I've only been in a couple of relationships, but I've been with a fair amount of girls. In high school, I was out of control, leading to my mom finding me in less-than-ideal positions with girls. However, I wasn't under such watchful eyes in college."

I am not surprised Jasper has extensive dating experience—anyone with eyes can see why. I have had my fair share of experience, but since losing Kai, my dating life has been nonexistent, so I'm rusty. Knowing he has been with more people than I have bothers me, although I don't understand why. I mean, it's not like we're together in his eyes... Are we? I can't read Jasper. I imagine he doesn't have many options here in the Cove, so maybe he's just lonely and I'm convenient.

"I can see you over there, likely overthinking as usual." He casts a quick glance my way as he pulls into Soi's parking lot, resting his hand on my thigh. "No need to overthink this, love. Let's start with something small. How about we go on a date?"

Love.

My heart does a little flip as I let the gravity of that word sink in.

Instead of feeling overwhelmed, I feel exasperated.

"I'd like that," I say quietly, unbuckling my seatbelt. I look at Soi's yellow logo and suddenly feel the urge to call in sick so I can spend more time in Jasper's car with my coffee and jitters.

"Let's plan on Friday night. I'll pick you up from your place at 6:00 p.m. Does that sound good?"

"I'm in," I say, opening the car door to leave. "Don't miss me too much in the meantime." As I walk inside, giddiness takes over.

I'm going on a date with Jasper Alcott.

TWENTY-SIX

JASPER

The last few days have been typical. Aged Emporium has received hundreds of followers over the past week thanks to Soi's impressive marketing efforts. Consequently, the shop has had more business than usual. We are not exceeding expectations by any means, but we do have a steady flow of customers daily, which is objectively fantastic.

Truthfully, I've been looking forward to Friday since Wednesday morning, the last time I saw Iris. It's strange. We went from strangers to colleagues to friends to... *this* much faster than I ever anticipated. Despite the speed at which we're moving, it still doesn't feel like we're moving fast enough. In previous experiences with women, I found myself rushing into it so I could rush my way out of it. With Iris, though, I *want* to take my time.

But I *can't*. After finding out she's had a lot of experience dating, I am going to make this first date something special. I refuse just to be another one of those guys.

I glance at the clock, and thankfully, it's closing time. After shutting the shop down, I stop by Little Falls for a quick errand then head home to prepare for my first date in years. I take a shower, losing track of time in a train of thought centered on *her*. I whip out a casual, but nice, outfit for tonight, composed of a brown sweater, black trousers held up by a black belt, and a watch. After putting a trench coat on, I spray myself with cologne, then drive over to her place. Upon arrival, I text her to let her know I'm here.

"You should honk," a voice startles me. "She loves that shit."

I skeptically look at Kai in my rearview mirror. "Seriously?"

"Seriously."

Kai knows Iris pretty well, so I give him the benefit of the doubt this time. I honk the horn a couple of times, resulting in Iris rushing to her window and looking down at me, scrunching her nose and undoubtedly urging me to stop. She hustles away before I can get a good look at her.

"Dude, you're so gullible for a realist." Kai wheezes in laughter. "She hates it when people honk at her from the lot."

Screw. This. "Hey, Kai? Eat shit. Who invited you?"

"You did," he gloats. "By inviting Iris, you essentially invited me, too. I'm so excited to see what you have planned for us."

He bats his eyelashes. I narrow my eyes, gritting my teeth. "Seriously, dude, you're relieved of your duties for tonight. Go play a harp or whatever it is you do in your spare time."

"Wait, you think I play the harp in my spare time? I'm touched—that's way cooler than what I actually do." Kai snorts.

"If you're so curious, you could've just asked. I like to go to the mountains."

I suppose it makes sense for him to go there—the mountains do tend to bring people serenity. "Great. Go take a hike."

"No can do, bro," he says, leaning back in his seat, making himself comfortable. "I'm going to hang out with you two tonight. Don't worry. You won't even notice I'm there." I made a terrible miscalculation in assuming tonight would be an average first date. I forgot to account for our permanent paranormal third wheel.

"Fine. Do me a favor. If Iris and I make out, please at least give her the decency of looking away," I huff, resting my hand on my forehead.

"That's one thing you don't have to worry about," he admits. "Rest assured, if you start making out, I am *out*."

No problem, I'll just have to initiate that earlier in our evening.

"But I'd be surprised if you make it that far tonight," he mocks. "From what I've gathered, she takes things slow."

We'll see about that.

"*Bro*, have you just forgotten that I can read your mind?"

"Nope, my thoughts were fully intentional." Suddenly, Iris appears in my line of sight. She's wearing a beige sweater with flowy sleeves, a plaid mini skirt, tights, and knee-high boots, topping the outfit off with a thick tan trenchcoat. Her hair is half up, half down, tied back with a black ribbon. Upon seeing me, a radiant smile stretches across her face, the authenticity in it taking my breath away for just a moment. I step out of the car to greet and open the door for her, but not before grabbing a hold of her waist and pulling her toward me.

"You look ravishing," I whisper, staring intently into her emerald eyes.

"You don't look too bad yourself." She smiles shyly, getting into the car and slowly settling into the seat. I walk back to the driver's side to begin the drive. The sun is still setting as we take off. I turned on the music before she joined me in the car. After a few moments, I notice she keeps pulling down her skirt.

"No need to cover those thighs on my account, Greene." I glance over at her for a second to catch her blush, then chuckle. I hear obnoxious gagging sounds from the back seat. I glare at Kai through the rearview mirror and see him smirking.

"Everything okay?" *If only Iris weren't so observant.*

"Yeah, all good." I hide my grimace, focusing my attention on the road. It's a good thing Kai is already dead.

"So, where are we going?" Iris purses her lips.

"It's a surprise."

"Ugh, *fine.*" She rolls her eyes. She stares outside the window, watching the sky as it melts. We arrive at Marble Grove precisely when I want to. I get out to open her car door, then head to my trunk to pick up the goods. I grab the basket and hand it to Iris, then grab the blanket I packed. Her jaw drops.

"Are we having a picnic? At night?" I grin in response, not wanting to give it away.

We approach the white gazebo we spent time in just a few days before. Marble Grove is striking during daylight hours, but it's something else entirely at night—I figured a night picnic surrounded by gleaming holiday lights would be the perfect way to spend our time together. I lower myself to unfold the blanket and set up the basket on the ground of the dimly lit gazebo. My eyes flicker up to Iris, witnessing her staring at the lights lining the gazebo and pond beyond us in awe. My chilled heart warms a fraction at the sight.

"Wouldn't have pegged you for a romantic, Jasper," Kai whispers directly in my ear. I scratch my jaw and attempt to bite my tongue, then look at him as he locks his eyes on Iris. While watching her reaction to the atmosphere, he grins. His eyes glisten. "I haven't seen her look this free in a while."

For the first time since meeting Kai, I finally get it. His contentment is driven by hers. Her happiness means more to him than I can even understand. For that reason, Kai and I are tethered together—differently from how he and Iris are, but still tethered. We both want her to feel *free*.

Once I set the sandwiches, grapes, and wine up on the blanket, I pull out a loaf of fresh-baked bread and stand. I reach out for her hand. "Before we begin eating, I say we pay the ducks a visit."

"Fresh-baked bread for the ducks? This is officially the most wholesome evening I've ever had." Her eyes sparkle as she snags the loaf of bread from my hands and sprints out of the gazebo toward the pond, dragging me along right behind her. As we run together, I catch a quick glimpse of her ass in that short plaid skirt and suddenly feel weak. *Damn.*

I catch up to her, reaching the water's edge. Iris begins clicking her tongue. "Here, little ducks." She glances around. Unfortunately, the ducks aren't coming out to play—something I stupidly did not take into account.

You can't let her down, Jasper.

"Here, one sec," I say, gently taking the loaf from her. I venture into the darker part of the grove, near the stones and evergreens, at the pond's edge covered in shadows. I'm certain some of the ducks are camped out around here.

"Jasper, what are you doing? It's way too dark over there, it's fine. Let's just throw out some bread along the edge here for the ducks to eat when the sun comes out." She catches up to me, lightly tugging me back.

"Greene, I'll be damned if you don't get to see at least one duck." I stalk forward, deeper into the dark—alone. I trek down the rough dirt path, looking everywhere I possibly can for a lone duck. I'll settle for even one duck sighting at this point. Hell, a duckling would suffice. Just *something* to make this date memorable.

"C'mon, man, she won't be bothered if she doesn't see a duck. She's already so happy with everything else," Kai's voice disrupts me. I turn to my right to see he's walking right next to me. "Turn back around."

"I'm good." I keep walking, further and further into the dark.

"No, you're not. I'm serious; it's not worth it. What you're doing right now is more triggering than it is helpful." He halts in front of me, stopping me in my tracks and urging me to turn back around. I gaze over my shoulder to see her standing along the water's edge, her arms folded defeatedly. "Take a deep breath. I've seen her go through enough to know when someone isn't doing okay. Breathe, man. Breathe, then turn back around."

His hazel eyes pierce mine, but not in his soul-searching way. In a genuine way. Deciding it truly isn't worth it, I turn back around, determined to bring her smile back. "Sorry, Greene," I say, stepping behind her and wrapping my arms around her. "I got caught up in the moment, forgetting why we're really here."

She glances up at me, taunting me with her twinkling green eyes. "Glad you came to your senses, Jasper. Are you okay?"

"I am now, love."

We tear the bread into pieces, tossing them onto the ground near the pond. These ducks will be eating fresh-baked bread all day tomorrow. After scattering the pieces, Iris and I walk back to the gazebo through a thin layer of snow, holding hands. We both sit on the blanket across from each other on the wooden floor and dig into the sandwiches and wine, talking about everything from Truman to our college days.

Kai leans on the pavilion for most of the conversation, watching us under the dimly lit lights. Instead of looking at us with concern in his eyes like usual, his eyes fixate on us with a sense of...longing. Several moments later, he says, "Hey Jasper, I will take off. Keep her safe tonight, okay? I mean, I'll be here if prompted, but promise me I can trust you."

I promise. He walks away, fading into the night, and I'm alone at last. With Greene. *My girl.*

TWENTY-SEVEN

IRIS

As a child, I often envisioned my ideal date taking place in a meadow surrounded by blooming flowers and luminous light. I imagined a boy kissing my hand under the sun, telling me I was pretty. Little did I know, my ideal date as an adult would take place in a grove at night, enveloped by whispering trees and sparkling lights. Instead of kissing my hand under the sun and calling me pretty, he kisses my forehead under the moon and tells me I'm *ravishing*.

Jasper Alcott crossed off an item on my bucket list that didn't even exist before tonight. A night picnic is just what my clouded heart needs. After finishing a glass of wine and the chicken salad sandwiches he kindly prepared for us, I rise to my feet to lean over the gazebo's edge, overlooking the dark waters. I gaze up toward the sky, resting my eyes on the moon. The sun used to rule my world until that dreadful day. Now, I feel more comfortable under the moon's watchful eye than the sun. How fitting it is for our first real date to take place under a night sky full of twinkling stars.

He joins my side, pressing into me. I lean into his touch, continuing to admire the sky and stars and moon and everything in between. "Would you believe me if I told you I used to like mornings?" I whisper, still entranced by the moon itself.

"Nope, you're bluffing," he teases. "I mean, you've woken up pretty early while at my place this week."

"Yeah, well, that's unusual, to be honest. I used to enjoy waking up before the sun rose. Sunrises were my favorite part of the day. I loved greeting the sun."

"What did you love about them?" My heart pounds. I haven't told anyone about this. I don't even know how to say it, but my heart is telling me it's time.

"The sun has always reminded me of my brother," I admit quietly, still fixing my gaze on the moon.

"It sounds like you and your brother are close." Jasper grins, intertwining his fingers with mine over the white wooden railing. "I've always wanted a brother or sister. I'm glad you got one of the good ones."

It's time. Tell him.

I turn to face him. "He really *was* one of the good ones. He passed away." Tears prickle my eyes, threatening to cascade down my cheek at any given second.

For a fleeting moment, time stops. *I can't believe I told him.* Jasper stares into my eyes. He lets go of my hand, causing my heart to pause. Instead of turning away like my unwelcome thoughts suggest he will, he reaches up to gently brush a tear off my cheek that must have escaped.

"I'm so sorry, love." He closes his eyes, leaning his head toward mine until our foreheads meet. I follow his lead, closing my eyes and allowing myself to embrace only a fragment of the pain lingering inside my heart. He runs his fingers through my hair and kisses my forehead. "I'm so, so sorry."

"Thank you, Jasper. I think about him every single day and miss him like hell, even though it's been years." My voice comes out more broken than I expect, to which I scoff, opening my eyes. "I'm a mess."

"Grief is messy, but that does not make you a mess." Jasper opens his eyes. "When you're ready to talk about it, I'm here, Greene. I meant what I said the other day—you can hit me with whatever you've got. I'll be waiting."

"I'll keep that in mind." I tightly wrap my arms around him, pulling him in for a warm hug. I don't feel ready to give him all the nitty gritty details yet, but knowing he is here for me means more than he will ever know. While holding him, his scent fills my nose—pine and sandalwood. My favorite scent these days. I rise on my tiptoes to kiss his cheek, then fall flat on my feet. Before I can pull away, his grip tightens as he leans in, parting his lips to meet mine. We kiss, but it's different from our last one—it's more heated. I slip my tongue into his mouth, dancing with his, taking pleasure as we explore each other's mouths. A groan escapes from him. I push my hips forward, pressing into him. Taking me by the small of my back, he turns me, placing my back against the gazebo's post. He slides his hands to outline my waist. His lips inch their way down to my neck. I lift my chin, granting him full access to my neck. I can't help but gasp in pleasure.

"*Fuck*," he groans. "You're so beautiful, Greene." He leans back, and I see the hunger in his hooded eyes. For just a moment, I'm ready to let go and fully give in. I find myself wanting *more*. Labels be damned. Now, it's my turn. I kiss his neck, heat rising in my chest when suddenly, he pulls away. He looks off to his left, breaking me out of my reverie. I hear quiet footsteps. He steps out of our trance, placing himself in front of me. I follow his gaze and see a man in uniform heading toward the pavilion.

"Don't want any trouble, folks," the middle-aged groundskeeper says while holding a flashlight. "But the Grove is closing for the night in about ten minutes, so it's time to pack up."

"No problem, sir, thank you," I hastily respond, heat spreading across my cheeks. Jasper sighs in disbelief.

"I can't believe they're curfewing us," he grumbles, running his fingers through his dark waves.

"I haven't felt this young and alive in years." I squeal excitedly, rushing to pack up our things. "Do you take all your hometown dates here?"

"You'd be the first." He folds the blanket. He hands the basket and wine to me, wrapping his arm around my neck as we venture out into the dark night. "I can't remember the last time I went on a real date, honestly."

"I used to date a lot, but I can confidently say I've never been on a date quite like this one," I giggle. His eyes narrow for a millisecond before his energy shifts.

"Yeah, it's not every day you get busted by an elderly groundskeeper while making out," he smirks at me.

"Hey, I would not consider him elderly! He doesn't look a day over 50," I argue.

"To each their own," Jasper taunts. "And let's not forget the time I told you you'd get to feed the ducks fresh bread only not to meet a single duck. This first date couldn't be more perfect, huh?"

My heart skips a beat. "*First* date?"

"As long as you're up for another, hypothetically speaking." We step in front of his car. I tug on his arm, stopping him.

"I think I agree with you," I whisper, kissing his lips softly. "Our first date couldn't have been *more* perfect." I settle into his car.

"Maybe tonight doesn't have to end yet..." Jasper drawls as he turns the car on. I glance at him with curious eyes.

"What do you have in mind?"

"Let's go on a drive." He casually rests his hand on my upper thigh, barely below the hem of my plaid skirt. We drive around the bend for a few minutes, and then he pulls off onto the side of the road near the forest, shutting the car off. I anxiously bite my lip and climb over the armrest to straddle him, wasting no time. I've been down this road before; I know the ins and outs of good old-fashioned car make-outs, but my heart is racing. I gaze into his hooded eyes for a moment before his hand cups my behind, pulling me closer to him, leaving me no choice but to meet his lips.

As he caresses my lower back, I rotate my hips in sync with his, letting my skirt roll up above my waist and losing my breath at the hardness of his cock against me. My lips graze his chiseled jawline down toward his neck. I stroke his neck with my tongue, letting out small gasps as I roll my hips and grind against him.

"*Iris*," he rasps while gripping my waist hard. "Do you feel how hard I am for you?" I moan in response as he hardens even further, tightening my legs around his hips. With our bodies pressed against each other like this, my arousal skyrockets, leading me into a state of euphoria. Eventually, we untangle, and I sink back into the seat breathlessly as he drives us home.

As my mind wanders, I reflect on our evening. Tonight, I told Jasper about Kai, and I found consolation rather than dread in talking about him. Jasper is patient beyond words, stubborn, but more compassionate than I could've ever guessed. I attempt to suffocate the persistent butterflies that won't leave me alone, but yet again, I predictably fail.

I lay my hand on top of his, grasping it in mine, then lean my head against the headrest and realize one more thing about our evening.

The quiet didn't defeat me tonight.

Twenty-Eight

Iris

I prance across the stage, smiling brightly from ear to ear. Upon accepting the piece of paper I have worked so ridiculously hard for, I glance out to the audience.

First, I notice my brown-haired father, typing vigorously on his phone. The screen's light shines brightly onto his tan skin. On his right sits my blonde mother who's currently wearing an unreadable, rather blank expression. To my father's left, sits the happiest-looking guy in the room—my brother, Kai. He claps without ceasing, whistling, roaring my nickname for the entire auditorium to hear. Watching me accept my diploma, he doesn't even blink, not daring to miss a second of this. Instead, his grin stretches as wide as my own. He peers to his right for only a second to share his excitement with her. Katherine cheers as loudly as Kai does. I fight back tears as my eyes shift back to Kai. He claps even harder as I walk off the stage.

After throwing my cap in the air and officially saying goodbye to late-night study dates and dreadful group projects, I immediately begin my search. Finding Kai typically isn't too challenging—he's almost always the tallest in the room. I turn right and bump right into him, to which he immediately turns our encounter into a bear hug. "You did it, Irie! I'm so proud of you!"

While we embrace, Katherine tugs on my gown, pulling me into a warm hug. "How are you feeling?" Katherine's genuinely caring nature never fails to touch me.

"I'm feeling...relieved," I answer candidly, peeking over her shoulder to find my mom standing alone. I approach her slowly, swallowing a lump in my throat.

"Thanks for coming," I say quietly.

"It's my daughter's college graduation. I wouldn't miss it," she says frankly, looking around.

"Where did dad go?"

"He had an emergency business call he couldn't miss," she says. For a second, I think I see remorse in her gaze, but I must be mistaken.

"Honestly, I'm just thankful you both showed up." I smile softly. "Thank you so much."

"You're welcome."

"Mom, isn't Irie so badass? She graduated in the top ten percent of her class." Kai hooks his arm around my neck. "Not as badass as me, objectively speaking, but still. Pretty badass."

"Language, Kai." Mom shifts uncomfortably, breaking into a subtle smile. "I'm going to head out to beat traffic." She reaches out to Kai first, hugging him tightly. As an afterthought, she pulls me *in for a hug, too. I yearn for the hug to last longer but accept the hand I've been dealt.*

"Drive safe," I shout as she steps away. I know a parent attending their child's college graduation may be a bare minimum requirement for most, but for me, this is monumental. I can't remember the last time my parents both showed me support publicly, so this feels good.

"C'mon, Irie, let's go get dinner." His hands grip my shoulders from behind, ushering me forward through the crowd as Katherine follows closely behind him. She laughs as Kai clears the way for her, using me as a human shield against the herd of people.

A ringing disrupts my dream, forcefully pulling me back into reality. A reality he no longer exists in. I sigh, wishing I could've spent more time in the memory—just this once. I shut off my phone's alarm and instantly turn on music. I normally would sleep in on Sunday, but Callie and I are dress shopping this morning for both Katherine's wedding and the masquerade ball—two very different events that require very different dresses. I figure Callie's help is absolutely necessary, as I can't remember the last time I went shopping for formal dresses. Typically I wear whatever formal wear I already have available in my closet for events I orchestrate, but I figured this would be a good excuse to go shopping. I slip on a black hoodie with a pair of leggings today. After throwing my hair up in a messy bun, I check my phone.

Jasper

Good morning, Greene.

How is it that a simple text from Jasper can make my heart race?

Iris

Good morning :)

191

Truman's aggressive meows signal an overdue breakfast. I feed him, then check my phone.

Callie

Good morning!! I'm on my way, see you soon!

I'm hopeful that Callie can help me gain clarity today. Obviously, I like Jasper and he likes me. I can admit that to myself, I'm not entirely dense. Not knowing how this ends concerns me more than I'd like to admit, though. What happens after we finish working together? How deep are his feelings? Where do we even go from here? Callie interrupts my spiraling thoughts, letting me know she has arrived. I meet her in the car, and we venture out of the Cove, southbound toward Seattle.

"So, what's up with you and Jasper?" Callie asks after taking a sip of her coffee. She doesn't waste any time.

"*Ugh*," I groan. "I don't know."

"You don't know?" She raises her brows. "Odd, it seems like you are dating each other."

"Well..." I pause, wincing. "We kissed. And made out."

"OMG, excuse me?!" She nearly slams on the brakes while on the interstate, to which I hold my breath and brace myself.

"Callie!" I shout, frustrated. "You can't do that."

"I'm so sorry, I know, I know." She casts an apologetic glance my way. "I'm just in complete disbelief you didn't mention the fact that you made out with our town's hottest resident sooner. I'm hurt, really."

"It all happened so fast. We actually had our first kiss on Tuesday night. Truman went missing and Jasper helped me find him, resulting in me spending the night at his place. We cuddled together next to the fireplace, and it just kinda... happened."

"Kissing that beautiful man doesn't just *kinda happen*, Iris Adelaide," Callie states. "Did you kiss him? Or did he kiss you?"

"Well, I guess I kissed him." I look away shyly.

"That's my best friend!" She cheers, giggling. "I knew you had it in you. Did he kiss you back? Was he like totally into it?"

"Um, yeah, I guess so?"

"Hell yeah, he was." She beams while taking a turn. "You don't understand how invested I am in your relationship. I've been rooting for you."

"Well, thank you, Callie." I stifle a laugh. "But I don't know... I can't figure out where to go from here. I have no clue how deep his feelings are or anything. I can't read him at all."

"Why don't you just ask?" she asks like it's the most obvious choice in the world.

"Easier said than done," I mumble. "I mean, he did take me on a date on Friday night..."

"IRIS!" She gasps. "A real date?"

"Yes. Not a fake one." She shakes her head while taking another turn.

"SMH, I can't believe you have been withholding so much valuable information from me, girl. I'm hurt."

I burst out into laughter. "I didn't want to text you all of this! That's why I'm telling you now."

"He really likes you, Iris," she says matter-of-factly.

"What makes you so sure?"

"Hm, aside from helping you rescue Truman, taking you out on a date, and making out with you..." She pauses. "He held onto you for a long time on Tuesday night."

I scoff, then begin to blush, remembering how indescribably good it feels to be held in his arms.

"I'm serious, Iris. You should've seen the way he was looking at you all night, too."

"How was he looking at me?"

"Like he would do *anything* for you." She sighs. "Trust me. This is real."

I let her words sink in. *This is real.* I can't imagine an outcome in which this situation ends well, which terrifies me. While fixating on what she just said, I suddenly feel my phone vibrate.

Mom

> Iris, your father and I will be dropping by your apartment on Thursday. We will bring a turkey and a couple of sides. Please provide dessert. See you then.

Oh, hell no.

Iris

> Sorry, I have to work.

Mom

> I highly doubt as an event planner that you'll be working on Thanksgiving.

Events director. Again, oh, hell no. As pitiful as it may sound, I forgot this Thursday is Thanksgiving. Why on earth are my parents coming to town to visit *me*? I've lived here for four years and they have only visited the Cove one other time, which was to attend one of Kai's games.

"Well, my mother just announced she and my father are visiting me this Thanksgiving, so that's just great," I announce, radiating sarcasm. Callie pulls into the mall's parking lot while dropping her jaw dramatically.

"The infamous Greenes are visiting you this week? If my life were half as eventful as yours, I'd be a happy girl," she jokes. "You'll be fine; I'm sure they won't stay long, seeing as they never do, right?"

Her words sting. I know she didn't intend for that, and it's hard for others to understand, but the fact that my parents don't care to spend time with me hurts. Regardless of the facade I display.

"Right." I force out a laugh. "I'll be fine!"

"With Jasper by your side, how couldn't you be anything less than fine?" she teases. I suppose she has a point. We walk into the mall and map out the shops we will visit today. I recently chose to accept Jasper's offer to be my date to Katherine's wedding. I didn't want to make a big deal out of it, so I just sent him a quick text to confirm his attendance. Today, my primary objective is to find a classy dress for the wedding in my hometown and a magical masquerade dress for Aged Emporium's fundraiser. My secondary objective may or may not be to find dresses that will leave a mark on Jasper, too.

TWENTY-NINE

IRIS

I am not in a great mood. Aged Emporium has been getting more business thanks to Soi's campaign, which is great. I couldn't be more excited for Jasper. He has been ecstatic the last couple of days, but because Aged Emporium is getting more business than usual, he hasn't been able to talk with me as much.

On top of that, he stayed at work late yesterday to install a new sound system to play festive music. Sure, it may have been my recommendation to play music, but I didn't realize how long it would take to install a sound system.

So, here I am, sitting in my office sulking on a Tuesday morning simply because Jasper hasn't graced me with his presence since Friday evening. I'm not one to usually mind alone time—in fact, I've spent so much time alone over the last couple of years, I like to think I've gotten used to it. At least, that's what I thought. Until I met Jasper Alcott.

I check my phone to see I don't have any new notifications and let out a dramatic sigh, deciding it's time to partake in *another* cup of coffee that will never live up to Little Falls' lattes. I saunter to the coffee machine, preparing a cup of the blonde roast brew.

"How's it going, Iris?" Joy asks, fetching herself a cup of coffee too.

"I'm doing well! How has your week been so far? Anything I can help with?"

"It's going great so far." She answers. "Do you mind if I ask you something not so work-related?"

"Oh, sure," I answer. "What's up?" My coffee finishes brewing. After I finish mixing in an assortment of sweet creamers, I grab the cup and take a sip of the scolding hot drink.

"So, I've been interested in romantically pursuing one of our clients." Joy breaks eye contact to mix her drink. "Is that against our regulations?"

"Well, there isn't anything in our contracts against that. Just so long as it doesn't negatively impact our professional relationship with the client, that should be fine." I set my coffee down on the counter, nearly dropping it.

"Got it! Thank you for the clarification." She grabs her coffee and turns to walk away, but not before my curiosity gets the best of me.

"Do you mind if I ask who you're interested in?"

"Oh, um, sure." She turns back toward me. "I'm interested in Jasper Alcott. I don't know if it's reciprocated at all, but I had a crush on him back in high school, so I figure I'd be doing myself an injustice if I don't shoot my shot, you know?"

My back stiffens. I had a feeling she would say Jasper, but hearing her confirm my suspicions aloud has struck me. How do I even respond?

"I see." I grin softly. She clearly expects me to say more, but instead, I forcibly keep my lips sealed, determining it's better not to say enough than to say too much here. I pat her on the shoulder and then walk back to my office, silently screaming. Physically, Joy is a beautiful, fit woman who's bright and full of life, whereas I'm like a car running on empty. How could he not take interest in someone as delightful as she is?

I hear a ping, realizing I've received a new message.

Jasper

> It's been too long since I've held you.

> Want to stay over tonight?

Iris

> I committed to Trivia Tuesday again.

> Want to join me then we can go back to your place?

Jasper

> I'm in, Greene. It's a date.

My heart flutters. *Finally.* Despite how thrilled I am to spend an evening in Jasper's company, I can't help but feel a little uneasy knowing Joy has feelings for him too, though.

Jasper is so much better at trivia than I am, it's not even funny. That man is a walking encyclopedia, full of random information ranging from who won the rowing portion of the 1994 Olympic games to who invented the breadmaker—that would be Joseph Lee, by the way. I'd be fooling myself if I claimed his level of intelligence didn't turn me on. Not that he really has to try hard to turn me on anyway. He isn't drinking this time—he has insisted on being sober throughout our time together tonight, given how he was last Trivia Tuesday. I wasn't originally planning on drinking, but intrusive thoughts about Joy got the better of me, so I ended up caving and deciding to drink just a little to take the edge off.

We've already played a couple of rounds of trivia, so we stepped away to take a break. Jasper is holding me in his arms against his bulge, careful not to let anyone get near me. Being cradled in his arms feels like serendipity personified. I used to make fun of couples who whispered sweet nothings in each other's ears because I never understood the allure—now, I do. And it's downright terrifying.

I want to let go and fall into *this*, but the idea of plummeting to the earth after the fall petrifies me as much as it entices me.

"You okay, Greene?" he whispers, tucking a strand of hair gently behind my ear. He kisses the back of my neck and rests his head on my shoulder while awaiting my response, still pulling my waist toward him.

"Yeah." I glance at him over my shoulder, smiling. He quirks an eyebrow at me, scowling.

"Sorry, Greene, I'm calling bullshit." He tightens his hold on my waist. "What's bothering you?"

"How can you tell if something *may* be bothering me?" I ask playfully, avoiding his question.

"I'd like to think I've gotten decent at reading you." He spins me toward him and stares into my eyes. *That makes one of us.* "You can talk to me."

"Are you interested in dating Joy?" I blurt out, to which his eyes widen.

"Why would you ask that?"

"Is that a yes?" I ask, breaking eye contact to look down at my feet. He tilts my chin up so our eyes can meet again.

"Iris, if you think I'm interested in dating Joy, then I must be doing something seriously wrong here." His gray eyes search mine. "I don't want to overwhelm you, but I need to be frank. You're the only girl I want, Greene. I don't see that changing anytime soon."

After an initial wave of shock, his confession sends me straight into a state of ease. *Thank goodness his feelings are real.* I lean into him, wrapping my arms around his neck. I part my lips, inviting him to kiss me, an invitation he hungrily accepts. Our tongues dance with each other momentarily before I remember we're in public. I gently pull away as heat fills my cheeks and stomach simultaneously. "The feeling is mutual, Jasper."

"It better be." He smirks. "Want to get out of here, love?"

I glance over his shoulder to see Callie still having the time of her life, crushing opponents in trivia. We make eye contact for a second, and she gives me a cheesy thumbs-up and grin, waving me off. I let out a giggle and nod, feeling weightless because of this man and this moment and memory. The pull I feel toward Jasper feels magnetic—otherworldly, even.

"I can't wait for our *planned* sleepover tonight," I joke from the front seat of his car. "I even packed my own change of clothes this time."

"That's a shame," he sighs, "I love seeing you in mine."

"Perhaps that can be arranged," I taunt as a blush spreads across my cheeks. "We'll see."

"That, we will." He casts a devilish grin my way. Jasper and I didn't spend too much time apart over the last few days, I know. But the amount of time we spent apart made tonight feel special. Upon walking into his cozy house, the air feels noticeably different. This home no longer feels like a stranger to me. As I walk inside, it embraces me in a way I haven't experienced before. In this exact moment, I realize—this is what it feels like to have a home. However, I don't think this feeling in the air is entirely due to the house. After setting my bag down, I turn around, looking at the real reason why this home feels the way it does tonight. Jasper has opened his heart to me. As terrifying as it may be, I intend to do the same for him. It feels unexplainably right.

"Do you want anything to drink? You know the drill by now. I have *gross* coffee, decent tea, and wat—" I collide with him mid-sentence, cutting him off. I grip his neck, crashing my lips into his. He wastes no time. His hand lowers down the slope of my back, pulling me into him tightly. My lips pull away from his.

"I want *you*, Jasper," I whisper breathlessly, gazing into his silver eyes. Caught off-guard, he staggers for a moment before speaking.

"Are you absolutely sure, Greene? There's no turning back once we go down this road." His eyes bore into mine with intensity as he drops his gaze to my lips. Although I'm typically the most indecisive person in the world, I have zero doubts about what I want right now. Finally, I feel certain about something. I want nothing more than to simply *be* with Jasper Alcott. I will no longer hide—not from him.

"Don't make me second-guess myself, Jasper." I bite my lip, toying with him.

"To hell with it," he breathes, parting his lips and slipping his tongue into my mouth hungrily. He tastes like mint, refreshing me with every swipe. I press myself against him, his bulge hard as it pulses against my stomach. His hands roam down, gripping my ass to sweep me off the ground into a straddle, carrying me through the hallway to his bedroom smoothly. Up until now, I've never seen his room. With a single lit lamp in the corner alongside a shelf of books and some Vinyl records decoratively on display, it's warmer than I anticipated—but now isn't the time to take note of his decor. He lays me across his bed and spreads my legs, kissing me *everywhere*. I take his shirt off and run my fingers along his stomach, resting them just above the seam of his pants, grazing his abs. Suddenly, his hands take hold of mine, pinning my hands to the bed over my head. He rapidly kisses my neck, nipping and sucking, too.

"I've been wanting this more than you know, baby," he groans, sliding his tongue down my neck. I gasp, trying to break loose from his grip so I can touch him the way he's touching me. A strand of his ebony hair falls across his face as he shakes his head. "I'm not done with you yet, Greene."

He runs his tongue across my collarbone inching his way down my body to the skirt of my dress. He lifts it up, gazing at my lacy pink thong. *Okay, fine, I admit it—maybe I was hoping this would happen tonight.* He gulps.

He slowly pulls my thong off, sliding it down my bare legs, then reaches upward to slip my dress off. His eyes slowly sweep across my body as he stands, seeming to take in every inch. He drags his gaze back up to meet mine.

"Oh my—*fuck, Iris*," he rasps, placing a kiss on my ear. "It's settled. You are a goddess."

I blush as he grips my waist, pulling me up to him. He releases a guttural groan while greedily massaging me. "Oh, you're more than a handful, aren't you, baby?"

I gasp in pleasure as his lips find my breast. He flicks his tongue hungrily seeming to plead for even more. I'm in pure bliss. I reach down to grab ahold of him, gripping his length the best I can given its size. Realizing he's still wearing pants, I push him away and pull them down, drinking in the sight of his defined body.

"What are we waiting for?" I gaze into his hooded eyes while stroking him.

"You have no idea how challenging it's been to wait for you," he admits while stroking my waist. "But damn, it's been worth it." Heat pools between my thighs as my body quakes, practically begging for him to take me. No longer able to hold back, we embrace each other, and our bodies melt together.

Although this is our first time, we act in desperation, as though it will be our last. We whisper sweet nothings into each other's ears throughout. In the moments after, we lay side by side in a state of nirvana—true, utter oblivion in the best way. He wraps me in his arms and gently kisses the back of my head, breathing in my scent as we drift off to sleep.

For the first time in years, I feel safe. I feel at home. I feel a sense of *peace*. I find myself never wanting to leave this moment.

THIRTY

JASPER

O h, I could get used to *this*. By this, I mean *her*, more specifically. Holding her in my arms feels natural, almost a little too natural. Her scent intoxicates me as I curl her into my arms tighter. I tried resisting her. I really did. But Iris isn't simply a 'want' for me anymore—she's a need. A necessity, even. I fight back a grin as I bury my head into her neck, kissing her soft skin and grazing the collar of her shirt—my T-shirt—with my lips. *She's mine.* I run my fingers through her deep brunette waves, letting myself get lost in them. She leans back into my touch, inhaling and exhaling slowly.

As I get lost in her, my mind starts to work overtime. Her parents aren't the best. She lost her brother, who she very clearly cherished. I don't know the details, but knowing she has been carrying this, seemingly all alone, kills me. What's worse is how skilled she is at hiding her grief. She's the type of person to laugh at someone's jokes despite how pitiful the jokes are. She often cares about others more than herself. She prioritizes everyone else's desires over her own needs. She wears the mask over her emotions as a shield, preventing everyone from discovering the true weight she bears. It all makes sense now—she needs a guardian angel to help her carry and embrace this weight. I still don't fully understand why I can see Kai. However, I'm starting to understand how pivotal his role in her life is. He has helped her a ton, although it is apparent he won't be around much longer. Sure, she can carry this weight alone; she's more than capable of it. But she shouldn't *have* to. I refuse to let her sail through this dark storm alone any longer. Now, she's stuck with me. I stroke her cheek, and suddenly, her emerald eyes crack open, peering directly into mine.

"Good morning, Greene," my voice comes out in a hoarse whisper. She reaches her hand up to cup my cheek.

"I cannot believe what happened last night." Her nose crinkles as her lips curve into a smile. "Were you expecting that?"

"Truthfully? I never know what to expect when it comes to you," I breathe. "But I was hopeful."

"So was I." She shyly breaks eye contact, running her hand across my back. "Surprising, I know."

I scoff, grabbing the small of her back and pulling her into my chest. "Well, what should we do now?"

"Right now, I need to get dressed and head home to take care of Truman," she says pointedly, turning away.

"You spend a lot of time with this Truman guy," I taunt. "I'll take you home. Just five more minutes of this first."

"I've really got to go, Jasper—"

"Please don't make me beg, love," I whisper into her ear. She caves, relaxing her body into mine again, pushing her back against me.

"It's been so long since I felt this...weightless." She exasperatedly sighs. "This feeling won't last much longer, though. Apparently, the Greenes themselves are visiting me for Thanksgiving tomorrow."

I quirk a brow. "*The* infamous Greenes?"

"That would be correct."

"Oh, wow. When was the last time you saw them?"

"Honestly, I don't remember." She pauses, contemplating. "Probably a few weeks after my brother's passing. They came to town to collect some of his belongings from his apartment."

"Your brother lived in the Cove?"

"Oh yeah, he is actually the main reason why I moved to Chrysocolla Cove." She drifts off, seeming to get lost in thought. "I never imagined moving to a small town after graduating, but he hyped up this place. I've really never considered my parents' house a home anyway, so I had zero desire to move back to my hometown. But I wanted to live closer to him. He's the only family I really ever felt close to; he was my best friend."

"I get that," I say. "It's nice living close to family, and considering he was your family, it only makes sense."

"You know how a lot of people claim their brother or sister is their best friend, but they don't really mean it? We weren't like that. We truly were best friends; he taught me how to drive, how to manage money, how to date. He taught me everything."

I grin at first, but my smile fades as the reality of her situation settles in. "I've gotta ask, Iris. Why didn't your parents teach you any of that? All of that is a pretty rudimentary part of parenthood if we're being honest here."

She glances over my shoulder, zoning out. "Truthfully... I don't know why my parents didn't take the reins in teaching me more about life. I have educated guesses, though. Assumptions, really. I think my dad was too absent to teach me much—he was always working. When he wasn't working, he put all his extra time into his relationship with my brother. My mom may have gotten too caught up in how different we are. She's always been bothered by how quiet I am around her. Little does she know, I actually hardly ever fall silent around those I'm comfortable with." She chuckles, turning to look into my eyes. "My brother, although entirely different from me, *tried* to understand me. In doing so, he loved me unconditionally. The way I always wished my parents would, I suppose."

Even while opening up about how insufferable her parents are, she manages to produce a laugh. How does she do it? How is she able to smile through it all?

"As you once said to me, I see you overthinking over there. No need to overthink this, love." She smiles softly, caressing my tense jaw.

I sigh. "You deserve more than this. All of this."

"Do I, though? What have I done to deserve better than the hand I've been dealt?" she asks, searching my eyes.

"Maybe I haven't known you long yet, Greene, but I *feel* like I've known you for years." I tuck a lock of hair behind her ear. "You deserve more. So much more. If for nothing else, for simply caring about others as fiercely as you do despite it all."

We look into each other's eyes for a moment; then an idea comes to mind. It may be a stupid one, but I can't resist offering. "How about I join you on Thanksgiving?"

"What?" She gawks, raising her brows. "Jasper, I will absolutely not subject you to the Greenes."

"C'mon, I'll show you." I nudge her. "I'm even better with parents than you are; just watch."

"Is that a challenge?" Her mouth quirks.

"Nope," I say firmly. "It's a statement."

"Last warning, Jasper." She arches an eyebrow. "You can't say I didn't try."

"I would love nothing more than to support you while you fend off your lame-ass parents," I say, to which she bursts into laughter.

"Fine." She sighs. "But won't your family be annoyed you're missing Thanksgiving with them?"

"Eh, my family is weird—we do a Thanksgiving brunch every year instead of a Thanksgiving dinner, so we should be done by noon. I'll head over to your place after that to help you prep."

She rises while my T-shirt barely covers her ass. *Holy Hell.* She peeks over her shoulder, catching my eyes lingering on her. "Thank you, Jasper."

"Told you," I can't contain my wide grin. "You can hit me with whatever you've got."

Work flies by. We forgo staying the night together again—her choice, not mine—so I'm not late to my parents' home for Thanksgiving brunch. I offer to bake a pecan pie using my mom's recipe for Greene's Thanksgiving feast. She obviously dreads seeing her parents. Consequently, I'm going to make sure it goes a hell of a lot better than she anticipates. I finish baking the pie and putting it in the fridge. Funnily enough, I prepared a better dish for her parents than my own.

"Surprise." An uninvited guest startles me after I shut my fridge. "Miss me?"

"Didn't even notice you were gone." I grimace.

"Jasper, I'm hurt. After all we've been through?"

I sigh. "What do you want, Kai?"

"Just wanted to catch up. She went to sleep early tonight, so I figured I'd stop by."

I stride over to my couch, slumping into it with a beer in hand. "Cool."

"Damn, you're dry as hell, man." Kai sits beside me. "I don't know if I see what Iris sees in you."

"The fact that she sees anything in me is shocking to say the least." I sip my beer, gesturing it toward him. "Want one?"

"Come to think of it, I haven't tried drinking as a guardian before..." He pauses. I shrug, handing him the bottle. To our utter shock, he grasps it, then slowly brings it to his lips, swallowing. Apparently, angels and ghosts are different from each other. Consequently, angels are able to touch objects if they choose, whereas ghosts can't.

"Holy shit!" Kai exclaims excitedly. "I can't believe I didn't try this sooner!"

Despite my efforts not to, I grin like an idiot. This man really is something else. He takes a few more large gulps, finishing off the bottle.

"Damn, dude, drink your own next time," I grunt, leaning back into my couch.

"I'm so sorry, man." Kai smirks, wiping his lips. "I haven't felt this way in so long. I didn't think I'd ever feel this sensation again, honestly."

"You only had one beer, Kai." I roll my eyes. "There's no way you're feeling it that fast."

"On the contrary, Jas." He waves his finger at me. "I experience practically *everything* more intensely now, so this may or may not be hitting me harder than it would've during my mortal life."

He stands, heading to my fridge to presumably grab another. I fixate on how this legitimately makes zero sense. So much for logic.

"Death defies logic, Jas," Kai leaps over the side of my couch, landing beside me forcefully.

"Would you stop calling me Jas? And stop reading my mind while you're at it?"

"Seriously? I can't call you buddy, can't call you Jas... I bet you'd let her call you Jas," Kai taunts me. "Speaking of Irie, I cannot believe you slept with her. You did the exact opposite of what I told you to, my guy."

"I'm sorry, what did you just call her?"

"Call who?"

"Iris?"

"Oh, Irie?"

"Uh, yeah." I quirk a brow, to which he waves me off.

"Iris, Irie. Same thing, really. Same person." Kai leans back onto the couch after downing part of his second beer. "No one really calls her Irie other than me, though."

"I see," I say, taking the beer out of his hand to drink some myself. "I think you should slow down on these. I wouldn't want it to affect your Iris spidey-senses."

"Eh, I'm not so worried about that. That girl basically has two guardians with you in the picture now." He grins, then drops the smile, seeming to sober up. "Serious question: how do you really feel about her? Don't bullshit me."

No point in holding back, considering he can read my mind anyway, sober or not. "I'm clearly not the most cheerful guy in the Cove—"

"We've established that," Kai affirms with a nod, crossing his arms and leaning back into my couch.

"As I *was saying*." I exhale sharply. "Moving back here made me feel like a failure. All I ever wanted was to leave this town, so having to come back to it felt wrong in so many ways. Since meeting Iris, though, my existence here has started to make sense. Instead of dreading this town every waking moment, I've begun to actually enjoy it. I feel comfortable with her. I find myself thinking about her every single day. She's grieving and carrying so much weight on her shoulders, yet she still manages to emit the brightest glow I've ever witnessed. I don't want to lose that light. I don't want to lose her."

Kai searches my eyes, no doubt refraining from exercising soulsight. I don't blame him—I'd want to make sure to get the truth, too. "I believe you, man."

He pats my shoulder, then rises clumsily. *Lightweight.* "I'm going to go back to Irie's now. Good night, bro." He saunters away, fading into nothing. I don't know if I'll ever get used to that.

THIRTY-ONE

IRIS

S torms brew both inside my apartment and outside in the sky. I glance outside, taking note of the grayness settling in over the Cove. My clouds are quite restless today. How perfectly ideal, given the visitors from the *Wicked West* joining me. I gulp some air, pacing away from the window back to the dining area. I've set the table using my only nice set of dishware, and odds are, it still isn't half as nice as what my parents are used to.

Growing up, my mom liked old-fashioned dinners. She cared a great deal about placemats and fine cutlery. My apartment has never seen such finery, and that won't be changing today. Truman leaps onto the bar I'm leaning against. I pet him gently, then cradle him in my arms, settling him down at my feet. "Not today, Truman. The bar is for people today."

Not today. As those words replay in my mind, I have an epiphany. I haven't used those two words in a while. In fact, I've been adopting a "today's the day" type of attitude over the last several days. I've talked more about Kai over the last week than in… years. Sure, I haven't *exactly* said his name aloud yet, but that's irrelevant. While setting the silverware, my eyes drift to his old spot at my table, and I reminisce on a different time. A time when my biggest concern was whether Katherine and Kai would get back together. A time when Kai didn't stop me from drinking too much, instead keeping a watchful eye over me, all smiles. A time when I didn't realize just how much I had to be thankful for.

If Kai were here now, I imagine he'd try to cheer me up in the way only he could, pulling me in for a bear hug and calling me the name reserved for him alone to use—*Irie.* It's mildly concerning how far I would go just to hear him call out to me just one more time. A knock at the door interrupts my wandering mind, and my heart lunges. I peek out my peephole, and instantly, my troubled mind calms. *He came.*

I open the door, beckoning Jasper inside. As he steps inside, he sets down his food on my counter and then sweeps me into his arms, pulling me into a tight embrace.

"Something smells heavenly, and it isn't the pie," he murmurs into my ear. "Have I ever told you how intoxicating you smell?"

"You may have mentioned it before." My face warms as I reminisce about our first night at the bar. The way he held me in his arms that night made me swoon… *Now's not the time, Iris. Focus.* "You have no idea how relieved I am to see you. My parents will be here any minute. Can you take a look at everything and let me know how it all looks?"

"On it, Greene." He salutes, scanning my dining table. His gaze shifts to my kitchen, then to me. "Everything looks great. Better than great, really."

I exhale, allowing myself to relax for just a second.

"Talk to me." His eyes pierce mine. "What's on your mind?"

"*Ugh,*" I groan. "I don't want to do this. I don't want to spend Thanksgiving with them. I don't want to force myself to host them with a smile plastered on my face."

"So, don't," he says plainly, sinking into my couch, leaning back with his hands behind his head.

"What do you mean, 'don't'?" I narrow my eyes.

"Don't force yourself to keep a smile on your face. They practically invited themselves over here—you don't owe them anything today. Quite frankly, they're lucky you didn't tell them to screw off," he grumbles. "I've got you, love. Just squeeze my hand if things get too overwhelming, okay?"

His gray eyes match the sky outside. I nod and take another deep breath. Suddenly, I hear a knock at the door. I don't even waste my time peering into the peephole, knowing exactly who is waiting on the other side. I open the door and greet them.

"Hey guys," I say. "Come on in."

My mom's blue eyes look me up and down, then she strolls in casually while my dad follows behind her, his brown eyes wide upon taking in my living space. He isn't on his phone yet—that itself is a miracle. My dad and I haven't ever been close by any means, but he at least throws me a friendly smile occasionally. As they walk in, Jasper reaches my side, stroking my hand. Truman pokes his head out of my bedroom, looks at my parents, then decides to scurry back into the comfort of his bed. I wish I could join him.

"Mom, Dad, this is Jasper." I gesture toward him. "Jasper, these are my parents." He shakes their hands and smiles at each of them politely. My mom flashes an obligatory smile his way, visibly impressed with his appearance. Appearance has always been a priority for her. My dad squares him up from behind her.

"Iris, you didn't tell us you had a boyfriend." She gapes.

"Well, I didn't mention that because he's not my boyfriend," I admit awkwardly, earning an eyebrow raise from Jasper. My parents nod knowingly as if it is obvious I'd never have a boyfriend like him. Deep down, I might agree with them.

"Ah, yes, that makes more sense," she says, sighing. "Jasper, it's a pleasure to meet you. So glad Iris has a *friend* like you in town."

"Actually, your daughter is holding back." He nudges me. "I'm sure she was just waiting to tell you until she was ready, but I can't help it. We *are* together."

For the second time within two minutes, my mom's jaw drops, but this time, mine does too. I'm unsure whether to laugh or cry at the shock in her expression. Similarly, my dad raises both of his eyebrows at us in surprise.

"I see," she says pointedly, glancing over at my dining table. "Well, is that where we're eating?"

"The table with all the food and plates? Yes, Mom, that is where we're eating," I answer, unable to hide my disdain for the question. "Did you bring the turkey? I saved a spot right in the middle for it."

My dad nods, setting the large dish on the rectangular table, front and center. My mom ignores me, instead turning her attention to Jasper. "So, what brings you to this town, Jasper?"

"I actually grew up here." He sits at the table, prompting me to sit next to him. My mom and dad sit across from us. "I recently moved back to take over my old man's business."

"Ah, how impressive," she remarks, pouring herself a glass of white wine.

"Owning a business is the way to go," my dad chimes in as he slices the turkey. "I always told my kids that, but they didn't listen. Maybe there's still hope for Iris, after all; she can learn a thing or two from you."

I pour myself a gracious glass of wine and sip. "Make sure not to get carried away this time, dear," my mom mumbles while taking a bite of her potatoes.

"Note taken." I raise my glass to her as an idea comes to mind. "Hey, why don't we go around the table and share what we're thankful for?"

My parents glance at each other in confusion. "Iris, we haven't done that in years."

"Well, in my defense, we haven't eaten Thanksgiving together in years either, so..." I say. Jasper rests his hand on my thigh and grips it once, giving me the encouragement I need to continue. "Let's do it. Here, I'll start."

I clear my throat. I'm unsure what's come over me, but it feels good. "I'm thankful for the Cove."

My parents burst into laughter. "Of all things, that's what you're most thankful for this year?"

"Absolutely," I pipe back. "The Cove brought me to Soi, Truman, and Jasper. So, yeah, I'm thankful for this tiny town you can't seem to stomach."

Her eyes bore into mine impatiently before flickering away to gaze at Jasper. "Jasper, what are you thankful for?"

"Trivia Tuesdays," he says firmly, with flat-lined lips.

"Trivia Tuesdays?" my mom asks, as my dad predictably types out a message on his phone.

"Yep," he affirms, not caring to elaborate. Now I let out a chuckle, knowing well why he's thankful for Trivia Tuesdays. He smirks at me, taking a bite of his meal.

"What are you guys thankful for? We've both taken a turn, now it's yours," I say, looking at my parents.

"I'm thankful for another good year of work," my dad proudly declares, to which my mom sighs. "Business is booming this year."

"We all saw that one coming," I comment. My dad has a stunned expression on his face that I quite like. "What about you, Mom?"

She contemplates, staring at her food before answering.

"I'm thankful to be here. Together." *Whoa.* Did not see that one coming. "Your brother would've wanted us to come together."

I gulp, then take a generous drink of my wine. My dad finally sets his phone down. "I'm thankful to be here, too."

I try to hold back, but before I can stop myself, I say, "Why don't you visit me more often then? If you're so thankful to be here, why don't you ever come?"

"Iris, you don't understand how difficult it is for us to visit you—"

"I *don't understand?* I don't? Why don't you try to understand for once," I bite back, not wavering despite the riptide of anxiety threatening to pull me under. "I reached out after he passed away. I offered to visit. Hell, I even found myself *wanting* to visit you for some reason despite knowing you two could care less."

"Iris Adelaide Greene," my dad says sharply. Jasper's grasp on my thigh tightens. "That's not true."

"Actions speak louder than words, Dad. He was the only person who ever truly cared about me." My mom breaks eye contact, visibly struck, and then she glimpses back into my eyes. To my utter shock, her eyes are glassy.

"Iris, when I look at you, I see *him*." Her voice breaks. "I know I've always been distant, and especially so in recent years, but it's harder than ever to be around you now."

Her words pierce me. I pause, collecting my thoughts. How could she possibly see Kai when she looks at me? Sure, we share the same last name, but other than that, our resemblance is slim. Most of my friends joked that our parents adopted one of us. Not only that, but our essences couldn't be more different. Kai shined bright like sunlight, whereas I always resonated with the clouds surrounding the sun. Subjecting Jasper to this conversation was not a part of my agenda for today, but something tells me he doesn't mind.

"That's the thing, Mom," my heart pounds, "it shouldn't have been so challenging for you to be around me in the first place. I'm *your daughter* whether you're ashamed of me or not."

"Iris!" my dad exclaims, radiating anger.

"Do *not* yell at her," Jasper says while gripping my thigh so tightly it nearly hurts. I realize, up until now, I haven't actually looked at him. Turns out, he is *seething*. "I'm entirely in favor of you all having a civilized, healthy conversation, but I will not tolerate yelling—especially when directed at Iris."

"With all due respect, son, this really isn't any of your business, so it's best if you excuse yourself before you say something you'll regret." My dad locks his eyes on him. Jasper clenches his jaw.

"I'm actually quite comfortable here," he says cooly then throws him a smirk, leaning back in his seat, still holding my thigh. "Carry on, Greene."

My mom glances between the two of us, and I swear, she suppresses a subtle smile. As I stare into her eyes, I notice the faintest hint of sympathy. Dare I say, she seems to be listening for once. I sigh.

"Believe it or not, I didn't accept your self-imposed invitation out of malice," I admit begrudgingly. "A small sliver of me may or may not have wanted to see you both, too."

"You're so much more like Kai than you realize, Iris," my mom whispers. "I wish he was still here."

"I do, too, mom." I break eye contact. "More than you know." We eat the rest of the meal and Jasper's scrumptious pecan pie in semi-comfortable silence. I thought the silence would be excruciating, but with Jasper by my side, it has become easier to bear.

After we finish the meal, I usher them out. My dad thanks me for hosting and hustles out the door and down the stairs, immediately answering a phone call and leaving my mom standing alone in the doorway.

"I've gotta ask," I begin. "Why did you both come here? Why didn't you just invite me over to your home?"

She glances around my apartment before answering. "We really did want to see you. We knew if we invited you, you wouldn't come, and to be honest, I wouldn't have blamed you for rejecting the invite."

I accept her reasoning for now. Our relationship may be broken, but at least we have a relationship to fix if we ever choose to. "Well, drive safe and take your time through the mountains."

"We always do." She nods. She turns to leave but stops herself abruptly, then—in a shocking turn of events—she embraces me. "I'm not ashamed of you, Iris. I know it'll take years, maybe even a lifetime, to prove that to you, and that's within good reason. Just know, I'm not ashamed."

THIRTY-TWO

JASPER

K ai. His name was *Kai*.

The room has been spinning for the last several minutes. Iris just said goodbye to her mom and slumped on the couch, leaning into me. "Well, that was eventful," she says. "I'm sorry you had to witness all of that."

"No need to apologize, Greene. I'm so proud of you for standing up to them. That was remarkable," I whisper, and I mean every word of it, but I keep getting lost in my own mind. Surely, it's a coincidence. Surely, her brother isn't her guardian. Surely.

Kai, Kai, Kai. Where is the bastard when I need him? I look around for him, but alas, he has been missing in action since about halfway through the dinner debate. He got a kick out of

Iris telling her parents off but vanished shortly after. "So, you mentioned your brother at dinner. Kai, is it?"

She pauses, fluttering her lashes. "Yeah, Kai. Loving Kai came easily to my parents."

"I'm so sorry, baby," I say, tucking a lock of hair behind her ear and peering into her eyes. "Do you have any pictures of him?"

"I do." She bites her lip. "I haven't looked at them in a while. Let me go grab some from my room—I have an old photo album I can share with you."

"Take your time, Greene," I call out as she prances away. As caught off-guard I am by the Kai-name-thing, I really am so damn proud of Iris. She stood on the frontlines and didn't force herself to hide, which is no small feat. *This woman.*

She strolls back into the living room carrying a thick maroon photo album in her arms. Iris is wearing a flowy floral dress today, and I can't get enough of how good she looks in it. Seeing her in this makes me even more curious to see the types of clothes she'll wear as the seasons change.

She sits down next to me. I wrap my arm around her, holding her tight. She opens the album and lands on a picture of her Kai when he was only a child. He and Iris are standing together, wearing corky costumes, grinning from ear to ear. "We used to dress up in coordinated costumes every Halloween." She runs her fingers along his face in the photo. "Here, I'll show you what he looked like as an adult instead."

She flips halfway through the album, landing on a different page; a group photo of the Cove's baseball team. I skim the image, and my eyes immediately land on a familiar bright face. *No. Please, no.*

"Jasper, it's imperative you do not tell Iris she has a guardian."

"Okay, so when I encouraged you to get closer to Iris, I meant as friends."

"As her guardian, her well-being means everything to me."

"I like her, man. I really like her." "I've known for a while, buddy. That's what makes all of this so much harder."

"No one really calls her Irie other than me, though."

"Who were you to Iris?" "No one."

"That's Kai." Iris points to the man I'm already staring at. "He coached baseball at the high school for a few years—he loved coaching so much. He always joked that it was his life calling."

"Mm," I mutter under my breath, at a complete loss for words. I grow rigid, suddenly feeling like I need to lie down. "Hey, baby, I've gotta get going."

"Oh, so soon?" She frowns adorably.

"Sorry, I have some things to take care of. I'll talk to you later." I rise, preparing to leave.

"Wait, Jasper," she halts me. "Did you mean what you said earlier? Do you really consider me as your girlfriend? Or were you just putting on a good show for my parents?"

I hesitate. Of course, I meant it—Iris is all *mine*. And I'm unequivocally hers. But everything feels chaotic and unfair at the moment. Instead of overcomplicating things, I answer candidly.

"I meant it." I put on the best smile I can manage at the moment, placing a kiss on her forehead. I don't want to leave, but I physically cannot stay any longer without bursting. "We'll talk later, Greene."

"See you later, love," she says. As I walk down the stairs, my heart races and panic consumes every fiber of my being. This secret I've been keeping from her is so much more important than I ever realized, and when she finds out, she will never look at me the same. I *feel* it.

Settling into my car, I attempt to steady my breathing as the world around me grows blurry. "Where the hell are you, Kai?" I mutter aloud, pulling out of the parking lot. Rather than turning down the road that leads to my home, I keep driving. I won't stop. Thirty minutes pass in the blink of an eye, and suddenly, I'm driving in the mountains. Unsure of where or when to stop, I veer off the road, parking on the shoulder. I get out of the car and take in the view. The sun will be setting soon, but I don't know where else to go, and this is where my subconscious mind led me.

"*I like to visit the mountains.*"

I gaze all around me, hoping to see an obnoxious fool on the horizon. After several moments of leaning against the mountainside railing, I accept that Kai isn't here. I turn back toward my car, stunned at the sight I see.

There he is, leaning against my car, glimpsing up at the sky. I don't think before disrupting his daydream.

"Kai, what the actual hell were you thinking? Holding back a secret like that?" I grit my teeth, trying my best to maintain composure. "Why, man? Why?"

He glances at me. As my eyes bore into him, I recognize remorse. Regret, even. *Good.*

"Jasper, I never expected you to fall for my sister." Kai sighs, rubbing his temples. "This has overcomplicated everything."

"Kai, please, I have not fallen—" He raises his hand to stop me.

"Bro, you're an honest man. You don't have to admit it, but please, do yourself a favor and don't deny it aloud." His words settle in my mind for a few seconds before he continues.

"Who the fuck do you think you are, Kai? What kind of guardian angel are you? Don't you understand how fucked up this is?"

"New drinking game idea: take a shot every time you say fuck," he chimes in smugly without hesitating.

"Screw. You." I break eye contact, running my fingers through my hair. "I can't keep this from Iris, Kai. It was already hard enough keeping your existence a secret, but knowing that you're her dead brother makes it nearly impossible."

"Nearly impossible, but not entirely," he says, glancing back up at the sky. "Jasper, while we're being open and honest here, I have another confession. I don't know how this story ends. I don't know where to go from here. I suppose you could say I've been *winging* it." He chuckles, defeatedly.

"Just answer me," I grunt. "Why didn't you tell me sooner?"

"Iris has always deserved more," he answers, boldly. "I didn't want to rob her of the chance to share her story. You're a smart dude. If I had told you who I was initially, you would've connected the dots fairly quickly. You would've known Iris has been grieving from the beginning without her ever getting the chance to tell you herself. Because you didn't know the significance of who Iris and I were to each other, you were able to discover those parts of her on your own without any sort of preconceived notions. Sure, you have gotten closer to her than I anticipated, but that's beside the point. You've known since the beginning that I was a guardian; I denounced being labeled an *angel* for a reason—I'm far from it. I've been holding back since day one."

In an instant, I'm feeling bad for him. *Damnit.*

"Well... at least you had a decent reason for holding back," I grumble. "For the record, you're a guardian angel, dude. No more sugar-coating it. The only thing missing is your wings."

"Yeah, I'm supposed to get those when I ascend or something. They are honestly just for show anyway. Who needs wings when I can teleport wherever I want whenever I want?" He grins cockily.

"Yeah, and you never let anyone forget it." I cross my arms. "Kai, I don't know what to do from here. I hate keeping this secret from her now even more than before."

He lets out a sigh. "I don't know, man. Just give me time to think of a plan. I need to do some research on my end, too—if Iris is going to find out I'm her guardian angel, I want to know the consequences of that reveal."

"How much time will you need?"

"I'm not sure…" He contemplates. "Just give me time. I will give you the green light as soon as possible."

"Kai, how am I supposed to spend time with Iris in the meantime?"

"You've never had a hard time figuring that out before." He folds his arms, rolling his eyes. "Just keep doing whatever it is you've been doing. Shockingly, it seems to work for Irie."

"Whatever, man," I say. "For what it's worth… I'm sorry."

"For what?"

"That your life was cut short. You were–*are* really loved, man." A look of understanding passes between us.

"I've come to terms with it. Besides, this side isn't so bad." A grin stretches across his face. "I'll feel better once she fully accepts all of her emotions. She's getting stronger every day. I'm so damn proud of her."

"That's one thing we have in common. How about the way she told your parents off earlier?"

"Oh, hell yeah, I was sitting on the couch, petting Truman and eating imaginary popcorn the entire time," he jokes. "She's fully accepted a lot of her emotions recently. Thank you for your hand in that."

"Nah, that's all Greene." I suppress a small grin. "Well, I'll try my best to hold onto your secret for a little longer, but no promises.

You have no idea how hard this is. The last thing I want is to betray her."

"Duly noted," he says. "I'll be in touch after I gather information."

"Will you be going to Katherine's wedding with us?"

"Wouldn't miss it for the world." He grins, looking down at his feet. "Catch you later, bro. I'm sorry for not telling you sooner. Really, I am."

"I understand why you didn't," I admit reluctantly. "See you later. Bro." His grin shines brightly in response as he walks away, venturing deeper into the forest.

My phone vibrates, and I see an incoming message from Iris. She sent me a picture of herself, staring into her bedroom mirror, gripping the bottom of her dress in one hand, carrying her phone in the other, looking cute as hell.

Iris

> I'm having the time of my life, thanks for asking.

For fuck's sake. How am I supposed to hide this from my girl?

THIRTY-THREE

IRIS

T he feeling in the air has been different since Thanksgiving. It's not necessarily bad, but it's not great either. Jasper and I have both been in work mode 24/7 for the last several days now that the masquerade fundraiser is less than three weeks away. His traffic has increased substantially, so he has opened Aged Emporium early and stayed late every night this week. He even hung up a masquerade fundraiser poster on his front door and has handed out flyers to every customer. Over a hundred people have RSVP'd on the event page, which is a major turnout considering the Cove's small population.

To my disappointment, we had to skip Trivia Tuesday because we were both busy. Not to mention, Jasper isn't my only client—I still have a couple of other smaller-scale events I'm overseeing, so my team has been heavily relying on me. Joy chose not to pursue Jasper, understandably so, given that he hasn't tried to keep our relationship private. She and I spoke about it recently. Thankfully, she has been extremely supportive. He dropped by twice this week, bearing gifts from Little Falls each time. Surprisingly, he planted a kiss directly on my lips for anyone and everyone to witness today, which was the first time he kissed me in front of my staff. One of the event planners dropped their physical planner, and an audible collective gasp cut our kiss short.

It feels nice to be so desired. I don't know if I've ever experienced this feeling before. Nothing compares to how it feels to be wanted by Jasper Alcott.

I can only hope he knows I feel the same. I've never been great at offering up words of affirmation, but with him, I try. Unfortunately, though, the quick Little Falls drop-ins are the only times I've seen him this week. Of course, he looks *damn* good every time he nonchalantly strolls into our building, which only fuels my desire for him. We're planning on spending the evening together tonight, which is just what I need, seeing as in less than two days, we'll be driving to Katherine's wedding in my hometown.

I feel mixed emotions about seeing Katherine again. The last time we saw each other was at Kai's funeral. She checks in on me occasionally, which I so dearly appreciate, but we aren't as close as we used to be. At one point, I thought she would be my future sister-in-law. I never imagined attending a wedding for Katherine without Kai standing across from her at the altar. However, if Kai were here, I know he'd be endlessly happy for her, so I've made an oath to at least *try* to adopt the same attitude.

Jasper proposed a "chill" date night composed of a movie marathon. As a movie enthusiast, I'm beyond ready for this. Of course, Truman is invited, so I'm bringing him along for the evening. Truman absolutely loves accompanying me to Jasper's home. After getting home from work, I change when my phone pings.

Jasper

> It's been too long, Greene. Feel free to forgo packing a bag. ;)

I hate how giddy those stupid winky faces make me. I'm obviously down hard for this man.

Iris

> I'll be packing a bag, but I can forgo the unmentionables?

Jasper

> Well, that's hot.

Iris

> I'll take that as a yes.

Jasper

> Hell. Yes.

I grin, recklessly choosing not to pack underwear or a bra tonight, changing into an oversized sweatshirt and leggings. It's only been a week since we last spent the night in each other's arms, but wow, I'm counting down the minutes till he picks me up at this point. Thankfully, he should be here any minute, so I won't be counting long. Upon arrival, he opens the car door for me. I wouldn't have pegged Jasper for being a romantic, but I've been proven wrong time and time again already, and we've only been seeing each other for a few weeks now.

We walk into his home, and it takes sheer strength not to drag him directly into his bedroom, skipping the movie portion of the evening. Before Jasper, I wasn't like this. I didn't feel these types of urges often at all. Since Jasper, I have admittedly had a challenging time fighting them off. My eyes drift down to his pants for only a second. *Yep, we are definitely on the same wavelength.* Warmth reaches my cheeks as I slump down onto his luxurious plush brown couch.

"It's crazy—your couch is even cozier than mine," I moan, sinking into it deeper, stretching my arms.

"It'd be best for you to refrain from making those noises until later, Greene," he taunts, falling on the couch beside me and folding me in his arms possessively. After a lengthy debate on what to watch, we settle for a thriller. I *live* for plot twists—I've always felt that the most epic endings are unpredictable.

Jasper lounges in the corner spot of his sectional, so naturally, I lay down, nestling my head into his lap. At first, he seems mildly unsure of what to do, but after a few minutes, we mold into each other, fitting perfectly together. Halfway through the movie, our lips meet. One thing leads to another, and before we know it, I'm straddling him on the couch in nothing other than my sweatshirt. He runs his hands down the slope of my back to my behind, tracing every curve delicately while sucking on my neck. A whimper escapes me, resulting in him hardening beneath me. *He is too good at this.*

"Let's take this to the bedroom, baby," he whispers with gravel in his voice. I gaze into his eyes and comply without hesitating. I wrap my arms around his neck, and he lifts me with ease, carrying me to his domain and setting me atop his silky white sheets. I grow wet with anticipation, bracing myself for the pleasure to come. Maybe this isn't the most unpredictable way to end our evening, but it's pretty *epic* if you ask me. Although, something still feels... off. I can't quite wrap my head around why I feel this way, so I voluntarily lose myself to the heat of the moment instead.

The day has come. I'm going to Katherine's wedding. With Jasper. As I apply my makeup, I'm feeling antsy for a multitude of reasons. First and foremost, this is my first public appearance with Jasper as my date. Considering we'll be in my hometown, plenty of people will have questions I just don't feel mentally prepared to answer. Secondly, again, this is *Katherine's* wedding. I know I should feel endlessly happy for my old friend, but I feel a sense of sadness and longing I can't fully explain or comprehend. Life doesn't feel exactly fair at the moment. Lastly, I'm quite nervous about the mountain drive. I haven't taken this route in a long time, and as always, I can't help but envision Kai's shining smile when I do.

One discovery I've had since his passing is how much it hurts to think about the one you lost in any capacity. Sure, sometimes a fun memory will pop up, and for a moment, you may find yourself smiling at the thought of it. As quickly as the memory sparks joy in you, grief robs you yet again, though, being the great thief it is. Grief takes memories and contorts them, causing people to want to avoid all the old moments—whether they be positive or negative—and the pain they inflict.

This drive brings back many memories, both tremendously good and unspeakably bad. Often, my body reacts before my brain does. I have no idea how I'll react because it's been so long since I last took this route. I can only hope Jasper will be okay with potentially witnessing yet another Iris episode.

I complete my makeup and look at my wavy hair, ensuring it's as smooth as possible for today's occasion. I chose a forest green long-sleeved satin gown with a classy v-neckline. The sleeves are slightly puffy but not over the top. It cinches in at the waist, funneling out into a long skirt with a high slit, putting nearly my entire leg on display. I take pride in having thicker thighs, so I figured it wouldn't hurt to showcase them.

Carefully, I slip on the dress, hoping it still fits how it did when I initially tried it on. Thankfully, it fits the way I remember it fitting. I turn toward my mirror, and immediately, I burst into an embarrassing grin. I feel so good in this gown, it's unreal. For the first time since opening the invite, I feel somewhat excited to attend the wedding. Jasper texts me, alerting me he's waiting outside. I gently kiss Truman before stepping out the door to meet my hot date.

As I approach him, I instantly blush upon seeing him in a gray suit and white button-up, complete with a green pocket square matching the exact shade of my dress. He put a product in his tousled dark hair, and his eyes currently resemble cloudy skies after rainfall.

"Wow, Jasper, you outdid yourself." I smile wide at him, biting my lip.

He simply stares at me in response, taking a deep breath. His skylike eyes drop to my thighs and slowly roam upward toward my face, lingering in some places longer than others along the way, ultimately meeting my eyes. "I'm at a loss for words. You've quite *literally* made me speechless."

I playfully nudge him, shaking my head, to which he grasps my hand. "I mean it, Greene. I don't care how cheesy this sounds. You take my breath away."

I unapologetically blush even harder. "Thank you, love."

We settle into his car, and he immediately holds my thigh on display, claiming me. I hope Jasper never tires of holding my thigh while driving because it has very quickly become one of my favorite things ever, along with Truman's cuddles and the sky itself.

About an hour into the drive, my body cringes, bracing itself for impact. I know what this means. *We're getting close to the site.* I begin to breathe rapidly but don't want to concern Jasper, so I attempt to regain composure silently—on my own.

Not today. I will not go there today.

Not today. I will not go there today.

Not today. I will not go there today.

Suddenly, a different thought crosses my mind: *Today's the day. You're going there today.*

Then, I realize the voice in my head is right. I *am* going there today. I've mustered the strength and am going there right now, whether I want to or not. My breathing steadies, but my heart is still racing.

"You okay, Greene?" He glances at me briefly before looking back at the road, but my body responds before I can. I instantly urge him to keep both eyes on the road. Visibly concerned, he pulls over onto the shoulder and then looks directly at me.

"What's going on? I'm here with you. You're not alone."

How surreal it feels to hear that. I've felt alone for so long that I have forgotten what it's like to lean on others. Right now, I'm trusting him—he deserves to know.

If the last few weeks have proven anything, Jasper Alcott will not sit idly by as I tuck away my emotions. He refuses to let me endure through this alone, becoming an anchor for my restless mind.

"Kai died in a car accident," my voice trembles as a tear slides down my cheek. "On this exact mountain almost two years ago. Soon, we'll be passing his memorial site. I—I think I lost myself when I lost him, Jasper. He wasn't alone in the car... I was with him."

Panic consumes me; I've never talked about the accident aloud to a single soul.

Inhale. Exhale.

Breathe.

"Truthfully, a part of me blames myself for his death. I turned up the music so obnoxiously loud and *let go*. As soon as I did, he smiled at me, taking his eyes off the road for just a second. The next thing I knew, we were spinning out of control. I remember screaming—I think I even screamed his name as we spun out. I also remember thinking, 'This is it. I'm going to die.' It all happened within a matter of seconds, but I was so *certain* I'd die. When we stopped spinning, I opened my eyes and gasped for air, amazed I was still breathing. I felt so relieved until I noticed his arm draped over me, unflinching... It was so quiet. And I was alive, but alone... so unmistakably alone. Without hesitating, I earnestly wished we swapped places. I couldn't bear the thought of living in a world without Kai. He deserved to live more than I do, Jasper."

I gaze down at my dress, assessing the small puddle of tears seeping into it, darkening its shade of green.

Inhale. Exhale.

Breathe.

"Baby, look at me," Jasper whispers. I slowly turn toward him, not daring to look into his eyes. He tilts my chin upward, so I have no other choice but to peer into his eyes, gray pools swirling with emotion. "You are not to blame for Kai's death. If he were here, I feel in my bones that he would want you to know it was not your fault. And I need you to take back that wish *right now*."

As I stare into his eyes, I feel a sense of calmness wash over me—almost like magic. Jasper's eyes flicker behind me for a millisecond before looking back into my eyes. "Do you take back your wish, love?"

Taking back that wish is no small feat. Truthfully, I've found myself wishing for this outcome on several occasions over the last couple of years. I couldn't comprehend how death could conquer someone as bright as Kai so early on in his life, leaving behind a dull storm cloud of a person like myself. For years, I've desperately tried to wear a smile on every occasion, careful not to let my gloominess show. But as of recently, rather than avoiding my inner turmoil like the plague, I've tried my hardest to embrace my emotions. In doing so, I've felt... lighter. Something I didn't know I could feel in a world without my sun. With all of this in mind, I consider his request deeply, making a choice that will alter the way I view my life.

"I take it back," I whisper defiantly as tears cascade down my cheeks. "I want to *live*."

"Not only that, Iris." He gently brushes my tears away, then grasps my face. "You *deserve* to live."

Thirty-Four

Kai

After an emotional but absolutely pivotal ride, we finally arrive at Katherine's wedding venue. I feel lame wearing a T-shirt and jeans, but reminding myself that Jasper is my *only* audience member helps a little. I'm feeling a huge sense of peace at the moment—Irie finally opened up to Jasper, and in turn, I can sense that the weight she carries has dropped significantly. So significantly, in fact, I don't know how much longer it'll be before my mission is complete. She seems to be embracing her emotions more and more every day. Yeah, it definitely won't be long now.

Speaking of happiness, I'm feeling immensely happy for my girl, Katherine. Sure, she may not technically be *my* girl anymore, mortally speaking, but I'll always feel that way about her. Irie and

Jasper walk into the chapel, holding hands. I never could have imagined how fulfilling it'd be to watch Irie fall in love.

They sit together on one of the benches at the back of the chapel, whispering jokes into each other's ear. I can't help but notice the way Jasper looks at her. He looks at Iris the way she looks at the clouds. Shit, maybe I should pursue matchmaking. I'll have to ask the Archangels if Cupid is accepting apprentices. There isn't space for me to sit next to them, so I stand in the back instead, preparing for the ceremony to begin. The venue is all decked out in earthy colors like brown, green, navy blue, and gold.

As if on cue, the lights dim, and classical music begins playing, signifying the beginning of Katherine's happily ever after. I walk closer to the front to get a better look at everything, then stop dead in my tracks, instantly feeling stunned. At the very end of the front row, I notice a reserved seat for Kai Greene.

I can't believe it.

Katherine and I were close friends throughout our teenage years but didn't actually begin dating until college. We dated for years, becoming best friends in the process. She cared for Irie fiercely, in the way I always hoped my partners would care for her. Breaking up with her would ultimately become the biggest regret of my life because not only did I lose my girlfriend. I lost my very best friend. At the time of my death, I was considering attempting to rekindle what we had. However, death waits for no one; it snuck up when I least expected it, otherwise I would've acted much quicker. Regardless, seeing that she saved a spot for me warms my heart.

We all rise, then watch the bridal and groom parties waltz in. Finally, Katherine enters, and I kid you not, my heart stops. She looks *radiant*. Her dress fits her in all the right places, not leaving much for the imagination. She smiles at each and every person she locks eye contact with, landing directly on someone for a second longer than the rest. I follow her eyes to see that Irie is tearing up—that's been a new thing for her recently. She's crying more than ever these days, and I'm loving it.

Eventually, her eyes linger on my seat. She gazes at the chair, then looks upward, her honeyed eyes landing on... me. I doubt she can see me, but I can't take my eyes off of her. Her inner and outer beauty has always stood out. During my guardian training, I briefly learned about soulmates. Mortals fantasize soulmates, but no one really knows whether or not they're real. I learned that soulmates are indeed real, but it's incredibly rare for someone to find their mate during their mortal life. A soulmate connection feels otherworldly—you can't fight the pull, no matter how hard you try. I know it's a long shot, especially since she's literally marrying someone else as we speak, but my connection with her feels so strong I can't help but wonder if we're soulmates. Maybe, in another life, it would've been us. I suppose I may never know, but regardless, I'm eternally happy for my girl. She chose love over fear, unlike what I did all those years ago.

I can only hope Irie does the same. She and Jasper have been getting uncomfortably close recently, but I still can't tell if she'll completely let herself fall for him. Likewise, Jasper is so stubborn I wouldn't be surprised if he denies the true nature of his feelings for an unbearably long time. Only time will tell.

As I watch Katherine say I do, I grin from ear to ear and clap proudly. I meant it when I told Jasper I wouldn't have missed this for the world. Seeing Katherine get her happily ever after makes our entire relationship, all the good and the bad moments, worth it. After the ceremony, Irie begins socializing with friends from high school, so Jasper catches up to me, prompting me to follow him into a grove of trees, away from people.

"It sucks you're so embarrassed to talk to me, man," I taunt. "It's hurting my self-esteem."

Jasper smirks, obviously stifling a laugh. "So, what's your history with Katherine like? I saw a seat reserved for you."

I sigh. "In short, she was my girlfriend for years. We broke up shortly before I died."

He nods in understanding, patting me on the shoulder. "I'm sorry, man. She looked over at Iris and then at your reserved seat with a lot of compassion. I can tell she loved you."

"She did. And I loved her too," I say firmly. A moment of understanding passes between us. "Thank you."

"Well, we really need to talk about something of dire importance," Jasper says dramatically, as music in the connected ballroom to the chapel begins to play. It must be time for dancing—the best part of every wedding. I used to get down and dirty on the dance floor in my prime. "I've got to tell Iris."

My heart skips a beat and *not* in a good way this time. "What? Why? Things are going so well."

"That's the thing," he runs his fingers through his hair. "I guess things are going well, objectively speaking, but I'm holding back a lot by not telling her the truth, man. My feelings for Iris are getting deeper. I can't keep this up."

"I hear you, Jasper," I sigh. "I did some research in the Archives of the Middle Realm to see what happens when the guarded find out about their angels, but before I could read up on it, I was cast out of the Ancient Library. I guess a lot of those records are private."

"I see," Jasper contemplates. "Well, I doubt this situation between us is common. You're not even technically telling or showing Iris you're here yourself."

"Fair point," I say. "I mean, I can't control you, Jasper. If you want to tell her now, go for it. Just know that this could impact her journey significantly. Whether that be a positive or negative impact is almost entirely up to her."

"I understand. I thought about what you said recently." He pauses. "About me falling for Iris. I feel like this secret is keeping me from finding out if I really have fallen for her. I need to tell her. Tonight."

"What the hell, tonight?" I exclaim. "Can't you wait till after the wedding?"

"Kai, with all due respect, I've been waiting weeks now to tell her. Iris is opening up to me in so many ways. You, yourself, agreed that she deserves more. Well, she *especially* deserves the truth."

I rub my temples and sigh. He is right. I can't even deny it. "Okay, do what you think is best."

He pats me on the back, then heads back to the reception hall, entering the ballroom. I have no idea how their conversation will go, but I can guarantee I'll be by their sides to pick up the pieces should things go badly. I gaze up at the sky in time to catch the sun setting over the mountains, giving the moon permission to light the sky for the remainder of the evening.

THIRTY-FIVE

JASPER

S oft music greets me as I stroll into the immaculate ballroom,
fashioned in an assortment of earthy tones. Several pieces
shimmer when the light hits them just right. My eyes scan the
room, searching for my favorite shade of Greene. I spot her
swaying her hips in tune with the music alongside some old
friends. As much as I want to steal her away, I take a seat and
patiently wait for her. I anticipate our conversation won't be easy,
so I'm glad she's enjoying herself for now. I sit in a seat assigned
to me and take note of the seat next to her seat, meant for
Kai. Katherine must have loved him deeply to honor him at her
wedding like this.

I can't lie. I often find myself wondering what it would've been
like to meet Kai under other circumstances. Our personalities

couldn't be more different, but our meeting would have been inevitable because of how much we both care about Iris. I wonder if we would've been friends. My eyes flicker back to her, and to my utter shock, she is suddenly dancing with someone. Not just anyone, either—it's the asshole from the Halloween party. I turn away for two minutes and, of course, he swoops in to steal her first dance of the evening. Of fucking course.

As they dance together, she looks stiff. I clench my jaw, restraining myself. His expression appears apologetic, but he still pulls her closer and whispers something in her ear despite her obvious disinterest. *That's it.* I toss back the rest of my drink and stand up, trudging to her side. Upon reaching them, I stand in between them and graze her back, drawing my lips to her ear.

"I'm here to steal you away," I whisper, to which her eyes light up.

"Please do," she mumbles. I grin, then turn toward the prick.

"Thanks for keeping *my* girlfriend company. You're free to go," I shout over the music, reaching out for her hand. He scowls at me, visibly outraged by my interruption. I bore my eyes into him, daring him to fucking try me. After a few seconds, he glances back at Iris. She responds with a simple shrug and a polite smile. *That's my girl.*

"I appreciate your apology, Jake." She takes my hand. "Take care."

I lead her toward the opposite edge of the dance floor as far away from him as possible. I don't know what came over me just now, but holding her close is already calming me.

"So, what did he have to say?"

"He wanted to apologize for the way he acted on Halloween. He acknowledged how ridiculous he was being." She trails off, looking down at her feet while our hips sway to the music.

"That's all?"

"And again, he asked if I'd be open to giving him a chance." She sighs. I'm not even remotely surprised.

"Ah, *there* it is," I smirk, "and you told him to piss off, I presume?" She chuckles in response, rubbing my back.

"More or less, but in a much more civilized manner than that," she jibes. I raise her hand above us, twirling her, watching her green dress flutter.

"Enough about him." I glance down at her. Her dress accentuates her eyes *and* body perfectly. She wraps her arms around my neck as we gaze into each other's eyes. Despite all the pain she carries, her emerald eyes glitter brightly against the dim lights in the room. The world around us fades, growing blurry. She slides her hands down from my neck to my back, pulling me toward her tightly as she leans her head against my chest. I embrace her, continuing to sway with the music. The melody grows fainter and fainter until it lingers in our ears as a mere echo of what it was.

At this moment, I can only register one sound: the rhythm of our hearts, beating in harmony as one.

She glances up at me. I frame her face with my hands and pull her in for a kiss, savoring her taste. We break away and lean back into each other, swaying again.

Don't tell her. You can't let her down, Jasper.

My heart stops beating. I've already been feeling uncertain about telling Greene about Kai, but knowing this could let her down eats me alive. The last thing I ever want to do is hurt her, but it feels like the longer I keep this from her, the more it will hurt in the long run. On the flip side, I have no idea how she will react knowing this information. It's not every day you find out you have a guardian angel who just so happens to be your big brother whom you idolized your entire life. This is such a screwed-up situation. We continue dancing, but Iris pauses, glancing up into my eyes again to search them.

"Everything okay? You look... off," she says worriedly. *That's an understatement.* "Honestly, things have felt a little off since Thanksgiving."

"Everything is okay, love. Let's go somewhere quiet to talk." I guide her off the dance floor, weaving us through the crowd to make it outside. I don't feel anxiety often, but damn, I'm feeling it right now. I lead her to the grove in the forest, the same area I spoke to Kai in earlier. I find a large sitting stone, wipe it down, and then prompt her to sit. I follow suit, sitting next to her. I take her hands in mine. I glance around to see if I can spot Kai, but alas, he doesn't seem to be here.

"Iris, I need to start by expressing how much you mean to me. Every moment we've spent together stays with me, right in here." I lay my hand over my heart. Then, I point a finger at my head. "But there's something in *here* I can no longer keep to myself."

I glimpse up at the stars and take a deep breath. "Have you ever wondered what happened to Kai after he passed away?"

She gazes at the stars and exhales. "Every day, he crosses my mind. I have no idea what to believe, but I'd like to believe he's up there, in the stars, shining brightly."

"I like the idea of that." I grin while my eyes remain fixed on the stars flickering in the cloudy night sky. "What if, after a person dies, they're given a choice between staying a little longer or crossing over? Do you think that's plausible?"

"I suppose anything is possible, considering no one really knows." She looks down. "Wherever and whatever Kai may be now, I hope he's found peace." I nod, then peer back at her as she stares at the stars. I don't want to tell her, but I know I need to. She deserves the truth—and not just fragments of it—the full truth.

"This is going to be a lot to take in, so I'm going to just say it." I swallow and run my fingers through my hair to distract myself from my racing heart. "I met your brother shortly after moving back to the Cove."

Her brows furrow as confusion crosses her features. "I—I don't understand." Her eyes search mine for answers. I tighten my grasp of her hand, rubbing it gently. "Are you like a psychic or medium or something?"

"No, Greene. Quite frankly, I never even believed in the supernatural... until I met Kai," I whisper. "Although your brother is deceased, he's still here. He's been here for years. He's your guardian angel now, and for some reason neither of us can explain, I can see him."

Her green eyes widen as her breathing shortens. "That's not possible, Jasper. My brother died. Two years ago. This isn't funny."

Her hands escape from mine as she pointedly turns away from me. My heart cracks at the absence of her touch.

"I know it sounds crazy, but this is real. After Kai passed away, he went to some place called the Middle Realm and the Archangels gave him a choice between immediately ascending or being your guardian angel for a period of time. He didn't hesitate—he chose to be your guardian because he could see you struggling. Throughout his guardianship, he has helped you countless times. You just didn't realize it," I say softly, stroking her back. "He introduced himself to me early on, but I swear I didn't know he was your brother until recently."

ERIN HALLI

"None of this makes sense," she mutters, shaking her head and burying her face in her hands. "Kai is gone. I've come to terms with that. How do I know you're being honest?"

"Well, for starters, I know Katherine is his ex-girlfriend—his one regret in his life is breaking up with her. He is unbearably protective of you, so much so that I resisted the urge to pursue you for *weeks* due to his nagging," I say, turning her to look at me again. Then, I see her eyes brimming with tears. "If that isn't enough, Kai slips up and calls you Irie when talking about you sometimes."

In an instant, tears stream down her cheeks. I brush them away the best I can, but they don't slow down. She still hasn't said a word. Instead, she silently cries, holding back all sound. I wrap my arm around her, pulling her into me. She leans into my hold and lets out a sob.

"I'm sorry." Her voice breaks. "This is just... a lot."

"Greene, what did I tell you about apologizing? There is no need. What can I do for you, love?"

"I don't understand... Is he here? Right now?" I look around and shake my head. "Why did he choose to stay?"

"Do you even have to ask? To help you get through this," I say. "Once you find peace, he will ascend."

She weeps and then shakes her head solemnly. "Then he will never ascend."

"Don't say that, baby, you've been making such good progress—"

"Progress? Am I a project in your eyes?" She narrows her tear-filled eyes at me. "Wait... Have you known since the beginning I was struggling?"

"What? No, of course not, Greene," I affirm. "I learned after we had already met that you had a guardian angel, but I didn't know the exact reason. You've never been a project for me."

"It's just hard to believe that, given the timing. Why now? Why tell me now? You've been keeping this to yourself just fine," she accuses.

"Baby, keeping this from you was eating me alive—I couldn't wait a second longer to tell you. Especially after I found out who he was to you."

"Well, why didn't you tell me sooner?" Emotion swirls in her eyes. My stomach drops. She's *hurt*. I don't think I've ever seen her so hurt. No, *no, no*.

"I wanted to, I really did, but Kai wouldn't let me. I swear, if I had known from the beginning who he was to you, I would've told you sooner."

"I am feeling so... confused," she says, tightly shutting her eyes. "Why can you see him? Why can't I? Will I ever get to see him?"

"I... don't know, Greene," I whisper. "I wish I had answers for you. When Kai first told me about his role in your life, I had similar questions, but he asked me to help you."

"So, you've just been talking to my dead brother this entire time? How do I know whether any of *this* is real or not?" Her voice cracks. "Have you only been getting closer to me to help him ascend or whatever?"

"What? No, absolutely not," I affirm. "This is real. I've never felt this way before."

"How do I know you're not saying that just to help me *find peace*?"

"Please, just trust me, Iris—"

"Jasper, I want to trust you. I want to believe you. More than anything," she says firmly. "But at this moment, my feelings are undeniably real, and right now, I'm feeling all sorts of emotions I can't fully understand. I need to honor my feelings and myself." She stands up, wipes her tears, pats her gown, and begins to walk away. Instinctively, I stand and reach out to grab her hand, pulling her back.

"I'm so, so sorry." Despite my best efforts to remain calm, my voice breaks. "Iris... will we be okay?"

She gazes back into my eyes somberly. "I hope so, but only time will tell," she says while continuing to wipe her tears away. "I'm going to hitch a ride home."

"What? No, please let me take you home," I plead. I don't know if I've ever felt so anxious in my life. This feeling—this pain, it's burning a hole in my chest. If Iris walks away from me tonight, I fear she won't come back.

"It's okay, man." Kai walks up behind her with sorrow in his expression. "She needs space."

She catches me looking at Kai over her shoulder.

"Is he here? Right now?" she asks frantically, looking around with a hint of hope causing my heart to break even more.

"He is," I answer, keeping my eyes locked on him. Her eyes follow my gaze. She glances directly at the spot Kai is standing in.

"I can't see him," she whispers quietly. She reaches her hand out, hovering near his shoulder. Kai stares intently at her with a mournful expression. "I can't—I can't even feel him."

"I'm here, Irie. I've always been here." He brushes a tear away. "We've got to go, Jasper. I'll take care of her tonight."

"Kai wants you to know he's always been here," I rasp. "I'll let you go tonight, love, but that does *not* mean I'm letting you go for good."

"I'll see you back in the Cove," she says. Kai wraps his arm around her, emitting a subtle golden glow and leads her away. The longer he holds his arm around her, the more her slumped shoulders rise. As I watch her slip away into the night, coldness seeps in, and suddenly, my world seems a hell of a lot dimmer than it was before.

THIRTY-SIX

IRIS

As I wander through the dim forest further and further away from Jasper, my mind spins endlessly. Angels are real. Kai is an angel. He is apparently my guardian angel. Supposedly, he has been here the entire time, meaning he never even really left. How is this possible? As a little girl, I used to fantasize about folklore. I could never have imagined any of the beings I dreamed about actually existing. Feeling lightheaded, I glance up at the crescent moon and close my eyes, attempting to steady my breathing. None of this makes sense. I stand outside the entrance to the ballroom and take a long, deep breath, collecting myself before walking back inside to retrieve my belongings. On my way back outside after grabbing my belongings, someone stops me. To my surprise, it's tonight's majesty herself.

"Iris, I'm so glad you could make it!" She smiles, but upon further observation of my tear-stained cheeks, her smile turns into a frown. "Oh, honey. Believe it or not, tonight has been emotional for me, too. I nearly lost it when I looked at the spot we saved for him." She rubs my back. If only she knew that this isn't the only reason behind my tears.

"Thank you for inviting me, Katherine—saving a spot for Kai meant the world to me." I smile warmly, masking my inner emotions as well as I can.

"Do you think he joined us tonight?" she asks, hope gleaming in her gaze. "I mean, I know there's no way to know for sure, but did you feel him here?"

My eyes water again. Of course. Just when I thought I was done crying for the evening. "I know he was here, Katherine."

Her honey-brown eyes brim with tears. "Please reach out if you ever need anything at all. I mean it." She pulls me in for a fierce hug. "I'll always think of you as a little sister."

"That means more than you know. I hate to leave early, but something came up." I pull away. "Wishing you all the happiness in the world." She sends me off with a big grin. Instead of hitching a ride back to the Cove, I do something uncharacteristic. I book a ride to a different location—one I had zero intentions of visiting anytime soon, but after the night I've had, all of my common sense has evidently evaded me.

I lift the third gray stone lining the pathway to the front door and pick up a single key. Then, I sneak into the pristine home as quiet as a mouse, stumbling through the dark, avoiding any and all objects blocking my path to his office. Once inside the office, I sort through all the keys in the top drawer of his desk. Thankfully, my parents aren't home, otherwise this could have been a rather uncomfortable situation. I couldn't bear to talk to them right now.

"Bet you're laughing at me as we speak, huh," I grumble to thin air. Why can't I see or feel him here? Why is it Jasper can and I can't? I would do anything to interact with him again. *Anything.* "Help your girl out—which key is it again?"

I'm met with silence. Predictably. Maybe I should've had Jasper give me a ride back to the Cove. After all, I would love nothing more than to have a two-way conversation with my dead brother through my boyfriend. I chuckle aloud at how insane that sounds. *Goodness, this can't be happening.* Once I find the key to my old car, I plan on driving it as fast as possible the entire way back to the Cove. Maybe then, Kai will reveal himself to me. This might be the perfect excuse to drive my old car again.

How many keys does my father have? *Finally,* I locate the key to my old car and hastily walk back toward the front door in the dark, bumping into a decorative statue on the way, nearly knocking it over. Right before reaching the front door, I catch sight of something I haven't seen in a long time. I walk toward the large painted family portrait on the wall. This portrait includes my brother, parents, and myself. In the painting, we all are gazing at Kai as he glows. I read the custom vinyl calligraphy below it.

Kai Nicholas Greene (1994-2021)
Our beloved son, brother, friend, and coach. May our son, who held the sun in his smile, rest in peace.

Suddenly, I feel cold. I can't pinpoint when I started crying again, but based on how wet my cheeks are, I'd say I started a while ago. Instead of walking out the front door, I backtrack, making my way toward the stairs. I barely land on the bottom step before my knees give out. In an instant, I'm crashing to the ground. My stomach twists in knots, then I hear low wailing, and to my horror, I discover it's *my* wailing. I rock myself back and forth on the bottom step and attempt to reign my tears back in, but it's no use. As my heart physically aches, I realize I can't breathe.

"Kai, where are you? Where are you right now? I need you," I whisper frantically as my breathing grows more and more rapid. "Kai, *please*," I beg. A few seconds later, I feel warmth spreading across my entire body, starting at my shoulders. I look up to see someone sitting beside me on the staircase, wrapping their arms around me. Through my tear-filled blurred vision, I realize who it is. It's someone I never would've expected to see.

"Mom?" I ask quietly. She continues to hold me tight, unwavering. She says nothing, but her hold on me is strong. Instead of fighting her embrace, I lean into it. She cradles me. After several moments of embracing each other, I break away and glimpse into her blue eyes.

"I'm sorry I broke in and attempted to steal my car back," I mutter. She barely cracks a smile, but nevertheless, a smile from her is a rarity, no matter how small.

"You would've gotten away with it, too, but your father and I both had a feeling we needed to get home immediately." Her voice trails off. "It was the strangest thing. Lo and behold, I find you here."

"I see," I say, recognizing exactly what this means. "Well, I should head back to the Cove; thank you."

"I insist you stay the night here; the mountain roads aren't safe—especially at night," she states firmly. "You can stay in your old room. It looks the same anyway." Do I want to stay overnight? No. But should I? Probably. I sigh and nod, agreeing to stay.

We head up to my old room, and she wasn't exaggerating; it looks like it hasn't been touched since the last time I saw it. One thing I can appreciate about my mom is she doesn't linger—as soon as she shows me to my room, she says good night, giving me the space I'm craving. I check my phone before settling in.

Jasper

> Please, tell me you're safe.

I could respond, but I don't have it in me right now. I haven't even started processing how I'm feeling about Jasper at the moment. I decide to wait to respond until I've had more time to process this, so I shower. As I rinse my hair, my thoughts immediately drift to Jasper and I feel a roller coaster of emotions all over again, starting with disappointment. I thought we'd be showering together tonight if I'm being honest. Then, I feel hurt because of this monumental secret he held onto throughout our entire relationship. Following that, anger finds me; the last thing I want to be is a project for someone to fix. Lastly, I feel... empty. I feel empty without him by my side. This emotional roller coaster cycles through itself about five more times before I finish my shower. I hop out and slip on a robe to a missed call from *Callie?* I call her back instantly.

"Callie, what's up?"

"Girl, are you okay? Jasper just called me asking if I'd heard from you."

"Oh, um.." I pause, "You can tell him I'm safe and just need space."

"Got it," she says. "But are you really okay?"

"I've had a long night, and I'd really rather not talk about it right now, but thank you so much for checking in on me, Callie. It means a lot."

"Of course, bestie. I'm always here if you need to talk. I'll let you go. Sweet dreams." We hang up. I plop down in bed to stare up at the ceiling, letting out an obnoxious groan. What on earth am I going to do? Instinctively, I reach across the bed, expecting Truman to join and comfort me at any minute.

Shit! I forgot about Truman! Without thinking, I call him. He answers immediately.

"I'm so sorry to reach out like this—I'll tell you right now, what I'm about to ask has nothing to do with anything that happened tonight."

"Understood, Greene."

"And I still need space and time to determine how or *if* we can move forward from here." A moment of silence goes by, making my skin itch. I may handle the quiet slightly better these days, but silence during this phone call? Painfully unsettling.

"Hit me with whatever you've got."

"So, I'm not going home tonight, and I totally forgot—"

"What? You didn't go back to the Cove tonight?"

"Um, yes. Anyway, as I was saying—"

"Where are you?"

"You'd never guess." I pause, getting irritated with his probing questions after our night. "Okay, to continue—"

"Your parents' place?"

I grit my teeth. "How could you possibly know that?"

"Uh, a little birdie told me." I scowl. *Kai.* Who knows what else he has been whispering in Jasper's ear throughout our entire relationship?

"Of course he did. Anyway, as I was saying, I forgot about Truman. Do you mind going to my apartment to make sure he has enough food and water to last him through tomorrow afternoon? I only expected to be gone for a few hours, not overnight, so I'm just a little worried," I admit.

"Say no more. I'll take care of Truman," he promises. "You just focus on getting a good night's rest, love. Take all the time you need... I'll be waiting."

We hang up and my chest feels lighter. Even when I'm frustrated with Jasper, he has the power to bring me back to Earth after my troubled mind whisks me away. Despite this, I can't move on from what happened tonight.

How am I supposed to know whether or not Jasper's feelings for me are real? He's known since the beginning how fragile I am. I wouldn't be surprised at all if he's been trying to "fix" me from day one. He has always been able to read my emotions, even when no one else can. Maybe the only reason he could see past my mask is because Kai has been whispering in his ear all along. My mind spins with all these possibilities, not knowing which possibility is the reality.

Ultimately, I am not certain about why I walked away from him tonight. Maybe I left because I felt hurt. Or perhaps being the first to leave hurts less than being left. At the time, I felt as though I had to walk away to protect myself from even more pain. I didn't want to hurt Jasper, but I couldn't stay—not while my thoughts were so scattered. Everything still feels unclear and murky. What I need now, more than ever, is true clarity. Something I struggle to receive in ordinary circumstances as is.

I turn off the lights and tuck myself into my teenage bed, contemplating everything. If Kai has been here this entire time, when has he helped me exactly? I wish I could pinpoint different moments he impacted. I wish I knew more about what Ascension really means. I wish I could interact with him the way he can interact with me. As I think about all of this, the quiet sets in. Instead of turning on my music immediately, I sit in silence. The quiet has not felt safe for a long time, but at this moment, it feels less like a stranger and more like a familiar friend.

Perhaps, rather than the noise I bask in to draw away my innermost thoughts, my soul craves the pure, relentless quiet I dread. After a few moments of drifting off into the quiet, my mind goes back to Kai and that dreadful icy day. Consequently, I revert back to my old ways, turning on music to drown out uninvited thoughts consuming my mind.

THIRTY-SEVEN

JASPER

The moment I found out I failed a course in graduate school, my heart sank. I felt like a screw-up. A letdown. A failure. The biggest joke in the world. In an instant, I re-evaluated my whole life plan. School was my thing—I liked college. Hell, I even liked studying. While working in the industry for a few years, I actually missed school. Shocking, I know. I've always valued knowledge above all else. Under the impression that wisdom is the only thing you take with you beyond life, I absorbed as much information as I could.

Throughout my life, I tried my damndest to emulate excellence. My parents worked hard their entire lives and didn't have much other than Aged Emporium to show for it. So, I set a goal to give them something to be proud of early on. At first, their words of affirmation were encouraging. They provided me with the boost of confidence I needed to step forward. However, as time progressed, I grew more and more critical of myself—if they didn't provide the same level of support for every accomplishment, I knew I let them down. Always being the person who volunteered to help when no one else wanted to, I bent over backward to exceed. After decades of striving for greatness, a fundamental part of who I believed myself to be cracked in half amidst my failure. Then, when I received the news about my dad's injury, I spiraled. Suddenly, the amount of schooling I underwent no longer mattered anyway. What mattered more was whether or not I could fill my dad's shoes, whom I hadn't ever intended to follow in the first place. If I don't excel in running Aged Emporium, I will let them down even more than I already have.

Letting people down doesn't sit right with me—it never has. But letting *her* down? The aftermath of that is un-fucking-bearable. On Saturday night, I accidentally passed out on her couch after watching Truman. To my utter shock, I awoke to an angel calling my name.

"Jasper? Jasper, what are you still doing here?"

I slowly peeled my eyes open to see her—yep, unquestionably an angel. "Good morning, beautiful." I smiled while squinting, reaching out to stroke her soft skin. Her breath hitched. I pulled her in for a kiss, but instead of giving in, she fought my pull—something she hadn't ever done before. It almost felt unnatural. Looking into her murky green eyes, I suddenly remembered how our evening went and hastily dropped my hand. "I'm so sorry. I know you need time. I didn't mean to—"

"I understand." Her eyes flickered to Truman, who was perched on the couch armrest, purring. "Thank you for taking care of him. I'll take it from here."

I ran my fingers through my hair and nodded, standing to leave despite my pounding heart pleading to stay. Her eyes glimmered with unreadable emotion. For once, I couldn't register what she was feeling, and it scared the living hell out of me. Since walking away, we haven't talked—at least, not like we used to. It's been five days. Okay, sure, she has texted me about our fundraiser event, but she has resorted back to calling me "Mr. Alcott." As much as I fancied that charade before, I have little taste for it now. Not to mention, Joy stopped by Aged Emporium *on her behalf* to solidify several event preparations this week. I told Greene I would give her time and space, as she requested. I keep telling myself that waiting will be worth it, no matter how agonizing this feels.

In the meantime, instead of sulking, I've tried to fill my days as much as possible. I've worked out more rigorously during the last several days than usual, spending hours in my garage weight lifting. I've also been taking care of any and every project I can at Aged Emporium. From relabeling a hundred vinyl records to cleaning every single stair step, I have continually kept myself busy from 8:00 a.m. to 8:00 p.m. I even started sifting through our boxes of old unclaimed letters dating all the way back to the mid-eighteenth century. After reading a few tragic love letters and thinking of her one too many times, I decided that was *not* the best use of my time. I had hoped the projects would distract me from this gaping hole in my chest. As usual, I was wrong.

I take another gulp of whiskey and sigh, staring at my ceiling. Iris isn't the only person I haven't heard from recently—Kai hasn't been around much, either. I've seen him twice since the confession. Both times were brief. I knew telling her everything was a gamble, but if I had known this would be the outcome, I can't confidently say I would've made the same choice. If only I could've told her in the beginning—then she may have been able to believe me when I told her I hadn't ever felt this way before, and it has nothing to do with Kai. Now, she's questioning everything I've ever told her. How will I ever gain her trust back? I'm an utter idiot.

I glance at the time, noting that they will be here soon. I sigh again. I'm *not* in the mood for company, but these guests are persistent and nearly impossible to avoid. Thankfully, I don't need to pretend to be cheery for my parents—they know I'm a grump at my core. Sure enough, I hear my front door creak open. I slowly saunter over to the entryway, greeting them with a nod.

"How's it going?" I help wheel my dad in.

"Better now that we're here." My mom winks, putting her purse on my entry table and hanging up her coat. I pick up the large casserole dish resting in my dad's lap, carrying it to my dining table. We all settle in around the table and begin dishing up our plates.

"How have you been, son?" My dad grunts, taking a bite of my mom's famous lasagna.

"I've been better," I grumble, taking another swig of my whiskey. My mom lets out a chuckle. My dad and I both side-eye her in confusion.

"Something funny, dear?" My dad raises his thick brows.

"You two are funny, grunting and grumbling over there," she teases. "I just love our family dinners. I'd love to do these every night if we could."

"Nope, we're good," my dad and I say in unison. I lock eye contact with him for a second, and we both crack a small grin.

"So, you said you've been better," my mom continues. "What's going on?"

Ah, there it is. My mom has the tendency to pry. Honestly, she's been doing this for so many years I don't even think she recognizes how much she pries at this point. I've gotten better at setting subtle boundaries with my parents, though, so I keep what I share with them fairly vague. "I screwed up recently, but it's nothing new at this point. I'll fix it."

"Jasper, you're always fixing something and a majority of the time, you're doing it on your own. I hope you know your father and I are immensely proud of you. If you need anything, we're here to help, okay?" I nod, taking a deep inhale. "Does this have to do with a certain someone who shares her name with a flower?"

"Thanks, mom, but with all due respect, it's none of your business." I cut her a sharp glance. She raises her eyebrows at me and I sigh. "I let her down. I'll leave it at that." She gazes at me with warmth in her eyes.

"I understand," she says quietly. "I'll stop prying. You should know you've never been a letdown to us. I can't speak for her, but unless she has told you herself, there's a decent chance you haven't let her down. Give it time. It will all work out the way it's meant to."

Unless she has told you herself, there's a decent chance you haven't let her down. I let that statement sink in.

"I appreciate that, Mom," I say. We continue eating, my dad commenting on how delicious it tastes every once in a while. I catch them up on how well Aged Emporium is doing. The masquerade ball hasn't even happened yet, and we've already doubled the business. In a shocking turn of events, I can hardly wait to see what Aged Emporium's future entails. My dad beams upon hearing that news. My mom begins discussing what she's planning to wear to the ball. After the meal, I rise from the table to walk them out, feeling woozy now as the alcohol finally hits me. As my mom hugs me goodbye, she whispers something in my ear.

"Don't give up," she urges. I pull away and glance at her in confusion. "I saw the way you looked at each other that morning. Fight for her, Jasper."

After their departure, I drain my glass. I've only had one drink tonight, but it was filled to the brim. I settle onto my couch and lean back, resting my hands behind my head. In all my years of dating, my mom has never encouraged me to hold onto someone, and she's met several of the girls I've talked to. Leave it to my girl to change my mom's old ways.

Am I even allowed to call her "my girl" at this point? I hid the truth from her, betraying her trust. I don't blame her one bit for wanting distance, but I'd be lying to myself if I said the distance wasn't killing me. I've never ached like this for anyone before, but Greene is something else. As I close my eyes, I envision her soft, supple lips brushing over mine like a feather. I hear her melodic voice calling to me like a siren's song. I feel her delicate skin, peppered with goosebumps as I caress her.

I need to hear her laugh, see her smile, feel her body against mine. I'm so damn hopeless, I'd even watch one of those wonky reality TV shows with her right now voluntarily. I need *her*.

But as much as I'm aching to be with her, I ache *for* her, too. If I'm feeling this lousy, I can't even imagine how she feels. Finding out Kai never really left her side has to be earth-shattering. I wish I could support her through this, but she's made her stance on our relationship as clear as day for now. I need to give her space... First, though, I have just one item to attend to. I begin to type out a message to her, going back and forth on whether or not to send it a few times, but in my laissez-faire buzzed state, I just send it.

> Can you please stop calling me Mr. Alcott?

> It's killing me, Greene.

As soon as I send it, I set my phone down and close my eyes again. I know she won't text back—she needs time. I've got to respect that. But I physically couldn't make it through another day of her addressing me as *Mr. Alcott*. She knows *exactly* what she's doing by calling me that incessantly. I begin to drift off when my phone vibrates.

Iris

> I'll consider it.

My heart skips a beat.

Hell, when did I become the guy whose heart stops upon receiving a text? I bite back an embarrassingly big grin. This message isn't much, but it's *something*. I will take anything she gives me. Anything.

Thirty-Eight

Iris

While strolling down the cobblestone road bordering the Cove's town square, I refrain from texting Jasper more than I'd like to confess. When he texted me casually on Thursday evening, my stupid butterflies returned with a vengeance. It felt wrong to ignore him blatantly, so I responded with a short, bland text. Working through my emotions over the past seven days has been challenging, to say the least. Not only am I working through this situation with Jasper and Kai, but I've thought a lot about my mom, too. For the first time, I feel somewhat valued by her. I can only hope it lasts. The more I've thought about my mom, the more I've realized she has a difficult time showcasing her vulnerable side with me. Being married to someone as absent as my dad can't be easy... I know this doesn't excuse her actions toward me, but it *does* shed light on why she is the way she is.

Shamefully, as I walk down the street, I poke my head around each corner, hoping Kai will manifest himself to me. I'm still holding on to the possibility that I may be able to see him if I squint hard enough. Part of me wants to stumble just to see if he'll catch me. *Maybe this is why it's better for people not to know they have a guardian angel.* Entering Little Falls for the first time this week, Davis's eyes widen upon seeing me. "Where have you been, missy?"

"I've been slammed with work lately." I grin. Technically, it's not a lie, but I suppose it isn't the truth in its entirety, either. If I were being honest with him, I'd admit that I haven't left my apartment for non-work related reasons in days. Every day, I've woke up, walked straight to work, and then straight home at the conclusion of the day. "I'll get the usual."

"Coming right up—it's on the house today, you look like you need it." He winks, rolling up his flannel's sleeves. I don't know if Davis realizes that isn't the most flattering sentiment, but knowing him, he meant no harm. I suppose he isn't wrong. I trudge over to a table meant for two and sink into the plush chair. I reflect on the first time Jasper and I ever met—he offered to give me a ride because of the rain. Little did I know, my brother was probably right there with us the entire time. Part of me can't help but wonder if the only reason Jasper accepted Soi's fundraiser opportunity was because of Kai, too. I rub my temples and lean my head back, releasing a frustrated sigh. How will I ever move past this?

"Iris," Davis shouts. I grab my order and thank him, then slip back outside, tightening my coat. As I take a sip of my latte, I peer up at the gray sky. The sun is nowhere in sight today. *Typical.* I continue down the winding road, focusing on the pitter-patter of my treading feet. After walking uphill for several minutes, the high school's peak comes into my line of sight. I wouldn't miss Callie's art exhibit for anything.

Upon walking in, I'm greeted with atmospheric indie folk music, setting the mood. I follow printed signs leading me to the school's quaint gallery. The gallery itself is smaller than an average classroom, but glass windows make up the entire front wall of the exhibit. A large tan, backless teakwood bench sits in the center of the room. Before Callie joined the staff, the gallery didn't have any seating, so she made it her personal mission to track down a high-quality bench for the gallery. I remember Kai telling me about it from his perspective—he was quite impressed she got the Principal to approve a $600 bench for *art students*. I chuckle to myself, remembering how much of a debacle this entire situation was at the time.

I arrive early to explore the exhibit, intending to leave before all the students and their families arrive. While walking to Callie's classroom, I hear laughter—it appears some of her friends arrived early, too. As I walk into her classroom, I see him currently occupying her attention, keeping his back turned to me. I'd recognize those dark waves anywhere.

"Iris! You're early!" Callie, fashioned in a highly colorful sweater dress, breaks away from her conversation, rushing to my side and bringing me in for a hug. "I'm so glad you're here! The students blew me away this year, I can't wait for you to see all their pieces."

As we're hugging, he turns around, piercing me with his eyes causing the room's energy to shift. Adorned in a black crewneck with dark jeans, he saunters over to us as Callie and I pull apart. Instantly, the homely scent of pine and sandalwood reaches my nose. I inhale, breathing in for what feels like the first time in days.

"Hi, Greene."

"Hi," I whisper, unable to avoid glimpsing at his lips. I can't believe I forgot Callie invited him to this back at the bar weeks ago.

"Well, I am going to let you two catch up." Callie scrunches her nose, grasping my shoulder before frolicking away. I grimace, not knowing what to say first. "Feel free to walk through the gallery now before it gets crowded! It's open."

"Shall we?" He reaches out his arm for me to wrap my arm in his. Linking arms is innocent—hardly intimate—so I cave. As I wrap my arm around his toned bicep, chills spread across my skin. *I've missed his touch.*

We walk inside the exhibit together, and I gaze at all the expressive colors surrounding us, instantly feeling as though we've been transported to a new place. The walls are entirely covered in canvases, both big and small, displaying styles of every variation imaginable. Underneath each piece lies a title alongside a student's name and age. After admiring several creative pieces, an oil painting in the corner beckons me.

Composed of intricate gray swirls, the sky complements a landscape of a meadow overtaken by wildflowers, primarily in pink, red, orange, and yellow hues. In the meadow of colors, a hydrangea sits at its center. Instead of illuminating a bright, warm color like the others, it blooms in a cool tone of *blue*. However, it remains as striking as all the other flowers in the grove alongside it. It's simply different. My gaze drifts down to the title.

THE MASKED FLOWER

My eyes begin to water for reasons my mind can't fully comprehend. I never would've guessed I'd resonate deeply with an art piece created by a seventeen-year-old, but here we are.

"Reminds me of you," Jasper's gravelly voice reaches my ear.

I glance up at him in awe. Once again, we seem to be on the same wavelength. "I do feel drawn to it."

"Is this an auction? Can we bid on it, or...?" He looks around, then bites his lip. It takes effort to stifle my grin. *Damnit, why does he have to be so hard to be angry at?*

"It's a high school art show, Jasper. We can't buy the art." I shake my head and continue walking, gazing at other colorful pieces.

"One point for Jasper, zero for Greene," he taunts in a sing-song manner.

"What? What is that supposed to mean?" I turn toward him, scowling.

"You called me Jasper." He grins brightly to which I roll my eyes. After everything that has happened, I have spent time processing my situation. During our time apart, it was necessary to enforce certain boundaries and formalities. I had no idea he would be so bothered by it... okay, *maybe* I had an inkling he'd be a little annoyed. Although a tad petty, I don't regret it.

"Fair enough," I quip. I take a seat on the teakwood bench, and Jasper sits next to me shortly after, his thigh resting against mine. He told me early on in our relationship that physical touch is one of his top love languages. I relate to him on that. Consequently, when he touches me, even in small ways, I can't help but feel a bit special. We sit in uncomfortable silence for a couple of minutes.

"I still need time," I finally say.

"I understand."

"Is he here right now?" I glance over his shoulder and then around the room.

"You might be surprised to hear that I haven't seen much of Kai recently since I told you about him," he says, staring at a charcoal piece of an astronaut on a mountain. At least, I think it's an astronaut—it may just be an abstract fish... "He isn't here right now. But I am."

A beat of silence passes between us as we prolongingly stare into each other's eyes.

"It's quiet in here, don't you think?" He raises a brow. "You're handling it well."

"I suppose I'm getting used to it." Suddenly, I stand up and tug on his hand, yanking him up, unsure of what's come over me. "Here, let me show you something."

We leave the art exhibit and wander down several different hallways until we arrive. We halt at a large display case. Inside lies some of my favorite things—my brother's coaching jersey, his helmet from college, and a glove with his name engraved on it.

"Every member of his baseball team signed his jersey," I whisper. "Those kids really loved him. Every now and then, one of them posts about Kai on social media."

"I'm starting to think *everyone* loved Kai," Jasper jokes.

"Well, that's because everyone did. Kai never had any enemies—sure, he had some rivals, but never enemies," I reminisce. "He bothered the absolute hell out of me on some days, but he never failed to make me laugh."

"I can understand that." He turns to face me. "I'd be lying if I said Kai hasn't cracked me up a couple of times. He's an odd one."

"It's so strange. I just can't wrap my head around why you can see him when no one else can. Wouldn't it make more sense for me to be able to see him, considering he is my guardian angel?"

"It would certainly make more sense for you to see him than me," he agrees. "Kai isn't sure why I can see him without even trying, but he told me he's been researching it. I don't know if we'll ever know, Iris." Suddenly, Jasper's eyes flicker beyond me. I imagine Kai might have just arrived. How did I miss this so many times before I knew about Kai? Jasper isn't the most discreet person I know.

"He's here now, isn't he?" I ask, to which Jasper nods. "How is he?"

"He's more concerned with how you're doing, Greene," he says. Of course, he is. Kai has always been more concerned about my well-being than himself, guardian angel or not,

"I'm fine," I say. Jasper quirks a brow, causing me to sigh. "Okay, no. I'm not fine. I'm confused. I'm overwhelmed. I'm conflicted. There, you happy?"

"Exceptionally." He grins cockily. I begin to walk away, but he grasps my arm gently, pulling me back to his side. "You never have to hide your emotions from us, Iris."

Us. I don't know how to feel about that statement. I know I don't have to hide my emotions from Jasper, and I would love nothing more than to have a real conversation with Kai, but it's not the same. I want to hear his voice. I want to hear his laugh. I want to hear him tell me himself he's been here the whole time because, quite frankly, I still have a hard time believing it.

"I'm going to head home." I smile curtly, heaviness coating the thick air between us. "Big week ahead of us, with the ball and everything. I'll see you next week."

His shoulders droop, but nonetheless, he lets me go. When he said he would wait for me, I wasn't sure if I believed him initially. However, I'm starting to think he meant it. He *will* wait for me.

THIRTY-NINE

KAI

Well, my favorite person in the world is heartbroken. I've watched her grieve. I've watched her succumb to depression. I've watched her go numb. Now, I've watched her heart break, and I would go to the ends of the earth to put the pieces back together. But as much as I want to take matters into my own hands, it isn't my place to fix their relationship—it's up to them to figure their situation out. I just wish they'd figure it out sooner rather than later because the secondhand heartbreak is excruciating.

I glance out of Irie's bedroom window to gaze up at the twilight sky, noting the balance of stars, clouds, and the moon. My eyes catch on her sleeping soundly with little Truman nestled in the crook of her neck. It could be an older sibling thing, but I've

272

always been a solid helper. As a kid, my parents praised me for how good I was at helping others. Sitting idly by as Irie and Jasper attempt to overcome this is not ideal. Truth be told, a big part of me blames myself for their demise.

Why did I force Jasper to keep this a secret for so long? I should've known from the moment he laid eyes on my sister that he was done for. As much as I hate to admit it, I shouldn't have stood between them for as long as I did, forcing them apart when they were clearly meant to be together. They weren't ever *just* friends—not really, at least. Damnit, I was such a cock-blocker-kill-joy-dick in the beginning, too.

After several minutes of wallowing in self-pity, I decide I need to help somehow. It's my duty. I'm going to figure out why Jasper can see me. Maybe that knowledge will help us all out of this big mess. I stalk out of her bedroom, setting my thoughts on the one place that holds the answers we need, not caring about the consequences. When I open her front door to slip outside, I find myself back in the good ole Middle Realm.

I'm no stranger to the Middle Realm. At this point, I've visited dozens of times. After dying, I stayed here for a period of time, too. But this is the first time I've visited with a strict agenda—another mission of sorts. I walk through the opulent doors with my head held high, careful not to capture unnecessary attention. I spent some time here in the Ancient Library recently but was cast out after not sleuthing to the best of my ability. That won't happen this time. There's too much at stake now.

I continue walking through the grand hall, heading into the main foyer. Located centrally in the Middle Realm's stunning headquarters, the foyer is surrounded by grand staircases, all leading to different places within the Middle Realm.

To put the Middle Realm into simple context—most of its inhabitants spend their days at headquarters fulfilling whatever role they are assigned to while opting to spend evenings in their homes, usually located just outside of the main building in the living quarters. The living quarters built upon the clouds themselves span a few miles beyond the perimeters of the building. Some angels choose to live in simple homes, others choose apartments, and the lucky ones live in mansions. All of the buildings in the Middle Realm are technically indoor, though, seeing as a thick pane of glass separates this realm from the Golden Realm.

Only a handful of angels stay in the Middle Realm, working as guardians, hunters, officers, watchers, and educators. Archangels run the place. Some angels stay by choice, others by force. Don't get me wrong, the Middle Realm is otherworldly in the best way, but I can't imagine being *forced* to live here while having a front-row seat to the Golden Realm. Then again, I don't love being told what to do, so maybe it's just a personality thing. Who knows.

While walking up the first set of stairs, I focus on the doors to the Greeting Center. I found myself in that space when I first awoke in the Middle Realm. All newly dead angels awake there in a dome-like room with a perfect view of what lies beyond those walls. As I mentioned before, I was utterly stunned by the undeniable beauty of this realm, but I couldn't stomach leaving Irie in her most vulnerable state. I don't visit this area as often as I'd like to, but soon enough, I should be able to behold the full enchantment of the afterlife. Well, if we can help Irie find peace, that is. I refuse to give up on her.

I walk up another flight of stairs, passing several new guardian recruits and my old mentor, Matt, walking downstairs toward one of the training arenas. I flash him a peace sign, to which he nods back at me, his lips tugging upward into a cocky smirk. His wings are so rad—they're silver. I keep trekking casually until I land at the top of the third staircase, reaching the Ancient Library's entrance. This time, I'll be as inconspicuous as possible.

Don't be suspicious, don't be suspicious, don't be suspicious. I chuckle at my own train of thought, then remember my purpose. *Damnit, why does that jingle have to be so catchy?*

I press my finger to the sensor and wait for the tall golden doors to open. After a moment of silence, I press my finger against the sensor again, pushing extra hard for good measure, then back away, tucking my hands into my pockets. After another minute of daunting silence, I hear footsteps approach from behind me. I peek over my shoulder to see another angel walking toward the library. Her jet-black shoulder-length hair shimmers under the crystal lights, complementing her light-bronzed skin tone and shimmering night wings composed of black, gray, and navy blue feathers. Fashioned in a pencil skirt with a flowy light blue blouse, she looks... put together. *Too* put together. I gulp, attempting to hide my nerves.

"Having trouble?" she asks, eyeing the large closed doors in front of me.

"Oh, er, yeah." I scratch my head. "I'm thinking the sensor stopped working. Do you mind giving it a whirl?" Her eyebrows raise as her lips curl upward, just slightly, before dropping back into a firm line.

"A *whirl*?" she questions. I gawk—she'd have to be ancient to not understand that expression. Am I dealing with an Archangel here? A solid lump forms in my throat. "Sure, I'll give it a *whirl*."

She presses her finger to the sensor, and sure enough, the doors open for her. How strange... Why didn't that work for me?

Without saying another word, she struts into the library like she owns the place, not even acknowledging my presence. I sneak into the massive two-story library behind her, catching up to her quick pace.

"Hey, thanks," I say. "I don't know why it wouldn't work for me."

"Well, you clearly don't have access to the library, but it would've been a pain to bring the Archangels into it, so consider this my gift to you, Kai Greene." She continues walking without missing a beat. Now, I know what you're thinking—it's strange she knows my name. Truth be told, I used to think things like that were odd, but in the Middle Realm, angels just seem to know things. Especially more advanced angels like this one. I can't figure her out, but I can confirm she isn't a novice angel like me.

"Wait, since when do I not have access? I thought all guardians have permanent access to the library."

"Take it up with the Archangels; I don't have time to break it down for you." Damn, who pissed in her cereal? But shit, if she's right and I no longer have access, how will I get past the second sensor to the Archives room upstairs? My access must have been revoked after my failed sleuthing in the restricted area last time. I've never been good at sneaking around. That was always Irie's thing. However, this time, I'm focusing on historical records in the Archives instead. Hopefully, that's less suspicious. She saunters away like she means business, but I intercept her, stepping right in front of her to gaze into her eyes.

"I don't suppose you have it in you to do me one more favor?" Before I can register what's happening, I accidentally use my soulsight on her. A series of images come to mind, including an unsettled sea of blue and dozens of dragonflies, and an immense feeling rushes over me: a feeling of... guilt. Ah, *crap*. I didn't mean to pierce her soul. I haven't ever lost control like this. Rather than reacting to the soulsight, though, she just sighs like she's bored.

"If I do one more favor, will you leave me alone?" Her brown eyes peer into mine. Her irises have microscopic flecks of gold. I wonder if she knows that.

"Promise." I hold three fingers mimicking a scouts-honor symbol. She rolls her eyes, prompting me to continue. "Can you use your extra special finger to get me into the Archives?" Rather than answering, she pushes past me and begins trotting up the spiral staircase, swaying her hips casually with every step. We arrive at the top of the staircase outside of the Archives. She raises her hand, pressing her small finger up to the sensor and the door automatically opens for her. I'm honestly a little hurt the library doesn't like me anymore.

"As you requested, you're relieved of your duties. I'll officially leave you alone." I salute her with a wink. She smiles firmly and then turns to walk away. Before I can think better of it, I catch her arm softly to stop her. "What's your name?"

Her eyes drop to my hand grasping her arm, then flicker upward to meet mine. "I thought you said you'd leave me alone."

Ouch. She is not the friendliest angel, is she? I chuckle softly, flashing her my best grin. "Okay, okay, you're right."

I walk toward the Archives, accepting defeat, when a voice from behind me says, "Cleo."

I turn back to throw her a smirk, but to my surprise, she's gone. Deciding I've wasted too much time already, I stride toward the scrolls to begin searching for an answer as to why Jasper can see me when no one else can. After spending about an hour searching, I finally locate a scroll that may be relevant titled "Astral Anomalies."

Cleo. I like that name.

FORTY

IRIS

Several days pass in a blur. We have spoken a few times this week, but my primary focus is fundraising. Aged Emporium just hit three thousand followers on socials, and over one hundred and fifty people have bought tickets to the ball at Marble Grove. Consequently, we've already raised hundreds of dollars for Aged Emporium in ticket sales alone. We will accept further donations at the event itself, highlighting every person who donates. I anticipate this event will do wonders for Aged Emporium, which brings me great joy, considering how much Jasper's family deserves this.

With the ball taking place tomorrow evening, I sent out a majority of our event planning team to Marble Grove to decorate and set everything up. I stay behind at the office, finalizing all the other details. As I scan my planner, it looks barer than it once did, causing me to realize something. I haven't been thinking about work when I'm away from work nearly as often as I used to. I attempt to pinpoint when this changed and discover that it all leads back to Jasper. While spending time with him, I don't feel the need to hyper-fixate on work. Instead, I tend to hyper-fixate on us, not wanting to blink so I don't miss a second.

I sigh. I've done a lot of contemplating. I'm not angry at Jasper for withholding this from me anymore. I understand he had his hands tied, and it seems like he wanted to tell me but couldn't. Unfortunately, though, I've concluded that there is no concrete way for me to determine whether or not Jasper only pursued me to help Kai. I also recognize that my feelings for him are far deeper than anything I've ever felt for anyone. It hurt like hell to lose Kai because of how close we were. Grief is merciless. I can't even fathom how deeply it would hurt to lose Jasper if something were to happen. So, he may not realize it, but choosing to walk away is for both of us. I figure it's best to cut the rope now before his feelings mirror the intensity and complexity of my own. This is the only way to protect our hearts.

My phone rings, and a familiar face pops up on my screen. I hurriedly answer. "Lena?"

"Iris! I'm here! Well, actually, we're here! We both came—we figured a ball would be the perfect excuse to dress up, and I wanted to support you during your first major fundraiser."

"Oh, this is the best news ever! When can I see you?"

"Tina has insisted we go on a hike today." Lena audibly gags into the phone. "I am not a hiker, but love makes you do crazy things, I suppose. So, we will probably need to catch up tomorrow. Can we get ready together? In-person this time?"

"I'm so in!" My grin widens. "I have to get there early, as I'm sure you already know. Want to swing by at around noon?"

"We will be there. I've got to go. We're heading to baggage claim, and it's quite crowded. See you tomorrow!"

After saying goodbye to Lena, I can't stop smiling. I haven't seen Lena since she moved away several months ago. The idea of getting ready for an event together like old times excites me—this is exactly what I need.

"I can't believe we haven't seen each other since March." Lena applies the final touches of her makeup masterfully. While Lena and I share my bathroom mirror, Tina is currently in the kitchen baking homemade cookies. She doesn't wear much makeup or apply heat to her hair, so she is in no rush to get ready.

"It is wild," I agree while putting on mascara. I've settled on a bronze and black makeup combo for tonight, using a pop of copper in my inner crease.

"So, what's going on with you? Something seems to be bothering you," she says, putting on deep red lipstick. Of course, Lena can tell. She always can. She's the one person I can't bullshit—aside from Jasper.

"Well, if you *must* know, I have been dating someone—his name is Jasper—and everything has gotten jumbled and so confusing, I don't really know if we'll be moving forward after tonight," I confess.

"Ah, I see. What makes you think you won't be able to move forward?"

"It's just... hard," I sigh, sparing her the complexities of my love life. "I don't know how deep his feelings for me are, but mine are quite deep. In fact, they're deeper than I'm even comfortable with, so I'd rather cut it off before we hurt each other even more."

Lena pauses applying her makeup and turns toward me abruptly. "Do you think you've fallen for him?"

"No... Maybe... I don't know, Lena, everything is so mixed up." I rub my temples and let out a loud, tired sigh.

"Iris, if even a fragment of you feels like you could love him, please, listen to me." She grabs my shoulders and locks eye contact with me. "You have every right to walk away after tonight, but please, do yourself justice and tell him how you feel before you do."

My heart skips a beat. Until now, I chalked my feelings up to caring for him deeply. I avoided considering it could be love. Do I love Jasper Alcott? Is that what this tugging feeling in my chest is? Could this be the root cause of the gaping hole left in his absence? Is this why butterflies have taken permanent residency in my stomach, and I can't think straight without him near? I'll admit, he has made himself irreplaceable. The idea of losing him makes me sick, but if I truly love him, then the unavoidable loss will be impossible to face.

"I'll keep that in mind—thank you," I say sincerely. We turn back toward the large rectangular mirror, completing our makeup and hair, as the aroma of oatmeal raisin cookies invades the bathroom. "Tina, those cookies smell heavenly!"

"Thanks, honey!" she shouts from the kitchen. "They're Lena's favorite."

I catch a glimpse of Lena, who's subtly blushing. "She's a keeper, Lena."

"I'm pretty lucky. Who knows, maybe your boyfriend is a keeper too." She winks. "Now, for the moment of truth. Let's see your dress for tonight."

I nearly trip over Truman on the way to my closet. *I wonder if Kai kept me from fully tripping just now.* I scoff, then carefully pull out the most magical gown I've ever owned. If I dressed up as an angel of clouds and light on Halloween, tonight, I'm masking myself as an angel of the starry night sky. The black sheer-sleeved ball gown is covered in microscopic crystals. When light hits the dress just right, it shimmers. The sleeves are form-fitting with a floral lace design, giving the sheath dress a chic look. I chose to wear my hair half-up and half-down, leaving some wavy whisps down to frame my face. I finish the look with a delicate black lace mask. Tonight means more than what meets the eye—it's everything. My gut is telling me the choices I make tonight will have lasting consequences.

While walking onto the stage, I absorb all my surroundings. The elegant room smells of pinecones and candied cranberries. Aged Emporium's winter masquerade ball has taken the word "whimsical" to a whole new level. A large, frosted artificial tree sits in the center of the dance floor, just below the magnificent crystal chandelier. No, not a classic Christmas tree—an oak tree, barren of leaves. Instead, it's entirely frosted, completed with a few lanterns dangling off its limbs. Intricate centerpieces lie atop each table, featuring slender white candlesticks in onyx candle holders alongside vases full of white hydrangeas. Several other realistic barren trees adorned with lights and frost line the walls of the ballroom. Our staff spent hours hanging up solid snowflakes directly from the ceiling using invisible wire so the guests could witness snowflakes gently floating in mid-air amidst fairy lights twinkling throughout the grand room. I glance around to see everyone mingling amongst themselves, in good spirits. This is everything I could've envisioned and more. I don't see him, but I imagine he's around here somewhere. Nevertheless, the show must go on, so I place myself on center stage to greet all our attendees with as much grace as I can muster.

"Good evening! Our team at Soi couldn't be more thrilled you all made it. At Soi, we prioritize giving back to our community when possible, so when we learned about the Alcott family and Aged Emporium, we immediately chose to take action. You're supporting a local business and family that truly deserves it by being here tonight." I pause, noticing him in this sea of bodies, standing beside his parents. My face and heart warm simultaneously. "I've had the absolute privilege of working closely with Aged Emporium's newest owner, Jasper Alcott, throughout the last several weeks, and I can confidently say no one in town is more deserving than him. You should all be very proud of yourselves for supporting such an amazing human being."

My eyes glisten, leading me to cut the speech short. "Please, enjoy the drinks and good company, and be sure to greet the Alcott family while you can. Cheers." I hastily step off the stage, eager to breathe in some fresh air, but a hand intersects my path before I can slip outside.

"Care to dance, Greene?" I slowly peel my eyes away from the door, looking at the man holding out his hand instead. Jasper is adorned in an all-black tuxedo fashioned with a pocket square. True to his nature, he chose to forego a formal tie or bow tie. His black mask accentuates the flecks of silver in his eyes. My breath hitches—he's devastatingly handsome.

"Sure," I answer softly, deciding I can slip outside later.

The music decrescendos slowly, growing fainter with each passing movement as several couples waltz around us. I glance at his masked face and trace the outlines of it with my eyes. As his hand roams down my back, my mind wanders to the first time he stroked my back at the Halloween party earlier this fall. To my surprise, the way he's looking at me tonight isn't too different from that evening.

"What do you think of it?" I ask.

"Your gown reminds me of the midnight sky." His lips inch closer to my ear, whispering, "You look exquisite."

"I meant the ball, Jasper." I blush, looking away to hide my smile as he chuckles to himself.

"The ball exceeded every single expectation I could've had as your client."

"If I didn't know any better, I'd think you were trying to win me over, Mr. Alcott," I quip. He sweeps us closer to the edge of the dance floor near the windows, giving us a view of the gardens outside.

His grin—almost feline—stretches as he murmurs, "Who says I haven't already, Greene?"

I part my lips in awe. He takes me in his arms, and we simply dance. Our footsteps move in harmony with each other as one. He leads, and I follow without missing a single step. As we dance, our eyes meet, focusing only on each other's gaze. His hand slides even lower down my back, settling mere inches just above my rear. He pulls me into him tighter. At this moment, nothing else matters. I forget why I needed space. I forget why I ever walked away. I forget why we aren't kissing right now at this very moment. I lean in closer, studying his breathing, which is growing more rapid by the second. He feels this, too—he *has* to feel this.

I'm walking away for the both of us.

In an instant, my senses return to me with vigor. "I'm sorry, Jasper, I—I can't do this."

I break away, running aimlessly, bumping into everyone in my path and apologizing to each bystander with every step I take. At first, Jasper moves to follow me, but he is quickly intercepted by several women who I'm sure are just as intrigued by him as I am. I stumble outside, nearly missing the step down into the courtyard, and close the patio door behind me. My hand instinctively rests over my heart as I inhale deeply, trying to catch my breath. I continue stumbling for several more feet for what feels like ages until I frantically land on my knees. It's so quiet. So unbearably quiet. I vaguely analyze my surroundings, but through my blurry vision, I'm at a loss as to where I ended up. Instead, I rip off my mask and wrap my arms around my bent knees, cradling my head between them.

"Kai, I'm not sure if you're here right now," I whisper. "Honestly, I guess I can never tell when you're here. I must not be intuitive enough. I can't ever seem to feel it—feel *you*," I rasp as tears coat my cheeks and my throat tightens. "I miss you, Kai. I know Jasper says you've been here with me all this time, but if that's the case, why do I miss you so unbearably much? Why does my heart ache constantly? Am I actually *broken*?"

I take a deep breath and choke out a sob. "Knowing you're still around has... changed something in me. Now that I know you're here, I don't ever want you to leave. So, if that means I won't ever find peace, then so be it because I need you. I'll always need you, Kai."

I weep. I just want him back. I want Kai back. Why can't I feel him? Where is he right now? Can he feel my heart breaking at the mere thought of him? Can he feel my body quivering out of anxiety, fear, and despair in his absence? While rocking back and forth, my hands grow numb, succumbing to the elements.

Gradually the air begins to shift. Despite the bitter cold surrounding me in this gazebo I've grown so fond of, warmth finds me. It feels as though a current of heat swims through every inch of my body. I slowly lift my head, and to my utter disappointment, I see no one... but I cannot deny that I can *feel* something. And it's a feeling I'm not unfamiliar with.

It's the same feeling I felt when I sorted through his belongings in his apartment after.

The same feeling I felt on the first Thanksgiving without him.

The same feeling I felt when I thought I was going to get hit by a car but unexpectedly gained my footing and rose instead.

The same feeling I felt when I had a panic attack at Aged Emporium.

The same feeling I felt when I thought I lost Truman and searched throughout the Cove for him before showing up on Jasper's doorstep.

The feeling is not what I anticipated—it's not grand or obnoxious. It's a comforting essence, similar to that of the sun's warm rays on a radiant day.

This is Kai. I don't get to feel him whenever I want in whatever capacity I choose. I feel him in the moments I'm *breaking*. I reflect on all the other times I've felt this comfort, realizing that perhaps he has truly been here all along.

FORTY-ONE

JASPER

H er soft hand slips out of mine in an instant, shattering the illusion of peace that came over me just moments earlier. She walks away for the second time in the last two weeks, making my heart physically ache. I reach out my hand to catch her, but she's too swift.

When she walked onto the platform to thank our guests for being here in that starlit, tantalizing gown, I lost my mind. At that moment, all I could think about was her—the most beautiful woman I've ever known. The need to hold her in my arms took over, leading me to intercept her path the second she finished her speech. I should've known our moment of peace would be short-lived, but I'll be damned if our story ends here. I stride down the path she carved, but someone halts me. Too many people stand between me and that door she just exited through.

"Jasper, I love your shop," a blonde girl with a blue mask shouts over the music toward me. "Can I get you a drink?"

"I'm fine, thanks," I answer sharply, fixing my eyes on the door. "If you'll excuse me." I continue walking when someone familiar blocks my passage.

"We did it, Jasper!" Joy swings her arms around me. I appreciate the sentiment but now is simply not the time.

"We did," I say politely. "I've got to go, I'll catch you later."

"Joining Iris? I saw her slip outside." She inclines her head toward the door as my stress levels increase by the second. I run my fingers through my hair, nodding.

"Here." She grabs hold of my hand, ushering me through the crowd, barking orders at everyone in our way. Multiple people attempt to stir up conversations with me as we approach the exit. I can't blame them—I know I'm being the world's biggest ass right now, but I've got to get to Greene. I can't lose her. I won't.

Joy halts us in front of the exit, her grin widening as she opens the door. "Go get her."

"Thanks, Joy." I grin at her, wasting no time sneaking outside into the dark. It's far more cold and quiet out here than it is in there. Good riddance. I used to love loud parties, but those days are behind me. Now, I just want to spend time with my girl. I scan the snow-covered courtyard and gardens, tirelessly searching for her. Gradually, I feel drawn to the same gazebo where we spent our first date. As I get nearer, I spot Iris. To my dismay, she's currently cradling herself on the ground, nestling her head full of dark curls in between her knees. I approach her as quietly as possible, careful not to disrupt her. Upon getting nearer, I hear her whispering.

"*...I don't ever want you to leave. So, if that means I won't ever find peace, then so be it because I need you. I'll always need you, Kai.*" As her voice rasps and turns into a sob, my heart shatters. Everything in me wants to run to her side and help her through this. I step toward her, but someone catches my arm, pulling me back. I turn toward Kai, who's smiling softly.

"This is it, Jasper," he whispers, his eyes overfilled with tears that haven't yet fallen. "I know you're here now, and brother, I trust you. Let me do this for her. Our time is running out." Stunned, unsure of how to feel, I nod solemnly. He walks past me, straight to her side. He wraps his arms around her tighter than I've ever witnessed, squeezing his eyes shut as he embraces her. I watch the yellow glow of his power funnel into her gently, mimicking the way a stream flows down a mountainside creek. As he holds her, he rests his head on top of hers. His hold tightens, emitting the brightest light—so impossibly bright I have to shield my eyes. After a moment, his light dims, and tears evade him. He pulls away from Iris slightly and breaks out into a huge grin. I glance at her to see her looking up directly into his eyes. She may not be able to see him, but it's clear as day she *feels* him.

"Kai?" she calls out quietly after a moment of silence. Kai peers at me, motioning me to join them. As I step out of the shadows, she jumps, visibly shaken.

"Sorry to disappoint." I approach her side, slipping off my mask as she isn't wearing hers anymore either. I sit down next to her, allowing our thighs to touch. "Kai is here too, love."

Her bloodshot eyes widen. "That means—that means I felt him. I actually felt him."

"He just gave you the most obnoxious hug I've ever seen," I joke, glancing at Kai, who rolls his eyes in response.

"Jasper, can you tell her something for me?" His expression sombers. "She thinks the key to solving her problems is for me to come back, but really, *she* needs to come back. The world without the true Iris isn't whole. Even after I ascend, I'll still be watching, just from afar. She won't be alone. Ever."

I repeat his exact message. Her eyes brim with tears again as she rests her hand over her heart. "Jasper, what happens when you find your safe place, your home, in a person, and you lose that person? When I lost my safe place, I think—I think I lost myself, and I haven't found my way back because I don't feel like I have anywhere to call home anymore."

"I'll be your home, Iris." I place a gentle kiss on her forehead. Kai rises and walks out of the gazebo, leaving us. Her lips tremble as she shakes her head.

"I'm not asking for a new home. I just want my old one back. You can see him, talk to him even, maybe that's enough. Maybe we can continue this for years, and eventually, I'll somehow find peace—" I lift her chin mid-sentence, then stroke her damp cheek with my thumb.

"Greene, I won't ever replace your old home. I know Kai. I can't compare our relationship to the relationship you had with him. Sometimes, though, we have to build our own safe place and search for true peace there. I will keep you safe. I will give you space when you need it. You don't ever have to put a smile on your face when you're hurting, especially not in my company. It is *not* your responsibility to hide your grief from others. I'm sorry I didn't say this sooner, Iris, but I'm saying it now because I can't wait a second longer before sharing *my* truth with you."

I tuck a strand of hair behind her ear and gaze into her mesmerizing mossy eyes subtly reflecting the moonlight. "I've never felt this way. I've been racking my brain, trying to determine how to proceed from here, but there is no other way to describe the depth of my feelings. I love you, Greene. I've loved you for quite some time now. I've walked through life without the privilege of your company for nearly three decades, and I can't fathom taking another step without you. Not anymore, love."

Our eyes remain locked on each other. At this moment, nothing matters more than how she feels. If she wants to walk away one final time, I'll respect that. I will always trust her judgment. Similar to my friend Kai, I just want her to find peace. If her peace can only be found elsewhere, then so be it. She deserves nothing less. Eventually, I break eye contact. "I'll respect whatever decision you need to make here. Hit me with whatever you've got."

A few seconds later, she breaks the silence with a whisper saying, "I wasn't sure how you felt, and I can't stand the thought of losing you. But what if hypothetically speaking, my feelings mirror your own?" She looks away, biting her lip and intertwining her fingers in mine, holding my hand. "I've felt like a burden for years, but in your arms, I feel weightless—lighter than a feather. I *love* you, Jasper. More than I ever could've imagined possible."

My heart stills. She loves me. *Iris loves me.*

In an instant, I rise, pulling her off the ground of the dimly lit gazebo. I embrace her with a fierceness I've never known and inhale her scent of honeyed vanilla.

She is *mine*—my love, my light, my everything. I soften my hold and lean back to look at her, my hands resting on her waist. Slowly, her smile fades away.

"But I just feel like I already know how this will end," she rasps. "If I ever lose you... Jasper, I'm so scared."

Hearing her admission strikes a chord deep inside me. I gently move my hands upward, following the slope of her back all the way up to her neck, eventually cradling her soft face in them. "I'll admit, I'm scared too. But if feeling afraid is what it takes, I'd rather feel terrified than lose you."

Then I lean in, parting my lips, and kiss her hungrily. I've missed her taste so fucking much, I'm already feeling weak in the knees, and she hasn't even slipped her tongue out yet. She has made a mess of me. Our lips break apart, leaving us breathless. I crush her against my chest, then pull back to gaze into her eyes again.

"*The only emotion that equates to love is fear,*" she mumbles to herself quietly. "Kai said that once."

"Really? Kai said that? How uncharacteristic, but eh, I guess it's fitting for the occasion," I quip. I search for him and take note of the eerie silence. "Hey, it's quiet as Hell out here, Greene. How are you feeling?"

"About the quiet? I feel okay. Not great, but not anxious." She gazes around, then continues, "About us? I *may* be squealing inside a little."

We both burst into laughter. Ah, I love this girl. "Do you mind if I ask why the quiet bothers you?" We walk over to the outer edge of the gazebo, leaning on the railing.

"No one has ever asked that before." She pauses, stroking her hand up and down my back. "Then again, I think you're the only person who ever caught on to how much I loathed the quiet. I suppose I found comfort in chaos and despair in quiet moments. I embraced chaos and greeted it as if it were an old friend, even. The quiet was not welcome, nor would it ever be. Or so I thought. Then, you came along."

I caress her arm and urge her to continue. "I found comfort in chaos because the last time I ever heard Kai's voice was amongst a sea of chaos. I didn't lose him in the chaos. I lost him in the lingering stillness that came after. That same stillness settled in, making itself at home. I've avoided that side of myself for so long because every time the quiet takes over, I think of Kai and the moment he took his last breath. To me, accepting the silence equates to letting him go." My gut clenches at the thought of how painful this has been for her.

"Remind me—didn't you say that you and Kai were listening to music in his final moments? Didn't he smile at you?" I ask. She looks away, and a subtle smile reaches her lips. She nods. "How did you feel at that moment?"

"I didn't have a care in the world," she admits. I hear footsteps and see Kai approaching us.

"I didn't either, Irie," he says, grinning. "I loved that moment. It was the perfect ending to my life on Earth."

"Greene, Kai says that moment was the perfect ending to his life." I continue to gaze into her eyes. She lets out a quiet laugh as tears cascade down her cheek. "Baby, I'm proud of you for embracing and releasing your emotions. You can hold onto your memories with Kai forever and still let this weight go when you're ready. You deserve to feel joy—true joy." We sit in silence for a moment. Instead of fidgeting, Iris stands up straight and smiles at me.

"Thank you, Jasper," she says. "For everything." I glance over at Kai, telling him to get lost with my eyes, to which he shrugs and folds his arms.

Seriously, Kai. Unless you want to watch your sister and me make out, it's best you move along.

What? I thought you guys had an event you're both hosting to tend to. I'm here to remind you.

Why are you mind speaking to me? She can't hear you anyway.

Mind speaking is fun. I don't know how much longer I'll be able to do it.

I sigh, rubbing my forehead.

"Everything okay?" she asks.

"Yes, everything is just fine, I'm just getting a headache from dealing with your brother, that's all." I smirk at Kai, who's currently rolling his eyes harder than ever. "In all seriousness, he did remind me that we're hosting the event inside. Do you care? If not, I'm happy to take you home for some real fun."

"What? Of course, I care! Don't you?" She gawks.

"Well, I care about the cause, sure. But truthfully? I want nothing more than to have you all to myself for the rest of the night." I gaze at her, taking note of the sudden pinkness of her cheeks.

"For Heaven's sake, Jasper," Kai gags obnoxiously. "I'm still here!"

And whose fault is that?

"Here, I've got an idea," Iris unknowingly interrupts our conversation, putting her lacy black mask back on. "Let's go back inside and dance together one more time—to make up for our last two dances together, of course. Then, we'll head home."

"I'm in, Greene."

FORTY-TWO

IRIS

As we follow the rocky path back to the roaring ballroom hand in hand, I sneak a quick glance at Jasper. Moonlight beams directly on his chiseled face, illuminating his bright eyes and sharp jawline. The moon suits Jasper, similar to the way the sun suited Kai. Upon thinking of Kai, a dozen memories come to mind all at once: hiding Halloween candy from our parents, sneaking out for midnight fast food runs, cheering him on from the sidelines of his baseball games... and for once, I don't push the memories aside. Instead, I embrace them and crack the slightest of smiles in his memory. The pain remains, but now, a sliver of joy lingers along with it, too.

"What are you smiling about over there?" Jasper nudges me coyly.

"I'm just feeling... light." I smile even brighter, causing his grin to stretch. I catch his arm and turn around to peer at the pond behind us. Now, confusion crosses his features. "The only thing that would make this moment better is catching some ducks in action."

Jasper lets out an exasperated breath and smirks, wrapping his arm around my neck tightly and kissing my ear. "Those damn ducks ruined our first date." I laugh mischievously while leaning into him.

"Oh, please, those ducks couldn't have ruined our first date even if they actually tried." I bite my lip. He loves me. Jasper *loves* me. And I love him. I never would have imagined this would be the outcome of our business partnership. He straightens his matte black suit jacket and then holds the door to the ballroom open for me. We slip inside, unnoticed, save for two people who happen to matter very much.

"Where have you been?" Jasper's mom approaches us, gazing at us knowingly while standing behind his dad's wheelchair. She motions for me to wipe my lips. *Thank you,* I mouth in response while fixing my lipstick.

"Admiring the moon," Jasper says nonchalantly, stepping behind me and tightening his arms around my waist, causing several guests to gawk at us in curiosity.

"I see," she grins, her eyes twinkling beneath her burgundy mask. "Well, we just wanted to thank you, Iris. You've changed our lives in more ways than one." She pulls me in for a warm hug.

"It was no problem at all, Mrs. Alcott," I say. She waves her hand.

"Please, call me Irene." She winks.

"You two have fun." His dad nods at us, smirking. As they stroll away, our audience still sneaks glances at us. My eyes search the crowd for Joy, but instead, I find Lena sitting with Tina at a round table in the corner. Our eyes meet, and her face softens as she gazes between Jasper and I. *Proud of you*, she mouths from afar, causing my eyes to water in response. It's ridiculous; two months ago, I hadn't cried in ages, and now I cry over just about everything. I smile and nod at her just once, then quickly glance away to avoid bursting into even more tears. I continue my search for Joy, finally finding her nearby, next to the F&B (food and beverage) table. I trudge through the crowd toward her, tugging him right behind me.

"I think this has been a huge success." Her smile glows. "Is there anything else I can do to help? I've been keeping an eye on the F&B table while you stepped away, we were running low on cream puffs, so I went ahead and asked Maurice to refill that tray, but other than that, we are good." I peer behind her at the refreshments table, taking note of how perfectly placed every single porcelain tray is. I glance around the room to see an endless amount of beaming faces, some familiar, some strange, but all filled with light.

"I'm so proud of you, Joy! This is one of the most successful fundraisers we've ever hosted, and it all started with you. I can't thank you enough. Would you be up for taking the reins for the rest of the evening?" Her jaw drops, and then she breaks out into a huge, outrageously contagious smile.

"Is that even a question? Of course! Leave it to me." She grins. "I'll get on it. Thanks for the opportunity!"

We say good night, and I turn to see Jasper swaying to the music with a smug smile on his face. *Well, that's sexy.* He extends his hand to me while dipping his head. "Let's see if we can get through one full song together."

"Let's." I take hold of his hand. Rather than letting fear dictate my next move, I follow his lead, careful not to break away. He twirls me and brings me back to him, holding me closer to him than before. I close my eyes and lean my head against his chest as the music whispers into my very soul. For the first time, we dance in true, uninterrupted *peace.*

No longer am I questioning the depth of his feelings for me, nor my own feelings for him.

No longer am I wearing a mask to conceal my emotions.

No longer am I a prisoner of my grief. Instead, I'm its master.

Today's the day. I will go there today.

In a swift movement, I let go of his hand and shed my lace mask, flinging it across the room. Breathlessly, I fall into weightless laughter and gaze into his eyes, embracing the storms held within them. He gazes at me in awe, joining me in my delight. His hands roam to the curves of my waist, pulling me closer to him and swaying us to the rhythm of the music. Observers may think I've gone mad, but I am simply unconcerned.

I am free.

At this moment, I make a vow, a promise to myself to keep until my dying breath: I will not lose myself again. Never again.

Jasper and I sneak out of our own event early. I wish I could say I was sorry, but for once, I'm not feeling sorry. I'm ready to spend time with my boyfriend. Honestly, the term "boyfriend"

doesn't do the feelings I have for him justice. Since our very first encounter, I've felt drawn to him.

We settle on returning to my apartment—I would rather not leave Truman alone if I don't have to. As we drive back, Jasper rests his hand on my upper thigh. A moment later, I notice him gazing into his rearview mirror, making strange facial expressions. No *way*.

"You know, it's not nice to leave people out." I pout. "What are you guys talking about?"

Startled, Jasper peers at me in the corner of his eye, then sighs. "Sorry, Greene. I forget I don't really have to hide this from you anymore—" Jasper pauses as if he was interrupted, then rolls his eyes. "If you recall, it is *your* fault I had to hide this from her in the first place. You and I both know keeping this from her didn't sit right with me, but you practically begged me to."

Well, isn't this fascinating? I'm picking up bits and pieces based on my limited context, but if I were to guess, Kai *really* likes bothering Jasper, and that alone makes me giggle. Failing to suppress a chuckle, Jasper cuts a glance my way.

"What? What is it?" Before I can respond, he scowls while looking in the rearview mirror. "Shut it, Kai."

"What? What did Kai say?" My heart leaps; it feels nice knowing Kai is here. After tonight, I don't know how much longer I'll get to hear from him through Jasper's... gift. I'm not sure what to call it.

"He said you were laughing at me."

"Oh. Well, he's right," I tease. "I just find your relationship dynamics mildly entertaining, that's all."

"Thanks, Greene," he huffs.

"Anytime," I joke, stroking his arm. "So, is Kai a third wheel on all our dates? And is he always sitting in the back seat? Oh, and did he happen to figure out why you get the pleasure of seeing him when no one else does?"

"Whoa, whoa, whoa. First, Kai doesn't like being referred to as a third wheel." I bite back a huge grin. "But yes, he is constantly third wheeling with us. He's done it several times at this point, proving to be a pain in my ass—" He glares at his mirror.

"Again, he insists we do not classify his company as 'third wheeling.'" He glowers, turning down my street. I glance over my shoulder to the backseat, disappointed to see nothing, but nod nonetheless.

"You've got it, Kai." I chuckle.

"Anyway, yes, Kai tends to tag along, but he isn't always around. Sometimes, he isn't present during our time together at all. Actually, he has a sixth sense connecting him to you, so if you're in danger, whether it be emotional or physical, he's alerted. Meaning that he can step away whenever he'd like because he can teleport back to you instantly if something is wrong. Yes, he sits in the back seat during our drives when he rides with us, but again, he isn't always here." Jasper's brows pull together in confusion. "As far as your final question goes, he says he has determined why I can see him when no one else can, but it's best we go over it back at your place for some reason."

"So, I guess he is heading upstairs to hang out with us for a bit then?" I grin mischievously as Jasper pulls into my apartment's parking lot.

"Guess so."

"I don't mind the company—I'll take whatever we can get while we still have him," I smile softly, fidgeting with my dress. Jasper gently grabs hold of my hand, leading me to glimpse at him.

"Believe it or not, me too," he begrudgingly admits.

My heartbeat increases rapidly with every step upstairs to my apartment. I want nothing more than to be held in his arms all night long.

FORTY-THREE

JASPER

I play with her long, wavy locks while lounging on the sofa with a mug of black coffee in hand. Because it was so chilly outside, she insisted on brewing coffee for us as soon as we entered her apartment—of course, she filled hers with every creamer imaginable. Truman greeted us, brushing the entirety of his stout body against my leg. I bet down to pet him, earning a soft purr. I've always been more of a dog person than a cat person, but Truman has grown on me. I love that little troublemaker.

I stop messing with her hair and toss my arm around her shoulders, tucking her closely into my side. She leans her head against me and rests her tired eyes. She has had a long night, but it's far from over. While counting her freckles, Kai clears his throat.

"Jasper, every moment counts—I need to tell you something. Both of you." Kai plops down on the floor. Truman wastes no time in rushing to his side to say hello. As Kai strokes him, Truman leans into his touch.

"Greene, Kai would like to share something with us," I whisper into her ear. She gazes back at me with heat in her eyes. Damn, it's been too long.

Kai, can it wait?

"Nope, let's talk now. There will be plenty of time for you two to do... whatever it is you do... after this." Kai cringes, folding his arms.

"You ready?" She nods, looking directly in Kai's direction.

"So, why can Jasper see you when I can't?" she boldly asks.

"Alright, Jasper. I need you to listen closely and reiterate all of this information the best you can to Irie." I nod, urging him to continue. I haven't got the slightest clue why I can see Kai, so I'm just as intrigued to know as Iris is. "Do you remember the Middle Realm? Well, I visited that realm recently to see if I could gather more information from the Archives on why you can see me when other mortals can't. I meandered into the Archives with the help of another angel. After she walked out of the area, I began sorting through records. Eventually, I came across a basket of scrolls containing information on cases in history in which this occurred. One in particular struck me."

Kai bobs his throat and swallows. "A deceased woman named Jenna chose to be a guardian angel for a man in his 30s who was riddled with crippling depression in New York back in the 90s. He resorted to drowning himself in alcohol to block out his emptiness and nearly got lost in his addiction before she came along. She spent months with him, helping him to heal. He was making great progress. One day, they took the subway together.

While on the subway, she noticed someone staring at her—it wasn't uncommon for angels to run into each other while in a city as large as NYC—nothing like the Cove. Jenna assumed the woman was an angel, so she smiled. Upon closer look though, Jenna realized the woman was not an angel at all. Stunned, she teleported out of the subway to the surface for a moment to get fresh air. She chose to wait for her guarded at his stop, feeling he would be safe on the subway—I guess the subway was safer back then than it is now or something.

"Twenty minutes later, the man exited the subway. She approached and noticed him laughing for the first time in months. Once she got closer, she recognized the same woman on the train walking in step with him. Stunned yet again, Jenna crouched behind a pillar and waited for them to pass, choosing to follow behind them at a distance. She was positive the woman had seen her, so when the woman and her guarded started dating, she felt skeptical and kept her distance as much as possible. But as time went on, her guarded became lighter and lighter. She even became friends with the woman. On their wedding day, Jenna's time with her assignment was up. She recorded all her findings, hoping one day someone would be able to explain the phenomenon.

"So, considering you are able to see me without my help, I took it up with the Archangels myself after learning about Jenna. They weren't pleased I was seeking out such confidential information, but I played it off. I acted like I was just researching out of mere curiosity. I'm sure they bought it. Anyway, I asked them why a mortal would be able to see a guardian angel when other mortals can't, and you'll never guess the answer." Kai's hazel eyes lock with mine. "Now that you believe in angels, hopefully, it'll be easier for your skeptical ass to believe this too. Soulmates are real. Most people aren't lucky enough to find their soulmate in their lifetime, so they unite with them in the afterlife instead.

"However, there is no doubt here. You and Irie are soulmates—bound to find each other in every lifetime at every cost. Considering this occurrence is extremely rare, there isn't a ton of research on it, but the reason you can see me when no one else can is because of how strong your bond is. You're in tune with her—in mind, body, and soul."

Soulmates. I am in tune with Iris—in mind, body, and soul. I nearly drop my cup of coffee as goosebumps spread across every inch of my body. I quickly set it down on the coffee table to avoid it from spilling as my mind spins in every direction.

She turns toward me with concern in her eyes. "What? What is it? What did he share?"

Right. She can't even hear him, so it's up to me.

"Kai says the reason I can see you is because—"

"Um, Jasper? Hello? Are you not going to share any of the background details I so *graciously* risked everything to gather for you?" Kai glares at me. I let out a sigh.

"Well, Kai said he did some research and found evidence of this happening another time a few decades ago, and in that case, it was because the person who could see the angel was actually the guarded's... soulmate," I say. "Soulmates are real. Kai believes we are soulmates, bound to find each other in every lifetime at all costs."

I let that information sink in as I hold her in my grasp, breathing slowly. Finally, she asks, "Well, what do you believe?"

"I could ask you the same question." The corner of my lips tugs upward into a smile.

"I don't know, Jasper. Would it be crazy if I felt like this explanation actually makes sense?"

"Yes, absolutely crazy," I say, watching her nose crinkle. "First, we learn that angels exist, and now, we learn that soulmates do, too? I'm not buying it. What will it be next? Demons? Warlocks?"

Silence hums between us. "Oh... so you don't believe we could be soulmates?"

I rest my head in the crook of her neck, letting my lips brush against her ear. Then, I whisper, with the intent of my quiet words reaching her heart. "The moment I watched you waltz into that coffee shop like you owned the place, I knew I was in trouble. I've felt inexplicably drawn to you since that very first moment before I ever even knew your name. Every time I've seen you since then, I've felt the pull grow stronger and stronger. *You're* the reason I believe in soulmates, Greene."

Her breath hitches, then she turns to gaze directly into my eyes. I peer into her green irises, allowing them to unravel me. "You're mine," she declares, wrapping her arms around my neck.

I lift her chin to steal a kiss. Our lips join together for a perfect moment of serenity. Then, yet again, we are interrupted by her pesky brother clearing his throat.

"Well, I'll see myself out, I guess." He stands up, placing his hands on his hips. "Be safe, kids." He waves a finger at me sternly. I throw a couch pillow at him irritably. He chuckles maniacally and shows himself out. "I'll see you both tomorrow. Keep her safe tonight, Jasper."

I *always will.*

After he fades away, I embrace Iris in my arms. *Soulmates.* Ever since meeting the Greenes, all the logic I stored inside my mind for years on end has been thrown out the window. Oddly enough, I couldn't care less. If letting go of logic is what led me to hold my soulmate in my arms, then I'd give it all up. Without warning, I scoop her up and carry her to the bedroom relinquishing in the sound of her laugh. She jokingly tells me to put her down, but we both know that isn't *really* what she wants. Upon walking into her room, I realize I haven't taken a good look at this room since her apartment flooded nearly two months ago. Her walls are lined with loads of art and decor, and a night mask alongside a jewelry box rests on the nightstand. My attention is pulled away as her body is calling my name.

I lay her on the bed and trace the outline of her body with my hands, pressing firmly along the curves of her hips and thighs. Her starlight dress clings graciously to her body. She really does embody the midnight sky right now. I've said it before, I'll say it again: this woman is a *goddess*. I motion for her to rise. After she stands, she turns away, prompting me to unzip her gown. As I slide the zipper down her backside, my eyes linger on the slope of it. The starry dress falls to the ground, pooling around her ankles. From behind her, I pull her into me and hoarsely whisper into her ear. "Do you trust me?"

"Yes," she whispers.

I glimpse at her nightstand. "Close your eyes, Greene."

She obliges, fluttering her eyes closed.

"Good girl," I whisper in her ear before wandering over to the wooden nightstand and picking up her sleep mask. I gently lift her head and slip it on, shielding her eyes from any trace of light in the room. I wish I would've brought a blindfold, but after putting the mask on her, it's clear this will work just fine. I guide her to the bed and lay her down on the cotton sheets, ready to worship every inch of her. She lets out a breathy moan as my lips graze her waist. *For fuck's sake*—I'm already so hard I'm throbbing, yet we have just begun.

After tasting nearly every part of her body and still craving more, I suck on her delicious breast. My hand roams down, finding its way between her legs. I push my fingers against her center and rub circles around it for as much time as she can take eventually slipping a finger in, and she moans louder, making my head spin. I fall into a steady rhythm, eventually adding a second finger into the mix, all while keeping my thumb pressed directly on her, resulting in Iris fisting her hands in my hair. As she tugs on my hair, I break away from her breasts, allowing a guttural groan to escape my lips. "Greene, you're *mine*. My *everything*."

I slip the mask off of her with my free hand, wanting to look directly into her ethereal green eyes as we bind our bodies together. Her hooded eyes bore into mine.

"*Please, Jasper*." Pleasure shoots up my spine upon hearing her breathe my name.

"Say no more, baby." I pull my fingers out and taste the faint trace of her left behind, causing her head to roll back in pleasure. She tastes *delectable*. I need more. I mount her, planting my knees on either side, pressing myself against her. "I'm all yours, Greene."

Lights dance in her eyes as her wet lips curve into a smile. "And I'm yours." That sentiment alone is my great undoing. After a *mindblowing* night, I cradle her in my arms with our legs tangled under the sheets. I hold her all night long making a silent vow never to let go.

FORTY-FOUR

IRIS

"Jasper, where are we going?" I ask for the third time since jumping into his car. He insists he can't tell me, but he and I both know he could tell me if he wanted to. He's simply refusing to cooperate here, and as endearing as he is, I can only find ignorance blissful for so long.

"Can't tell you, Greene." He bites his lip. He seems nervous which is unlike him.

"Can't? Or *won't*?" I goad him.

"Both are the same in this instance, really," he remarks coyly while his lips curl into a smile. I haven't been able to take my eyes off the fullness of his lips since last night. Waking up in his arms today felt better than it ever has. However, he interrupted our slumber, absolutely adamant about taking me on a drive. As we wind around the mountain, I recognize our surroundings well. Too well.

"Are we going where I think we are?" I ask hesitantly.

"We are." He sighs, taking his eyes off the road for only a second to glance into mine. "I'm here. I won't leave your side."

My heartbeat quickens as I process what this means. I thought I would get more time. How foolishly naive I was to think time would be merciful. We pull around the one last bend, nearing a rustic wooden plaque resting on the shoulder's edge. I avoided looking at it the last time Jasper and I passed by, but this time, I can't take my eyes off of it. We slow down and come to a stop on the shoulder next to the railing, overlooking the picturesque mountain range covered by a sheet of glistening snow. Jasper walks over to open my door for me. I gaze into his eyes as he reaches for my hand. "It's time, Greene."

I slip my hand into his and allow him to pull me out of the car. I approach the memorial and run my fingers along the plaque's rim, my eyes fixated on the image of my brother. My best friend. "This is my first time stopping here," I admit in a whisper. "I honestly didn't know if I'd ever be strong enough to."

"He's here," Jasper says, pressing a kiss to my temple. "He wants a proper send-off. He figured it'd be best to do it here."

I peer over the mountainside as dozens of memories of my road trips with Kai flash before my eyes. "Why here?"

"He says he wants his guardianship on Earth to encapsulate the circle of life thing, and because this is where he died, it's only fitting," he jokes. I choke back a defeated laugh.

"Kai always did love *The Lion King*," I reminisce. "He said we were like two of the characters."

"Which ones, Simba and Nala?" He raises his brows.

"What? Oh, no, of course not," I scoff. "Timon and Pumbaa. He said I was like Timon and he was like Pumbaa."

He barks out a laugh and quickly covers his mouth, attempting but clearly failing to hold it back. "Sorry, it's just... I can totally see it." He wraps his arm around me.

"Well, I'll just take that as a compliment." I look away, withholding a smile. "Timon was always the sensible one anyway. Pumbaa was too boisterous for my taste."

"Sounds about right." He rests his head on mine. "Kai apparently thinks Timon was a stick in the mud compared to Pumbaa. He says he's a 'Pumbaa Supremacist.'" I burst out into laughter, but it trails off as I get lost in a series of memories circling around Kai, both good and bad.

"Jasper, I don't know how to do this..." My eyes burn.

"How about you talk to him directly? Pretend I'm not even here. I'll just be his mouthpiece." He keeps his arm wrapped around me. "He's standing right in front of you, looking into your eyes. Say what you need to say; I'll repeat his exact responses, okay?"

Acknowledging this is the only way I'll be able to do this, I nod and pull away from Jasper. Currently, my only focus is connecting with Kai. Squeezing my eyes shut, I try to envision him standing in front of me. If I could see him, I imagine he would be towering over me. He'd probably be wearing a T-shirt and jeans. His golden skin would shine effortlessly in the morning sunlight, and a single lock of his light sandy brown hair would fall, resting above his defined eyebrows. At this moment, he'd flash his pearly white teeth at me in that infectious grin he always had. This is how I remember my brother. Keeping my eyes closed, I speak, not caring to filter what I share. If this is all we get, I'm not holding anything back.

"None of this is fair, Kai. This isn't how our lives were supposed to go."

"How were our lives supposed to go, Irie?"

"We were supposed to do more late-night fast food runs. We were supposed to watch more new movies together and make fun of the actors' facial expressions. We were supposed to go on more scenic drives. We were supposed to sit side-by-side at more awkward family dinners. We were supposed to be at each other's weddings. We were supposed to grow old and complain about our crappy neighbors." I hold back my tears, refusing to let them fall. "Together."

A gentle breeze sweeps across my face before he responds. "You may not feel me as strongly after today, but I assure you, I'll be watching. When you're craving greasy tacos at one o'clock in the morning, you better go get those tacos and savor them. I'll be there. When you go to the movies, laugh extra obnoxiously at all the ridiculous facial expressions those actors use. When you miss me, go on a mountain drive and turn up the stereo. The louder you play that music, the better. Oh, and you better believe I won't ever miss an opportunity for an uncomfortable evening at the Greene Household. And Irie, Heaven and Hell can't stop me from attending your wedding. Hell, I better be Jasper's best man." As Jasper speaks, his voice fades away—instead, I only hear the voice of my big brother, comforting me as he always has. "But Irie, fate is real, and this was my fate all along. This is my place now, and you can't imagine how free I feel knowing that you're finally embracing your emotions. If this was my life's purpose, I got damn lucky because despite how awful our parents were to you at times, I've always known you were something special."

No longer able to hold back my tears, the floodgates open. Soon, my cheeks are coated. A thumb strokes my cheek, brushing tears away while I keep my eyes shut to hold onto the illusion just a little longer. "You'll be okay, Irie. I've been your guardian for years now. You're stronger than I ever was. I'm confident you'll be invincible by the time we meet again."

"I miss you so much, Kai." My voice breaks. "I'll never stop missing you."

"I know," he answers softly. "The grief won't ever fully subside. But as time goes on, you'll find it feels different. I have a feeling you're already noticing a small difference in the way your grief feels now than it felt initially, right?" I nod. "See, that's what I mean. Accepting the full weight of your grief used to be scarier for you than it is now. You're already doing what I couldn't, Irie—you're choosing love over fear. In embracing your feelings, you're choosing to love yourself. I'm so beyond proud of you. Even if you did end up falling for a dude like Jasper."

I let out a small chuckle and wipe my cheeks, which is no use, considering I can't stop weeping. My throat tightens. I know I shouldn't ask. I have no right to after all he's done for me, but the words spill out nonetheless. "Kai, can I please see you one more time? Just once? *Please*?" A moment of silence passes between us.

"The truth is, seeing me won't make the pain go away, Irie," he says lightly as a gentle breeze surrounds us again. "Here, keep your eyes closed. I can actually see the image in your mind. Hold onto that."

I keep my eyes closed and await something—anything. Then, I feel warmth spreading throughout my body, similar to last night. Only, this time, the warmth feels more defined. It feels like... him. I envision Kai engulfing me in his arms while keeping my eyes sealed shut. I feel him holding me the way he used to. He towers over me, resting his head atop mine gently while holding me fiercely. Wasting no time, I raise my arms and wrap him in the tightest embrace I can.

As I bury my head into my brother's chest, I give in and let it all go. Uncontrollable sobs escape me. Kai has always been the sun in my cloud-filled sky—his embrace brightens the darkest corners of my heart. While he holds me, all our memories flash before my eyes, including the accident itself. Rather than pushing them away, I watch them replay in my mind, engraving every moment. How lucky I am to have had a brother like Kai.

"I know it's cliche as hell, but it's not goodbye," he whispers into my hair. "I'll see you later. As much as it kills me to say it, you're in good hands—I know *Truman* will keep you very safe."

I burst into laughter, accidentally opening my eyes, and to my utter shock, bright hazel eyes peer back into mine. My jaw drops as I quickly glance to my left and see Jasper staring at us in reverence, with tears in his eyes. Shocked at the sight before me, my lips tremble. "Kai? You're—you're really here?"

"I told you—I've been here all along. I wanted you to see for yourself just this once. Consequences be damned." He grins, then turns around to overlook the mountains. "I've got to go. My mission is complete. I want you to promise me to live every minute, Irie."

"I promise, Kai." I say, finding I actually mean it. As I stare at him, I memorize his features, accepting this is the very last time I'll ever see him on this side. We share a smile, then he breaks eye contact and glimpses at Jasper while still holding me in his arms.

"Thank you, brother." His voice cracks. "You are enough, Jasper—more than enough. I would've loved to have gotten to know you under better circumstances, but that wasn't in the cards for us. We'll catch up on the other side, buddy."

"I'm going to miss you, bro." Jasper swallows. My heart aches watching the two of them say goodbye to each other. "More than I'd like to admit."

"Aw, I'm so glad you finally admitted it." He beams, yanking Jasper into our embrace. I find myself wishing this moment could last a lifetime. I never want to let go of them—the two men who mean more to me than life itself. "Time's up. I'll be waiting, you two."

Kai winks at us and pulls away, fading into the sky where he's always belonged.

FORTY-FIVE

JASPER

It's been way too quiet for my comfort recently. Look, I know Iris used to loathe the quiet, so this is her thing. But somehow, the annoying angel who insisted on constantly referring to me as his buddy may have grown on me. So, when Kai kissed this world goodbye, he kissed my ass goodbye, too—rather abruptly, I might add. I've spent an excessive amount of time with her over the last several days—no complaints here—and I've found myself actually looking for him. This is uncharted territory for me. I didn't know him during his mortal life, but I got to know him extensively during his afterlife, so saying goodbye was hard. Period.

If I'm being honest, I'm a little worried about him. He told me the number one rule of guardianship was to remain discreet.

By the end, he broke the most important rule, revealing himself to her. Of course, Kai being the idiot he is, even declared the consequences can be damned. It's tearing me up not knowing what happened to him after our fateful encounter.

"What's got you looking so serious over there?" she asks with mischief in her eyes while she packs her suitcase.

"Baby, this is just my face," I answer nonchalantly.

"Jasper, maybe that's what the world sees, but we both know that isn't what I usually see," she says while packing a dainty little yellow lingerie set. I'm going to have a *fan-fucking-tastic* weekend.

"Fair enough." I sigh, plopping down on her bed. Truman immediately jumps onto my lap, obviously expecting to be pet. I stroke his orange fur, deciding to confide in my love. "Well, there's no point in hiding it. I guess I'm still getting used to not seeing him around."

She pauses mid-action, then rests her hands atop her luggage. She peers up into my eyes from her position on the floor. "You're missing Kai."

"I guess," I grunt. She joins me on her bed, letting our thighs touch.

"Why do you think you're feeling this way?" She rubs my back gently, leading me to wonder how I ever survived without her touch.

"I don't know. He drove me crazy. He crashed all our dates, tried to force us apart at first, drank my beer without asking, and constantly called me 'buddy,' despite my protests." I scoff. "He was a pain in my ass if I'm being honest. I don't know why I feel like this."

"Jasper, you should know by now what this means." Her hand roams from my back to my front, resting on my heart soothingly. "You're grieving."

"I'm grieving a guy I never even knew before he died? Nonsense." I ignore the sinking feeling in my chest.

"Just give yourself time. I'll be here to talk when you're ready." As I think about her statement, my head hurts. *That's* what this unbearable feeling in my chest is? I can't even begin to comprehend how she navigated through this seemingly alone for years.

"Okay, Greene. You may be right," I whisper. "I guess I'm grieving... This is my first time losing him, and to be frank, it's heavy. But yes, I think I just need some time to process it."

"I'll always be here. I miss him, too," she says with tears in her eyes. "Ugh, I cry over *everything* now. It's exhausting."

I chuckle and wrap both of my arms around her, pulling her toward me and whispering, "Well, I love it."

She rolls her eyes and elbows me, wiggling her way out of my grasp. I reach for her again and miss. Her eyes shine bright with victory as she sinks back down to the floor to resume packing. We're heading to her parents' home for the holidays—shocking, I know. It certainly wasn't my idea. It wasn't her idea, either. Her mom actually invited her, and for once, she sounded excited to host her daughter. I wasn't sure about going at first, but after seeing the hope in her eyes, I knew I had to support her in this.

If she wants to work on mending the relationship she has with her parents, I'll walk with her every step of the way. If she chooses to cut them out of her life forever, I'll stand by her side proudly for that, too. Wherever Iris goes, I'll follow.

Thankfully, we could both take a couple of days off of work to enjoy the break. Business at Aged Emporium has been booming since the fundraiser. We received thousands of dollars in generous donations, a majority of which is going toward a major renovation of the shop. One of those renovation projects includes the installation of an elevator. When I told my parents the news, my mom immediately burst into hysterics, which wasn't shocking. To my surprise, though, my dad choked up, too. He loves Aged Emporium with all his heart; he deserves to be able to wander to whatever corner of the shop he pleases without limitation, and in a few months, he will.

With all the extra business, Aged Emporium is already exceeding expectations. In other words, we're no longer in the hole. In fact, we're nowhere near the hole. I'm hoping never to get close to that hole again, plainly speaking. And while I'm on the subject, I have to admit, managing Aged Emporium has grown on me. Lately, instead of dreading spending my days there, I look forward to them.

We're planning on spending the weekend with Greene's folks, then we're heading back to the Cove early so I can get her all to myself for the remainder of our time off. *I. Can't. Wait.* We prioritized being back in time for Trivia Tuesday—Callie will kill us if we miss another anytime soon.

"Hey, do you mind grabbing me a Tupperware set from the kitchen?"

"Um, sure," I answer, raising an eyebrow.

"What? My parents never keep leftovers, so they don't even own good Tupperware," she answers defensively.

"Whatever you say, Greene," I taunt, strolling out of her bedroom toward the kitchen. As I open the fridge, I see an unopened bottle of beer. I reach for it and realize it's a beer from my home.

"Hey, did you grab one of my beers from my place before we got here?" I shout from the kitchen.

"Nope, why?" If Iris didn't grab this, then... I scoff, realizing how impossible *this* seems. Now Kai is just screwing with me. He knows I'm a skeptic, so he probably assumed this would drive me insane. Instead of being driven to insanity by this, I'm actually feeling a sense of relief. I remember the first time we drank together all too well. I don't need an explanation this time. Instead, I crack open the bottle and swallow, choking back tears.

Damn. Kai was something else.

"Well, that was an eventful day." Iris sighs as she settles into her teenage bed that barely fits the both of us. "I'm already ready to go home."

"I'm always ready to go home at this point," I grumble, climbing underneath the sheets next to her, wrapping her in my arms and breathing in her scent. "Speaking of home... I want to give something to you, Greene."

"Oh, baby, as much as I would love ownership of your home, I'm in a little over my head as is at the moment," she taunts. I roll my eyes in response, resulting in her barking out a laugh.

"You're relentless," I say.

"So I've been told," she jokes. I love seeing this side of my girl. Ever since Kai ascended, she has been more airy than ever.

"I'm being serious, though. Here, sit up." I rise, leaning my back against the wooden headboard and reaching over to the nightstand to grab a small gift box. At first, Greene protests getting up, insisting she is already comfortable as is, but upon seeing the little box resting in my hand, she gets up, resting her back alongside the headboard next to mine.

"I know we haven't been together long, and this might seem crazy, but I've found that I throw all logic out the window when it concerns you," I admit, glimpsing into her emerald eyes and tucking a strand of hair behind her ear. "Drifting off to sleep to the sound of your voice is the lullaby I never knew I needed. And I mean that—I *need* you. I need to fall asleep to the sound of your voice and wake up to the feel of your body against mine."

I hand her the little velvet box, and her cheeks blossom in response. She unwraps the gift, revealing a set of keys. "Here are the keys to my house. I know you love your apartment, so I won't force you to move in right away, but I want you to know I'm all in, Greene. My home, my heart—they're yours. *All* yours."

"Jasper, I don't know what to say..." She pauses, twiddling the keys in her hand. "I've never felt like I had a physical home. Even the home we're in right now isn't a comfort to me. It's just a house I lived in around people who truthfully didn't cherish me until they lost their other child. To call your home my home means everything."

I pull her into my arms and peer into her eyes. *Those eyes.* Have I mentioned how bright they have been lately? They're gleaming like emerald stardust these days. A beat of silence passes between us as I anxiously await her response.

"So, when can I move in? How does the third weekend of January sound? I don't have an event that weekend," she teases. *This girl.* She never ceases to surprise me.

I pull her in for a kiss, savoring the taste of her full lips. For years, I've felt like a letdown. I've lived a mundane life without caring what happens next, then they walked in. Since encountering the Greenes, my life has been anything but mundane.

Knowing I'm enough for Iris means more than she even knows. After trying so hard and feeling like a failure for so many years, she swooped into my life and filled me with a feeling I didn't realize I was missing: *hope*. For the first time in my life, I'm feeling optimistic about what the future holds. My buddy, Kai, may be her angel, but she is mine.

If Kai taught me anything, it's how pivotal it is to embrace my emotions and treasure those I hold closest to my heart. While I cradle her in my arms, I kiss her head and breathe in my favorite scent—*her*.

Quite frankly, I didn't know it was possible to feel this way. Now that I have the privilege of accompanying Ms. Iris Adelaide Greene through life, I refuse to take another step for granted ever again.

FORTY-SIX

IRIS

I awake in a quiet room, glimpsing down to see his strong arm wrapped around my waist, reminding me of another moment of time that wasn't quite like this. As my mind wanders, his gentle breathing on my neck anchors me, pulling me back to the shore while giving me goosebumps simultaneously. I lie awake, deeply contemplating how I got here.

On a chilly autumn day in a small, seemingly inconsequential town, I stumbled upon my soulmate. He walked into my life like an angel in disguise, stealing pieces of my heart every moment we shared together. Then, several weeks later, he gave me a key to his home. Little did the gray-eyed thief know, he stole the key to my heart long before he gifted me his.

I offered to move in the next month, and I think he thought I was teasing him when, in actuality, my offer was genuine. I'd gladly move in with him next week if I didn't have to work some things out with my apartment complex. I've never felt more certain of anything.

From his passion for vintage antiques—regardless of whether or not he admits to liking them—to his love for cooking and learning, to the sound of his intoxicating laugh, I have fallen hard. I have plummeted to Earth face-first, and in an odd twist of events, I have no fear. No, instead, excitement rushes through me at the thought of what lies ahead for us.

Cutting a glance at my old baby blue alarm clock resting on the yellow nightstand, I realize the sun will be rising soon. Who would've thought I could wake up before the sun without an alarm? I attempt to wiggle out of his arms as wearily as possible, careful not to awaken my love. As I adjust his arm to slip away, I hold my breath. After managing to get loose, I sit up, stretching my arms, when an arm yanks me backward, causing me to crash into his chest.

"What are you doing awake, baby?" His husky voice breathes into my ear, giving me chills. Words can't describe how it feels to be cherished by this man. I turn to face him and hold him in my arms tightly. His eyes haven't even opened yet. My fingers trace his jaw, gliding over to trace his lips.

"Just wanted to catch the sunrise," I whisper softly. "You can go back to sleep."

"Not without you," he answers groggily, keeping his eyes shut tight and his grip on my waist even tighter. "Not anymore."

"Someone's being dramatic," I tease, running my fingers through his dark waves. "I'll be back soon."

He sighs, loosening his grip on my waist. "I'll be waiting, Greene."

If there's one thing I know about Jasper, it's that he will always wait for me. Some might consider me the luckiest girl in the world for that fact alone. I stand up and slip on a thick olive green bathrobe. I sneak out of the bedroom, creeping as quietly as a mouse across the hallway, careful not to wake my parents. Instantaneously, I'm transported to a different time—a time full of wonder, not so different from this one.

"Hurry up, Irie! We're going to miss it!" he whispers frantically, dragging me across the dimly lit hallway. "Be as quiet as a mouse, they can't know we're doing this."

"Kai, you're the one who's being loud." I pout. I've never been much of a morning person, but especially not before the sun comes out.

"Shhh, Irie, listen to me just this once," he says as we stumble down the stairs. We're young. So young. I follow Kai across the home as he leads me toward the back door.

"It's so cold, I don't wanna go outside," I whine. He mutters under his breath and slings his robe over my shoulders, and then we slip outside.

"Look, Irie! Do you see that?" He points to the dusty sky.

"See what?" I squint my eyes, hoping to see what he's referring to. "All I see are stars..."

"Yes, exactly! Guess what those stars are right there?" He points to a group of stars clustered together.

"Um... the Milky Way?" He shakes his head in amusement.

"Those stars are Santa and his reindeer. They just finished dropping off all our presents, and we caught them in the act right before they disappeared." He grins proudly. "See? The sun is starting to rise, so they're slowly fading away."

"Wow!" I gasp, holding onto every word.

"Look, Santa is giving us this sunrise, too." He smiles. I watch as the sky slowly blends into an array of colors, ranging from midnight blue to lavender to pink. My eyes drift across the sky to the moon. The moon always brings me comfort, and right now, it is covered by fluffy clouds.

"Do you think Santa wants us to watch the moon and the clouds too?" I ask hopefully.

"Of course, Irie." He grins, his eyes fixated on the mural in the sky. "He wouldn't want us to miss a minute of this."

"I want you to promise me to live every minute, Irie." His voice echoes in my mind.

I scurry downstairs quietly, remaining mindful of all the sleeping souls in the home. Adrenaline fills me as I rush toward the back door, hoping I haven't missed it. I open the door and step outside, greeting the brisk winter air in haste.

I close the door behind me and gaze up at the sky. A cluster of twinkling stars capture my attention. As I watch them begin to fade, I close my eyes, reminiscing on all the Christmas sunrises we shared together. Then, my eyes shift to the moon, lighting the darkest part of the sky as opaque clouds grow more visible by the second. Warm tears stream down my cheeks.

I didn't want to lose Kai. I blamed myself for his early departure, feeling an endless stream of guilt rushing through me constantly. As I sunk deeper and deeper into the chasm of grief, I wished I could've taken his place, not valuing my life as much as I valued his. I couldn't bear the insufferable quiet, always choosing to embrace chaos because the noise reminded me of our last moments together.

For years, I avoided building new relationships out of fear that I'd inevitably lose them—I couldn't bear any more loss.

No, I couldn't *survive* it.

When the sun set on that quiet, snowy day two years ago, the moon claimed the sky and the clouds as its own, and I didn't want to accept it.

But if I hadn't lost the sun in my sky, I may have overlooked the moon.

Suddenly, defined arms wrap around my waist from behind. I tilt my head, staring at the man holding me.

In his arms, I feel safe. In his arms, I feel warm. In his arms, I feel *unbreakable*.

My loss led me to the love of my life, my soulmate, and that cannot be coincidental. Fate *is* real. I will miss my brother every day for the rest of my life, but in the meantime, I want to make the best of every minute I get to share with my loved ones—particularly this one. Every moment of life is precious. Perhaps life is not meant to be lived alone.

"You didn't have to get out of bed." I chuckle softly, leaning into his warm embrace. While the sun rises, owning the sky, the snow-capped mountainscape serves as the most striking backdrop.

"As much as I need my sleep, I need you far more, love." Jasper's soft lips graze my ear as he moves to place a gentle kiss on my temple. I breathe in his scent and close my eyes. This man was made for me. I've determined that the depth of our love is abundantly worth the inevitable loss to come. "Are you okay, Greene?"

For years, I've hidden. I've told countless people I was fine, masking my emotions with the widest and brightest smile I could muster. But with Jasper, I don't need to lie.

He sees right through all my masks, and he still loves me.

"I feel happy," I say, granting myself permission to smile. He spins me to look at him, then cradles my face in his palm. I lean into his touch and gaze into his stormy eyes. His hand roams lower down my back, pulling me closer and holding my waist, his lips curling into a smile.

"What are you waiting for, Jasper?" I challenge him.

Without hesitation, his lips crash against mine like a tidal wave, stealing my breath away. He grabs my waist and pulls me into him even tighter, rightfully claiming what's his. I slip my tongue out to join his and run my fingers through his soft hair, etching this kiss into my mind and stowing it away with all our other kisses.

Bliss takes over, entirely consuming the very core of my being, as it tends to do with Jasper's touch.

I always considered Kai the sun in my sky, keeping life bright and cheerful. If he is the sun, then Jasper is unequivocally the moon, lighting the dimly lit, cobblestoned path when the dark gets too perilous to endure alone. Against all odds, I've prevailed with help from my angel along with my soulmate.

Now, I'm like a cloud—simply floating across the sky without a care in the world.

EPILOGUE

KAI

ROUGHLY TWO YEARS LATER

Let me start off by saying: I'm okay. I know, I know, it's not about me—it's about Irie. It's always been about her. So, let's get to the good stuff, shall we? Chrysocolla Cove is thriving, the flowers are in full bloom, and the sun stays out longer during thesc toasty summer days. Little Falls remains the top destination spot for Cove locals and tourists alike. The high school is closed for the rest of the summer, and with it being event season, Irie is busier than ever.

"Let's go, people!" She motions toward her team, ushering them into the event venue. "We are running five minutes late; we don't have a second to waste."

She gazes around the large hall, taking in her surroundings and jotting down some notes in her planner. The event isn't until tomorrow, but she knows better than anyone how procrastination can bite you in the ass. So, she hustles around the room, making sure every piece of decor is accounted for, all the tables are set with the delicate lacy table runners she selected for this event specifically, and each chair is wrapped in ribbon.

"Boss, I really think it'd be best for you to take a breather. We've got this covered." Joy smiles at her warmly.

"Oh, please, Joy, I'm just fine! Do you know how much coffee I've had today?" Irie lets out a jittery laugh. Joy nods, then walks away, pulling out her phone. Irie resumes, barking out orders left and right, when suddenly, her phone pings.

Jasper

> You need to rest, Greene.

She blushes, biting her lip. Years later, Jasper still gives her butterflies.

Iris

> Can't, I've got to finish this job, love.

Jasper

> Non-negotiable. I'm waiting outside.

Her jaw drops. *What?* She marches outside, seeing him leaning against his car. Fashioned in a charcoal crew neck and blue jeans, he smirks at her. He has some facial hair now, but don't fret. It's *very* well-kept, as per her request. Today, he looks extra cool. *Ugh.* He has the effortlessly cool look down.

"What are you doing here?" She scowls, folding her arms. The breeze blows strands of loose hair out of her face. Her hair is a shade lighter than it once was, thanks to the summer sun.

"Isn't it obvious?" He quirks a brow, then walks toward her, wrapping his arm around her neck and kissing her temple. "I'm taking you home for the day."

"Now is not the time for jokes." She stifles a laugh. "You know I can't go home, they need me here—"

"I've been assured they can take it from here, Greene," he affirms, pulling her closer. "Let's go."

Her green eyes flicker from the venue to the car to Jasper. Obviously, she feels torn. Usually, I'd side with her, but Jasper and the others are right this time. She has been working too hard. She needs a break. I knew leaving her in his hands would work out well. Eventually, she sighs and agrees to go home, settling herself into the front seat of the car.

While they drive down the mountain roads back to the Cove, she gazes out of her passenger-side window. "I don't see what the big fuss is about."

He bursts into laughter, wheezing, "Baby, you're something else."

She huffs a puff of air and officially accepts defeat, melting in the way she always does in his presence. A sparkle catches her eye as she rests her hand atop his on her thigh. She has allowed herself to get lost in this at least a hundred times, and the glimmer of the gem never ceases to take her breath away. I have to admit, he did damn good.

They spend the rest of the day together, laughing about ridiculous jokes that no one else seems to understand, cuddling on his comfy ass couch, and reminiscing on the last couple of years they've spent together. Their home is filled with photos of them and Truman now. Looks like Jasper is sentimental after all—at least, he is when it comes to her. Despite their usual sleeping arrangements, Jasper sleeps at his parents' home tonight for tradition's sake. They both need to be well-rested and knowing them, they wouldn't get much sleep tonight if they slept together.

I am at a loss for words. I'm speechless. And I'm *never* speechless. I thought Katherine's wedding was grand, but this? This is *immaculate*. From the greenery cascading down the walls to the delicate lace decorations to the familiar faces, I couldn't imagine a more perfect ceremony. Don't get me wrong, I loved the way Katherine honored me at her wedding, but my sister has blown me away. Not only did they save me a seat in the front row, but they insisted on saving a space for me to stand in between Jasper and his other groomsmen.

He chose me to be his best man.

I'm sure the wedding guests don't understand it. Why would they choose me? In their eyes, he and I never even met. They probably assume this is just a sweet gesture for her, without an underlying deeper meaning. They couldn't be more off-base, though.

These two love birds may not be able to feel my presence anymore, but I've been watching from afar the entire time, just like I promised I would. Amidst all the chaos, Jasper and I became more than friends too—we are brothers now, whether he likes it or not. I couldn't have picked a better person to be by her side, even if my afterlife depended on it. They are the epitome of true soulmates. As I proudly stand by his side, my heart races. Suddenly, the lights dim, the violin music softens, and the crowd turns toward Marble Grove's huge fancy wooden doors. In an instant, my heart goes from racing fast to barely beating.

Her half-up, half-down hair is pinned back by a small tiara with a cream, sheer veil. The smile on her face is priceless; it warms my heart, filling my soul with pure light. True to her independent spirit, she chose to walk herself down the aisle in a vintage cream dress with a lace train. As much as I love the choice, I can't help myself from stepping in true to my obnoxious nature. I walk directly down the aisle and meet her halfway. No one can see me anyway, so it shouldn't matter, right? Upon reaching her, I link my arm to hers and walk alongside her the rest of the way. Up this close, I can see tears brimming her eyelids. From this angle, I also capture a look at Jasper's face.

She isn't the only one with tears pooling in her eyes. He gulps then blushes, beaming at her with the most intimate smile I've ever seen him wear, awestruck by her, by this moment of true solace. For Heaven's sake, I can't handle how happy I feel right now. I might explode.

As we land at his feet, I let go of her arm. For a split second, she glances right at me, and her lips part as if she could feel the absence of my touch. That shouldn't be possible, but then again, if I've learned anything over the last several years, it's that nothing is impossible for a Greene.

They choose to keep their vows short and sweet—I'm convinced it's because they want to become husband and wife as soon as humanly possible. They deserve this. After everything, they deserve every ounce of happiness in the world. Choosing love over fear changed their lives forever. I'm so unbelievably proud of them both.

"...You're my home, Jasper," she whispers, gazing into his eyes.

"And you're my *everything*, Greene." He lifts her chin, not breaking eye contact for a single second. This is the moment when I realize these two are the actual main characters—we're all just living in their world. I can't wait to see what their next chapter holds. Selfishly, I'd love to become an uncle soon. I mean, can you imagine it? Uncle Kai giving little Charlie piggyback rides? Although, my set of wings might make piggyback rides a bit harder to maneuver... I could also see Truman getting jealous, and we can't have that, can we?

Speaking of wings, I know you may be curious about the Middle Realm, Archangels, Golden Realm, and everything in between. I don't blame you. I'd be curious, too. In fact, I was very curious before my mortal life ended, so I get it. I really do. However, knowing exactly what comes next after this life won't do you much good. If you know all the details, living in the moment will be more challenging. Besides, where's the fun in knowing what's to come? As far as my personal afterlife experience goes, that's *definitely* a story for another day. For now, let's live in this moment shared amongst soulmates and sear it into our minds so it lasts a lifetime.

ACKNOWLEDGEMENTS

I cannot thank you enough for wandering into Chrysocolla Cove with me. By taking the time to read this book, you've helped me accomplish a lifelong dream I never would've imagined possible. Iris, Jasper, and Kai all hold a very special place in my heart, I can only hope they touched your heart as much as they've touched mine.

To my husband, thank you for believing in me so fiercely from day one. Thank you for supporting my dream and pushing me to step beyond my comfort zone. I appreciate you listening to my endless rambles and 'what ifs.' I truly cannot imagine embarking on this journey with another living soul. Thank you for your undying support. You have my heart.

To my sisters, thank you for always expressing how proud you are of me. I have felt so loved by you both throughout this process. I appreciate you listening to me talk endlessly about my novel ideas with patience and love like Mom always listened.

To Kristen, thank you for giving this story a chance and Alpha reading it from the first to the last page. Without you, I genuinely don't know if I would've ever completed this book. Thank you for your constant encouragement and words of affirmation.

To Kayla Hobbs, Samantha, and Myrika, thank you all so much for reading the book early on and providing essential critiques, edits, and more. Your words of support helped keep me going on my darkest days of writing and editing. Thank you for loving these characters as much as I do. Each of you helped make this story what it is today.

To Bella, Kayla Crowe, Sophia, Niya, and Shelbie, thank you all for beta-reading the book and providing me with fresh perspectives and the words of affirmation I needed more than anything. This book wouldn't be the same without the insights you shared.

To Lara, I couldn't have dreamed of working with a better artist or friend on this beautiful cover. You brought my vision to life in the most striking way. Thank you for sharing your wonderful talents with me and this book. I'm honored that you designed The Masked Flower's cover.

To you, my readers. Firstly, I'm sorry that Kai died. Similar to how Jasper imagined an alternate universe in which he and Kai met while he was still living, I often find myself lost in similar trains of thought with those whom I've lost. However, the intent of this story was not to keep him physically alive, no matter how lovely that story would've been. No, instead, the intention was to keep his memory alive through those who loved him most. If you find yourself resonating with Iris, I'm sending all of my love to you. I am with you. Thank you for accompanying her on her journey to true peace. I hope that you can find peace, too, if you haven't already. And if you have found peace, I am so proud of you.

With all my love,

Erin

ABOUT THE AUTHOR

As a grieving wanderer herself, Erin Halli writes stories encompassing authentic journeys through grief-long, cumbersome paths. Additionally, she has a background in journalism, copywriting, and blog writing. Her objective is for readers to find comfort in knowing they do not roam the lonesome isles of grief alone. Her debut novel, The Masked Flower, is a story of grief, triumph, hope, healing, and, of course, true love. Erin resides in Texas with her husband and two small dogs.

You can keep up with Erin by following her on Instagram and Goodreads and subscribing to her newsletter.

www.erinhalli.wordpress.com
Instagram: @erinbooklore